Shackerstone rang Ian Yardl

"Ian Yardley." The respons
with sleep.

"Sir. It's Brian Shackerstone. I need to brief you on Klingsor."

"An arrest?"

"Yes."

"I'll just move to another room, hold on. I don't want to disturb the missus." Shackerstone heard some movement before Yardley's voice came back more clearly. "Okay, Brian, what have we got?"

"Another girl impaled, but this time in the boot of the suspect's car."

"Tell me it was a good stop by uniformed cops."

"It was. They thought it was a drunk driver. A good result, except that the suspect is a police officer."

"Local?"

"Very, it is DC Dastra."

"Dastra? Bloody hell. Where is he?"

"Here at Wemstone."

"And the victim?"

"No ID yet. White female like the others. Young."

"It's not that girl with the eye patch, is it?"

"No eye patch, but another hazel rod by the look of it, bent over to get the body in the car. The body and the car have been photographed at the location of the stop, but we'll need more work during the day. We've seized Dastra's clothes and it looks like he's got soil on his shoes and knees, as well as some sort of grease on the back of his jacket. The police surgeon says he's not fit to detain because he whacked the side of his head when he piled his car up, and twisted one of his testicles. The doc says it's pretty swollen."

"That's the sort of injury a woman gives to a man."

"Quite. Anyhow, he's in hospital under guard."

"So his custody clock has stopped."

"Until we get him back."

"Thank God for that."

Shackerstone phoned Gordonstown next. The phone rang for ten rings before Gordonstown's voice answered wearily. "Hello."

"Sir. DCI Shackerstone, sorry to wake you…"

"This better be bloody important."

"It is. There's been an arrest for Klingsor."

Gordonstown's voice became more earnest. "Why wasn't I informed there was going to be…"

"It wasn't by the team. It was a uniformed stop."

"Really?"

"A good one. The suspect had the body in his car."

"Nice one."

"The not so nice bit is that the suspect is a cop—DC Dastra."

Champagne Books Presents

The Piano Room

By

Harry Hindes

Champagne Books
www.champagnebooks.com
Copyright 2012 by Harry Hindes
ISBN 9781927454855
October 2012
Cover Art by Trisha FitzGerald
Produced in Canada

Champagne Books
#35069-4604 37 ST SW
Calgary, AB T3E 7C7
Canada

Dedication

For Peter.

One

Question (Detective Inspector Graham): "How were the victims' bodies disposed of?"

Answer (Suspect): "They needed to disappear for good... a deep grave certain to be built over and sacks of lime to eat them away."

Q: "Then we found them."
A: "You forget. This was last year. You didn't find them. Lucy found them..." (Noise of tape ending)
(Extract from evidential tape transcript.)

A pair of yellow-white anklebones swung down like a heavy pendulum above a settling cloud of fallen sand and earth, glowing under primitive twelve-volt lights. Tough sinews suspended the swinging tibia and fibula, with attached foot, in a series of oscillations that described a diminishing arc across the upper half of the narrow bore. Two students in the tunnel scurried backwards from the grim, unheralded fall from the roof. The third, a redheaded girl of about twenty, spat soil from her mouth and tried to clear dirt from her eyes.

Lucy Aybrams caught her breath, saying nothing. Her vision cleared slightly and she witnessed the last tiny swings of the bones as they came to a standstill. Through the settling clouds of earth, she spied more bones in the lining of the tunnel roof. The shape of a woman's shoe stood in relief from the soil.

Lucy scuttled backwards, her eyes suddenly stinging. The

soft tissues of her eyelids seared with a wave of pain. She cried out in her clear American accent. "Something's burning my eyes. I can't see. I need help." She reached back, fingers splayed, trying to feel her way.

"This way, this way," said a voice behind her. Lucy touched the hairy arm of one of the road protestors, and gripping it in fear, allowed herself to be guided back towards the short shaft to the surface. She saw a jumble of blurred shapes above her, and then her sensitized eyes were pierced by rays of sunlight falling through the canopy of trees above.

"Don't rub them," said someone. "Get some water, quickly!" came another voice, further away from her. She felt many arms lifting her up and laying her out on the soft woodland earth. Large strong hands cradled the sides of her head as her eyes recoiled from a gush of still mineral water jetted straight from a plastic bottle inches from her face. Her eyelids refused to open, despite her willing them apart. Out beyond the burning in her eyes, Lucy heard the chants of protestors echoing through the treetops mixed with radio chatter from the advancing line of riot police.

"Excuse me!" shouted the man who held her head, "we've found a body or something in our tunnel." Lucy heard heavy footsteps approach.

"What's happened to her?" said a deeper voice.

"Her eyes are burning. It's from the tunnel. We've found a human skeleton, well, bones or something."

"Is that a cop?" interrupted Lucy.

"Yes," said the voice.

"I need a hospital, quickly."

"Okay, love. I can sort that out. There's an ambulance on standby up by the road."

"In case you beat one of us up?" said a male voice.

"No, in case *you* beat one of *us* up!" said a voice next to Lucy, which then spoke into a police radio. "Get the paramedics down to the main clearing in the woods. We've got a female protestor with some sort of burns to her eyes. Over."

"Received."

"There's also a report of possible human remains in one of the protest tunnels. Can we get CID informed? Our confined spaces team will take a look to confirm. Over."

"All received."

The gnawing sensation in her eyes clouded the passage of the next few minutes. Lucy could hear the diminishing protest in the woods around her. She guessed that the police and bailiffs had overwhelmed the protestors, for now the main source of noise in her ears was the shriek of gasoline powered bolt-cutters slicing through the chains with which they had bound themselves to trees. Two paramedics arrived at Lucy's side and after a battery of questions they set to work on her.

"I'm going to put some drops in your eyes to help you open them. This will ease the pain."

"Good," Lucy gasped. She felt fingers in thin plastic gloves force her swelling eyelids open and dribble the liquid into each eye. The relief was sudden, and she found she could open her eyes slightly. Prompt irrigation of her eyes with saline solution lessened the burning still further, but panic set in as she heard one of them on the radio to a hospital requesting advice from an ophthalmic specialist.

~ * ~

When she had arrived in the woodlands on that bright but misty spring morning, the Wemstone bypass protest had seemed the most important thing in Lucy's world. Now, lying on the ground with her head between someone's knees while trying to remain calm, the sudden turnaround of fortune hit her like a truck. The unattainable Lucy Aybrams, one of the most desirable students at Oxford, was now having her face eaten into by something both sinister and deliberate. How many times had she said she wished she were less physically attractive so that the academic world would take her more seriously? Her casual wish was apparently being answered. Her face, the very thing she had hoped people would look beyond, felt as if it were peeling off around her eyes. She had fended off dozens of handsome and eligible young undergraduates. Then the uncomfortable thought now surfaced that she might henceforth be lucky to attract the plainest of men, and perhaps even then only after a few pints of Dutch courage. This brought useful tears to her stinging eyes.

Think clearly—change your train of thought. A skeleton—

yes—think about that. However, this was no ordinary grave. There was no graveyard here. This little strip of land in the hills between London and Oxford was ancient woodland. That was precisely why she had joined the protest.

Lucy started considering the huge improbability of a grave being found from below. In all the billions of graves back through time, had it ever happened before? What figure could be put to that probability? This was the sort of obscure question that graced Oxford entrance examinations: "Discuss the contention that atoms from Socrates's cup of hemlock are now in the body of every living human."

No doubt missed by someone, a dead woman had been occupying this fought-over patch of soil, but at the time of her burial, discovery was the one thing Lucy knew the woman had been put here to avoid.

The bones changed everything. The police had been the "enemy" until this moment. She was now fully aware that her life was taking a dark and unwanted turn into their world.

"I've just spoken to the hospital," said a voice. "Given the circumstances in the tunnel and all your symptoms, they're suggesting you've been burnt by calcium oxide or calcium hydroxide."

"Lime?" asked Lucy.

"Yes, it's a strong alkali. We have to get you to hospital on the hurry-up."

"Or what?"

"There's... there's a possibility of long-term damage."

"Blindness?"

"Let's get you to hospital. There's an ophthalmologist already waiting for you."

"What about my face?"

"Eyes first. There's a lot can be done with skin. Nobody can mend eyes."

Two

Question (DI Graham): "Listen. The tape is about to run out and I think we could all do with a break from this interview. I hope there's nothing else you want to add."

Answer (Suspect): "I do. They clutch at straws, anything to spin it out. They try to make desperate deals with you at the end. 'I'll do anything you ask... anything. Please don't kill me. I won't tell anyone.' And then, when they see how they are going to die, they go off their pretty heads. They kick. They scream. It's a primal scream. It echoes on and on in your mind. It's a real turn-on..."

Q: (Long silence) "A turn-on?"
(Noise on tape of suspect moving his wheelchair and striking table surface with his hand.)
A: "Yes." (Pause followed by laughter.)
(Extract from evidential tape transcript.)

Superintendent Ian Yardley wove his broad frame through the cluttered desks in the Criminal Investigation Department at Wemstone police station. The CID main office was deserted apart from two detective constables working intently at computer screens and oblivious to Yardley's presence. He arrived at the door of a small side office with a brand new blue plastic nameplate on it: *Detective Chief Inspector Brian Shackerstone.* He eased the door open. A heavily built man with dark mahogany skin and thick forearms bulging from the rolled up sleeves of his white shirt, looked up from a pile of papers on his desk.

"Brian."

"Good morning, Guv. I suppose you've got more work for me?"

"I'm afraid so."

"I hate Mondays. Stick it on the pile, sir. I'm up to my eyeballs writing my troops' annual reports. I hadn't realized there was so much crap for a DCI serving on a local division."

Shackerstone looked down and carried on working, but then noticed Yardley hadn't moved from the doorway. Shackerstone looked back up. "I'm sorry. I just…"

"It's not that sort of work. Our bypass protest has just unearthed a skeleton."

Shackerstone's eyes widened. "Oh, right. That's interesting. Is it old?"

"Recent, according to the uniformed cops out there."

Shackerstone rose heavily from his chair and plucked his crumpled suit jacket from a coat stand. "I'll take a look, but in a few hours, my ex-chums from the Force Major Inquiry Team will be all over it. Detective Superintendent Joshua Gordonstown will have the chance to gloat again when he takes the crime scene off me the way he took my bloody job at F-MIT."

"It's your crime scene until he gets there. If you want to show him what you're still made of, now's the time."

Shackerstone angrily pocketed his mobile phone. "What? Show him I'm still married to Central Southern Police? Maybe if I hadn't been, I'd still be married to Joanna and I wouldn't be living in a one bedroom flat in Marlow, half broke from putting my boys through private schools."

Yardley turned silently away and made his way back through the office. Shackerstone followed for a few paces, surveying the empty desks.

"Where's Reshard Khan?" he shouted across to the two detectives.

"With a prisoner."

Shackerstone hurried downstairs. He tapped an entry code into a panel and entered the custody suite.

He glanced at the empty chair behind the sergeant's desk, then caught the sound of laughter echoing in the cell corridor. He pushed a heavy wooden door ajar and looked through the gap. Detective sergeant Reshard Khan and the custody sergeant were standing with a third officer watching a cell door. An arm was dangling through the small opening in the cell door, trying to catch the cell door handle with a belt. At the third attempt, the belt caught the door handle, and with a jerk, the door opened.

"Nothing to it," said a fourth police officer emerging from the cell. The others seemed about to applaud when Shackerstone swung the passageway door open, deliberately framing himself in the doorway, bullet headed and stocky.

"Detective Sergeant Khan. We've got a crime scene. Suspicious death."

"Bugger!" he heard one of the officers exclaim under his breath. "It's the new DCI."

Shackerstone waited at the end of the cell passage while the officers trooped past him, the escapologist buckling his belt. He didn't ask what they were doing—he had been in the force long enough to realize that the harmless mischief he had once got involved in had not died out. The officer from the cell had a fresh and spotless uniform that captured Shackerstone's attention.

"And who are you?"

"Police Constable Dastra, sir, David Dastra... but usually known as Barney."

He held out his hand, and Shackerstone shook it, saying nothing but looking intently into his eyes for a moment. Then, "Barney Dastra, eh?"

"No, sir, it's just Barney. It's got no handle to it. Some of my former parishioners used to call me 'PC Barney'."

"Some of mine used to call me "PC Black-as-stone", but times have changed... I hope." Shackerstone frowned and looked away as Khan's cultured British Pakistani accent gained his attention. "It's his first day, sir. Ex Met detective constable, he's come from Harlesden."

"Harlesden? What has Central Southern Police done to deserve you as a transfer?"

"I've just inherited my parents' place out at Henley. Travelling to Harlesden was getting a bit expensive and..."

"And you gave up being a detective so you could cut down

your travel?" Shackerstone winked at Khan.

"Not for too long, I hope. I know it's the rules: I have to do a year back on the beat."

"Have you ever kept a decision log, Barney?"

"Yes, of course."

"Good. Get your kit together and come with me. On day one in the force you're always waiting around like a spare part."

~ * ~

In his dirty white Citroen, Shackerstone drove Khan and Dastra across a grassy field of parked chartered tour buses and minibuses amid knots of aimless and thwarted protestors. The car scattered a group of crows from the grass and they wheeled away squawking. The dejected road demonstrators cleared a path slowly for the car as if making a final token protest. Shackerstone parked it by a group of police vans close to a pathway leading through to the protestors' encampment.

Shackerstone opened the back of the car and took out sealed sets of blue paper coveralls, gloves, hard hats and overshoes, tossing them to Khan and Dastra who ripped open the packages and began donning the suits. Shackerstone rummaged around in the back of the car trying to find an XXL size suit, but without success. He squeezed himself into an XL, sure of it ripping the first time he bent over. With Khan and Dastra following, he then picked his way towards the tunnel entrance through lines of unevenly spaced uniformed officers and police-line tapes cordoning the clearing. Shackerstone noted that the woods were marred by an abandoned web of boards, placards, banners and ropeways up amongst the branches and discarded first aid wrappers on the ground. He saw two uniformed officers standing over a large rectangular hole in the ground reinforced with old wooden pallets. One spoke as he approached. "It's the left hand tunnel, Guv. The confined spaces team has shored up what they can, but you can't go in there without safety specs, sir."

"I'll be the judge of that," muttered Shackerstone.

"One young lass is in hospital... could be blinded. The confined spaces team reckon there's quicklime down there, but as you say, the decision is yours, Guv..."

Shackerstone nodded. "Okay... so some smartarse says I need bloody safety specs. Given that I don't keep spare pairs in my car..."

"I have some here, sir," said the officer, producing three pairs still in plastic wrappers. He handed them out. "They were issued in case our protestors started throwing urine and stuff..."

Shackerstone had overplayed the gruff DCI to the uniformed officer, and adopted a more conciliatory tone. "Oh, thanks. Good call. Right, let's go in and take a look. Dastra, get scribing."

Dastra theatrically folded back the cover of the decision log. "Sir!"

Shackerstone climbed down an aluminum ladder into the hole. He crouched down for the left tunnel and felt a seam on the paper suit split. He crawled along under bright new timber and metal supports until he could see the bones dangling from the roof. Here the tunnel had been left as it had fallen, with earth and planks in a haphazard pile.

Even with a clear idea of what to expect, the first view of the bones took a few moments for him to digest. He focused beyond the leg hanging from the roof. He could see embedded in the roof the shape of another three bones, just proud of the surface. Khan crawled into the space behind him and knelt upright, with Dastra peering over his shoulder. Shackerstone shook his head. "There's more than one set of bones here. Note the small piece of gray nylon rope looped underneath the furthest two, loose from the ankles, and a woman's shoe."

Khan and Dastra strained their necks to get a clearer view.

"Right, Reshard, I need the following. Dastra, get all this down with reasons: Firstly, I will treat this as suspicious, as opposed to some archaeological find... until proved otherwise. I need a specialist forensic team with a Crime Scene coordinator to handle evidence preservation. This will require at least three Scenes of Crime officers."

"Does this force have that many SOCOs?" asked Dastra.

"Well, we haven't got a limitless supply like the Met, but three shouldn't tax us. They'll need a forensic anthropologist for the bones and a chemist from the lab to do a hazardous substance risk assessment and figure out whatever this stuff in the soil is. I know they will ask surveyors' department to shore this lot up because of the risks, so we can ask for them now to save time. My decision is that a thorough forensic examination of the site takes place with the bones in situ, before we get hold of a Home Office pathologist to view them, also in situ. Then we will recover them carefully for a post mortem. I need a photographer and video unit to record the scene. I need an exhibits officer. We'll need sniffer dogs and a specialist search team to dig the site over to see if there are any more bodies. I need detectives here to take statements from the protestors. Who was in here during the fall?"

"Three protestors in all," Khan replied. "Two have gone back to the police station by van and one to hospital."

"They will all have to have forensics done on them for elimination. Make sure their clothes are kept and the police vans are swept. We will need hair samples and mouth swabs from them all so we can eliminate their DNA from any we find here. I want statements from all three before they go home. We also need to know which other members of the Great Unwashed have been down here previously, so get a Police Support Unit of one inspector, three sergeants and eighteen PCs up here so they can sift the protestors. We could have hundreds to eliminate."

"We've got two units already here from the eviction, Guv, but they're still in riot gear."

"Of course. Get them back into ordinary uniform and get one unit talking to the protestors, and the other to guard the perimeter. A tent needs to be put up over the shaft in case we get a lot of rain. Have I missed anything?"

Dastra spoke up, "Site mapping, sir. It's a complex plot. At the very minimum you need a plan sketcher. Someone who can do computer mapping would be handy."

"I like it. Reshard, see what we can do."

"If you get stuck, I'm a failed geologist, and I can do computer mapping," offered Dastra.

"But you're back on the beat, eh?" Then Shackerstone's attention drifted to the shoe. "Ah, perhaps this *can* be for you, "failed geologist". Is the soil we can see lodged in the ribs of the soles different from the local stuff?"

Dastra eased himself round Khan and Shackerstone, past the dangling leg bones and examined the bottom of the shoe.

"Yes sir, it seems to be. Very fine alluvial clay, not sandy like the surrounding soil."

"Then we'd best have a mud man."

"There's a clear band of color, sir," interrupted Dastra, pointing up at the two bones crossed by the rope, "coming out between the feet, a dark stain in the sand." They moved closer. Shackerstone moved until his face was only inches from the rope. "Okay, well spotted. It goes on up between the legs."

~ * ~

Back on the surface, Shackerstone returned to his car with Dastra and dictated some notes for the decision log while Khan busied himself on his mobile phone summoning the specialist help needed. Shackerstone watched Khan make his way across the field to the Inspector in charge of the riot officers.

"He's a good DS, Khan. Even an ex-Met boy like you should be able to pick up a few tricks from him."

"If I get the chance, sir."

Nearly an hour went by while Shackerstone watched the sun drive away the last threads of mist hanging around the woods. He watched the uniformed officers taking statements from the protestors, and daydreamed of his own early days in uniform in the seventies. The arrival of a small white van bouncing across the field brought him back to a state of alertness.

"That's Malcolm."

"Malcolm?" asked Dastra.

"Force photographer. Top bloke. And he's beaten all the other specialists to it."

He swiveled out of his seat, marshaling his thoughts for the briefing he intended for the photographer, but as he got to his feet his mobile phone chirruped somewhere under his overalls. He fumbled about to find it, and eventually plucked it out through the split he had sustained in the tunnel.

"Brian, it's Joshua Gordonstown."

"Hello, sir."

"What have you got?"

"Two sets of human remains in the roof of a tunnel dug by our bypass protestors. One person to hospital with burns to the face and eyes."

"A copper?"

"A protestor. One of the confined spaces bods reckons it could be quicklime."

"Serves them right... maybe that'll put them off digging holes."

"If you say so."

"Look, Brian. I know there are a few issues between us right now..."

"Like spending my final months in the force back in a local bloody CID office juggling crime figures."

"Final months?"

"Yeah, I'm retiring at thirty years."

"But you'll only be fifty."

"I'd have gone to sixty if you had kept me at F-MIT."

"I'm sorry you feel that way... it wasn't personal. This really isn't the time. For what it's worth, Ian Yardley wants you to take this one on until I finish with my current job at court."

"But do *you*?"

"Yes, and I'll stay out of your way. When I'm done at court I'm having a determined crack at the Chief Superintendent's promotion process in the autumn."

"But you've got plenty of other Detective Chief Inspectors."

"All used up on other jobs. Anyhow, you're still a damned experienced detective, even if you feel you can't work with me."

"I'll need a Detective Inspector. I can't run this and take a DI out of the office at Wemstone. It's understaffed as it is."

"I've a brand new DI. I'll send her over tomorrow with any detectives I can release to you. We haven't got time to break her in, so an attachment to F-MIT's first black DCI will do her good."

"I suppose it might, but I've got a whole cast of specialists on their way to me now who will each need a thorough briefing. I don't need to be wet-nursing a new DI when I come in to work tomorrow."

"Do you want her or not?"

"I suppose beggars can't be choosers, sir."

Shackerstone closed the phone, sighed, and ambled towards the photographer's white van for the first of his briefings.

Three

Question (DI Graham): "For the record, how did Lucy become a victim?"

Answer(Suspect): "She wasn't supposed to get her face burnt. Nobody was supposed to find the…"

Q: "You misunderstand. For the tape I need you to describe why you chose her as a victim later on."

A: "Because she was a perfect fit, and the piano room was the perfect location. (Pause) And revenge, of course."
(Extract from evidential tape transcript.)

Shackerstone parked his car in the police station yard. "Is it okay if I finish now?" asked Dastra, opening the door to get out.

"This isn't the bloody Met… you'll still be here at midnight and I'll be here signing your overtime. You remain at work 'subject to the exigencies of duty' as regulations have it. Reshard, find him a witness statement to take. Give me the log."

"Guv."

Shackerstone tucked the decision log under his arm and hurried in through the rear doors of the police station.

Sitting in his office about twenty minutes later, writing more entries in his decision log, Shackerstone heard a lone voice in the main CID office. It was Khan on the phone to someone. "Get yourself up to CID; I've got an action for you."

He heard Khan put the phone down and within thirty seconds, there was the sound of footsteps coming up the stairs.

"Sarge," came a newly familiar voice. It was Dastra.

"You've drawn the short straw, new boy. The lady in Wemstone hospital with the chemical burns. She caused the fall in the tunnel, and she's a Yank."

"On a protest here? She's got some nerve."

"You can ask her all about it."

"I bet she's a fat, mouthy, gum chewing lesbian."

Shackerstone got up and stopped just inside the main office. "With a burnt face, Constable Dastra. According to witnesses, it was a very pretty face until this morning. A little humanity, please?"

"Okay, sorry, sir"

Shackerstone watched as Khan handed Dastra some evidence bags. "Get full details, seize her clothes, and find out from the hospital when she will be fit to make a witness statement."

"I'll need a car," said Dastra

"None to spare. Have you got your own here?"

"In the station yard."

"Guv, will you authorize Dastra's car for him to claim mileage?"

"Sure," said Shackerstone, sitting on a desk and folding his arms. "Cop the details. If the engine's over eighteen hundred, he'll get the higher rate."

"How big is it?" asked Khan.

"Five thousand CC." replied Dastra.

"Five *thousand*? What the hell is that?"

"Porsche 928, I inherited it from my dad."

"I don't think mileage will cover starting her up, will it?"

"Eighteen to the gallon on a run. I guess it would be better if I drove it more slowly."

"You don't drive a sports car around at thirty. If you've got it, flaunt it. You'll need all this overtime to keep the tank filled up."

"Don't get carried away," Shackerstone cautioned. "This part of the country is dotted with speed cameras, and don't ask me to write off any of your speeding fines because you were on police business."

"No, sir."

~ * ~

Lying on a hospital bed, Lucy Aybrams strained her ears as

the silence was penetrated by the distant sound of a dripping tap echoing off hard walls and shiny floors. Through the pad covering her eyes, she could just make out the dim fluorescent glow of the lights above her bed in a room on the observation ward. She listened as a distant noise slowly crystallized into the rolling of a trolley along a hard floor, with accompanying light footsteps. The trolley stopped and Lucy heard female voices echoing along the corridor. She tried to listen but their conversation was indistinct, fragmented by the many surfaces on the path the sound was taking to her ears. Heavier footsteps with slightly squeaky shoes approached the voices, and a man interrupted the conversation. He spoke for short time, and then the squeaky-shoes sound began moving along the corridor towards her room. She tried to estimate how far away they were.

"Miss Lucy Aybrams?" said a deep and softly spoken voice somewhere by the door.

"Hi. Yes. Who is it?"

"Police Constable Dastra. I'm here to get your details and seize your clothes."

"Seize my clothes?"

"Sorry." The voice moved nearer. "Your clothes need to be examined forensically."

"I think they're near me somewhere. Is there a cabinet by the bed?"

"Yes, there is. I'll take a look."

Lucy heard the click of a cupboard door opening, followed by a grunt of satisfaction.

"Police Constable Dastra, do you have a first name?"

"It's Barney."

"Barney Dastra?"

"Just Barney... B. Dastra has an unfortunate anagram."

"Oh. Yes... that could be..."

"Awkward."

Lucy heard an unfamiliar crackle. "What's that noise?"

"Evidence bags. I'm bagging up your clothes."

She listened carefully, trying to visualize what he was doing.

"Anyhow, where are you from?" he said. She heard the clicking of a pen.

"San Francisco."

"How come you're on a bypass protest in England?" His voice was slightly muffled. She thought that perhaps he was looking down and writing.

"I'm in my second year at Oxford, reading history. There were no lectures today. I guess I've always been protesting about something or other. But this was my first road protest."

"Not a good start, then."

"I don't imagine I'll be going down any more tunnels for a while. Maybe I'll stick to trees in future. I guess it's harder to hide bodies in trees."

"Yes. Look, I know this can't be easy. Have they said whether you will be okay? I mean…"

"Will I go blind?"

"Well… Yes."

"They don't know. Your colleagues say there was quicklime poured all around the bones, but most of it has changed to ordinary lime because of rain."

"So it isn't as bad as it could be?"

"That's what the doctors say. But lime still does a lot more damage than acid."

"Gosh. Does it?" The pen clicked again.

"The ophthalmologist told me that acids form a protective layer on the eye. Alkalis eat into the cells."

"I'm sorry to hear that." She felt him touch the back of her hand. "Does your family know you are here?"

"No. I want to find out how bad it is going to be before I phone home."

"What about friends at college?"

"The local cops have left a message for my flatmate, but she'll be out tonight and tomorrow."

"It's not a good time to be alone."

"I've got nurses and doctors."

"And cops."

"Yes. The occasional cop named Barney. I wonder if… What do you look like?"

"Sorry?" She felt him draw his hand away. Lucy remained quite still.

"I want to know what you look like so I can recognize you

when I get rid of this dressing."

"But they'll send a detective next time. I'm just a plod, sorry, a uniformed officer."

"I might run into you. You never know. Perhaps on another protest, or when you return my clothes."

There was silence, followed by the sound of the rubber-tipped legs of a chair being dragged across to the bed. Lucy heard Dastra sit down on the hard plastic seat. "Okay. I'm male, white, five-ten, twenty-five years old, medium build, dark wavy hair, brown eyes, hooked nose, high cheekbones. People sometimes say that I'm a bit Jewish looking. That should be enough to pick me out of an identity parade. Okay, now it's your turn."

"My turn?"

"I can manage female, white, uh, American, twentyish, shoulder-length straight red hair, slim build, five six to five seven...but I can't see your face."

"Bright red and burned."

His voice softened and he slowed down. "I mean, uh, on a normal day, when you're not lying on your back in Wemstone General."

"Okay. Sorry. Dark blue eyes, I hope, reasonable sized nose."

"There you go. If we run into each other again, we just might recognize one another." Lucy heard him rise from the chair. "I must go now, so..."

"Haven't you forgotten something?"

"I have?"

"My name and address? My date of birth?"

"I got them from reception on the way in."

"Oh... so you have to leave now?"

"I'm all finished here."

"Listen, Barney. As you said, it's a bit lonely lying here, worrying about my sight. I wondered if you would stay a while."

"I need to get home..."

"So do I..."

There was an awkward silence.

"Are you still there?"

"Yes. Sorry. That wasn't very sensitive."

"That's okay. Don't cops have to be good at talking to people?"

"They do. But sometimes the selection procedure lets someone like me in."

"Are you shy?"

"No..." She heard him sit down. "Okay. I admit I used to be. The job has changed me. It has to."

Lucy wanted to ask him if he had decided to stay, but she felt he hadn't made his mind up yet and she didn't want to precipitate a decision.

"Can you tell me about the bones? I *did* find them."

"It's confidential, but yes, just general stuff."

"That's okay."

"Well, if this is murder, then it's a mercifully rare method of body disposal."

"In what way?"

"Not a run of the mill killing where the victim is left where they died. Most of us never get near a case where steps have been taken to hide the body. It is unlikely to be a domestic killing, if it is two women..."

"Two? I thought there was just one. I guess everyone at the station house will be working on finding out who they were."

"Yes, there will be some really painstaking work on the forensics tonight, then weeks of chasing up leads and statement taking."

"Lots of procedure... just like in the States."

"Then it all has to be logged in on HOLMES...that's a computer database."

"HOLMES? Is that named after Sherlock?"

"In a way. It stands for Home Office Large Major Enquiry System."

"Large... major...that's tautological."

She detected a soft laugh from him. "It is, but you can have a *small* major enquiry. A cut and dry domestic murder for instance. HOLMES was invented about twenty years ago, after the Yorkshire Ripper case. A lorry—truck—driver went all over the north of England murdering prostitutes."

"I've been here long enough to know what a lorry is.

Anyway, go on, please."

"In those days, everything went onto a card index. When he was eventually caught by a bit of good patrolling by uniformed officers, it was discovered that his name had been in the system all along. An officer had even recommended that a senior detective interview him. So HOLMES was created to avoid that happening again."

"So it's worth all the effort?"

"It is, when it works." There was silence for an interval and then they then both tried to break it at the same moment.

"Will…" began Dastra.

"Can I…"

"Sorry."

"Sorry, you were about to say something."

"I was going to ask if you will be okay for help over here if your sight is damaged."

"I don't know. I'll try not to think about it."

"And how about the shock of finding dead bodies?"

"With nothing else to see just now, it's hard to get the images out of my head."

"Talk with someone if you need to… a good friend or someone like that."

"Is that what you do?"

"Yes, I… no, I don't really. I guess it may be a man thing… you just bottle stuff up and deal with it alone. Anyhow, I have left my friends back in the Met, sorry, the Metropolitan Police. I've just moved out of London to this police force so I can take over my parents' house near Henley."

"Oh?"

"They both died a little while back."

"I'm sorry."

"Thank you. That's kind of you."

"How long ago was it?"

"Only four months…back in February. They were in their seventies."

"You must have been a late-life baby. Do you have brothers and sisters?"

"None at all. I was adopted after they discovered they

couldn't have kids."

"They were a bit old to adopt weren't they?"

"Yes, but I was in a kids' home, which wasn't a good place for someone like me. Mum and Dad fostered me when I was seven. Then they had a long battle to adopt me... indeed because of their age."

Lucy created a mental picture of a determined but devoted couple fighting bureaucracy. For a moment, she imagined a small cottage with them living happily together.

"Did you keep their house because of memories?"

"There's more to it than that. It is a grand place in its own grounds. It has been in the family for over a century. Dad wants, uh, wanted me to pass it on to my children."

"Uh... and you have made no progress in that direction?"

"No, not at all. I was born to be single."

"Is there someone? Sorry, that's intrusive of me."

"Nobody special. It's not that I'm gay or anything like that, I'm just generally a bit of a slow starter with the ladies."

"You're doing just fine with me. How long have you been a cop?"

"About four years. Up until last week, I was at a place called Harlesden. It was violent, but I bet it's not like San Francisco."

"Most of it is relatively safe, but there are thousands of homeless. They come from all across the States because they hear that San Francisco is very liberal. In fact it's so liberal that people pretty much dislike the police."

"Do you?"

"Do I what?"

"Dislike the police."

"I've never been very comfortable with cops."

"But you still asked me to stay."

"Yes. I did. You sounded...interesting."

"I hope I've lived up to expectations. How about you? Are you interesting?"

Lucy heard Dastra's chair give a squeak as if he were shifting his weight to relax.

"I'm still really at school. Life has been pretty sheltered until now, although Oxford has brought other opportunities."

"Such as?"

"Meeting different people. You see, everyone back in my neighborhood came from much the same background. I guess we were all white, middle class, and hiding in a liberal pocket of white, middle class, Little America. I know that Oxford is unique, and pretty elitist even by British standards, but it is still a world away from home."

"Just a streak of rebellion in you then?"

"I suppose, yes, I am rebellious."

"Hence your presence on protests. Have you been arrested yet?"

"Geez, yes, nearly, but I charmed my way out of it."

"Which is probably just as well. I don't think the courts over here would be too impressed by American students militantly taking on local issues."

"I have often thought of that, but it's the risk. I need to protest. So long as it is something I believe in, I'm always ready to wave a placard and shout. Like today... I think you British should be proud to preserve your heritage."

"But it's only some old patch of woods."

"It's ancient woodland, and it'll be lost forever under pavement."

"But there are loads of woods round here. It's not like some old cathedral or a college in Oxford. I mean, I can relate to preserving old buildings—you could say I've got one myself."

"Of course, and so you must appreciate architecture."

"Architecture? I suppose so." He paused, "Yes, I suppose I do. In fact, thinking about it, I used to travel to different cathedrals as a young teenager, taking photographs and doing sketches."

"Really? That's wonderful. Do you still have them?"

"Yes, back home."

"Perhaps when I can... when I can see again...I could come and look."

"Okay. If you like."

"Aren't you going to ask me about my family?"

"I was getting round to it. What are your mum and dad like?"

"Both are in their late forties. Dad's a nuclear physicist, Mom was, too. They met through his work. She gave it up when they had me. But..."

"But?"

"They're not happy at the moment... heading for divorce. Maybe. I guess, if I'm blind it might change things."

"I wouldn't rely on that. Disability can add more strain to a relationship. And anyhow, you said you were trying not to think about it."

"I'm sorry. I jumped to the worst outcome then tried to find a silver lining. The thought of divorce is upsetting. Dad is very dedicated to his work. He's never home. I expect you see a lot of that in your job."

"Yes. A lot of police marriages go down the pan for that reason, as well as too many opportunities to meet people at strange hours in strange places."

"Makes sense."

"What about Oxford. You mentioned a flatmate."

"A girlfriend, Michaela, from Nottingham. She's on the same course. You could meet her."

"If we ever run into each other again."

Lucy heard Dastra get up from the chair. "Are you going?"

"I'm sorry, but I've got to get your clothes booked in."

"Thanks for staying for a while."

"It's a pleasure."

Suddenly, she felt him take her hand and hold it in both of his.

"All the very best for the future, Lucy. I hope everything works out okay for you."

"Thanks."

He lowered her hand slowly to the bed and she heard him walking away.

"Barney?" she called after him. His footsteps stopped, paused, and then came back towards her. "Barney, I just wanted to say I'm sorry we couldn't... I mean, I wish we'd met before today."

"Me too."

Four

Question (DI Graham): "Why Wemstone?"
Answer (Suspect): "Proximity to the house. That was all."
(Extract from evidential tape transcript.)

The morning after the skeletons had been found, Dastra made his way up to the third floor of Wemstone police station to the newly opened incident room. He checked through the wired glass in the wooden doors to see if anybody was about, and saw two men busy at computer screens. Dastra pushed the door open and one of the men looked up. "Can I help, mate?"

"I was looking for DS Khan." said Dastra, making his way towards the officer's desk.

"At home in bed... he was up all night."

"Gosh, they were quick." He picked up some photographs of the bypass scene.

"Sorry? Were you there then?"

"PC Dastra. I did Shackerstone's log and generally helped a bit at the scene yesterday. I dealt with the girl in the hospital... the one who caused the collapse."

"Pleased to meet you"

"Call me Barney."

"I was on annual leave yesterday, Barney. I missed the discovery."

"Any news from the post mortem?"

"Due this afternoon..." came the voice of the other man, seated at a HOLMES terminal. Dastra noted that the man didn't look up, but stared intently at the computer screen. He was in his early fifties, graying and well built. "If we get the bodies out this morning," he added.

"By the way, I didn't introduce myself. I'm Martin O'Donoghue, and this is the older Brian, Brian Calver. We're still taking the soil out a teaspoon at a time."

"I prefer "Retired Brian"," said Calver, turning to shake Dastra's hand.

"PC Dastra, everyone calls me Barney."

"So you're Barney."

"Yes, where's the rest of the squad?"

"Still being formed, but we've got the basics and even a shiny new Detective Inspector. She's going to the post mortem with Shackerstone. You already know DS Khan."

"Yes, I went to the scene with him and the DCI."

"A lot of the others are getting some shuteye. Shackerstone's at the scene with six officers fresh this morning. Surveyors are going to dig the whole lot over when we finish to see if there are any more bodies."

"More?"

"You know there was a third, on top of the others?"

"A third? I don't suppose you need another detective on the squad?"

"Speak to Khan," said Brian. "He was trying to fight your corner late yesterday evening with Shackerstone before he went home. I wouldn't hold your breath though. Check your e-mails. He might have left you a note."

With his spirits lifting at the possibility of getting back into the CID, Dastra found a computer in an empty office and logged on to his internal messages. There was nothing from Khan, but there was a message asking him to be at the superintendent's office at 10 a.m. He logged off despondently. At 9.55, he went up a floor to the superintendent's secretary's office and waited for his appointment. He was mildly irritated at being kept waiting, but eventually at twenty past ten, a squat, heavily built, large faced, dark-haired man in his mid-forties came out to meet him. Dastra stood up, recognizing the uniform markings of a superintendent.

"Hello, I'm Ian Yardley" said the man, with a strong

Cockney accent. "Welcome to Wemstone, David." He shook Dastra's hand vigorously. "Pleased to meet you. Come in to my office."

"Thank you, sir."

They entered the office and he offered Dastra a chair. The walls were covered in old group photographs from different police training courses, much like other similar offices in London.

"I understand from Mr. Shackerstone that your colleagues in the Met called you Barney. Do you mind that? You know we are less keen on nicknames than we used to be... bullying and all that stuff."

"I like it, sir. To be honest, I've grown fond of it. There are too many 'Davids' in The Job."

"Yes, my second name is David."

"Oh, I didn't mean it like that sir. I..."

"That's all right, Barney. You are right. I was on a relief with six 'Mikes' on it. Policing is full of 'Mikes' and 'Daves'. Perhaps someone should do a thesis on it at the Police Staff College at Bramshill. Anyhow, why Barney?"

"I was in care until seven. My old team decided it must have been

Dr. Barnardo's, so they nicknamed me Barney."

"Yes. 'Local Authority Care Home' would have been a tad long-winded as a name. Mr. Shackerstone tells me you have made yourself useful at the crime scene."

"Thank you, sir, that's the sort of work I like... being a detective in the Met. That was my field. I would like to get back..."

"Yes, moved from the Met. You've got a big, expensive house out Henley way?"

"I inherited it. Dad wanted to keep it in the family."

"That's good. I see you are single; still playing the field then?"

Dastra blushed slightly and smiled.

"You've spent a day working with Detective Sergeant Khan."

"Yes."

"I'll tell you what, Barney. Khan's been a busy man over the last twenty-four hours. A job like yesterday's is always a battle to get a spanner on jelly, but he and Shackerstone have really got a grip on it. Khan was still here at seven this morning when I came in. That's when he spoke to me about you."

"Sir?"

"Look, you were still a relatively new detective in your old force." Yardley got up and looked out of the window. "Central Southern Police Force's policy is that everyone who comes to us on transfer does twelve months on uniformed shift work getting to know the area. This is so that you get used to geography, people, systems and procedure. It also gives us a chance to look at your performance."

Dastra stared bleakly at the floor.

"The problem is we are short of uniformed officers, but shorter still of detectives, especially ones who have seen the sharper end of policing. Therefore, I've told Mr. Shackerstone to expect you tomorrow at 0800 on the murder squad, third floor incident room. Finish your induction day, Barney. You were in the right place at the right time yesterday. Some of us make our own luck... so keep it up."

"I'll do my best. Thank you sir."

Five

Question (DI Graham): "So how does one come to terms with killing in this way?"

Answer (Suspect): "Dehumanize them. If you treat them like you are breaking up an old machine, like an old car or something, then it becomes easy."

Q: "Easy?"
A: "Yes, the key is to have no empathy at all. Treating their lives like nothing, like slaughtering an animal in an abattoir. Then the job gets done."

Q: "Job?"
A: "Yes, a job of work, like Nazis in extermination units. Part of you just gets on with it, yet you remain 'decent' as Himmler put it."

Q: "Decent?"
A: "You feel detached from any sense of wrongdoing... sinless."
(Extract from evidential tape transcript.)

Detective Chief Inspector Brian Shackerstone sat in his car in the mortuary car park munching a banana sandwich. A red Renault Clio driven by a white brunette of about thirty-five trundled into the car park and parked in one of the marked doctors' bays. Shackerstone caught a glimpse of her face and long neck. He smiled to himself.

"I wouldn't mind being her patient."

He watched the driver's door open and two slender legs in smart red trousers swivel out of the car. The woman stood up and made her way towards him. He lowered his electric window.

"Hello there, can I help?"

"Hello Mr. Shackerstone. Don't you remember me? I was a DC on operation Nunney with you."

"DC Graham?"

"Detective Inspector Graham."

Shackerstone got out of his car and shook her hand firmly. "Nicola...uh, Nikki, of course, right? What are you here for?"

"I'm your new DI."

"Super! On promotion?"

"Yes. Just finished my course."

"You'll be on top of all the new policies then. Good."

They wandered across the car park and into the back entrance of the mortuary building. A voice echoed in the corridor. "Down here!"

"We'll get some gloves and suits," replied Shackerstone. A minute later, in paper coveralls, they were in the main mortuary. He hated mortuaries, but treated them as an unpleasant professional necessity. He had prepared himself for the smell with a bit of Vick's Vaporub up each nostril but in the event it was unnecessary; the smell was of damp soil, as the remaining flesh on the bodies had been desiccated by quicklime.

Shackerstone folded his arms and surveyed the room. Under bright fluorescent lights, each set of remains, with an amount of soil, lay on a separate table. Beneath each body was the plastic sheet in which it had been wrapped for removal from the protest site.

The photographer had mounted a video camera on a tripod to make a continuous record, but concentrated on obtaining high quality stills using a Hasselblad roll film camera attached to the same tripod head by a short bar. He had set them up at the end of the table nearest to the door. SOCO White was bending over and peering at the remains with the pathologist who was standing with him near the head end of the table. There were mutterings from the pair of them, but their words were muffled by the hum of powerful extractor fans in the ceiling. They finished with the area they were working on before either bothered to look up from their work and acknowledge the entry of the two detectives.

"Ah, there you are. Colm O'Toole, pathologist. I'm sorry I can't shake your hands. You must be the new DI."

Shackerstone replied, "This is DI Graham. Detective Superintendent Gordonstown is stuck at court."

"Detective Inspector Graham," said O'Toole, politely. "I'm pleased to meet you. Evidently you are as new to your job as Mr. Shackerstone thinks I am to mine."

"I've been on F-MIT for a week."

"I've been in medicine in one way or another for seventeen years, if you count medical school, but your boss feels thirty-five is too young for a Home Office pathologist. He likes us old and a bit frayed round the edges."

"Can we get on?" whispered Shackerstone.

"As you wish. I estimate there's at least five days' work here. And I'll need a forensic anthropologist."

"I know," intoned Shackerstone, with an air of resignation. "It's in hand."

"So all you get today is a preliminary look, but usual rules apply."

"A general view, nothing you'd swear to in court."

"Precisely." O'Toole flicked on a voice-activated tape recorder, placed it next to the first set of remains, and began. "Three bodies, probably females between the ages of sixteen and thirty, approximately. All found in sandy soil." He looked at Shackerstone for confirmation. Shackerstone nodded.

"All three have been buried in quicklime, but it's the trap so many killers have fallen into; lime doesn't eat bodies away quickly, indeed, it mummifies them for the first few months. Where each body has been in the lime, the skin is shriveled back onto the skeleton. What has caused most of the tissue loss is action by creatures that have burrowed into the unaffected flesh and organs. All three have had the remains of gray nylon rope recovered from them and where separate this has been removed at the scene by police. I must comment that the first body we are looking at still has the cord around the wrists and ankles. If I lift the pelvis here,

Malcolm, you will get your shot."

Shackerstone moved out of the way, as the photographer moved his tripod and took a number of pictures, replacing the back of the camera with a fresh pre-loaded roll-film holder when it ran out.

"Beginning with an overview of this body: As you can see most of the top of the skull has been crushed, although the teeth are intact, as is some tissue around the lower jaw and neck. Most of the skeleton is complete. There is quite a bit of saponified flesh at the front and side of the left hip, but the inner organs have been a feast for burrowing creatures. Tibia and fibula and feet bones are all intact. At a guess she was sixteen to twenty-four, slim, but at present I can't even tell you what part of the planet she came from. If I hadn't got a pelvis, I wouldn't have been able to tell you the gender."

"Apart from foot size and a shoe."

"You're the detective."

"Take some general shots, Malcolm."

The photographer continued on his business, with SOCO White standing idle.

"Done enough, have you?" asked Shackerstone.

"Uh, yes, Guv. Most of the samples I needed I got at the scene."

After about twenty-five minutes or so of picture taking and general anatomical observations from O'Toole, they moved across to the next body. O'Toole brought his tape recorder and pushed his glasses firmly onto the bridge of his nose.

"Number two is the best preserved of the three: European female, mid-twenties to early thirties, five-foot-six to five-foot-seven inches tall, slim build, red hair, long strands still adhering to pieces of flesh on the skull."

The photographer needed no cue and continued his work.

"Have you got some hair samples?"

White nodded.

"Her teeth are intact and she has only one small filling. I will try for a dental impression later. There are some remarkably well preserved tissues around the windpipe area and although there is little left of the skin on the neck, damage to the cartilage there is consistent with either strangulation or crushing, and this may be before or after death—it is impossible to determine which. I'm going to lift up the rib cage to show how animals have eaten the internal organs right down to the spine. I get the feeling the hole was limed first and she was dumped in it with body one, both on their backs as we saw at the scene. Number three was placed face down on top of the others, but lying the other way, then lime was added, hence all three have the greatest chemical action to their backs and arms, which were still tied behind them at the time of burial. Good job the rope was nylon, or we would have lost that too."

The photographer moved in and took more shots. "That's interesting," he said, with his eye still pressed to the back of his camera. "There are scores on the inside of the ribcage."

"That may help identify her... they might be from an operation. Let me have a look. Can one of you hold the ribs, here?"

Shackerstone nodded to Graham, and she pinched the ribcage awkwardly, avoiding adhesions of saponified tissue. O'Toole moved round to the other side by the photographer. He pressed his glasses back onto the bridge of his nose and screwed up his face.

"Yes, most interesting. There are score marks inside the right fourth and fifth rib, blunt gouges about half a centimetre wide. Too big for nibbling creatures. Perhaps done accidentally during excavation, but certainly if any older, done not much before death. There has been no healing of the bones."

O'Toole became more animated and crouched down to get a clear look from near the level of the slab.

"We may be going off at a tangent here, but if these marks are associated with the cause of death, then a long bladed weapon from the back may have made them."

He paused, drawing himself up and returning to his composed academic manner.

"In any case, and this is strictly conjecture, the vertical aspect of the scratches suggests the blade came from below, perhaps the lower back, outside of the ribcage. That is if these marks are in any way evidential at all. You can lower the ribcage now."

He moved on to the lower part of body.

"Not a great deal of tissue at all in the pelvic area and some bone has been lost to gnawing by rodents. However, the femurs are both fine specimens, with up to five centimetres of tissue depth in places and farther down where the tissues have gone this lady has suffered a broken right lower tibia, which has healed well."

He pointed out a thickening of bone around the blackened right ankle, and the photographer moved in to record it.

"Wood... we found some wood," said White.

Shackerstone frowned, "Sorry, Jim?"

"We recovered wood fibers in the soil from the ribcage, and some bits of well-rotted wood from the lower abdomen. We thought a plank or something had been placed over the body, and had fallen into it as it decomposed."

"So the damage to the ribs may have been done when these were removed, or when the plank rotted through the body?" asked Shackerstone.

"Unlikely," O'Toole replied. "These abrasions are from the rear. However, thank you for the thought Jim. We need all we can get here." O'Toole suddenly stepped back to the first body, lifting the ribcage and peering in. He said nothing and then moved round to the third body.

"Well, as Saint Stephen would have said, 'Stone me.'"

"What?" asked Shackerstone.

"Body one has the same marks, but slightly over to the right. Number three, when we come to examine her, has a severe amount of damage between the scapula and rear ribs."

"And?" said Shackerstone impatiently.

O'Toole didn't change his tone, but carried on looking at the second body. "You have all the ingredients: the dark lines in the soil, coupled with the traces of wood, suggest a long wooden rod. Three rods in fact; one for each body. I would go so far as to suggest that each rod might have had a sharp end which has ended up pressed against these ribs, or in the third case, it has exited the body just behind the shoulder."

"You're not suggesting..."

"I am. These three young ladies have been impaled on wooden spikes."

Shackerstone looked intently at O'Toole, trying to imagine the kind of deaths the victims had endured. Only the humming of the fans broke the minute or so of silence that followed.

Eventually, O'Toole raised his eyebrows and continued as if

there hadn't been a break. "Of course, it may not be possible to determine that this was the cause of death, especially with the suggestion of strangulation. I would concentrate on impaling as part of a general Modus Operandi. If you get the wood to the lab, they should help you see if there is a lot of human blood in it."

Graham asked, "Has anything like this been recorded before?"

"Some paedophile doing babysitting did the kids on railings back in the seventies, I think. But otherwise nothing I know of recently," replied O'Toole, "but it used to be a method of execution in the old Ottoman Empire, and of course, by Vlad the Impaler."

"Vlad the Impaler?"

"He was medieval Romanian warlord, and famed for impaling anybody for just about anything. He even impaled a lazy woman for failing to mend her husband's clothes."

"So he wasn't all bad," Shackerstone mumbled.

O'Toole carried on poking around the body. "It is said that the crime rate in his fiefdom was zero. The Dracula stories are loosely based on him. I believe they even called him Dracula in his time."

"So we are looking for a modern day Vlad?"

"Subject to further forensic analysis, as always."

Six

Question (DI Graham): "The Modus Operandi was discovered by our pathologist. He said it would have been a slow and extremely distressing death."

Answer (Suspect): "Yes, but stimulating... the victims' attempts to move about, to achieve a last shred of comfort... it makes them slide down the rod faster. That's the bloody irony of being impaled."

Q: *"And you enjoy watching this?"*
A: *"What do you think?"*

Q: *"I asked you."*
A: *"Yes. Death is a spectator sport, as it was for the citizens of the Roman Empire. That's why it's best to do the first killing in sight of the next victims. The Romans did it that way. When the next victims see the one in front turn to meat and they know they are next in line, it's real drama."*
(Extract from evidential tape transcript.)

Shackerstone could detect a restrained air of morbid interest on Wednesday among the forty-five police and support staff crowding into the incident room. He sensed them cautiously eyeing the scene and post mortem photographs on three large display boards, and sat down on a vacant swivel chair in front of the photos, facing his investigation team as if challenging them to look beyond him. Sitting to his right, he knew that criminal psychologist Dr.

Robert Holt would provide far more interest to the team than photographs of the skeletons. Rumors about the murder method had spread round the station, but nobody wished to appear to be keen to find out the details, even though it was human nature that it was the main thought on many minds.

Gordonstown and Yardley were both in the room, as were other representatives from the uniformed majority of the division. Gordonstown had been one of the last to arrive, and had ended up sitting on a desk. Morning sun streamed in through dusty Venetian blinds and two officers noisily tried to adjust them in order to reduce the glare.

Superintendent Yardley began. "Good morning, everyone. For those of you on loan from the Force Major Incident Team, I'm Superintendent Ian Yardley, the sub-divisional commander for Wemstone. Those of you who have been on this investigation since Monday will know many of the ins and outs of it, but for everyone's benefit, we are having a full briefing.

"I know this is all a bit unusual, but Mr. Gordonstown's Detective Chief Inspectors at F-MIT are all working to their limit on the reinvestigations ordered by the Chief Constable to make sure we haven't any hidden messes like the Stephen Lawrence case. We happen to have one of their recent losses as our new DCI, so I've got agreement for him to run this one, and in return, I've agreed to staff a murder squad here, but with the loan of five F-MIT officers in key posts.

"DCI Shackerstone is a seasoned murder detective, and when I heard he was leaving F-MIT I snapped him up. Brian and I go back a long way, to the days when it took a great deal of courage for a black officer to go out on patrol." Shackerstone acknowledged the comment with a nod. "Headquarters has sent us DI Nicola Graham to be Deputy Investigating Officer and Mr. Gordonstown will be in charge overall.

"Our investigation strategy is to identify, locate, and detain the suspect or suspects for these murders, minimizing further risk to the public and ourselves. The investigation will be done in a manner consistent with the force's statement of common purpose and values… which means we will be as open as we can, with, of course, a particular eye to our reputation. We don't want to get panned by a public enquiry several years down the line like our colleagues in London have with Lawrence. Now, before I let Mr. Shackerstone continue, I must request that you all remain focused on the wider political picture. The burial site has provided a convenient way of moving the protest on. However, as the site is now necessarily open for our purposes, the contractors are worried about a reoccupation. Please be thorough, but I would like to get the site sealed off and fenced as soon as possible. I'll hand you over to Mr. Shackerstone."

Shackerstone rose from his chair.

"Right, listen in, everyone." He turned and surveyed the photographs then turned back to his audience.

"On Monday during a protest on the new bypass route, the partial collapse of a tunnel dug by protestors revealed two sets of human remains. Further work at the site has revealed another set of remains in the same grave. A lot of excellent forensic work and manual labor by members of this team has established the following facts.

"One: All three bodies are female, still unidentified. Two: At or about the time of death they were impaled on wooden shafts, and this is the most likely cause of death. One body has evidence of a ligature to the neck. Three: We have no crime scene yet for the deaths. Bloody clay on a shoe suggests elsewhere than the burial site. Four: They were placed in the ground at approximately the same time, and were certainly buried at the same time. Five: Quicklime was used in a vain attempt to speed decomposition and we've recovered a corner of one of the bags it might have come from. Six: There are no clothing remains, except one shoe, but some pieces of nylon rope used to tie the wrists have been recovered. Any questions?"

"Yes, Guv," asked a DC. "Do we know which way in the shaft went?"

"Can't tell; there isn't enough left in the pelvis areas to help."

"That's a pity."

"Right, we have no intelligence on this at all. No index in the country can give us any help on impalers, as you might expect. The only two we know of are doing life for the murders of children. Missing persons have almost drawn a blank, but we are hopeful of one possible, and dental records are being sought now. To summarize Mr. Yardley's strategy, we are going to treat this as murder and catch the bastard who did it. This will be achieved from two opposite directions. Firstly, forensic work from the discovery site should help us to establish possible murder scenes and with luck, where the quicklime was bought. Secondly, establishing the identity of the victims should give us a steer into the knowledge we need about their movements. This will inevitably bring us into contact with their families and a difficult and emotional time for them and us. The Met is being beaten up at the Stephen Lawrence Inquiry over the poor performance of family liaison. Only two officers here have had any training in this at all, but I don't want to get into the same scenario. Keep full records of contact with the families and keep them informed. Please retain your best professional demeanor at all times. The movements of the victims should assist in providing information about how they fell into the hands of the murderer and should assist in leading us to the murder site. When we have established this, we will be halfway to catching our killer."

Shackerstone stopped and stroked his chin. "I have agreed with Mr. Gordonstown to withhold the MO from the press for the time being, at least until identities have been established for the victims and next-of-kin informed." Shackerstone put his hands in his pockets and looked at the floor briefly before continuing. "We can't assess whether the victims were killed at the same time, so we have to treat this with an open mind. It may be a one-off, with three victims, or three separate events. The latter seems unlikely because of the risks of storing the bodies. We have nothing to suggest that these are part of a series, and until any other bodies are found, we can't say for definite that this is part of the work of a serial killer. What we *have* done is to employ a psychologist recommended by the National Crime Faculty to try to give us an offender profile. Dr. Robert Holt assisted us with the A4 rapist, creating a fairly accurate picture of the life and habits of a night worker at Heathrow Airport.

"You all know it was a good police stop that eventually caught him and Rob was proved to be spot-on. He has looked at what we have got and has a reasonable view that we are looking for a lone male killer, on the basis that you don't get a lot of impalers about, and the likelihood of two teaming up is pretty remote. The rest I will leave to him in a minute.

"Right, the following are the key roles within this team: DI Graham will be office manager and Deputy Investigating Officer. DS Shanter will be the Receiver. DS Khan will run team one and DS Walsh, team two. There are lists on the wall for the rest of you. Finally, the name we have come up with for this investigation is operation Klingsor. Right, now if Dr. Holt would take over, please. Rob?"

A tall, skinny, balding white man of about forty-five rose and clasped hands behind his back. "Thank you, Brian. Well, there are a number of details I would like to have been able to glean from the post mortem examinations, particularly the point of entry of the stakes into the bodies. With no information one way or the other, I have concentrated on impaling as a general method. Since yesterday afternoon, I have studied all I can find about impalers available from sources all over the world. Apart from descriptions of impalement as a method of execution in countries in bygone centuries, the only personality we can look at with any reliable certainty is that of Vlad Tee-Pish—spelt T-E-P-E-S—the medieval Romanian warlord. This approach of course would only be valid if impaling was the primary motive for the killings. More recent crimes involving impaling have used the impaling as an afterthought, often to cover previous harm against the individual, or to mount a body as a trophy to terrorize the finder. This clearly isn't valid here, as there was a concerted attempt to hide the three bodies. We should, I believe keep an open mind as to whether the impalings are subsidiary to an earlier sexual offence. Nevertheless, impaling appears to have been done for the benefit of the killer and for his eyes only.

"My interest in the point of entry is quite important. The disorder often referred to as Vagina Dentata, whereby the sufferer believes women's vaginas contain teeth that will eat his penis, has been documented. It is true that sufferers have become involved in intense violence on female genitalia, often culminating in murder. This should be kept in mind when the point of entry is established.

"My preferred theory—and I must emphasize that it is only a theory—is that anybody who needs to kill three women in this manner in one session is a spree killer at the very least and probably a potential serial killer. With this in mind, I have looked closely at

Vlad Tepes, who by numbers alone is the greatest killer of this type.

"Apparently he was handed over to Ottoman Turkey by his father as a hostage against his father's potential disloyalty. The Turks at that time used impaling as the Romans did crucifixion, and young Vlad was doubtless made to witness such events, possibly creating a series of early traumatic experiences. As he grew up at the Ottoman court, he started to amuse himself by impaling small creatures. He started with insects, before moving on to small mammals. When he returned home to inherit his kingdom, he ruled it with only one capital punishment: Impaling. He had successive wars with German settlers crossing the Transylvanian Alps, and with his old captors, the Turks. In one war, he lined their route to his stronghold with the impaled bodies of his own people in order to unnerve his enemies, and he once impaled a whole town of people for complaining about taxation.

"He enjoyed the slow death he inflicted on his victims and this appears to have been the prime motivation for his behavior. He was a loner, without compassion or scruple, with little or no loyalty or regard for those around him. A young princess tried to trick him into marrying her by telling him she was pregnant. When he discovered she was not, he had her abdomen cut open from top to bottom with a T-shape incision while she was still alive, and had her hung up for everyone to see. He treated women as little more than animals. Even his eventual wife threw herself to her death from their castle as their enemies closed in and he ran off to Hungary.

"He didn't believe in letting the vengeful children of his victims live. He is even reported to have impaled a mother and had her suckling infant sewn by its lips onto one of her nipples."

Holt checked the room for reactions, but the officers listened on, cold and impassive. Shackerstone gave a slight nod of his head, signaling Holt to continue.

"My own view is that we now need to proceed on the basis of a worst case scenario that our man *is* a serial killer and has struck elsewhere, or will do. He may be suffering a Vagina Dentata type of psychosis. If it is a one-off spree killing we have little to lose by exploring the serial option, with the added benefit that we will be prepared for the worst." Holt paused for effect. "Serial killers tend to be white, male, heterosexual, sexually dysfunctional, and often socially inadequate. Generally, they tend to murder within their own ethnic group. Many insert themselves into the police inquiry in some way, in order to exercise some control over the event they fear the most: discovery. Insecure by nature, they will not vary their Modus Operandi significantly, and the more recent killers have exhibited a high degree of forensic awareness. These are early days of course, and our picture will grow more accurate as time goes on. What I do feel, is that three will not be enough, and that others may be lying undiscovered. This chap isn't proud of his work. He has gone to a lot of trouble to hide these three. For a serial killer, pride is the enemy. It makes him predictable and ultimately self- destructive, because he needs to tell someone. Think about that. He has a personality, habits, a life somewhere, friends, family, who knows?"

That was a good note to end on, thought Shackerstone, rising from his chair as Holt sat down. "You know where we are, and you all have actions to be getting on with. There's just one thing: I don't want this bloke being nicknamed Vlad. It would be unfair to the victim's families, the case would gain a high profile far too early, and the resulting pressure it would bring on this case from the media would be enough to cause us to take risks and make mistakes. Is that understood? *No nickname.*"

There were nods from around the room. "Thanks, that's all for now." Chattering filled the room as people drifted out or returned to their desks. Shanter made his way towards Shackerstone. "Guv, we've got problems with HOLMES. The increase in the number of new terminals has overloaded the server."

"What does that mean to a layman?"

"It means we've got to spend some money getting the computer bods to install a bigger drive."

"How much?"

"Three grand."

Shackerstone shook his head. "That's nothing on a job like this. Just get it done, pronto. HOLMES needs to be working for us."

"Guv." Shanter turned and picked up the nearest phone. Shackerstone scanned the room and saw Gordonstown approaching. "Who's the new boy?" he asked.

"Transfer from the Met."

"He looks a bit wet behind the ears."

"He has come from Harlesden. For my money and Ian Yardley's, we could do with more like him."

"What's his name?"

"Dastra, Dave Dastra, but everyone calls him Barney."

"Call him over."

"DC Dastra, step this way." Dastra joined them.

"Detective Superintendent Gordonstown, meet DC Dastra."

"Pleased to meet you, sir." said Dastra, offering his hand. Gordonstown didn't take it, but for an awkward moment looked intently at him, while Dastra slowly lowered his arm. Gordonstown spoke.

"If there's one thing in this world I hate after criminals, it's the magnificent bloody Metropolitan Police. What have we done to deserve you?"

Dastra's face reddened. "I'm sorry, have I offended you in some way?"

"I find everyone in the Met offensive."

"He's not in the Met now," interjected Shackerstone. "He's one of us."

Gordonstown grunted, turned on his heel and headed for the door with his hands in his pockets.

"Sorry about that, Barney. Perhaps you can see why..."

"Why you fell out with him? It wouldn't be difficult."

"Don't take it to heart... he's like that with everyone at some point. You just got it in the neck for being from the Met. Anyhow, on a happier note you can spend up to two thousand on a mapping computer and software. Speak to purchasing at HQ and discuss what we need. They reckon they can fast track it."

"That'll be a pleasure, sir. I'll get right onto it."

"Not before you've dealt with this action item," interrupted Khan, handing Dastra a small slip of paper. Dastra read it with an air of resignation. "Obtain witness statement from Lucy Aybrams." He sighed. "But she can't see what she's signing. It would be better to..."

"She has recovered the use of one eye. Collect her from the hospital at 11:30, bring her back here for a statement and then get her back to her digs. Then you can go gadget hunting."

"Yes, Guv, thanks. Just one more thing..."

"Yes?"

"Klingsor? It sounds like a skin disease."

"A magician in an opera. Now go and work some magic for me."

Seven

"Make a friend of what you fear
The shrieking ringing in your ear
Tell yourself you love the screams
That haunt you in your waking dreams."
(Extract from small red notebook, exhibit BS14, seized from suspect)

A voice woke Lucy from her daydream with a jolt. "Hi, Lucy… looks like you get to see me again after all."

Lucy Aybrams, wrapped in a hospital dressing gown was relaxing in a chair by her hospital bed. She tilted her head back and lifted the bandage over her right eye. "Barney?"

"That's me. My self-description wasn't bad, then."

"No, not bad at all."

"They've told me you are fit to give a statement and then I can run you home."

"Except you've got my clothes."

Dastra held up a Marks and Spencer shopping bag. "I bought you a tracksuit. It was that or a police paper suit."

Lucy let the bandage drop. "That was very thoughtful of you."

"I gave the lady in the store a description of your height and build, and she gave it her best shot. We erred on the generous side, and I'm afraid you'll only have plimsolls, sorry, tennis shoes from the police lost and found box."

"Thanks. How does my face look?"

"Less red than last time."

"How long will my statement take?"

"Four or five hours, I'm afraid."

"That's fine. Can you call a nurse to help me get dressed?"

~ * ~

With her eyes still under a bandage, Miss Lucy Catherine Aybrams sat on the table in an interview room at the police station, swinging her feet in boredom. The black "plimsolls" as Barney called them, which she had been given to replace her shoes, were slightly too big, and she let the backs slip down as her legs swung forwards. The slow process of Dastra typing her statement into a computer was now over. She had read through a printed copy with her good eye, signed it, and then he had taken it upstairs for checking. He was quick to return.

"To use an old cliché, your chariot awaits."

"Thanks, Barney." She slid off the table.

"Have you got all your stuff?"

"Everything you'll let me have at the moment."

"Good, then come with me." He led her out to the rear yard, carefully guiding her between vehicles. The pad over her left eye and right brow meant she only had vision to her lower right, and tilted her head back to see where she was going.

They stopped at a large black sports car.

"Is this yours?"

"Does it make me more interesting?" Dastra opened the passenger door for her. She didn't reply. He helped her into the car and did up her seatbelt. She heard him get in and start the engine, waiting a few seconds for the oil pressure to rise.

"Back to Oxford then?"

"Yes, please."

Dastra let the car glide slowly out of the yard and through the one-way traffic in Wemstone town center. Despite the quietness of the car, there was no conversation for several minutes. Lucy broke the silence.

"This is a lovely car. Is it British?"

"No, it's German, a Porsche 928."

"They must pay you well."

"Sadly, no, I inherited this too. Dad was a bit of an enthusiast."

"Have you got some music in this car?"

"Yes, sure." He switched on the CD controller and instrumental music filled the cabin. "Sorry, I didn't intend that. I thought the next disc…"

"That's Beethoven's third symphony."

"Yes, but I was expecting a track from the rock band Genesis."

"This is fine; I'm a real Beethoven nut. Do I take it you like Beethoven?"

"Actually I have come to, very much. I have a lot of him at home, over fifty CDs. I inherited them too."

"Wow."

He eased the heavy sports car down the slip road onto the M40 motorway, but kept it at seventy miles per hour in a knot of rush-hour traffic. The music played on through a crescendo, with Lucy listening intently. She was aware that Dastra was letting the speed creep up to ninety-five miles per hour along clearer stretches of the motorway as it wound through the Chiltern Hills.

"Do you think…?" Lucy began.

"Do I think what?"

"Do you think music, I mean, no… I'll say what I think."

"Off you go."

"I think that music is a kind of searchlight into the soul. If two people have similar tastes in music, especially this sort of music, I think that it points to great similarities between them. At a deeper levels, anyhow."

"Really?"

"Well, try this. Do you know Sibelius's second symphony?"

"Yes, very well. It was one of my mum's favorites."

"Does it keep you awake? I mean, can you get it out of your head after you play it?"

"Funnily enough, now I think of it, you're right. I can't."

"That's how it has always been for me. So what I am saying is that deep down we are likely to be very similar."

"Yes?"

"Well, we might get along well together. You know, we could become good friends."

Dastra drifted the car off the motorway at the Oxford turnoff.

"I'll need directions from here. I'm still new to this force."

Lucy gave him directions as best she could, but as she did all her road travelling by bicycle she didn't make allowances for the different directional flow of the cycle routes she used and nearly took Dastra down a one-way street.

Finally, they drew up outside a large Edwardian semidetached house of three stories. He went round to open the passenger door for her.

Lucy made her move. "Come on in with me. Michaela should be in this time of day."

She led him indoors through a large black and white tiled hallway and up a wide staircase to her flat on the second floor.

"Hi, anybody home?" she called, opening the door.

"Where have you been?" said a familiar female voice in a broad Nottinghamshire accent. Lucy didn't answer, but ushered Dastra in. Lucy's flatmate, Michaela, curly brown haired, leapt up from the soft brown leather sofa where she had been writing in a large binder. "Lucy... what has happened to your eyes?"

"Chemical burns. I've spent two nights in hospital. By the way, this is Barney, he's a cop."

Dastra nodded stiffly. "Pleased to meet you."

"I have a big alkali burn to my left eye, and as you can see, a lot of blotchy skin."

"But how..."

"I was down one of the tunnels at the protest site and there was a fall just as the police came to remove us. We found some human bones in the roof. It looks like they had been buried in lime and I got a face full of it."

"What will happen? I mean, will you get better?"

"They say the skin burns will eventually go. They've given me a steroid cream."

"And your eye?"

"They don't know yet. There's a big gray burn right in the middle and I'll be wearing a patch for a while."

"But Lucy, it's such a..."

"Disfigurement? Yes, I know. I'll have to get used to it."

There was an awkward silence before Michaela replied. "Oh, I didn't mean... I meant, well, only for a little while. You'll soon be back to normal, I'm sure. What do you think, Barney?"

"Time will tell."

"Barney's been a big help. He's a great guy. His visited me in hospital, bought me new clothes, and drove me back in his big German sports car."

"Very flash," said Michaela.

"And he has a massive collection of Beethoven CDs, haven't you Barney?"

"He'll get on with you, then. Sit yourself down Barney. I'll make you both a drink. Tea or coffee?"

"Tea, please."

Dastra sat down on the sofa and relaxed. Michaela got up and put a kettle on to boil in the kitchen, while Lucy went off to shower.

"Have you got a shower cap?" Lucy shouted back to Michaela, "I need to cover my dressing."

"In my soap bag," came her reply. As Lucy undressed in the bathroom, she heard Michaela striking up a conversation with Dastra. "Have you been in the force long then?"

"This is my first week in *this* force. I've just moved up from London."

"How long in the police then?"

"Four years."

"What did you do before?"

"I was at Liverpool University, doing Geology. I blew my first year, so I joined The Job—the police."

"I don't think I could do that."

"Sorry?"

"Join the police. I don't think I could do your job."

Lucy heard the kettle click off.

"I've never given it much thought. Once you are in, The Job takes over."

"It were tea weren't it?"

"Please." Lucy heard Michaela's feet on the kitchen floor. "How do you take it?"

"Julie Andrews."

"Julie Andrews?"

"White, nun."

"Oh, very good. I must use that one."

Lucy, naked apart from the eye bandage and a shower cap, cautiously felt her way into the shower, and turned on the water. A shower pump whirring behind the wall drowned out any further conversation between Dastra and Michaela, as soothing jets of water washed away the last physical traces of any soil from the tunnel collapse.

Lucy returned to the main room from her shower, barely dry and dressed only in a knee length white toweling dressing gown. Dastra looked up and she saw him steal a glance at her face, then look back down, gazing vacantly at the top of her left leg, which was partly uncovered. His eyes flicked back up to meet her good eye and she smiled. He looked away, blushing slightly. Lucy went into the kitchen and collected a coffee while Michaela settled down on the sofa with her tea and her binder. "Would you like some music, Barney?" Lucy asked.

"Well, yeah."

"Beethoven okay?"

"Nothing too heavy… it can be a bit of a conversation killer."

Lucy was glad that at least he wanted to keep talking. "Piano concerto number one?"

"That would be nice."

Lucy crossed the room to a portable CD player on a low unit and bent over at the waist to put the CD in, giving Dastra a glimpse of the back of her thighs as her dressing gown lifted. The opening bars of the music began to roll out, and Lucy sat down on the sofa on the other side of Dastra from Michaela. Dastra leaned back and Lucy touched his left wrist.

"I like the last movement best."

"Yes."

Michaela got up. "I'm going off to my room. I prefer Madonna, and I've got some headphones. Nice to have met you, Barney."

"Thanks for the tea."

Lucy relaxed with her head resting back on the cushions at an angle. She tried to catch Dastra's eye, but he was clearly distracted or uncomfortable for some reason. "Listen, I think I had best get back. I've got some computer stuff to order."

"No, don't…" Lucy was suddenly flustered. "Stay and enjoy the music, it's just…"

"But I don't want your boyfriend to come bowling in here and find me here with you in your dressing gown and your eyes bandaged."

"There's no steady boyfriend. I did have a lot of men after me, but, well, I guess there will be a lot fewer now…"

"Lucy, you'll recover and they'll be back. When you have got your degree you will go back on some path to a powerful job, or some rich handsome lawyer will marry you, and you'll have loads of lovely kids in some huge sunny house."

"But will I see *you* again?"

"You might. Why?"

"Because I want to."

"You want to? But I'm not part of your world; I live in the world of hard knocks, shift work, blood, guts and trauma. I know it all sounds fascinating to an outsider, but that is my life. That's what I have chosen to do. What I guess I'm trying to say is that we are virtually socially isolated from one another. This is very pleasant for me, and I can see it is for you too, for now anyway, but I know it is just a chance encounter that can't realistically lead anywhere."

Lucy looked back down at the floor, trying to make some sense of her feelings. She felt a strong attraction to Dastra, and believed that he had been more intimate in his conversation with her than perhaps he had been with anybody, and he hadn't been opening up in order to impress her. Now he had erected a barrier. She sat up with her right side to him. Dastra said nothing. Beethoven moved onto the next movement. Lucy let a tear drop to the cushion. Dastra put his hand on her shoulder. "It's been a hard experience for you. The sooner you get it behind you the better. My staying here can't help because I'm part of it."

"Please stay. Stay until the end. Please." She looked across at him, her right eye filled with tears.

"Okay, until the end."

"Promise?"

"Until the end."

They stayed there silently listening to the music. There was an occasional exchange of glances. Dastra got up from the sofa as the closing bars came. Lucy looked up sadly at him as she rose to her feet.

"That's the end."

"It was lovely wasn't it?"

"It was," he said quietly, "and I had best be off."

"Thanks for the lift and the clothes and well... everything."

"Thank *you*, you have been a great help to us."

"Us?"

"The Old Bill."

"The Old Bill?"

"Sorry; that's slang in London for police."

Dastra moved sideways to the flat door, clearly unsure of how to say goodbye. Lucy looked wistfully at him, her eye pleading for him to stay.

"Well, goodbye, then." He put his hand out to shake hers. She offered hers and he lifted it to his mouth. As he kissed it politely, she just caught a glimmer of a tear in his eye. She watched him stiffen his lips as if to avoid any show of further emotion.

"Will you be okay?" he asked.

"Yes, I will. Will I see you again?"

"You might. As I'm on the murder squad I might need to knock you up." There was a slight tremor in his voice.

Her mouth fell open then quickly closed. "Pardon me?"

Too late, he remembered the North American meaning of "knock you up." He cleared his throat. "Call on you, 'subject to the exigencies of duty'."

"Exigencies of duty?"

"The requirements of The Job—the investigation and all that."

"Of course. You've got my number." Lucy was about to ask for his, but the awkwardness of the moment stopped her. "Bye then."

"Yes, bye, lovely to be with you."

Dastra went out of the flat door and Lucy followed him in dressing gown and bare feet down to the main door. He turned and gave her a last look as he undid the latch. As he turned away and headed off for his car, Lucy shut the door and ran back upstairs to the flat. She pressed her face against the window to watch him leave.

He waited in the car for a minute before starting it and then Lucy heard the engine come to life. She stood at the window watching him drive away, tears running down her right cheek.

She knew he had been right about their future, but at least she would forget the skeletons in the tunnel for one evening.

Eight

Question (DI Graham): "So what then?"
Answer (Suspect): "Once the hunt was on, the first job was to throw you off the scent. Y'know, it was nerve jangling at times."

Q: "It was?"
A: "There were lighter moments. The television coverage was great."

Q: "Why?"
A: "The fear it must have caused. Every woman in the country must have crossed her legs a bit tighter when they heard about Vlad. There are parents who still don't let their daughters out alone. Mass feminine terror and mass publicity."
(Extract from evidential tape transcript.)

DCI Shackerstone settled down on a comfortable chair in Yardley's office. "Okay Brian, give me what you've got."

"I'll be quick, boss. I've got something bubbling at the moment."

"Progress?"

"I hope so, on the identification front. All persons reporting local missing females over the last six months are being visited for dentists' details for comparison of dental records with the teeth in the remains. We've begun with the missing persons reported nearest the body site, followed by those at gradually increasing distances.

"One has been identified as a missing twenty-five year old

newlywed from a village near Princes Risborough: Anne-Marie Bassington. She had been married just five months, and the report was for record purposes only. Her husband badgered the local nick, I think Princes Risborough police station, for more action, but he couldn't show that she hadn't walked out on him leaving no forwarding address.

"It has been established that she was last seen leaving home to go to a squash club in her blue Nissan Primera in March. According to the club's computerized booking in system, she never arrived. On the basis that the three bodies had been buried at the same time, I called Khan's team back in and got checks done on missing persons reported in a period of two weeks straddling her disappearance.

"There are no reports of the Nissan on the Police National Computer, so I'm working on the basis that it's been concealed somewhere. Today I've had a sweep of the locality of the bypass project done by helicopter. There was initially no joy, but they've spotted the shape of two cars under the surface of a lake about six miles out of town. One is blue."

"That's precisely the sort of luck we need."

"The downside is that I've already booked a slot on television on Crimewise at 9:30 tonight for an appeal for information. If the car is hers, I've got a race on to arrive at the BBC studio with hard information. At the moment I can't even get hold of any police divers."

"I can help there. The Met's diving team owes me a favor."

"Good. DS Khan has been down to the lake with Tim Hunt, and a crane has been ordered for this afternoon. There's no point in my going along until divers have had a look."

~ * ~

Shackerstone stood by the shore of the lake, the reflections of the surrounding trees broken by the ripples of diving activity beneath the surface. Tim Hunt ambled over to him. "Guv, this is going to be a goldmine. We can confirm Bassington's car is there, and a VW next to it."

"Good."

"It gets better. There's a third car deeper in the water, a dark blue Ford Fiesta. It was covered by weeds and stuff. They're going over every inch of the bottom to see what else they can find."

"Have we got any license plates?"

"Yes, all three have still got plates on. The Primera is Bassington's. The Golf and the Fiesta plates I've phoned in to the incident room for Police National Computer checks. The Golf is registered to a man in Maidenhead, but there is an interest report on it for a missing person in the right timeframe. Maidenhead is faxing us the details."

"Maidenhead! It would have been another week before we reached there."

"Oh, and Guv, the Fiesta check has come back as *Licensing Authority notified last owner no longer the keeper.* We're getting a call done to the old keeper to see who they sold it to."

"Bloody good work. We've been on the case just over a week and we've got three cars."

There was an echoing shout from a head in the middle of the lake. Shackerstone couldn't make out what was being said, and cupped his hand to his ear.

"What was that?" shouted Hunt.

"Another car!" shouted back Khan.

"Bloody hell," muttered Shackerstone.

An exchange of shouts went on between Khan and the diver, and three more divers surfaced. They swam slowly to the shore by Khan, so Shackerstone made his way over to them.

"Hello, I'm DCI Shackerstone, the acting SIO."

"Hello, Guv. Sergeant Richards. Yes, there's a brown Citroen BX down there too. It could be that this is a regular dumping ground, but none of them has been in there long. All of them are seeping petrol and oil. You can see the rainbow effect on the water."

"Have you got an index number?"

"One better!"

"What?"

One of the other divers produced an index plate from behind his back.

"It was on the bottom, but it fits the car."

"Tim, run a Police National Computer check on it."

"Guv."

Shackerstone wandered along the shoreline with his hands in

his pockets, and watched as the divers went under water again with bulky photographic gear. Tim Hunt's mobile phone burst into life and Shackerstone watched his eyebrows raise as he took the call.

"Guv! Guv! It's from Older Brian, we've got a result!"

"The Citroen?"

"Missing student from Uxbridge, a Tracey Kennedy, eighteen. The Met have been treating it as a full enquiry. She was supposed to have a history of depression. Her dental records are already on file. Missing Persons Bureau is trying a match with our two bodies now."

"Date?"

"Night before Bassington, March the twentieth."

Shackerstone turned to Khan.

"It looks like we've got our three victims. I'm going to need their families visited by 6:00 p.m. and I want to go on television tonight with names, ages, pictures, last movements, the full Monty. You go back to the police station and get moving on that. I'm going to speak to Gordonstown about going public over the M.O. Has Dastra got his big old sports car in?"

"I think so. Why?"

"Get him to run us both to the BBC studios in London. I need every edge I can get tonight."

~ * ~

At six-thirty, Shackerstone rang Ian Yardley at home. His wife answered, and she shouted to him to pick the phone up in his study. "Hello, Brian." came Yardley's voice on the line.

"Hi, boss. We've had some more progress."

"I heard the divers were good."

"Yes, thanks for that. We've got a possible match with a missing girl from Maidenhead, one Bridget O'Riordan, married, aged twenty-one, but no dental work in the UK. I've had an urgent message sent to the Garda in Eire to obtain records from her former dentist in Dublin. She also suffered a broken right ankle some years ago, and she was a redhead. Martin O'Donoghue has been down with a Family Liaison Officer to speak to her husband, and arrangements have been made for the Garda to call on her parents if news is bad. I've got a photo from hubby.

"The other is a Tracey Kennedy, definite match on dental

records. She was a full enquiry missing person at Uxbridge. They've done a good job, with a full account of her final known movements. We've got local detectives round with her parents to get a photo for the BBC's Crimewise program, which we'll pick up en route. Mum took it very badly when they broke the news, so they'll sit with her through the TV coverage."

"That's good."

"Their only daughter... and her fifteen minutes of fame."

"And yours. Good luck and do well, Brian."

~ * ~

At 9:29, Shackerstone was seated at a desk next to the presenter, John Micklewhite. There was a countdown to the program going on air and then the title music struck up. Shackerstone's throat began to go dry, as he realized how much this TV appearance could bring to the case. He knew that back at Wemstone the whole squad was in the office waiting by phones for calls from the public, while watching the program on a small monitor.

Micklewhite took viewers through other cases of the week, concentrating initially on a Dutch businessman whose return to Amsterdam from London was several months overdue. Most of the program was devoted to operation Klingsor and Micklewhite described the last known movements of each of the victims, and then showed pictures of them and the types of cars they owned. Finally, he turned to Shackerstone. "I'm now going to introduce Detective Chief Inspector Brian Shackerstone, from Wemstone police, who has some more facts on the case. What more can you tell the viewers at home?"

"Well, John. We have established that all three victims went missing on the nights of the twentieth and twenty-first of March. Each was alone in her car, and all three cars were recovered together today from a lake near Wemstone. My team will be conducting forensic tests on the cars tomorrow."

"I know that there is something important you wish to tell us about the method used in these killings."

"Yes," said Shackerstone sounding flat and unemotional. "It appears from initial examination that the victims may have been killed by being impaled on sharpened stakes, although we have not established this as the cause of death."

"Impaled?"

"Yes, it appears we are looking for a particularly vicious individual."

When the program had finished Shackerstone thanked the producer and collected the photographs. This was the darkest part of the investigation for him. His obsessive nature drove him to become attached to the memory of the victims, and he knew his sleep patterns would be disturbed by trying to imagine their last moments. He sat in an anteroom looking at the photographs, trying to bring the personalities to life in his mind. Shackerstone had always had to give himself an edge over other officers, right from his first day as a recruit. He felt, as a black officer, that he had to show everyone else he could not only go the extra mile, but also that he needed to rebut associations of failure with his racial origin. His consequential obsession with determined hard work and success had brought dividends to investigations, even if it had ruined his marriage.

Now it was part of an ingrained pattern of behaviour. For him this visualization of victims he had never met, living blameless and ordinary lives, was an essential part of the process of investigation. He needed to grieve over them. He needed to become sad and gloomy for a while. Only then would he be empowered to give of his best.

~ * ~

During a thunderstorm that rolled through the Chilterns on the following afternoon, Shackerstone was called to Yardley's office.

"Sorry, Brian. Problems."

"Problems?"

"The coverage in the papers this morning…"

"Christening him 'Vlad'. I half expected that."

"No. It's got worse. The local MP has asked questions in the House of Commons. The Home Secretary has badgered the Chief Constable and now he's breathing down my neck, and Josh Gordonstown's. Josh is talking about this screwing up his chances of promotion. We need to be able to give them a bit more."

"Okay. I'm going to run witness roadblocks in the vicinity of each of the disappearances, and we'll be checking every female missing person record in southern England who has gone missing with her car."

"Have you got enough staff?"

"I could use a few van loads of uniformed officers for a few days."

"I'll sort some Police Support Units out through HQ."

"Now that we've got some approximate times and locations, I'm having the cell phone sites checked for their last calls, if any, and to see if any common numbers come up for our man's phone. It's always a long shot..."

"And a lot of work for some poor sods. Have you got anything else?"

"We also have a result. The last owner of the Ford Fiesta has been spoken to, and he sold it on to a well-spoken man of about twenty-five years of age, five-foot eight-inches tall, who he described as foreign looking with heavier than average build, short black hair and blue eyes. No female present or mentioned. The man paid cash, and gave his name as Roland Smethers of an address in Watford."

~ * ~

On a brighter Friday, Shackerstone sat writing up his decision log in his office when a gentle knock on the open door disturbed him. He looked up to see DS Khan.

"Sorry, boss, Smethers doesn't exist at that address, and never has. A Mr. and Mrs. Gold live there. It looks like Smethers gave bogus details."

Shackerstone looked at the floor before looking up.

"Another dead end... that's three today."

"Three?"

"No trace on criminal records of any *Vagina Dentata* psychos, and the gray nylon rope is sold in virtually every DIY store in the country. When you've given your result to Tony Shanter, you can help young Dastra to get his mapping machine working. It arrived this morning."

"I know. He says it'll take a day to load the data and get it running."

"Tell him to come in tomorrow. The office is lightly manned as it is."

"On overtime, Guv?"

"All right. On overtime."

"Are you in tomorrow?"

"Not if I can help it." Shackerstone leaned back and put his hands behind his head. "I do a little fly fishing when I need to think. It's therapeutic. This Saturday I intend to be as far from policing as I can be— subject to..."

"The exigencies of duty."

Nine

Question (DI Graham): "So, but for Lucy Aybrams none of that would have happened."
Answer (Suspect): "Not like that. No. There was no point."

Q: "Let me just get this clear then. The discovery of the bodies by Lucy triggered your contingency plan."
A: "Yes. The plan was that the bypass would cover them up permanently, and in any case, the lime should have done most of the work. There was always a bit of risk. That's why there was a plan B, but it hadn't been thought through far enough. Y'know... all plans have flaws."
(Extract from evidential tape transcript.)

Lucy had planned her trip to Wemstone carefully. The excuse she had needed was the collection of her clothes, and once she had established they were ready, she waited a few more days for the red blotches to disappear from her skin. Her only blemish now was her clouded and dull left eye. Any attempt at using it uncovered was impossible, as all it did was blur her vision. She had remedied this with a small black eye patch bought after a long hunt round the pharmacies and opticians of Oxford.

She stepped down from the bus in her tightest jeans, a white blouse and with her hair as clean and natural as she could manage without getting shampoo in her bad eye. She was determined to make an impression on Dastra. Before crossing the road to the police station, she called from her cell phone.

"Wemstone incident room. Brian Calver."

"Hi, it's Lucy Aybrams. I'm across the road. Is Barney available? I'd like to pick up my clothes, if possible."

"He's here and he's fixed the computer, so he's free. Come to the front counter and tell them you're here to collect your clothes. I'll send him down."

Calver got up and stood looking out of the front windows of the office. He nodded with satisfaction and made his way back to his computer screen. The phone rang again. He was first to it, so Dastra got up to make the tea.

"Jolly good, I'll send him down," came Brian's voice. He put the phone down.

"Barney?"

"Yes?"

"Front counter. Another witness. That's down to you."

"I'll make the tea when I get back."

Calver watched him leave the room, and then turned to Mark Whitehouse. "Give him half a minute to go downstairs and then find us both an excuse to go to the front counter."

"What for?"

"It's that American bird, the one who found the bodies. She phoned yesterday, she sounds like she's got the hots for him."

"So? Hasn't she had her face burnt?"

"She had. But she's just entered this very nick—Wemstone police station, wearing a black eye patch and a very lovely face underneath it."

"How do you know that's her?"

"She phoned just now. Anyhow, I've dug out the telephoto shots taken of her by the public order mob before she went down the tunnel. I think someone from public order intelligence wanted to make her a film star. Half the early footage of the protest is of her. She was an absolute stunner, like a film star with bells on."

~ * ~

Ian Yardley and Councilor Trevor Thomas strolled up the steps at the front of the police station. Yardley pushed open one of the plate glass doors and ushered Thomas in. Dastra was locked in a long kiss with Lucy Aybrams at the front counter.

"Ah-*hem*!" Loudly, Yardley cleared his throat.

The pair separated and Dastra blushed with embarrassment. "Ah, sorry sir. I..."

Yardley went straight over to Lucy and offered his hand, blushing slightly himself. "You must be the lady who found our skeletons. Miss Aybrams, isn't it?"

"Hi. Yes. That's me, I'm sorry..."

"I'm Superintendent Ian Yardley. I hope this detective is looking after you well." He raised one eyebrow and looked at Dastra.

"Yes, well. He is. You've all been very helpful. I have come for my clothes. Officer Dastra here dealt with me."

"Yes. So I understand. It looks like you've made a fairly good recovery. How's your eye?"

"The cornea has a permanent burn."

"I'm sorry to hear that. I must say, for what it's worth... you look good with an eye patch."

They heard the security door lock open. Yardley turned briefly to Dastra, winked then ushered his guest in.

"Detective Constable Dastra," echoed Calver officiously, from somewhere beyond the station's front desk. "Take an early refreshments break... forty-five minutes unless you can find some more witness enquiries to do. When you come back I will have the young lady's clothes ready."

Dastra stepped away from Lucy. "I'll just get my jacket. Would you like to come up to the incident room?"

"Sure, I'd like that very much."

"Buzz me in, please."

The door unlocked and he showed Lucy through. "How did you come up from Oxford?"

"I took the bus."

"You came up on the bus? To see me?"

"Is that so bad?"

"Gosh, no. It's just, well, I'm flattered."

Calver followed them into the lift with Mark Whitehouse. Nothing was said. The door slid open on the third floor and Dastra let the other two officers go on ahead to the incident room in order to cover the more unpleasant photographs.

"See what I mean?" whispered Brian.

"Not half. And it looks like he's pulled it too! Jammy git.

What has he got that I haven't?"

"A 5 litre Porsche 928?"

"That's just a penis extension."

Dastra wandered in with Lucy. "I'd best introduce you. This is Older Brian, and this is Mark Whitehouse. Gents, this is Lucy Aybrams."

They both shook hands with her.

"We've spoken on the phone," commented Calver.

"Oh yes, thank you," said Lucy.

Dastra's eyes narrowed and he eyed Calver. He gave a knowing nod. Lucy cast her eyes around the room. "All this work!"

"I know it looks like chaos," said Calver, "but it all works to a fairly rigid system, in case we have to merge with another investigation."

"So who does what?"

"The most important jobs are the SIO—Senior Investigating Officer, that's DCI Shackerstone at the moment. And then the Receiver, DS Shanter, who sits over here when he's in. The SIO runs the investigation, but all the evidence and completed actions come back through the Receiver. In many ways, the Receiver knows more than the SIO. We have other people like me to index stuff and input onto the computer."

"HOLMES?"

"Indeed. The largest part of the team works away from the office following up actions the inquiry throws up. And that's what takes the time. Inputting can be slow, too, and that's the real bottleneck when the investigation gathers pace. The other big job, which is still going on, is gathering all the exhibits from the crime scene and any from the actions. There are officers who do nothing but gather exhibits all through the investigation, and others who do nothing but log them on HOLMES."

Dastra found his jacket and then took Lucy downstairs in the lift. Lucy didn't care where he was taking her. She just wanted to be with him and to have time to talk. He opened the passenger door for her, helped her to sit down and swing her legs in and he shut it firmly. She watched him stride happily around the front of the car. He eased himself into the driver's seat, started the engine and then slowly moved off towards the gateway. Calver strode out towards his car, right hand raised, and with a large evidence bag in his left. Dastra stopped and lowered the electric window.

"Young lady's clothes. Save you bringing her back up. I'll chuck them in the back."

"Cheers, Brian. And thanks again."

He opened the back of the car and put the bag inside, then went to the passenger window. Dastra clicked the switch that opened it, and the window eased down.

"Just need your signature here, Miss."

Brian handed Lucy a pad of receipt forms and a pen, pointing out where to sign.

"Thanks. I'll trust you that it is all there."

"It's all there, and if it isn't I'm sure you'll be back. The boss only authorized this young man's overtime to fix the computer. I think that means he is off duty now."

"Thanks, Brian." Dastra engaged *Drive* and let the car roll out of the yard and into Wemstone's Saturday shopping traffic.

Ten

Question (DI Graham): "So, the choice of venue."
Answer (Suspect): "The family residence, you might say."

Q: "Yes."
A: "It was so perfectly isolated. You could have killed dozens up there without any risk of anyone hearing you."

Q: "So you would think, but as we discovered, the woods can get quite busy at night."
A: "Really?"

Q: "Game. Good poaching country."
(Extract from evidential tape transcript.)

As Lucy and Dastra talked, he drove up through the Chilterns and then down a winding road off the western escarpment. He turned left at a main road at the bottom, signposted towards the M40 motorway.

Lucy's mind wandered. In her heart, she knew that Dastra would be the one. She knew at this moment that she wanted him. She let herself fantasize over how it might be. A great room somewhere, an open fire in the hearth. The second movement of Beethoven's fifth Piano concerto would be playing gently in the background. Barney would kiss her all over and then she would yield to him.

"Stop!" she cried out.

He slowed, jerking toward the side of the road. "Pardon?"

"Sorry, something walked over my grave. Can we park somewhere?"

"Sure, but, would you like to... uh. How can I put this without seeming too forward? Would you like to come up to my house?"

Lucy was caught on the horns of a profound dilemma in her feelings. On the one hand she knew she wanted him. On the other she felt she was being dragged step by step towards the bedroom as Barney's unwitting accomplice.

"Well, yes... that would be nice."

"You'll like it. Mock Elizabethan. At least, partly."

He started to drive faster, crossed under the motorway through a wide cylindrical tunnel and poured the car into corner after corner through the villages, then took a left turn into a road leading back up onto the escarpment.

Lucy shook her head to loosen her hair. "You know, since starting at the university I've only seen snatches of English countryside on my way to places like Wemstone. It's great to see it like this. It's so different from my part of California... so much less dry and rocky."

"Parts of England are rockier. This part has just got fairly settled geology."

"But even the patterns of roads and real estate are so different. None of the towns around here seems to be laid out in blocks. Roads wind all over the place, even when they are right in a town center."

"That's because the roads are so old. They weren't planned for motor cars."

"And there are so many tiny parcels of land, and even some of the poorest houses out here look older than the USA."

"Well, mine isn't. It's only about a hundred and twenty years old."

They turned into a country lane with a field to the left, and then turned again down a wooded lane. He stopped the car at some iron gates on the left. Lucy noticed a tall ivy covered brick wall running along the lane from the gates, and a similar one going left into the woods. Set into the wall on one side of the gate was a cast iron plate with the words *"Prospect of Peshawar"*. After opening the gates, Dastra got back in the car and let it glide forward through the entranceway.

"Prospect of Peshawar?"

"Peshawar was a place in old India, during the days of the Raj, northwest frontier and all that. It's in Pakistan now. The family named the house after one they had there."

They followed a rising gravel drive with woods on both sides. This gave way after about thirty yards to a wide lawn on the left, roughly cut, but becoming neater as the drive rose and crossed it. In the shadows of trees there appeared to be a stable or garage on the right, but Lucy's attention was diverted as the car looped around a large flowerbed in front of a broad, if neglected, country house.

"You're putting me on. This isn't yours. How can a cop...?"

"Like I said: Rich parents."

They got out of the car and Lucy walked back to the other side of the flowerbed to look at the house.

The central part was a mock Tudor two-story building with dark wooden framed sections on dirty brown backgrounds that had probably once been white. These were punctuated by more modern expanses of Victorian brickwork and the entire frontage of this part of the building was at least sixty feet across.

There were two incongruous additions to the left and right. The house sat along a ridge, and the only viable directions for extensions had been further along it. Lucy could see from the general lie of the land that it fell away at the back down a slope into trees. To the right of the house, at the southern end, was a large conservatory with a thin white metal frame rising to the windows on the first story. This had been built for views to the south and west out through a great gap in the trees. To the left of the house was a more substantial structure that seemed to belong to another style altogether. This consisted mainly of a large hipped roof, falling from above the second story of the main building down to a veranda, in the shadows of which were a series of French doors.

Dastra crunched across the gray gravel.

"A bit of a monstrosity, eh?"

"It's lovely. How do you look after it?"

"I have a housekeeper who makes fleeting visits on weekdays, a gardener twice a week to keep the worst of the plant growth back and an odd job man who calls to keep the dilapidation from overtaking."

He unlocked a heavy green door and led Lucy in to a wide but musty wood paneled hallway with rooms leading off into the shadows and a brown-carpeted staircase rising on the right. Lucy spied doors and passages off a landing upstairs. A low buzz sounded from a panel on the wall and Dastra tapped a number in to silence it. "Security. This place is a bit isolated."

"But so much space."

"A lot of the rooms are shut up. It keeps the dust down."

"And you live here all alone."

"For the last three months, yes. I'm tidying it up, after a fashion. I might rent out most of it and convert the piano room into a flat for me. Like I said, I don't want to be forced to move away."

"Where's the piano room?"

"That's the odd bit on the end, with the veranda and the big roof."

"Has it got a piano?"

"Yes, a big ebony-black grand. Do you play?"

"Oh, yes."

"Come on then, I'll do you the quick tour and we can end up at the piano."

"Great. Say, Barney, that's an interesting picture." She was looking up at an odd brown-colored reclining nude hanging near the foot of the stairs.

"It's one of mine. I mean, I painted it about, what, six years ago. There are a few of my nudes hanging about the place, interspersed with quite a few *proper* expensive paintings. I guess I could sell a few off to keep the place going. A bit pretentious of my dad, hanging that one there."

"It's very good. Who is she? An old flame?"

"Not at all. Just a paid model. Dad used to pay them to come up and pose for me in the piano room. It's north facing so the light's right."

"Have you painted many?"

"A dozen or so."

"And since you've been a cop?"

"Just one. Two weeks back. She came up here with a

minder."

"Minder?

He smiled. "A chaperone, I suppose you could say. And I can understand that—can't you? This place is isolated. I'll show you the painting later."

"Please."

He guided her into a yellowing sitting room on the right. The furniture was covered in white sheets, and the wood panelling on the walls was dry and dull. She noticed some butterflies in framed cases on one wall with a fine but slightly out of perspective pencil drawing of the central lantern of Ely cathedral.

"You did that too, didn't you?"

"Yes, a long time ago. I think I was only about twelve."

"A lot of talent for a twelve-year-old."

"That's what Dad thought."

He led on through to a study and on into the conservatory. The bright sun had made it hot so Dastra opened doors and windows. The few plants in the conservatory looked sad and dry. Some of their shed leaves were scattered dry and brown across the blue tiled floor. He led her out through a different exit and into a dining room at the back of the house, which opened out to a kitchen. The kitchen had a large Aga cooking range and an assortment of old wooden cupboards against drab, light-brown walls. Dastra led back through the dining room into the hallway, then into a library back near the front door. "This leads through into the piano room."

"So many books."

"Yes, over a hundred years' worth."

There was a full-length portrait of a couple in Edwardian dress hanging at one end of the room. The lady was wearing a high-necked white dress with leg-of-mutton sleeves, and a tiny, corset-constricted waist.

"Who is the beautiful lady?"

"Great, Great Grandmother, or should I say adopted Great, Great Grandmother?"

"Great, Great Grandmother. I think people become like the family they live with. Blood isn't as important as people say."

He looked into her eye and in doing so let a moment of silence show his apparent appreciation of her remark. "Now, on to the piano room. I've missed out all the bathrooms and stuff like that on this floor."

He led on through another sitting room and into the piano room itself. It was brighter and entirely different from the rest of the house. The room had no partitions or dropped ceiling so the inside accorded with the outside walls. Most of the inner surface of the hipped roof was a vast area of off-white boarding supported by four long oak trusses running up from a thick oak rafter, which bisected the room. Lucy estimated the room to be over fifteen feet high at the center. French doors marked the line of the verandas outside, and a tall cream colored plastered wall, showing signs of a bricked over window on the first story, marked the side of the main house. Amongst assorted paintings, a large fireplace had been set into this wall, linking up with an older chimney within the house. There were assorted bits of furniture, a sofa, and in two corners of the room, there were wide black objects about a meter tall that looked like oversize convection heaters. The grand piano stood towards the rear of the room. "This is it. Make yourself at home. Tea or Coffee?"

"Coffee please."

"Milk and sugar?"

"Just milk."

Lucy watched him go to the back of the room, past the piano and into a short passage that led back to the kitchen. She was eager to try the piano, but explored the room first. The floor was of polished wood with scattered throw rugs. Under the center of the beam there appeared to be a large double hatch in the floor, about eight feet square. Lucy guessed that this had once been some sort of basement storage room. She was more at ease here than in the main house, which felt creepy and lifeless. This room at least seemed lived-in. She examined the paintings, and recognized Dastra's nudes among them. She imagined herself sitting there, savoring the smell of linseed oil and turpentine, him with messy hands concentrating on every detail in emotionless detachment. She compared the paintings with the room for clues as to the settings. Something in the background of a picture of a small brunette caught her eye.

She had noticed them when she came in, but they hadn't really registered. They did now, and in fascinating clarity. She turned to peer up at two domed glass displays on the top of the great beam, sitting squarely equidistant from the middle of it. Within each container was a lifelike display of brightly colored butterflies settled upon a plant. Dastra came back in. "The Aga is a bit slow to boil the kettle."

"Who likes butterflies?"

"Me. I bought them in a house clearance a few years ago. There are a few more specimens around the house. Nothing sophisticated, I just like the patterns."

"Do you still collect?"

"No, I've moved on to other things."

"Like painting."

"Well, yes. But rarely." Dastra hesitated "The Job doesn't give you a lot of time for hobbies. I guess the car and this place are my pastimes now. Music of course. Please try the piano. It's a Bluthner."

He went off to make their coffees and Lucy sat herself down and lifted up the cover from the keyboard. He made his way back with coffee in a cafetière on a tray with two mugs and a small jug of milk. Lucy was playing Beethoven's Moonlight Sonata. "It's a beautiful piano."

"Yes, it's only about twenty years old."

"Like me then."

"Yes." He sat down on the sofa and put the tray on a small table. She watched him push the plunger on the cafetière down through the coffee and pour it out into the mugs. He said nothing, but listened to her play. She stopped at the end and closed the cover. She rose from the piano stool, sat down on a sofa and Dastra handed her a mug of coffee. She stared distantly out past the piano and through the French doors at the back.

"I can understand your parents loving it here."

"Especially this room, their favorite. In fact this was where they died."

"How did they…?"

"Accidental carbon monoxide poisoning, a bird's nest had blocked the flue of that old gas fire and they drifted off in each other's arms."

"I'm sorry."

"Don't be, it was their favorite place. They'd have wanted it to be here."

"How can you convert it to a flat then?"

"I don't think I could, but I've got to keep this place in use somehow... of course, my life has changed a bit today."

"Hey, for the better I hope."

"For the better."

"It's strange, but it's as if I've always known you."

"Well, there is a theory... that we project part of ourselves onto others, and we are guilty of self-love."

"That would be a pity."

"Yes it would... but I can't think of any bits of me I like that well."

"Barney, how can you say that? I love all of you..."

"You can't... you mustn't... not yet. You don't know all of me. You're forgetting that we have a lot of getting to know one another to do."

She looked into his eyes "I have got a gift for you."

"Me?"

"There's nobody else here."

She produced a CD from her bag. "Beethoven. Mass in C. I hope you haven't got it."

"I'm sure I haven't. What's it like?"

"It was Beethoven's own favorite, but one of his least known works."

"I'll put it on."

After a few moments, the soft voices of the opening harmony drifted out from the corners of the room and Lucy realized that the strange black objects were loudspeakers. The sound produced was of an amazing quality to her ears, and this took her mind off her emotions for a while.

"That sounds very good."

"Electrostatic speakers. Dad was really keen on having all the top stuff. The trouble was he got hypercritical. He listened too hard for the faults."

They sat and listened over the next forty minutes. They touched, they hugged, they kissed and kissed again. As the piece finished Dastra took her chin in his hands and looked directly into her good eye. "I'll never be able to listen to this again without thinking of you."

"Good. That was my plan."

Lucy spent an idyllic Saturday afternoon with Dastra, in love, in total privacy, and the outside world of Oxfordshire might as well have been another planet. They walked around the garden. They relaxed in different rooms. They discussed each other's likes and dislikes, their lives and experiences. Later, she played the piano, and in the evening, they prepared a meal together, eating it, at Lucy's request, in the dining room. Dastra played the servant to Lucy's lady of the house. To Lucy it seemed that they were constantly interrupted by their own emotions driving them to touch and hold one another, almost as if they were checking that the flame still burned brightly.

After a glass of wine back in the piano room, she cuddled up with Dastra on the sofa as a quiet section of the Sibelius second symphony drifted up over the great beam that bisected the room. Modeling for Dastra crossed her mind again. She suppressed the thought for a moment, but it wandered back, and she felt a tremor of arousal at the thought.

"Barney?"

"Yes?"

"Would you... would you... do you want to paint me? I mean..."

"Of course. I'd love to. I don't mean..." Lucy sensed Dastra's sudden awkwardness, as if this were the first time a woman was opening up to him. He paused, clearly agitated. "Yes, Lucy. I would love to get your clothes off!" His hand went up to his mouth. Lucy sensed a slender moment of destiny, but Dastra let it pass. "Sorry, I... I..." Then he slumped, deflated, as if he had suddenly lost his boldness. "But yes, you would be, well, a terrific model. If you're happy with..."

"I've never done that before, but... it would be for you. Does it take long?"

"Several hours and in daylight. We could make it our next date."

"Good. Yes. Wonderful." He could hardly have missed the disappointment in her soft reply as the room fell silent.

Dastra rose to close the curtains. "It's nine-thirty. I suppose you will have to go soon."

"I guess so."

"Michaela will have expected you back hours ago."

"I'm okay with that and she's used to it."

"It's been lovely having you here with me. It has breathed a bit of life back into the old place."

"I'm glad."

"Back to Oxford then?"

"If I must…" Lucy felt that she should find a way to continue but wasn't sure how. He extinguished the lights in the piano room and then in the connecting rooms as they both made their way back to the hall.

"You haven't shown me upstairs yet and I have a question."

"I didn't think it was quite the done thing. Not having, well, not on our first day together."

"I can understand that."

"What was the question?"

"Is there a four-poster bed *up there*?" Lucy's voice broke and it ended with a croak.

"Yes, a grand old one. With carved wooden spiral posts."

"Gosh."

Lucy looked longingly up the staircase and past the row of paintings. This could be the moment. She would make a play and let fate decide.

"Would you like to sweep me off my feet, throw me on the four-poster and ravish me?"

He blushed and raised his eyebrows. "Yes, please." He opened the front door.

"Well why don't—"

He cut her off, laughing. Lucy stepped out over the threshold, trying to hide her inner frustration, and Dastra pulled the door to behind them both. He opened the car door for her, and she soon found herself being driven out of the gates. He got out to close them. Lucy couldn't hide her exasperation and said the first thing that came into her head. "You should get electric gates."

"They're being made. I wanted the same design, but the current ones cannot be reused. I should have them in two weeks or so."

There was silence for a while, broken only by the purr of the engine and the rumble of the tires on the road surface. As they approached the roundabout at the bottom of the hill leading down to Wallingford, he heard Lucy give a deep sigh.

"Barney?"

"Yes."

"I know you are being very polite, but…"

"Yes?"

"I kind of thought you could take me back to Oxford tomorrow afternoon. Perhaps we could do the painting tomorrow if you have a canvas."

She leaned across the center console and put her hand on the top of his leg.

"Ah… I've got quite a big canvas."

"Good." Lucy paused and bit gently on her bottom lip. "I've never done this before. I don't want you to think I'm easy. Right now I just need…"

"Say what you want. You know I'll give you any…"

"I want us to be together tonight. I know you… you won't take advantage, will you? I mean… I'm frightened, but I…"

"Are you frightened of me?"

"No. I'm frightened of *us*! I also want to take this step by step. But I know… at least I think I know… where we… need to be tonight."

There was a sensible pause. "I believe I know as well… now. I'll turn the car around."

Eleven

Question (DI Graham): "So Lucy hadn't been part of the plans?"

Answer (suspect): "Not then. Not at all. She just kept turning up like a bad penny. Criminals and cops have one thing in common... cynical opportunism, so there had to be a way of using her to the best result, but Shackerstone forced the pace of things, and that was the undoing... control was lost to him."

Q: "To DCI Shackerstone?"
A: "Yes. Blackness isn't always only skin-deep."
(Extract from evidential tape transcript.)

Lucy awoke to dappled yellow sunlight streaming through gaps between curtains in Dastra's master bedroom. He was beside her in the four-poster bed, fast asleep. She was more aware now of the musty smell of the room than she had been when he had brought her into it. She slid out of the bed, slipped on her eye patch and opened a wardrobe to look for something to put on. The wardrobe was dark and empty, and Lucy crept out along the landing to find Dastra's usual bedroom, where she helped herself to a police shirt. She then found a bathroom, showered, then made her way downstairs to fix breakfast.

She took it up to Dastra on a tray and woke him up with a kiss. They ate, but Lucy didn't get dressed, preferring to float around the house in his shirt. For his part he went about his home in shorts and a T-shirt.

He was uncertain how to approach the promised modeling session, but while mulling it over in the kitchen he heard Lucy call from the piano room. "Barney?"

He trotted through to find Lucy reclining languorously on the sofa, her head propped up by one arm. "Time to paint?"

"If you are ready."

"Ready and willing."

Lucy watched him set up a studio easel with a large canvas of about three by five feet in one corner of the piano room, and set up some old boxes as a dais for her to sit on in the center of the room. He covered them in cushions and a dark piece of velvet before wheeling in an old tea trolley with his paints and brushes. His pallet was an old slab of marble covering the top of the trolley, with tubes of paint and dozens of brushes on a tray beneath. He positioned the trolley by the canvas and set up a stool for himself.

"Ready when you are."

Lucy stood up, expecting him to walk over and unbutton the police shirt. He watched intently, but said nothing. She took the shirt off, and dropped it behind her on the sofa before approaching the dais. "How should I sit?"

"I'll show you what I think now, but I might have to move you about a bit." He guided her as she sat down, and positioned her for a side-on pose. To Lucy it seemed that he went through a period of concentrated detachment, treating her like his previous models as he set her pose. He acted in a brusque and business-like manner, but once settled behind the canvas, he relaxed and returned to normal conversation.

"What about my eye patch?"

"Take it off."

"But you can't paint this…."

"I won't. I will mirror the other eye. You'll look like you should."

"Thank you."

"This is going to give me a lot of pleasure… if it is successful."

Lucy kept her head in profile, but tried to see him out of the corner of her eye. "What are you painting now?"

"I'm doing a basic outline in brown to get your proportions

right. It takes a while, and then when I'm happy, I'll start on the underpainting... big areas of color to give the top layers some luminance. Then I'll paint the details of your body and face."

"How long will this take?"

"The underpainting takes a couple of hours before it can take another layer."

"So your girls sit for how long?"

"Three or four separate sessions are usual. Spread over several weeks."

"Weeks?"

"When you pay your models you can make them sit as long as you wish. That way I can play the old master with deep glazes in oil and long drying out periods between layers. Today I'm using acrylic paint. It dries much faster than oils, so it will be mercifully swift. The whole thing will be done in one day... *Alla Prima*."

"Do I get a break?"

"At lunchtime. Also the light will be more diffuse after midday, because the sun will be over the house and all the light reaching into here will be indirect by then. Let me just do this."

"The horrors come when I try to do your face... you get a likeness about one time in six and the rejects look like freaks."

"So what do you do?"

"Scrape you off with a sharp palette knife and start again."

Straining to watch him sideways with her good eye, Lucy saw him begin with his larger brushes in an almost vague way across the hidden face of the canvas, but as the day moved on, he shifted to smaller and smaller brushes. The sitting gave Lucy a lot of time to think, but it was several hours before she realized how relaxed she felt naked under Dastra's gaze. That he appeared in no way aroused by the sight of her, caused her to fret on the state of her facial burns, but as the hours drifted by she persuaded herself that he was in a similar state of professional detachment to that of a doctor examining a patient.

~ * ~

"That's it, I've done you, so relax. I just need to capture a few background details."

Lucy got up and hurried over to look without reclaiming the shirt.

"That's brilliant! Honestly... it is me down to a tee. That's how I should look with two good eyes. It's even better than the others."

"Well, you have a certain quality which, I'm sure you are aware of." He filled in vague background details. "This will take another twenty minutes or so, then it's done."

"I'll make some dinner." said Lucy, buttoning her borrowed shirt.

She used the available food she found in the kitchen and Dastra eventually came in to wash his brushes.

They ate dinner after dressing properly then drove back through light rain to Lucy's flat in Oxford. Michaela was back at the flat and was not surprised to see Lucy with Dastra. Lucy watched again as he drove off, but with an uplifted heart.

Michaela was standing at Lucy's shoulder and watching the lights of the car pass out of view down the wet street. "So it all worked out?"

"Like a dream." Lucy turned to Michaela and took both her hands in hers. "I totally surprised him at the station house. He was like a big kid, then he got some time off. That guy on his squad clearly hadn't told him anything. He took me back to his house, and, like it's a mansion!"

"Really?"

"Right out in the country, in a forest somewhere, mock Tudor. It has a sweeping drive and more rooms than I saw: a library, conservatory, dining room, huge kitchen, magnificent bedrooms upstairs... It's strangely lovely, if a bit creepy. It's called Prospect of Peshawar."

"Isn't that in Pakistan or somewhere like that?"

"I think so. There's some family connection from the days of the British Raj. Anyhow, he lives there all alone, and Michaela, it really needs a woman's touch."

"And you think that Lucy Catherine Aybrams is the right woman?"

Lucy drew the curtains and they both sat down on the edge of the sofa. Lucy's nose twitched and she scratched it thoughtfully. "It's got this huge tall room on the side with a grand piano and this terrific hi-fi system. He's got a great collection of music, some amazing paintings on the walls—quite a few done by him, and... a four-poster bed."

"Which you decided to try out?"

Lucy blushed copiously. "It just happened. He actually started to bring me home on Saturday night. I had to insist that he turned around and I don't know if he just doesn't pick up on my signals, or if he's just very polite. Earlier on, I even suggested that he should ravish me and he laughed it off. I only got him back to the house by offering to model for a painting."

"A painting?"

"He painted a fantastic picture of me."

"But sleeping with him... surely..."

"No. I guess deep down I already knew he wouldn't."

"So... you've not quite finally done it?"

"Well, not quite, we did sleep together, but..."

"Heavy petting?" Michaela raised a single eyebrow.

Twelve

Question (Detective Inspector Graham—Interviewing): "Has sexual intercourse ever been normal for you?"
Answer(Suspect): "What is normal?"

Q: "Love between male and female, but without you murdering her later on."
(Excerpt from police tape transcript.)

On Monday, Brian Calver waited until the office was nearly empty before approaching Dastra, who was apparently busying himself getting the burial site mapped out accurately on the new computer. "Did you pull it?"

He didn't look up from the computer. "Oh, yes. I owe you one. I've pulled her, hook, line and sinker."

"Are you shagging it?"

"I'm sorry Brian. I wouldn't tell you if I was. Nothing personal… it's just…"

"No. I understand. Most of you lads in The Job are eager to share your conquests, but for what it's worth, I'd be like you." He put a hand on Dastra's shoulder. "Very lovely though, even with a pirate's patch."

"Oh, yes. She modeled for me."

"What, photographs?"

"No. I paint. I painted her."

"Painted? You are a dark horse indeed."

~ * ~

Brian Shackerstone came in later in the day, stopping briefly to dump his bag in a side office, and then returned to the main room.

"Can I have everyone's attention please?"

Just under half the murder squad was in the office, working hard on getting exhibits listed on HOLMES. Officers stopped conversations or dutifully swiveled their chairs away from their computers to listen.

"We've got some results. The wood in the bodies was saturated with blood, so it was in them at or soon after death. The bods at the lab have identified the wood as natural hazel, and not seasoned. It would be worth knowing where it might have come from.

"We've also got the lab to look at geological evidence of the unusual mud from the shoe. They tell me it is mostly of fine gray alluvial clay, local, but not at all widespread. This should really help narrow things down. Barney, can you map this stuff?"

"Just give me the data, Guv, and I'll make some calls."

"Get on it right away."

~ * ~

Dastra was in Shackerstone's office just after lunch on Wednesday.

"Guv. I've got some results."

"The clay?"

"Yes, it's better than we thought. I got hold of geological mapping data and put it on the machine. The clay in question is localized to a band only a hundred yards or so wide, running intermittently along hills for about three miles either side of Goring, mostly in woodland and fields. I was on to it within an hour of getting the data loaded up."

"So why the delay in telling me?"

"I couldn't get hold of you yesterday. I shoved it on HOLMES, but then I did a bit more, to help us narrow the area down. I've been on the internet searching for more mapping data from forestry sources. There wasn't a lot to be had at first, but I found that a project on tree diseases at University College London has mapped the tree types to the north of Goring. I went into London yesterday afternoon and they gave me a disc full of their work. I spent last night putting the plots onto the system manually, and now I have the hazel as an overlay on the clay data. There are only six fairly small areas where the clay and the hazel can be found together. Look, I've printed a map." He unrolled a large sheet of paper as Shackerstone cleared a space for it on his desk. They looked carefully at the six areas Dastra had identified.

"Bloody good work, Barney. It can't be more than a day's work for three pairs to do a walk through all of them. Take an action. Go and look tomorrow with Tim Hunt at these two bigger sites. Meanwhile I'll get some actions sorted out for the others. If yours take longer, then take Friday as well."

"I was going to ask you about that."

"What?"

"Friday. I'd like the day off if I can, and Saturday. My... girlfriend has invited me to an end of term party down in Oxford tomorrow night, and I..."

"You'll be too tired or too hung over to come in on Friday."

"Something like that."

"Get the sites looked at... properly... on Thursday, then you can have the time off. You've helped us jump ahead right and proper."

Thirteen

Question (DI Graham): "So can we go back to the woods?"

Answer(Suspect): "Yeah. The investigation was that close, then near misfortune led to a brilliant opportunity. It was too good to miss."

(Excerpt from evidential tape transcript.)

A fierce wind tugged at their clothes as Hunt and Dastra worked their way methodically across the second of the two sites they had been allocated.

"At least this site is accessible." Dastra shouted above the roar of the wind in the masses of leaves above them.

"I'm sure you're not bothered about having to leave the other site to a police search team. At least you'll get away to your bit of stuff."

"So we'd best do a good job on this one, or Shackerstone will think I blanked the first site deliberately. I'll start taking the soil samples."

"Listen, you get on with your geology bit and I'll make some inquiries."

"Here? Whereabouts?"

"There was a sign to a campsite down the lane. It's the only place on this site with any sort of habitation."

"But campers come and go…"

"But campsite owners don't." Hunt tapped his temple with an index finger. "Detective ability."

Hunt turned away and strolled off through the woods towards

the lane. Dastra's police radio burst into life. "DC Dastra from DS Shanter."

Dastra pulled the radio from his pocket and shielded the mouthpiece against the wind. "Go ahead."

"Barney. We've drawn a blank on the fragment of the lime bag, which really reduces the lines of inquiry from the burial. Thought you'd need to know. Shackerstone will be relying on anything you can get from the soil."

"Listen. Tell the other teams they'll need to dig down about a foot to get below the organic stuff from the trees. Stick to the grids I drew up. The lab will be able to localize our murder site with a bit of luck."

"I'll get on to them."

"Thanks."

Dastra put the radio down on a tree stump, checked his map and began to dig. The radio crackled again. "DC Dastra from DC Hunt."

"Go ahead."

"No campsite owner about. There are a couple of trailer caravans there, but they're all locked up. I'll try another day."

"Come back and give us a hand with this digging."

~ * ~

Lucy's doorbell rang promptly at 8:00 p.m. "Barney, I'll be down in a second."

Lucy slipped on a short black shift dress, having tied her hair into a single plait that ended in a small black ribbon. She ran down the stairs, opened the front door, threw her arms round Dastra's neck, and kissed him. "Sorry to keep you waiting. I was trying to find the right shoes."

"That's okay."

"Do they look okay with this dress?"

He moved back, looking down. "They look fine. So do you. You look wonderful. Do I look sufficiently student-like?"

"Barney, I don't mean this in a nasty way, but I think you look more like a seedy history lecturer."

"Perfect. I guess I won't seem out of place then."

"Don't worry. Nobody will care. They'll be too glad that this year is over. Perhaps we could go shopping tomorrow and get you some more fashionable clothes."

"I'd like that." He opened the passenger door of his car for her. "I have tickets to a concert tomorrow night. Beethoven, here in Oxford, would you like to...?"

"Oh, that's wonderful!" she said, settling into her seat.

Dastra got into the driving seat and started the engine. "I'll leave the CD off."

"Great. You can tell me how your case is going."

"It's going along fairly well. Since the weekend we've managed to localize the unusual soil we found at the scene. That's where I was working today."

"Why is the soil unusual?"

"It's quite a story."

"Go on. I'm interested."

"In testing my knowledge?"

"Perhaps. But I'd like to understand."

"Here goes, then... Once upon a time, thousands of years ago, the river Thames didn't run down from here towards London, but looped round to the north. The last ice age blocked this route and caused the Thames to fill the Oxford basin with a huge lake. At the same time, fine clays created by the grinding action of the glacial ice cap on the rocks beneath got washed into the lake. Eventually the lake burst over the hills at Goring in a great set of rapids, cutting the Goring Gap, carving a new line for the river and creating the London basin. The rapids deposited the fine clay in eddies along their course, mixed with distinctive rougher particles ground from the local rocks. This gives us our unique clay, and might just have helped us a step closer to chummy."

"Chummy?"

"Vlad.—our murderer."

Following Lucy's directions, they found an off-license for some drinks before arriving at a house on an estate in the south suburbs of Oxford. Loud music thumped from within as they approached the front door. Lucy rang a plastic doorbell that hung on corroded screws from peeling paintwork on the door surround. A girl with frizzy hair answered the door that led on to a hallway crowded with young drinkers and reverberating with rock music.

"Lucy, darling. Come in. Who's your friend?"

"This is Barney. He's…."

"The new man in your life?"

Lucy nodded. "Oh, yes! He is."

"Pleased to meet you, Barney. I'm Katie. I guessed Lucy was up to something. She's been hiding you from us. Take your drink through to the kitchen. The others are all over the place. Help yourselves to booze."

They picked their way through loose knots of students who were variously lying, standing, dancing, or cuddled together. For Lucy they were mostly familiar faces and pleased to see her. For Dastra, Lucy realized that she was the only familiar face, and he followed her politely, exchanging pleasantries with new faces where appropriate. A distinct odor of cannabis sharpened the air in the first room off the hall and she thought that it would have been easier for him if he had taken her to a police party among the familiar company of his former station. He soon showed disinterest in the people around him, and focused his attention on Lucy. She was bright and extroverted, and only had to step into a room for a group of people to gather round her like rabbits in the beams of car headlights. She was eager to introduce him to everyone she knew, and tried hard to tell him as much as she could about people in order to make him feel at ease.

They found the kitchen, and awkwardly helped themselves to drinks while a group of gay men there eyed Dastra up and down.

"It's nice to be looked at as the attractive half," he whispered in Lucy's ear. She cupped her hand to her mouth to stop herself from laughing as she glanced back over her shoulder at the men. Barney had just finished pouring his lager when Lucy wrapped her arm around his neck and pressed her lips to his. She gave a long slow kiss, fighting his tongue with hers. She eventually moved her head back and with her good eye looked up into his face from under her long lashes.

"That'll show them who you belong to… in every way."

They picked their way from group to group and conversation to conversation around the house, eventually settling in the relative quiet of the downstairs back room. Dastra sat propped against the wall, with Lucy lying on the floor with her head against his breastbone. A pair of bleached blond men came into the room and one of them announced, in a deliberately effeminate voice, "Darlings! Paul and I are trying to guess everyone's future job. We've done the other room. Paul wants all the chaps to be hairdressers and all the girlie types to be air hostesses. I've tried to make him be more realistic, so he has agreed to keep it shut and let me do the guessing in here. Right, Charlotte's easy." A mousy haired and skinny girl standing near the doorway with a heavily-built, bearded man waited for the judgment on her. "You're going to be a motorcycle pillion tester-outer, and Mark will be a dispatch rider. So all that mechanical engineering from your degree won't be wasted: you can fix your bike. And you, Lucy darling, you'll have to be a pirate... no, a history teacher. History degrees are good for little else, and your hunky new paramour, he's got a job, hasn't he? He's a piggy-wiggy. I wonder if he's ever arrested me for cruising in a gay bar."

Dastra met the man's eyes and glowered at him. The atmosphere in the room seemed to change, but the camp young man continued his course around the room until he had chosen everyone's career. He and his partner then retreated to the kitchen. "How did they find that out?" Dastra asked.

"Uh, sorry... I told them."

He sat up, forcing Lucy to sit upright. "How daft can you get? A cop is going to be about as popular here as a pork pie at a Jewish wedding."

"You're different from other cops."

"They don't know that."

Lucy jumped up and hurried from the room, tears already forming in her eyes. He followed her, but she darted upstairs and into the bathroom just as someone came out, jumping the queue in the process.

"Hey!" protested a large dark-haired girl at the head of the queue.

Dastra stepped round her. "Sorry. I've upset her."

"Well, you can un-upset her or she'll have the US Air Force carpet-bombing Oxford."

He knocked on the toilet door. "Lucy, it's Barney."

"Go away!"

"Look, I'm sorry. Please come out."

"Go away."

"Okay. But there are other people here, waiting to use the loo. Come out and talk. Please."

"Go away. I'm drying my eyes."

"Look. I'll go away. Right away. I'm not staying. I'll wait outside in the car to take you home."

He trotted downstairs and out to his car. Eventually Lucy emerged from the room, collected herself and made her way out to the car, her face expressionless, but with a sliver of wetness clinging to the bottom of her eye patch. He got out to speak to her, but she stopped a few feet short of him and spoke politely, but with no emotion. "Will you take me home please?"

"No problem. You know I will."

"Don't say anything. Please. Just take me home."

"As you wish." There was no conversation on the way back, other than him attempting to open one by asking occasional directions. He parked directly but slightly awkwardly on an exposed corner by Lucy's flat. He got out to open the passenger door but she hurried out of the car and brushed past him, tears forming again in her eyes. "Sorry. Good night." She continued walking on towards the communal door.

He followed, disoriented and uncertain about to what to do, if anything. "Sorry, Lucy. Is this it?"

Lucy let herself in and tried to shut the communal door in his face. He put his foot in the door. "Lucy, I'm sorry. Please. Let's talk."

"No. I don't want to talk. Go away." He eased his foot out of the door and Lucy shut it hard. She ran upstairs and let herself into the flat. Michaela was out. Lucy stomped through into the bathroom and started to undo the braid in her hair.

"Damn you, David Dastra! I cared about you. If only you knew. And you think I'm daft. What was so wrong about telling everyone you were a cop?"

She slipped the black dress off and let it slip to the floor with her briefs. She flicked the dress up onto a small vanity unit with her foot, pulled her eye patch off then angrily pushed her hair into a shower cap and started the shower. She tested the water temperature then stepped in and pulled the curtain behind her. "Men!" Fumbling for the shower gel, she gasped as she glimpsed a dark unfamiliar shape beyond the gray translucence of the shower curtain. Her heartbeat quickened and she backed away, sliding her hands across the tiles behind her to keep her balance. *And I left a cop outside.* The water from the shower and her clouded left eye obscured her view even more, and made her uncertain as to whether the shape was moving. She was sure she was alone in the flat. She had undone the mortise lock herself. She took deep breaths to calm herself, but it was a minute before she cautiously pushed the curtain aside, praying that the shape was Barney.

It was her dress on the vanity unit. She sighed loudly with relief, but the event had driven her anger away and now she wished he were in the flat with her.

"Barney, I'm sorry. I hope you haven't driven off. Please God! Let him still be outside in his car." She turned off the shower, wrapped a towel around herself, and hurried across the darkened main room of the flat and up to the window. The curtains hadn't been drawn, and Lucy peered out into the orange sodium glow of the street to look for the Porsche. Her heart sank, but then she caught sight of the front bumper and a short length of hood peeping out from behind a hedge. She half dried herself, slipped the black dress back on and ran barefoot into the street.

Lucy knocked on the passenger window and Dastra got out of the car and went round to her.

"Hi."

Lucy said nothing but took his hand and started to lead him towards the flat. He flicked the remote control to lock the car and let Lucy guide him forward. Once through the door of the flat and into the darkened lounge, he began to speak. "Look, I'm sorry."

Lucy gently put her hand over his mouth, turning to stand toe to toe with him. "Shhhh... I wanted to argue. I wanted to hit you. But I can't... I just can't." She peeled back the jacket from his shoulders and dropped it to the floor as she pressed her mouth to his.

He wrapped his arms around her. "So I'm back in your good books?"

Lucy nodded. "Carry me to the bedroom." Dastra made as if to lift her, but Lucy stopped him. "I just need to do one thing first... music."

"Music?"

"Yes." She found a CD and leaned over the portable stereo as she had done on the day she had first met him, but now she let the short dress reveal the soft shadows between her buttocks. The music started.

He thought quickly of something suitable to say. "Fifth piano concerto, second movement?"

"Yes."

He swept her up and maneuvered her through the doorway to her room. She flicked the light off as they went past and he laid her down gently on the bed.

~ * ~

Something woke her in the early daylight and she found him gone from the bed. "Darling?" He appeared at the door, naked, with the sound of a toilet tank filling somewhere in the darkness beyond. He slipped into the bed with her and she was conscious of the natural odor of his body for the first time. All sensations when she had brought him into the flat earlier had been suppressed in her urgent desire to make love to him. She wondered for a moment if she had bled as a result of it being her first time and gingerly felt herself. She felt a warm liquid running out of her and panicked, swinging her legs out of bed and sitting up.

"Darling, are you okay?"

"It's okay, I thought I was bleeding."

"Are you?"

"I might have a little bit last night. It's just, well, you're running out of me. Is that supposed to happen?"

"I don't know."

"You don't?"

"No. I've no idea. I guess I thought it would all stay inside you."

"So you don't know if this is right or not?"

"No. But it must be."

"But you must know."

"Lucy. I've a bit of a confession to make…"

Lucy cocked her head to one side. "Yes?"

"You weren't the only virgin in this bed last night."

Lucy said nothing but leaned over and kissed him on the

forehead.

"Is that shocking?"

"No, my darling. It's perfect."

Lucy got up, tiptoed out to the portable CD player in the next room and restarted the music.

~ * ~

They awoke in the late morning and Lucy made breakfast. "Shopping!" she said, brightly, drying the last of the dishes.

"Shopping?"

"To buy you some decent clothes for tonight."

"Lucy?"

"Darling?"

"This is a bit difficult."

"You're going to tell me you're gay."

"No. Be serious for a minute."

"Okay."

"I know this is a delicate matter, but what are we going to do about contraception? I wasn't expecting... well... we slipped up a bit."

"No we didn't. It's too late in the month for me. Don't worry. I know what I'm doing."

"Good," he sighed.

They were just leaving the flat when Lucy realized that she needed to go back for something. Dastra went on down to the car, and when Lucy finally came out of the front door she saw him sitting in it, window wound down, watching her every step as she crossed the road and made her way round to the passenger door. He started the engine as she got in.

"Don't I get the door opened for me now that you've had your wicked way with me?"

"Sorry. I was miles away." They pulled away, heading for the center of town. "I was wondering if you'd like to come up to the house again."

"Tomorrow?"

"After the concert, if you wish. It's up to you."

"Oh?"

"I've bought another canvas."

"Really?"

"Are you up for another session?"

"Sure."

~ * ~

Tim Hunt's phone rang in the office late in the afternoon. "Hi Tim, it's Barney."

"Hello, mate."

"Listen, I've got a bit of grief. Did you see whether or not I brought my police radio back in yesterday?"

"Come to think of it, no. I can't remember you bringing it back. I'll check to see if you've booked it back in."

Hunt went over and opened a binder by the radio cabinet, before checking the cabinet, then Dastra's desk, finally returning to the phone.

"It's not been booked back in and it's not immediately obvious."

"I think I know where I left it. It was on a tree stump close to that site where you checked the campsite. I'd best go back and try to find it."

"You should, yes."

"It's a right pain in the butt. I'm taking Lucy out to a concert tonight."

"What time?"

"I need to be back for seven-thirty."

"You'll do it easily in that car of yours."

Fourteen

"And then comes the morning
And the memory of the darkness
Is washed away by the light."
(Extract from small red notebook, exhibit BS14, seized from suspect)

Lucy wrapped a towel round herself and checked the bedside clock as she lifted the telephone receiver. 6:15 p.m.

"Hello."

"Lucy. It's Barney. I'm nearly where I left the radio."

"But you've not…"

"Not yet, but I know exactly where I put it. The only thing is that I'll be in a bit of a rush when I get back. I'll sound the horn when I arrive. Come straight out to the car."

"Okay. Be quick."

"Love you."

Lucy put the phone down and returned to getting herself ready, while listening for the sound of Dastra's car. 7:30 came and went. No horn sounded. With rising anger, she tried his mobile phone. There was no reply. As the hours passed, both she and Michaela tried calling him again. They tried telephoning his house. Lucy telephoned the police to see if there were any accidents reported. Nothing. She went off sadly to bed at around eleven.

~ * ~

Brian Shackerstone's bedside telephone rang at 1:15am. Khan was on the line. "Guv, Reshard Khan. It's Barney; he's been nicked near Goring. He's got a dead body in the boot of his car."

Shackerstone sat up in bed and shook the sleepiness from his head. "You're pissing me about."

"Tim Hunt said he telephoned in about leaving a personal radio at one of the sites they looked at. He was found by local Old Bill near there; he was driving erratically and the officers watched him ground his car on the verge. It sounds like they let him get out, thinking it was a drunk driver. He said he was busting for a leak so they let him have one. One of the PCs spotted blood on the back bumper of his car and then they found a woman's body in the back, impaled…"

"Impaled?"

"Yes, and plonked on a canvas."

"A canvas?"

"An artist's canvas… for painting."

"Where's Dastra?"

"They've brought him straight back here and the scene is all preserved. DI Graham was on call, she's taken it."

"Which leaves Dastra to us."

"Yes, but we will need someone from police complaints."

"I know. Do you think Dastra is Vlad?"

"I don't know what to think. The more you compare him with the profile we have, the better he looks."

Shackerstone mulled over all the possibilities. "Does Gordonstown know?"

"Not yet. He's on a weekend away at his pad in Scotland."

"Studying for promotion, no doubt. Good. Right, yes. I'll come in and sort some things out. What time was Dastra nicked?"

"About midnight, detention authorized back here at 12:43 a.m."

"At least that gives us the first twenty-four hours. We might have to get before a magistrate on Saturday afternoon if we can. A superintendent will only be able to extend custody up to midday on Sunday."

~ * ~

Shackerstone rang Ian Yardley at 1:43 a.m.

"Ian Yardley." The response was whispered in a voice thick with sleep.

"Sir. It's Brian Shackerstone. I need to brief you on

Klingsor."

"An arrest?"

"Yes."

"I'll just move to another room, hold on. I don't want to disturb the missus." Shackerstone heard some movement before Yardley's voice came back more clearly. "Okay, Brian, what have we got?"

"Another girl impaled, but this time in the boot of the suspect's car."

"Tell me it was a good stop by uniformed cops."

"It was. They thought it was a drunk driver. A good result, except that the suspect is a police officer."

"Local?"

"Very, it is DC Dastra."

"Dastra? Bloody hell. Where is he?"

"Here at Wemstone."

"And the victim?"

"No ID yet. White female like the others. Young."

"It's not that girl with the eye patch, is it?"

"No eye patch, but another hazel rod by the look of it, bent over to get the body in the car. The body and the car have been photographed at the location of the stop, but we'll need more work during the day. We've seized Dastra's clothes and it looks like he's got soil on his shoes and knees, as well as some sort of grease on the back of his jacket. The police surgeon says he's not fit to detain because he whacked the side of his head when he piled his car up, and twisted one of his testicles. The doc says it's pretty swollen."

"That's the sort of injury a woman gives to a man."

"Quite. Anyhow, he's in hospital under guard."

"So his custody clock has stopped."

"Until we get him back."

"Thank God for that."

Shackerstone phoned Gordonstown next. The phone rang for ten rings before Gordonstown's voice answered wearily. "Hello."

"Sir. DCI Shackerstone, sorry to wake you…"

"This better be bloody important."

"It is. There's been an arrest for Klingsor."

Gordonstown's voice became more earnest. "Why wasn't I

informed there was going to be…"

"It wasn't by the team. It was a uniformed stop."

"Really?"

"A good one. The suspect had the body in his car."

"Nice one."

"The not so nice bit is that the suspect is a cop—DC Dastra."

"Dastra! That's bloody sweet, that is. At least he's not really one of ours."

"How do you mean?"

"A new boy from the Met. It won't reflect too badly on the force as we've only had him a few weeks. We need to turn this round so that none of us are tainted by association. Think what it could do to a detective's career if people knew he had been working with Vlad under his nose."

~ * ~

With long flowing ginger hair, a blood-drained white skinned female appeared to gaze vacantly upwards, dull eyed and lifeless from the stainless steel mortuary tray. Shackerstone noted that external blood and other matter had been washed away, but the offending stake still protruded from her.

"Here we go again," said O'Toole, pushing his glasses back and switching on his tape recorder. He glanced at the detectives and took a great breath as if preparing to deliver a lecture to the Royal Society.

"White European female, healthy, twenty to twenty-five years, ginger hair, hazel eyes. Average build, no clothing. Mode of death?" He cleared his throat. "On initial observation, this appears to have been caused by her being impaled upon a sharpened wooden spike and her body weight allowed to propel her down it. Absence of any hypostasis in the legs suggests that if she died in an upright position, then she didn't spend more than a few hours in that position—as it takes six to eight hours for the redness to develop under the skin. Indeed hypostasis on her back continued to develop gradually during the examination at the discovery scene last night, and is consistent with the position we found her in the back of the car. Take some photos, Malcolm. Get the whole body and the entry and exit points of the spike. Marks on the neck suggest she was hoisted up by a rope, although there are no blood vessel bursts around the face consistent with strangulation. Therefore, this wasn't a proper noose, although there is a knot mark. Her hands still show marks of being tied, consistent with the gray nylon bindings present when I examined the body in the car last night. These ropes have been recovered during forensic examination at the scene."

O'Toole wandered around the body, occasionally stopping to examine specific areas. The others stood back, watching. "There aren't any other marks on the body, not so much as a clothing pressure mark. No defense wounds, no bits of skin under her nails, nothing. It is as if she went through this almost... obligingly."

"Or at gunpoint," whispered Shackerstone.

"What about toxicology? She could have been drugged," said Graham.

"The results will be a few days off."

O'Toole prodded the body about. "Have we got an identity yet?"

"A possible," murmured Shackerstone. "A missing person reported yesterday morning from Reading. Missing since Thursday night. We're waiting for more information. Can you give me a time of death?"

"Only approximately. Core temperature suggested she had been killed in the early evening, about seven. I'm going to have to take her apart as soon as possible. If we don't have anybody en route to identify her, I propose to carry on, and stitch her up afterwards. My boys here will have her looking good for the relatives by teatime."

Shackerstone didn't like being reminded of food at times like this, and he surmised that O'Toole was preying on his discomfort.

"Entry and exit sites, Malcolm, and then we'll see what she had for dinner last night."

The photographer took several shots of the top of the stake while O'Toole moved the legs to allow a better shot of the entry point.

"Did you get swabs from her pubic area last night, Jim?"

"Yes, thanks."

"We'll need to get internal ones," mumbled Shackerstone, playing with the end of his nose as if expecting a sudden assault on his sense of smell.

"I'll get those later. Shall we have a break and a nice cup of tea? Adrian can open the chest and skull."

Shackerstone needed the break, but not the tea. Khan, White, James, and Graham took tea with O'Toole in a small clean kitchen area off a corridor. Shackerstone used the toilet. Adrian came out to them after about fifteen minutes and nodded to O'Toole, who led them all back in. The body of the girl was now far more extensively defiled by the mortician's implements than it had been by the sharpened rod. From her neck to just below her navel, Adrian had cut a long incision and folded the skin back wide all along this length. A triangular section had been taken from the front ribs to expose the lungs and heart. Her scalp had been cut in a wide arc behind the ears and pulled down over her face. The top of the skull was off and the brain was on a set of scales in front of a viewing window used by more squeamish observers. Shackerstone wished he were safely beyond that window.

"Now to follow the route of our stake." O'Toole, freshly gloved, started by moving part of the girl's large intestine clear, but some of it snagged on the stake, visible now inside the body. "Entry into abdominal space via birth canal, punctured close to cervix, ruptured the intestines but missed major arteries and the main aorta. Interesting." A strong smell drifted up from the body. Shackerstone, standing at the girl's head, cupped his hand to his mouth and nose. "Even though our spike has punctured her large intestine and small intestine, that didn't kill her; it was hitting a major blood vessel in her liver that did that. Get more photos, Malcolm."

The photographer moved in to record shots of the girl's ravaged internal organs. The only sounds the click and wind of the camera. There was a sudden movement at the head of the slab. "Excuse me," said Shackerstone, heading for the door. He staggered towards the toilets, as O'Toole's voice echoed after him. "He doesn't like dead bodies much."

Brian Shackerstone's stomach was still very much alive as a sweat broke out across his forehead and reverse peristalsis forced him to heave over one of the toilet bowls. After a minute or two to catch his breath, he went to one of the sinks and splashed water over his face and head. He stared at himself in the mirror, his eyes reddened. "Come on Brian, be professional. Get a grip."

~ * ~

By the time the girl had been identified as being Sarah Louise Carothers, twenty-four, she was neatly stitched back together. Her husband and parents were brought to the mortuary by Tim Hunt. Shackerstone waited nervously in the car park for them and as the car swung in at about 5:00 p.m., he took a deep breath and walked purposefully towards it. Hunt pulled the car up in a parking bay, and a brown haired man of about twenty-five got out.

"What do *you* want?" he said to Shackerstone, abruptly.

"I'm Detective Chief Inspector Shackerstone, the senior investigating officer in this case."

There was an awkward silence as an older couple emerged from the car with Tim Hunt.

"I'm sorry. I thought you were..."

"Press?"

"Something like that."

Shackerstone knew the man wasn't expecting a black detective. But this wasn't the time or place to make an issue of it.

"An easy mistake. I was a press photographer once. I must still look the part."

"Yeah, right. Sorry. I'm Jeff Carothers. These are Sarah's parents; Tom and Veronica."

"Not the circumstances I would have wanted to meet you under," said Shackerstone, ushering them across the car park. He led them through the main door to the mortuary and along a bleak corridor to the chapel. Before entering, he spoke to them quietly. He felt a natural need to be quiet near bodies, and crept about as if they were likely to jump up at him. This was interpreted by families as politeness and sensitivity, so it did no harm.

"This is the formal identification. It only takes one of you, but if all three wish to see her, that's no problem. We are satisfied from the photographs we have seen, that this is Sarah. I am so very sorry."

"We'll all go in," said her young husband after receiving nods from the parents.

Shackerstone let them go on in alone. Sarah was lying beyond a glass screen, and the lighting arrangement allowed Adrian to make her appear a healthier color. She was covered with a white blanket up to her neck, hiding her wounds and the work of the mortician. Her freshly brushed hair hid the cut round her scalp. There was no scream from anyone, just silence; a long, eerie, brooding silence. Her father started to sob first, which set the other two off. Shackerstone still waited outside with Hunt, giving them privacy. The three came out and the father nodded resignedly, supporting his wife.

As they left he spoke to Shackerstone outside in the car park. "By God I hope you get the bastard who did this."

"We are confident we already have, sir."

Fifteen

Question (DI Graham): "Why was the Piano Room so important as a location?"
Answer (Suspect): "It had the beam, the outside looked right, and it was isolated."
(Extract from evidential tape transcript.)

DCI Shackerstone drove to Prospect of Peshawar on Sunday morning with Khan, Martin O'Donoghue, Mark Whitehouse and SOCOs White and Gray.

Once their two cars were through the gates using the keys taken from Dastra on Friday night, Shackerstone set the mood. "Dastra's drum looks like Dracula's castle," he said to Khan, as he swung his Citroen round the island flowerbed.

"More of a decaying imperial mausoleum. I'd buy it if I had a couple of million spare, and time to brighten it up."

"Even if you knew there had been murders here?"

"To be fair boss, we haven't established a murder scene."

"No, but I have a feeling about this place."

They got out of their cars and Khan walked up to the green front door with a set of keys. The two SOCOs dealt out forensic paper coveralls and shoes to prevent cross-contamination and Gray unfolded a plastic sheet by the door for exiting officers to take their suits off over, in order to catch any fibers. With thin forensic gloves on, Khan opened the door carefully, so as not to disturb any victim fingerprints that might be on the painted surface. Khan deactivated the alarm and Gray immediately got down and dusted the front door for fingerprints.

Shackerstone gazed down the hallway. "I'm going to do a rapid survey of the scene with SOCO White in order to assess further resources I might need and the likely time the job will take." He briefly scanned the paintings in the hall. "These are his; Older Brian said he paints."

"And very well," added Khan.

"Interesting psychological angle, though. A collector of women—in representational form."

Eventually Shackerstone and White reached the piano room.

"Stone me!" exclaimed Shackerstone. "The bugger has got Quad electrostatic speakers."

"What? The two black slabs?"

"Yes. These are the dog's bollocks in Hi-fi; they must have cost thousands. My landlord, when I was a young PC, had a set. He used to make me sit up all night with him drinking Scotch and listening to Wagner. What has Barney got in his collection?"

"Let's have a look. It's mostly Beethoven, Sibelius, some Pink Floyd, Genesis, Thin Lizzy—pretty catholic tastes."

"And what do you make of those?" Shackerstone motioned with his head towards the two bell jar displays of butterflies on the beam.

"Impaled creatures... that's for you and Dr. Holt."

"Yes. Let's go back and see where the team have got to."

Despite the passage of over an hour, the rest of the team had not progressed beyond the entrance hall.

Shackerstone and White searched the cellar and the upstairs, but Shackerstone kept going back to the piano room, as if drawn to it like an unhealed wound that he needed to pick a scab off. He noticed the new painting, but not recognizing it as anything other than a portrait of a beautiful unknown he sent it outside for photographing. He sat down on one end of the piano stool and surveyed the scene slowly, taking all the detail in. It was the sort of room he would like himself. He liked the space, the verandas, and the huge roof. The beam made him feel uneasy. It wasn't that it shouldn't have been there—its place in the structure was entirely appropriate. It just troubled him deep in his mind. He sat motionless, staring blankly at it for several minutes. "All I need to find is..." He stood up and kicked back a rug on the floor. "Yes, a hatch. This is it. This must be the scene." He hurried the others in from the hall. Shackerstone pointed up at the huge beam and the two butterfly displays set upon it. "Just look again at the thickness of that beam! A man could stand on it."

They all looked up, waiting for Shackerstone's next piece of reasoning. He craned his neck up to look right into the top apex of the room. "Can any of you see a pulley?"

"Up near the apex," said White.

Sure enough, a single pulley was attached to the underside of the roof, but slightly off center. "But then you'd expect that over a cellar hatch," continued White. "Especially in rural buildings."

There were two small brass rings set into the floor and Shackerstone got his assistants to pull at them. With considerable physical persuasion and much squeaking from dry hinges, two great doors revealed a hole about eight feet square and giving access to a dark, isolated cellar, the floor of which was about seven feet below them down a steep wooden ladder.

"Although I like to keep an open mind, I reckon he could have hoisted them up on that pulley, and sat on the beam watching them slide down into the pit. See if you can find any rope, gents. Jim, get looking for blood."

White wasn't pleased with this sudden change of method. "Guv, can we finish the hall first? We can do this room next if you like. As crime scene coordinator, I can't have you going off at a tangent like this."

"Look Jim, I need best evidence, and I need it bloody fast. If I wait while we go over the whole drum, it will be next Sunday before we have anything. Start here. Now!"

White swallowed. "Guv."

The rest of the team drifted back to the hall to get bags and labels. Shackerstone poked around the piano room. Behind the sofa, Shackerstone stopped to peer at something on the floor. He took a packet from his pocket and leaned down to look more closely. White, as if he'd been watching him and sensed some unease, came over to him. "Got something, Guv?"

Shackerstone straightened. "I think so. Hairs on the floor here. It looks like they've got a bit of root on the end."

"Good eyesight!" commented White with a slightly questioning air.

"Yes. Perfect."

White moved round and crouched down at Shackerstone's feet. Five long ginger hairs, with root matter attached were loosely coiled on the floor. White scooped them up into a bag and sealed it.

"You could have seized them yourself."

"It will look better if you do."

"I'll have to say you found them."

"As you wish."

Sixteen

Question (DI Graham): "And what happened after Sarah Carothers had died?"

Answer (Suspect): "Her pulse was checked, the rod lifted out of the ground, snapped over—that took some force—and then she was shoved in the boot of the Porsche."

(Extract from evidential tape transcript.)

At 10:03 a.m. on Monday, freshly returned from hospital, Dastra stood again in front of the custody officer at Wemstone, his rights having been read to him again. "Can you contact my girlfriend, and I'll have a duty solicitor please, Sarge."

"I'll do better than that. You can call her yourself, if the SIO has no objections."

Shackerstone shook his head. Dastra tried the telephone, but got no reply. "Can you get an officer to leave a note at her flat?"

"Okay. Write the address down."

Dastra began writing the address as the custody sergeant continued. "I take it you'll want a solicitor."

"Please," said Dastra without looking up. "John Aaronovitch."

Shackerstone's brows arched in surprise. "Aaronovitch? Not for this, surely."

"It'll do him good to represent a cop," the sergeant said with a smile. "In fact it will be rather ironic, and we know he'll give you a run for your money."

~ * ~

In the interview room, Walsh leaned across the table and started the double tape recorder. Shackerstone read the necessary preamble across to Dastra, and then continued "I am DCI Brian Shackerstone, interviewing David Dastra, also present is DS Karl Walsh, DCI Joe Hooker from complaints and Mr. Dastra's solicitor John Aaronovitch, who has just spent the last three hours with his client examining the evidence I have disclosed to them. Is that not correct, Mr. Aaronovitch?"

"Indeed."

"Right, PC Dastra, you had best start with what happened to you when you left here on Thursday afternoon with DC Hunt. Please explain for the benefit of the tape recorder."

"Well, I went to the two sites I had been allocated with Tim Hunt. The first was a small section of woodland called Wyatt's Copse. It was inaccessible. The second was a nameless bit farther north, down a path. We called it site four on the map. It was near a small campsite. There wasn't much to see there either, just a lot of trees and very slippery clay soil. At one point I put my radio down on a tree stump while I dug out more soil, then Tim called me and I don't know whether I picked up the radio from the stump or not. I didn't realize it was missing until the next day. I phoned Tim in the office to check if he had picked it up then hurried back to site four. I was in a desperate hurry because I had tickets to go to a concert and I was picking up my girlfriend at 7:30."

"Can she confirm this?"

"I'm sure she can. And I was with her until five."

"Who is she?"

"Lucy Aybrams, the witness who found the three bodies."

"So where were you on the previous evening, Thursday night?"

"With Lucy—we went to a student party."

"She can confirm this?"

"Of course, so can a lot of the partygoers. There were some gays there—somehow it got out that I was a cop. It got a bit—well—unpleasant. That's why we left around midnight and went back to her digs."

"What did you do back at her flat?"

"We went to bed."

"And she can confirm that?"

"Yes."

"Did you leave the flat at any time during the night?"

"No, I stayed there well into the morning."

"And she can confirm that you never left."

"Well, yes. We were asleep for much of the night."

"Where did you go in the morning?"

"To the shops in the city center. Lucy thought I needed more fashionable clothes. She helped me choose some new gear."

"She can confirm this?"

"Of course, and I've got the gear to prove it. And receipts."

"But she could have bought it in your absence. Have you got credit card receipts?"

"We paid cash."

"Convenient. And in the afternoon?"

"We had lunch in a little café in the covered market. It was up a flight of stairs, and then we went back to her flat."

"What did you do there?"

"Well. We went to bed again."

"Okay. What then?"

"We got ready to go out to the concert."

"Who was playing?"

"The county orchestra. Beethoven's third piano concerto and his symphony number seven, they're very..."

"Thanks. I know a bit about German music. What happened next?"

"It was then that I suddenly realized that I hadn't taken my personal radio back the night before. I checked in the car, and then I called Tim."

"He confirms that."

"Then I left Lucy and drove back to find it. I remember driving down to Goring, or at least I remember driving through the edge of Reading. I got to the traffic lights where you turn off to the site where I had left my radio. I phoned Lucy while I was waiting at the lights. I remember driving right and down the road from there. It was still daylight but when I got to the site it was gloomy in the woods. Then I don't remember anything."

"How do you account for the dead body in the back of your

anner.

car?"

"Honestly, I can't, sir! The bang on my head has made it difficult to recall."

"The convenient bang on the head?"

"It hasn't been very convenient for me."

"You were found with a freshly impaled young woman dumped on a canvas in the back of your car and you expect me to believe that you have no idea how she got there?"

"That's right sir, I haven't the faintest notion. I think that whoever it was that banged me on the head killed her and put the body in the car."

"Your head injury was caused when you crashed. Your blood is on the steering wheel."

"No. The hospital people say I was hit on the back of the head. I bled on the steering wheel after I was injured."

"I will tell you what I think happened. You set out the previous night deliberately to trap a lone woman with intent to impale her. You raped her in your car and then held her captive at your house."

"Rape?"

"Yes, rape! Either you returned to Lucy Aybrams or you've primed her to cover for you. At some point, you returned to your house. And I know which room you did it in too, that big room with the piano in it. You hoisted her up and shoved a spike up her…"

"Rape! Inspector," interrupted Aaronovitch. "You didn't disclose this before the interview. I will need to consult with my client."

"No!" said Dastra, his face twitching "If there is semen there, it won't be mine. This will get me out of this mess. Carry on, Guv."

"I think you put a rope around her neck and stripped her. You hoisted her up and lowered her on to a sharpened stake." His eyes narrowed as he stared into Dastra's. "You enjoyed watching her die. Dr. Holt says your type hates women. You have a medieval dislike of their power to create life, like witch finders, so you bring death to them through the very place where life comes out. Why? You must have thought it was a right laugh being on the squad with us, even more so when you pulled Aybrams."

Dastra leaned back, smugly smiling. "When the suspect

DNA comes back from her, it won't be mine. You'll have to search for the real suspect. It won't be my semen." He stabbed his finger triumphantly in the air towards Shackerstone.

"We'll see about that. It was all down the front of your trousers."

Dastra pulled his chair up to the table and fidgeted nervously with his hands.

"Where have you hidden her car?"

Dastra said nothing.

"The suspect is making no movement or response. Is it in a lake like all the others?"

Again, Dastra said nothing.

"Where are her clothes? Are they in her car? Did you burn them in a wood somewhere?"

Dastra didn't answer; his mind was clearly elsewhere. Hooker looked at the floor and shook his head. Shackerstone didn't let up.

"Are there any others? How long has this been going on?"

"This is all conjecture, Inspector," said Aaronovitch coldly.

"I'm a Detective Chief Inspector! We've got blood from the lip of the hatch in the floor of the piano room. How did that get there?"

Dastra appeared to focus on this, thinking hard. "That might be my father's. He died in there, with Mum, overcome by fumes. I didn't see them." He swallowed. "I didn't see them in situ, but I understand he rolled onto the floor and there was some bleeding. You can check it out with the local..."

"Do you think he'd be proud of you now?"

"You bastard."

Aaronovitch jumped in. "My client states that he has no recollection of events on Friday night, he has helped you as far as he can. I suggest you are going to get no further evidence by questioning him, and that you should rely on other sources."

"One more thing." Shackerstone's eyes narrowed and he stared hard at Dastra. "We've found ginger hairs in your house. Long ones. Like Sarah's."

"Probably Lucy's."

"We'll get DNA on the roots. I bet they're Sarah's."

"Unlikely."

"Met records show you were on compassionate leave when the other three girls went missing. Where were you?"

Aaronovitch jumped in again. "Is my client under arrest for those offences too?"

"He's free to answer the question."

"Okay, I would be up at the house, arranging funerals and clearing out. My family solicitor would have seen me a lot, but for much of the time I was alone. I would have to check my diary for any appointments on those nights. It could be that there are phone records that put me at the house. I made lots of calls."

"In the evenings?"

"I guess not."

"Have you got amnesia there too?"

"Hardly, it was the death of my parents. Not something I could easily forget."

"Like impaling a stranger."

"I'm not taking the bait, Guv."

"Interview terminated." Shackerstone got up and walked out. Hooker followed him in to the corridor, slamming the door behind them. "Call that a bloody interview?"

"He isn't going to cough."

"It still wasn't professional. He was on your squad until last week. I went in there to make sure you didn't do him any favors, not to listen to you throw your own gut feelings onto tape."

Shackerstone put his hands in his pockets and walked away, turning briefly to speak. "Quite frankly, this is *my* job, chum, and I don't give a toss what you think."

He walked on and punched the key code in the security lock to leave the custody area. He wandered up to the incident room and found Nicola Graham in her office. He walked in without invitation and sat down on a chair.

"Did you get far?"

"No, it didn't last more than a few minutes. He's still sticking up this amnesia thing in my face. To charge him I really need the DNA tonight or tomorrow, and it's at least four days away."

"We've got the guy who sold the Fiesta to "Smethers", and the man who saw Dastra by the back of his car."

"Of course. Can you jack up a police line-up this evening?"

"Only if we call the Met and go to one of theirs. We'll have to supply our own uniformed Inspector and pay all the costs."

"We'll pay."

"I'll ring now."

~ * ~

After discussions with Aaronovitch, Dastra signed some papers before being transferred to Kilburn police station, the divisional station for Harlesden, in West London. Shackerstone didn't go with Dastra to Kilburn, although he would have liked to. A black detective never got a second glance in London, or so he had had been assured.

The only officers from the team who went were Whitehouse and Walsh, who collected the witnesses and took them to Kilburn, but were only allowed as far as a waiting room, to prevent any allegations of witness prompting.

Naturally, Dastra had never been on the receiving end of an identity parade before. There was much signing and checking of procedure to do beforehand with his solicitor and the uniformed Inspector responsible for organizing the parade.

The Inspector showed Dastra into a long room with one-way glass down one side. There was a bench on the opposite side with about twenty black-haired white men of his general size and appearance. Dastra and Aaronovitch were permitted to select the men who would sit on the line-up. The rest were shown out. Those staying were all given cards with letters on them and the Inspector entered a few lines of information in a book. Dastra was allowed to choose his position in the parade, and after the Inspector and Aaronovitch had left, a voice told everyone to sit up and that the parade was in progress. There was silence for about three minutes then they were told to relax. A voice told Dastra to move position if he wanted to, but he stayed put, confident of two negative results. Another two minutes passed and then Aaronovitch came back in with the Inspector.

"One all."

"What?"

"The first one picked you out as standing by your car."

"What about the second one."

"Total blank. He didn't even pause when he walked up and down."

~ * ~

At 10:23 p.m., Dastra was dozing in his cell at Wemstone when the new custody officer for the night shift fetched him out.

Aaronovitch, Shackerstone and Graham were waiting by the custody officer's desk. Dastra knew what to expect, and stood in front of the desk as the sergeant picked up the custody record.

"David Dastra, You are charged that on or about Friday, June nineteenth, 1998 within the jurisdiction of the Central Criminal Court you did murder Sarah Louise Carothers—against the peace. In answer to this charge, you do not have to say anything, but it may harm your defense if you do not mention something when questioned which you later rely on in court. Anything you say may be given in evidence."

"I didn't do it."

"In view of the seriousness of the charge I intend to keep you in custody for court in the morning, where I understand these officers will be objecting to bail."

Seventeen

Question (Superintendent Hinx): "So where was Dastra after charge?"

Answer (DCI Shackerstone): "Wemstone Prison. Wycombe would have been better for him, even Grendon, but that's the way remand seems to work."

Q: "Did you cover his alibi?"
A: "Yes, with an open mind. Her statement said he was with her from Thursday evening to Friday afternoon. We checked the shop they claimed to have gone to, but nobody could remember. We checked all the security videos we could find, but most had been wiped by the time we made the request on the following Friday. We identified the café from Lucy's statement. The staff seemed to think that they might have been there, but couldn't swear to it."

Q: "You say you got the DNA result. Can you expand, please?"
A: "Yes, the semen from Sarah's body matched Dastra's, as you would expect, so I had him further charged with rape."

Q: "For the purposes of this inquiry, can you deal with what you knew at the time, and not what you have discovered since. We don't do hindsight."
A: "Thank you. I'll stick to my decision log."

Q: "So there was no possibility of error in the semen sample results?"

A: *"No, even his blood group was a one in 20,000 job. His DNA was millions to one, and as you can see in the policy file, I had the team go right back to his birth to establish there was no possibility of any twin. Hospital and local registrar records showed that he was a single birth and his mum died having him. She was unidentified, but even if he claimed he had an unknown older brother by the same parents, the DNA would have been different. Evidentially, he was a regular Oliver Twist."*

Q: *"What about other forensic evidence?"*

A: *"It was impossible to use a lot of it, because he had been in legitimate contact with us all and in and out of police vehicles. His traces were everywhere, and however hard we tried, the defense would be able to shoot us to bits. There were traces of cotton around Sarah's mouth and hands, probably from being chloroformed. Dastra had traces of the same cotton under his nails. Needless to say, any trace of chloroform was long gone."*

Q: *"Yes. (pause) What about Sarah's car."*

A: *"In the river Thames—totally washed clean by the current, about a mile and a half from where Dastra was arrested."*

Q: *"What about Sarah's forensic traces?"*

A: *"There were the hairs from the house; I'll just check the decision log. (Pause) Yes, the hairs were the only major piece to prove where she was prior to her death."*

Q: *"But might they have proved to be defense evidence if he had claimed he had consensual intercourse with her?"*

A: *"Yes, but forensic traces suggested sex took place in the backseat of his car. Anyhow, he couldn't take that line himself. He had amnesia."*

Q: *"I need to come back to that."*

A: *"Okay. The only other bits of forensics were of no great value. The mud on his knees was the same as from the rod, which at least tied him loosely to the murder site—but we had no site. In* theory, he could have got the mud from an entirely different location... for example, one of the sites he had mapped out for us himself. As I say, it was of little use. (pause) You want some more, of course. We tried a roadblock round where he was stopped, to see if any other witnesses could be found. It didn't produce anything useful at that stage."

Q: "Did it not concern you that despite a weeklong Police Search Advisor examination of Dastra's house and grounds, you didn't get another piece of evidence?"
A: "That's the way it was. I had more than enough to charge him."

Q: "How did you feel about the amnesia?"
A: "At the time I was open minded. Holt said it was possible that he had psychogenic amnesia—that the trauma of his alleged crimes had caused his mind to block them out."

Q: "But what was your view?"
A: "Originally, I thought he was faking it. But as time went on, he became more consistent and convincing. We know the truth now."

Q: "What about the profiling?"
A: "Unfortunately it was spot on. He fitted Holt's idea perfectly—a bit of a loner—inserting himself into the investigation—the impaled butterflies and the nude paintings—same ethnic group—sexually inexperienced. The fact that he was paying women to come and model for him only added weight—the body lying almost symbolically on the canvas...it was a brilliant image to give to the jury."

Q: "Ah, yes, the paintings. He had done a nude of Aybrams."
A: "Yes. I didn't initially realize that it was her—a patch over the eye might have given me a clue—but I hadn't met her at that stage. I thought it might be another dead Vlad victim."

Q: "I've got to ask some questions about the search of

Aybrams's flat."
    A: "Go on."

    Q: "Just explain for the tape why the flat was searched."
    A: "He was there, so he claimed, up until the murder. I thought that there was a possibility that if the flat was thoroughly searched and forensicated, then later we might get a link to a scene."

    Q: "A crime scene?"
    A: "We hadn't formally established a scene yet, but I had to believe that we would eventually. If traces from the flat had then turned up at the scene, or vice-versa, then I could have linked Dastra to it."

    Q: "You didn't go yourself?"
    A: "No, a PolSA Inspector dealt with it. Jim White collected all the forensic finds."

    Q: "So the PolSA was in command when Aybrams returned from college to find her flat being searched."
    A: "Yes, I understand that she was very upset. Searchers had been through her personal effects. Someone found some acutely personal things. She tried to make a complaint against the police, but DI Graham was called and calmed her down. She's good at that sort of thing—that's how she came to be a hostage negotiator."

    Q: "So you didn't deal with Aybrams's complaint, then?"
    A: "No, I didn't. Also, one of the squad took her statement giving Barney's alibi. In fact, I didn't meet her until the trial in September. She went back to America for the summer, so she wasn't likely to cross my path until then. She flew back for the trial, just as they moved Dastra up to Brixton prison. She tried to visit him at Wemstone, but she missed him."

    Q: "Had you met her at all?"
    A: "No, never, I'd only seen the painting. I must admit candidly that I was (pause) taken with it, but I didn't realize it was

her. Later, the others at the search were discussing her, but I didn't take it in. Superintendent Yardley bent my ear about how lovely she was, even with her eye patched, but I really wasn't listening. He described her, you know, like a model or a film star: lovely figure, red hair. Her court appearance was the first time any of us had seen her in the flesh without her pirate patch—except Dastra."
(Extract from MPS enquiry into Operation Klingsor.)

At the entrance to London's Central Criminal Court, Lucy queued up for the X-ray and metal detector then had her bag checked. Inside she took off her coat and put on a pair of low strength reading glasses. With her hair tied back severely in a ponytail, and wearing a conservative suit, the spectacles would, she hoped, help her to avoid becoming a distraction, and help to hide the odd appearance of her mended eye. Expert ophthalmic surgery in the USA during the summer had replaced the burnt and clouded surface of her left eye with a corneal graft, but its accompanying microscopic stitching gave the occasional appearance of a sixteen-pointed star around the periphery of her iris.

She checked the lists of trials on the wall and made her way up to the waiting area outside number four court. Members of Sarah Carothers's family were sitting there, waiting to go up into the public gallery after talking with detectives. Lucy looked about for anyone she recognized and, straining her eyes through the spectacles, was pleased to see DS Khan.

"Hi, there," she said, trying to sound bright and cheerful.

"Oh, hello. Are you on this morning?"

"Yes, I've got to confirm that Barney called me on his cell phone."

"Shhh. don't discuss it here with me. It may cause trouble. You are the opposition."

"Opposition?"

"Defense."

"Defense... okay, which one is Shackerstone?"

"Fat black one, behind you, with the younger guy in the black suit. He's Detective Superintendent Gordonstown."

Lucy turned. Shackerstone was already turning towards her. Their eyes met.

"Hi, I'm Lucy Aybrams."

Shackerstone stared at her, saying nothing. His own face gradually softened into a sad expression and then, quite unexpectedly, through his deep mahogany skin, he blushed. Gordonstown walked off without giving Lucy a second look.

"Yes. Hello. Sorry. DCI Shackerstone. You're Barney's girlfriend."

"Yes, I am."

"His painting of you doesn't do you justice—good as it is. Did you come down by train?"

"Yes, from Oxford."

"Look, you need to know this." He ushered her away from the group outside the courtroom. "Sarah Carothers's family will be in the public gallery. Chances are you might get a hard time. Just be warned."

"Are you trying to put me off?"

"No, no, not at all. I just don't want you to be…"

"Upset?"

"Yes, that's it."

"You've done that already, *Detective*". Lucy made the title sound like an epithet as her eyes peered into Shackerstone's as cold and hard as she could manage. Shackerstone turned away and left her standing alone. Lucy, with her eyes now getting used to the spectacles, scanned the group, many of whom were looking at her. She felt distinctly vulnerable. After a while, she sat down alone. She waited nervously all morning, but there was no call for her until after lunch.

"Lucy Aybrams!" echoed the voice of the court usher. He showed her in and took her to the witness box. Lucy looked for somewhere to sit down, but there was no chair in the witness box. She scanned the courtroom and spied Dastra in the dock, smartly dressed and with short hair. She exchanged smiles with him.

The usher handed Lucy a bible.

"Please read from the card."

"I swear by almighty God that the evidence I give to the court will be the truth, the whole truth and nothing but the truth." Lucy wanted to add *"So help me God"*, but resisted the urge.

A man in a gray wig stood up.

"Hello, Miss Aybrams."

"Hi."

"I'm Mr. Robinson, representing Mr. Dastra, and my learned colleague Mr. Lambworthy is prosecuting this case. Now, I want to take you back to June and to tell us about what happened on the nights of the eighteenth and nineteenth."

"Okay. Barney and I went to a party on the eighteenth and he stayed the night at my digs, then we spent most of Friday together."

"What time did you go back to your flat?"

"About midnight."

"What did you do?"

Lucy's face reddened. "We went to bed."

"To sleep?"

"Not at first. But we did eventually."

There was a slight rustle among the spectators in court.

"Until when?"

"Mid- morning."

"Did Mr. Dastra have an opportunity to leave during that time?"

"No. We were cuddled up together."

"You are sure?"

"Well, I woke up in the night and he wasn't there. I called out to him. He came back in from the bathroom, I think."

"You think?"

"He was naked—and the toilet tank was filling up—I could hear it."

"Sarah Carothers went missing that night. Could Mr. Dastra have left and returned?"

"I don't think so."

"Where was his car when you got out of it in the late evening?"

"By the corner."

"And when you came out in the morning?"

"In the same, no, it was on the other side of the road. But he had left the house before me. I went back to get something. I figured he had turned it round to go."

"You figured?"

"He had time to."

"Was the engine running?"

"He started it as I got in. But he could have cut it to save fuel—it's a big car, and gasoline is expensive here."

"But you never heard him move the car."

"No. But it had a pretty quiet motor."

"Where did you go in the morning?"

"Clothes shopping for him, then we went to lunch."

"And then?"

"Home again. My digs."

"And?"

"Bed again."

"I understand you had tickets to go to a concert with Mr. Dastra."

"Barney had the tickets."

"But you had arranged to go to a concert."

"Yes, Beethoven's Third Piano Concerto and his Seventh Symphony."

"What happened?"

"We didn't go."

"Why didn't you go?"

"At about five he suddenly found he had lost a police radio. He was upset, because he would be in a lot of trouble. He said he would be back, but he never came. He gave me a call later to let me know he had been delayed."

"About what time was that?"

"At about 6:15 p.m., I think."

"Very good, yes, the prosecution evidence shows the time on his mobile phone bill to be 6:13 p.m. What did he say to you?"

"He said that he would be cutting it a bit fine but that he expected to make it by 7:30 p.m."

"How did he sound?"

"He sounded okay."

"How's that?"

"Well, you know, he was still happy, pleased we were going to the concert. He sounded bothered by being in a hurry, but then he would be."

"Did he say where he was?"

"Somewhere near Goring."

"He actually said Goring?"

"Yes, sir."

"Did that give you an idea of how long he would be?"

"Not really. I don't have a car and I'm not too familiar with the area."

"Thank you, Miss Aybrams, my learned colleague is going to ask you some questions now."

Lambworthy rose to his feet. "Hello, Miss Aybrams, I have only a few questions. Did Mr. Dastra inform you during a telephone call that he would not be at the concert?"

"No, he was definitely coming and he had the tickets."

"Are you sure he didn't tell you that he would be unable to make it, due to developments in the case?"

"No, it is as I have said. He was doing his best to make it by 7:30 p.m."

"Do you love Mr. Dastra?"

"Yes, I do."

"How long have you known him?"

"Since the day the first three bodies were found."

"So you had only known him about three weeks or so at that time?"

"That's right."

"How did you meet him?"

"He came to the hospital when my eyes were burnt by the lime in the grave. Later he took a statement from me about finding the bodies. Then he took me home."

"You say in the opening of your original statement that you have been involved in a lot of protests, is that correct?"

"Yes, that is."

"Is Mr. Dastra one of your protests?"

"No, he's not."

"You say you love him. Were you in love on the night of the eighteenth of June?"

"Yes I was."

"After less than three weeks?"

"I know this may seem very hard for you to understand but I fell in love with him within hours of meeting him and he did with me."

"Almost love at first sight then."

"Yes, although I didn't have any sight when we first met."

"Of course. So you felt pretty sure he would turn up on the evening of the nineteenth?"

"It wasn't a case of turning up. We had been together all day. He had stepped out. If it was humanly possible, he would have come back."

"In your opinion. You feel you knew him that well after only three weeks."

"Yes, I do. He was open and honest with me from the moment we met, that was part of..."

"Part of what?"

"Part of the attraction, as much as anything else."

"Do you still love him?"

"Yes, sir, very much."

Lambworthy paused and turned a piece of paper over. He looked away towards the jury.

"Are you carrying his child?"

Lucy felt the blood draining from her face. She looked across at Barney, who was staring, open-mouthed. Lucy's eyes seemed to plead with him for a moment, as if he still had some ability to come to her rescue. She had no idea how anyone connected with the case could know about her pregnancy.

"Miss Aybrams?" came Lambworthy's voice.

"Sorry, yes. I'm carrying his child," mumbled Lucy, looking at the floor red-faced.

Lambworthy's tone became more aggressive. "Firstly I put it to you that he left you at your flat on Thursday night, and the next time you heard from him was the phone call on Friday."

"No. We slept together... that's when I think I became..."

"As you have said, you noticed him gone during the night, and heard him return from the lavatory. Is it not possible that he could have been gone some hours, and you awoke to the noise of the flushing toilet just as he returned?"

"I don't think so."

"You don't think so? Can you put a time on when he returned to bed."

"Only vaguely. It was getting light. It could have been four or five."

"Which would have given him quite an opportunity, unless you were both awake until then?"

"We were asleep."

"From when?"

"Soon after one, I guess."

"Giving him up to three hours."

"No. That wouldn't be right. We were cuddled up."

"So you said. Where did he park his car on the previous night?"

"On the corner."

"You have said the car wasn't in the same place when you went out later?"

"I did, but he had just moved it, I guess."

"Miss Aybrams. The court doesn't deal with guesswork. Are you sure you remember the car at all?"

"Of course."

"Or have you just mistaken the position of the car because you never saw it and you never did get into it, did you? Mr. Dastra was gone."

"No, he, we were together."

"And furthermore, you are covering for him to the extent that you even went out and bought clothes for him."

"No. That's wrong. He was with me all that time."

"Except after five?"

"That's right."

"So, if we believe you, Mr. Dastra was only out of touch with you from 5 p.m. until 6:13 p.m. Thereafter he was unaccounted for... and even you, his lover, cannot alibi him... until his arrest."

"Yes."

"I put it to you then that if what you say is true, then this phone call was to tell you that he wasn't coming, and that he was delayed."

Lucy paused before looking up and giving a confident answer.

"No, he said he was coming. I got ready. I waited for him."

"Can anyone corroborate this?"

"My flatmate. She was with me. She had just returned from

seeing a boyfriend."

"Thank you, Miss Aybrams."

Robinson rose to his feet. "I'm grateful to my learned friend. Just one more question. Miss Aybrams, has Mr. Dastra exhibited any unusual behavior towards you?"

"Like what?"

"Unusual in any way. Even say, unusual in a violent or sexual way?"

"Nothing like that."

"Any other strange behavior?"

"None at all."

"Apart from falling in love with you at first sight perhaps?"

"Apart from that."

"Thank you, Miss Aybrams. M'lud, can the court release Miss Aybrams?"

"Yes, and thank you, Miss Aybrams, for the candid way you have given your evidence. The court appreciates your situation."

"Bitch!" came a shout from the public gallery. "She's lying for him." Lucy looked up searching the faces above, unable to focus through the reading glasses.

"Silence in court!" boomed the judge.

Lucy had had enough. She dropped her gaze and fled the courtroom.

Outside, the first figure she saw through her tears was Reshard Khan, but as she moved towards the windows Shackerstone caught up with her and guided her briskly over to Khan.

"Get her out of here. Take her home. Look after her."

"What's wrong?"

"Get her out of here before someone attacks her. Here, take my car. The code is the same as the back door of Wemstone nick." He handed the keys to Khan. "Walk her over the road to Snow Hill nick. You know where my car is. The press pack will be outside the court for photos, try to keep them off her. Bloody vultures."

"Said an ex-vulture."

"I've lost my taste for carrion."

Khan turned to Lucy. "Come on. I'm taking you back to Oxford."

"But…"

"Quickly."

Sarah's husband was marching over to them, his face reddening. He seized Lucy by the arm as she turned to go, and spun her round to face him, his mouth inches from her eyes.

"How can you lie like that, you American bitch? What about Sarah? That bastard took her away." Small drops of his spittle struck Lucy's cheeks and sprayed the spectacles.

"I'm sorry. He didn't do it. That's all." Lucy felt more tears forcing themselves up into her eyes, but she didn't look away from him. He pulled his hand back as if to strike Lucy and in doing so caught the spectacles, flicking them across the room. Shackerstone moved in quickly behind him. "That won't help Sarah," he barked, gripping the man's wrist from behind. "Go!" he ordered, and Khan ran, pulling Lucy after him.

"You're on their bloody side. Coppers looking after fucking coppers."

"Don't be an arse."

Lucy retreated to the ladies' room to wipe the tears from her eyes. Khan waited outside. When she came out after about ten minutes, he took her down to the front entrance. Lucy put her coat on. Outside the press pack was waiting as Shackerstone had predicted, and Lucy could see them waiting on the other side of the smoked glass.

"This is when you need hijab," said Khan.

"Hijab?"

"You know, the headscarf worn by Muslim women. They wouldn't recognize you with me... they'd think you were my wife."

"I haven't got anything like that with me."

"Then we'd best just walk out calmly and cross the road to Snow Hill. Just walk quickly and if a knot of them get in the way just walk at them. Ready?"

"Ready."

Lucy and DS Khan hurried out through revolving security doors. At first, they thought they had escaped attention, but suddenly a voice said, "That's her!"

A group of photographers began running after them as they walked up the hill to Holborn Viaduct. They were overtaken and flashguns began firing in their faces. Khan turned to take a diagonal across the road, and they marched briskly out onto the junction at the top. They wove through traffic on Holborn Viaduct and made their way along the far side to the small road called Snow Hill. Most of the group followed them the full way. Khan got Lucy into the Police station, and left the group standing on the steps. Once he had settled her in the canteen with a coffee, he went off to get Shackerstone's car from a multi-story car park.

It took fifteen minutes for him to return, and when he did so there were only two photographers outside. He parked on the double yellow lines and ran in to get Lucy. The photographers were ready for her reappearance. Khan and Lucy rushed down the steps and into Shackerstone's white Citroen, before speeding out onto the main Holborn Viaduct and back towards the west.

Eighteen

Question (DI Graham): "Did you read the papers?"
Answer(Suspect): "Oh, yeah. Unbelievable. You couldn't
have made it up."

Q: "What?"
A: "A totally innocent girl vilified by the press like that—
more sensitive editors might have felt a bit guilty when Lucy later
became a victim."
(Extract from evidential tape transcript.)

Michaela woke Lucy the next morning at 7:00. Michaela
never usually woke her, and Lucy's alarm was set for 7:10.

"Lucy?"

"What time is it?" Lucy opened her eyes. The morning sky
was overcast, and the dark curtains made it seem that it was still the
middle of the night. Lucy sat up.

"It's seven. Sorry, I had to pop down to't shop for some
milk. It's the newspapers. They've written about you and Barney."
She sat down on the side of the bed. "I'm so sorry." She produced
two tabloid national newspapers from under her arm, and put them
down deliberately in front of Lucy. Different pictures of her leaving
court were on both front covers. The first paper was almost entirely
taken up with the words "Beauty and the Beast" against a black
background. The second, which carried the larger of the two pictures
of Lucy, carried the headline, "Bride of Dracula?" Inside both
papers, there was extensive coverage of the trial and word-by-word

accounts of her exchanges with the lawyers.

"I'll make coffee."

"Thanks."

Lucy read on as Michaela went off to the kitchen to the coffee. Every so often Lucy would shout out a piece from the paper. "Listen to this from the comment page: 'Accused in the Vlad case, David Dastra has seduced a beautiful American Oxford undergraduate into providing his alibi. Is she prepared to join Myra Hindley and Rose West as one of the most hated women in Britain?'" There was silence from the kitchen. "How about this: 'American beauty Lucy Abraham—' they even spelled my name wrong— 'admitted to having fallen in love with sinister David Dastra after finding three of his victims while digging a tunnel on the Wemstone bypass protest. Abraham, twenty, from San Francisco, fell under his spell at their first meeting, and had only known him three weeks when she conceived his lovechild after steamy summer nights at her flat in Oxford. She told the court Dastra was making love to her at the time Sarah Carothers went missing. She went on to claim he was on his way to meet her on the night of the murder. Sarah's husband, who'd been married only three months, confronted Abraham outside the courtroom and police prevented a fight. He was restrained by detectives while she ran from the Old Bailey in tears.'"

"That was true, wasn't it?" shouted Michaela.

"Well, not quite. I'm not in tears in any of the photographs."

Lucy found that there were several pictures of her in each paper, and the coverage in one went for several pages with little printed text.

"Do you think you will go back for the rest of the trial?" asked Michaela, returning with two coffee cups and sitting on the bed.

"I can't. It would be too awful. Reshard Khan said I might even be traced to here. I'm terrified of Sarah's husband."

"You've got to give Barney up, whatever the outcome of this. It'll ruin your life."

Lucy looked down, understanding the logic of Michaela's thinking. "I'm carrying his baby. He's got nobody. And nobody believes him except me."

"That's not totally true."

"No?"

"Well, I know you're not daft, and you are usually quick to spot what men are after. I suppose I'm saying that if you trust him, and *you* think he's innocent, then I should back you up."

Lucy grasped Michaela's free hand. "Thanks, you don't know what that means to me… and to Barney."

Michaela smiled. "For you, he's still the safest boyfriend in the world while he's locked away."

Lucy didn't reply. She knew Michaela had read her on the basis of previous behavior, and although Lucy wasn't aware herself that she saw Dastra in this way, Michaela's views struck her as logical, reasonable and profoundly uncomfortable.

~ * ~

Dastra's trial ran until the following Wednesday. Like every other day of the trial he was brought from Brixton prison by security van. The journey in the prison van was one of confinement in a tiny cell, one of ten in the van. Neither the other prisoners, nor the guards, had the remotest regard for him, and he made no attempt at striking up a relationship with anyone. Indeed, it was common knowledge at Brixton that there was a reward on offer to any prisoner who could "mark" him on the face with a permanent scar.

At the Old Bailey, he was placed in the court cells, and like all defendants, on remand or not, accompanied in the dock by a guard. When he was brought up from the cells for final submissions, the gallery was packed with Sarah's family, the national press and police officers from the squad. DCI Shackerstone was seated in the body of the court behind Lambworthy. All stood as the judge entered. Then the jury filed in.

Lambworthy began, "Ladies and gentlemen of the jury. Over the last few days, we have all heard a weight of evidence about the matter before us. What I propose to put before you now is a simple and straightforward argument as to the guilt of the accused. I think you need little guidance from me in this matter, now you have seen all the evidence, however disturbing much of it may have been. The defendant, David Dastra, is not on trial for all of the so-called Vlad killings, neither would it be fair under the legal system of this country for him to be so. There is not a shred of evidence pointing to him in any of these other murders. Think what you may about those, and the sensational coverage that they have received in the press, they are not before us today. These cases should in no way color your judgment when deciding on the matter in hand... the rape and murder of a young and attractive woman at the very beginning of a successful career as a lawyer."

He paused for effect, holding his robe either side of his chest. "Who knows, Sarah may well have been destined for higher things. Perhaps in this very court, prosecuting the murderers of tomorrow. Sarah Louise Carothers was twenty-four years of age, and with a supportive family, here today in this courtroom at the Old Bailey. Her future was extinguished in a terrifying and agonizing way at a location that has yet to be found. I like to hope that, should the defendant be found guilty, that he will reconsider his position and indicate to his former colleagues where that crime scene is, in order that Mrs. Carothers's family may have some closure." Lambworthy cast his eye around the court, catching the eye of DCI Shackerstone. "The evidence, as we have heard from expert witnesses, is overwhelming. The defendant was stopped, by his police colleagues, driving erratically. In the boot of his car was the impaled, lifeless and broken body of Mrs. Carothers. Clinging to her body, both internally and externally, the irrefutable evidence of this man's semen. Clinging to his clothing, that same fluid.

"Where he had killed Sarah, and where he was going, we may never know. His lover, Miss Aybrams asserts that she was with him when Sarah went missing, and throughout the day until 5:00 p.m. But then who kidnapped Sarah that night if it was not Mr. Dastra—whose semen was found inside her? He needed to be free to take her and conceal her and to dispose of her car in the Thames. In which case Miss Aybrams's evidence is at best mistaken, or at worst a complete fabrication. A mistake may indeed be possible in part— but I believe her admitted infatuation with him means her evidence needs to be treated with caution. What is clear is that even if we believe all of her evidence it is not impossible for him to have slipped out of her flat, kidnapped Sarah and hid her somewhere, wherever that may be. There is also the issue of the hairs from Sarah Carothers that were found at Mr. Dastra's house. The defense have vehemently challenged this damning piece of evidence, as well they might. Without a clear confession from the accused, or an honest account of his actions, we may never know how Sarah's hair got there. What we do know is that it was indeed her hair, and provides a link between the house and the victim. In short, Sarah's hairs strongly suggest his house. We do have an independent eyewitness who has clearly identified him from an identity parade as standing by his car a number of miles away from where he was arrested."

Lambworthy stopped to take a drink of water from a glass, and moved on to a second piece of paper.

"He, as he has stated, and as the medical evidence supports, received a head injury, apparently inflicted by a heavy piece of wood. This piece of evidence supports neither the prosecution arguments, nor those of the defense. His defense rests on the basis of his having no recollection of events due to that blow. A man who remembers little of his crimes is still guilty of them.

"I put it to you, ladies and gentlemen of the jury, that he could have come by that injury by any one of a number of means. I would sleep better at night if I could believe that Sarah herself was the architect of that blow, and in doing so sealed his fate. Yes, the possibility exists that in her struggle for life she struck out at her killer. Later, he managed to get her body into his car before becoming sick and disorientated from blood loss associated with the blow. That same blow brought him to his downfall. In her own small way, Sarah herself reached out beyond her squalid and agonizing death and hamstrung her attacker, for more honest and diligent police officers to capture. Ladies and gentlemen of the jury. Sarah and her family have lost her future. All that the evidence before you demands is a guilty verdict."

Lambworthy settled down in his seat lightly, and Robinson got to his feet. "The accused, my client, Detective Constable David Dastra, has led an entirely blameless life. He is an accomplished and professional police officer, highly thought of by his colleagues and with no convictions for any crimes. He is *not* on trial for *all* the so-called Vlad killings and I thank my learned colleague for making that point.

"Nevertheless, in a way he is by association. Yet not a shred of evidence can be found to associate him with any of those killings. My learned friend has been permitted to put a conjectural story to the court, relating to the injury to Mr. Dastra. I crave your indulgence to be equally imaginative, and perhaps far closer to the truth.

"I have spent many hours with Mr. Dastra, and the medical evidence tells me that he is being truthful when he says he recalls nothing after going to the woods at a distance from where he was found, to search for his police radio. I also want you to concentrate on the transparent honesty with which Miss Aybrams gave her evidence. She has been most candid about their relationship, even to her acute embarrassment. There can be little doubt that Mr. Dastra spent the night with her. Her condition certainly testifies to the fact that she had a sexual relationship with him.

"I put it to you that it is entirely possible and from all the circumstances far more likely, that Mr. Dastra, a man who is undoubtedly attractive to beautiful women, met Mrs. Carothers at some time after a quarter past six. She had already been reported missing, and in some circumstances or other, Mr. Dastra became her white knight rescuing a damsel in distress. Perhaps she had gone missing in entirely innocent circumstances as thousands of young women do every week, usually to return home the following day. Whatever the circumstances, my client, a dedicated and professional police officer, went to her aid and took her home to sort out her problem, whatever it was. He and she were mutually attracted, and he, a man whose sexual appetite has already been alluded to, made love to her."

"Never!" came a male voice from the gallery.

"I will have silence here, or I will have the gallery cleared," said the judge, peering over his glasses.

Robinson continued. "The prosecution have frankly admitted that Sarah's body shows not a single mark consistent with a violent rape, neither have the police been able to find a trace of any drug used to stupefy her. The traces of cotton around her mouth may be entirely innocent and perhaps left there by Sarah when removing makeup.

"The forensic evidence only supports a totally consensual act of intercourse. Unluckily for both my client and the victim, an unknown third person, with their own motives, struck him on the back of the head later that evening, as he was assisting her further—perhaps taking her to her car—or driving her back to Reading. Certainly, he must have felt that her predicament justified standing up Miss Aybrams. This same third person then went on to carry out his wicked purpose on her, and to cover his tracks, put both parties back in Mr. Dastra's car.

"And then there is the matter of Mrs. Carothers's car. Yes, it was found in water, like in the other Vlad killings. Mr. Dastra, it has already been established, was incapable of driving his own car properly. How then could he manage to dump the other car if what the prosecution proposes is true? No, there had to be a third and guilty person. I have put to you a far more plausible and innocent set of circumstances that account for Mr. Dastra's situation that night, and consistent with all of the evidence before you.

"The law demands that the prosecution proves Detective Constable Dastra's guilt beyond all reasonable doubt. That reasonable doubt is plain to see. We do not contest that the semen is his—what we do contest is that it was placed there without consent. It is useful to note also, that the prosecution has no physical evidence to prove that my client impaled and murdered Sarah Carothers at any time. All that the best efforts of the detectives on this case could produce, after weeks of work, was little better than the evidence before the two uniformed officers who stopped Detective Constable Dastra that night.

"I put it to you that you should cast aside emotion in this case along with the horrors of the Vlad killings, and concentrate on facts. The only facts are that Sarah Carothers is dead from a brutal murder. Mr. Dastra's semen was found in and on her body. Her hair was found, by the detective leading the case, at his house. After a week of searching, trained police forensic teams found nothing else at the house that has been adduced here as evidence. It is agreed that she could not have been killed in Mr. Dastra's home. Sarah's body was found in the back of the defendant's car. Her car was found in the Thames and Mr. Dastra received a severe blow to his head.

"There is no more. I have painted a reasonable and rational explanation for these circumstances. The prosecution case therefore has not been proven beyond reasonable doubt. I ask you to bring back to the court the only fair and true verdict of not guilty."

He sat down. The judge turned to make a short speech to the jury.

"Before you go away to consider your verdict, I must caution you all that you should exclude totally from your minds the press coverage directed at the defence witness Miss Lucy Aybrams. When considering your verdict it is David Dastra who under scrutiny here, and not the relationship between him and Miss Aybrams.

"I must now request you to retire and consider your verdict."

The jury was shown out by the usher and the court rose.

~ * ~

Down in the court cells Dastra paced up and down waiting for the verdict. Robinson arrived at the cell door and the court jailer let him in. "I've come to tell you I think we have a small chance."

"A *small* chance?"

"Well, it wasn't an easy trial. Whatever we say, the background to the case will bear heavily against us."

There was a call from the corridor.

"The jury is coming back already. I expect it will be for some directions."

Robinson was let out, and Dastra was escorted to the dock. The judge and other counsel came back in. The gallery filled as the jury filed in.

The clerk went up to the jury foreman. Robinson nodded for Dastra to stand.

"On the matter of the rape of Sarah Louise Carothers, have you reached a verdict?"

"Yes."

"Is it the verdict of you all?"

"It is."

"On the matter of the murder of Sarah Louise Carothers, have you reached a verdict?"

"Yes."

"Is it the verdict of you all?"

Dastra's heart was nearly in his mouth. His entire future hung on a decision he had not yet heard, but that those twelve strangers now looking at him were already privy to.

"Do you find the defendant David Dastra guilty or not guilty of the rape of Sarah Louise Carothers?"

"Guilty."

"Shit!" said Dastra under his breath. Still, there was hope on the murder charge.

"Do you find the defendant David Dastra guilty or not guilty of the murder of Sarah Louise Carothers?"

"Guilty"

The gallery erupted into cheers. Gordonstown was smiling with an air of personal satisfaction. Shackerstone was shaking the hands of various detectives and Sarah's family in a strangely disinterested manner.

"Silence in court, please," boomed the clerk.

"Thank you," the judge continued, then waited for silence.

"Before I pass sentence, I thank the jury for bringing in an honest verdict on as serious and harrowing a case as I have ever had to judge. The forensic photographs alone would shock the most hardened member of the criminal justice system.

"Whether or not this man is the killer known as Vlad, we may never know. Nevertheless, you all have the satisfaction of playing your part in putting a dangerous and twisted monster behind bars for many years. I would ask the jury to stay for a little longer to hear sentence, after I have listened to the defendant. Before I pass sentence, do you have anything to tell the court?"

"I didn't do this, M'lud…"

The judge interrupted. "David Dastra, you have been found guilty of two terrible crimes, both of which are punishable by life imprisonment. So irrefutable is your guilt that there is no possibility of a miscarriage of justice. You will go to prison for life, and I will write to the Home Secretary to recommend that you serve at least thirty years before release on license is considered."

The gallery erupted into cheers again and Dastra sat down as his world crashed in on him. He now had a life of rule forty-three isolation before him, to prevent attacks by other prisoners. Being a police officer in prison was one thing. Being numbered among the "beasts" multiplied the threat. From now on, he would be associated with The Yorkshire Ripper, The Black Panther and the Moors murderer Ian Brady. His release would be opposed with all the venom that the unforgiving public regularly spat out when Moors murderess Myra Hindley was so much as suggested for parole.

Reflecting further on his predicament, he realized that his only friend and only hope was Miss Lucy Aybrams.

Nineteen

"David Dastra exhibits all the symptoms of psychogenic amnesia. He could be faking them, but if so his subterfuge is sustained and unremitting. If he genuinely has the condition, then he has, in my view, witnessed something of his own handiwork that even he has found extremely traumatic."

Extract from report by prison psychologist, HMP Wemstone. (MPS enquiry into Operation Klingsor.)

As a convicted prisoner in Wemstone Prison, David Dastra received his first visit from Lucy Aybrams at the end of September. Visits to him had to be made alone and in a room with a prison guard present. This was clearly a drain on the resources of a prison that was already understaffed, especially at weekends.

Dastra sat at a table in the middle of a visitor's room, eager for the door to open and for Lucy to be shown in. A warder sat in the corner, obviously bored, and got up very slowly when there was a knock on the door. He showed Lucy in and she did as she was directed and sat down opposite Dastra. The atmosphere was far from relaxed, and with a guard present, far from private.

Dastra spoke first, in a half whisper. "Hi."

"Hi."

"It's so good to see you."

"It's good to see you too."

"Oh, God. I've missed you."

"And I've missed you too."

"I've so wanted to see, just to see, your face again."

Lucy smiled but said nothing.

"You know, you're the only hope I have. There's nobody else out there."

"I know, I know." She slid her hand across the table so that their fingers touched.

"You should have told me about the baby. I'm so sorry."

"I didn't want you to worry about me. You've got enough on your plate in here."

"But this is *us*. Flesh and blood, our flesh and blood—you *are* going to have it?"

"Of course, whatever happens."

"How did anyone find out?"

"When they searched my flat they must have found the test kit. I did it that same morning before I went out. I figured that they were just fishing in court, trying to put me off my stride. They nearly succeeded."

"When, uh, did we…"

"The night before you were arrested, I think."

"Sorry. We cut that fine. I bet you wish I'd been nicked sooner."

"Not a bit. You must believe that. Please."

"Nobody, nobody at all, apart from you, believes that I'm telling the truth. You do still believe me don't you?"

"You know I do, I said so in my letter."

"I know, but I needed to hear you say it. I'm so alone in here. You trust nothing and distrust everybody. I need to see you in the flesh to know you are still on my side."

"I am, absolutely. I just know you didn't do it. I know the evidence is overwhelming, but in my heart, I know you didn't do it. I know you couldn't."

She looked hard into his eyes to show him that she meant it. His eyes were worn and tired. He had only been in prison a few months and it was clearly wearing him down by degrees.

"You've grown your hair."

Lucy shook her head slightly at the sudden change of subject. "Oh, yes. That's protest number one… I'm not cutting it until you are released. No, until you have been totally exonerated."

"It suits you. I don't think it's much of a protest."

"It will be when it's down to my heels."

"I was hoping to be out of here by then. The remand wing was a holiday camp by comparison."

"Why?"

"It isn't safe here. There are no friends, just enemies." His face twitched down the left side. "Sooner or later I am going to get seriously hurt."

"But, but…isn't it their job to look after you?" Lucy shot a glance at the warder in the corner.

"It is, in theory, but there is a strange culture here. It's not like a police station. It's all bad."

"Even the staff?"

"Not everyone. In fact, somebody here is trying to sort out some sort of counseling for me to deal with my amnesia. But the atmosphere must get to them, locked up in here with the prisoners all day. I'm coming to understand that in many ways they are prisoners with us."

"How do they treat you?"

"The screws? Some like to dehumanize you."

"How?"

"From the moment you arrive they start grinding you down. The day you come in on remand they take everything, strip you naked and search you. They search you everywhere. When you get convicted they give you this uniform."

"It's not very nice. I think it might smell a bit."

"That's putting it politely."

"What then?"

"They shut you in a cell with a worn out bed and half a foam pillow. I'm supposed to be on my own, but I'm in with a terrorist!"

"Why?"

"They said we had a lot in common."

"Like what?"

"He's protesting his innocence. He should have been released in the peace process, but he has refused. He says he was fitted up."

"Fitted up?"

"Framed. Refusing release is the only protest he can make."

"What's his name?"

"Peter Lynch."

"Do you believe him?"

"I do now. He's the only ally I'm likely to get in here. I'm still working on him."

"What about me?"

"You?"

"Are you still working on me?"

"Oh, Lucy, if only... if only I were out. I would be working on you night and day."

"Like the press."

"I'm sorry about that. Have there been many more story offers."

"Two... ten thousand pounds each."

"And you said no?"

"I said yes if I could tell your side of the story and get it into print. They weren't interested."

"Typical."

"They'd like me to model though—before I get too fat. I've had several agencies after me. I could earn a lot in that field if I wanted that life, but then I always knew that."

"Are they at your flat?"

"Nearly every day. Things are getting strained with Michaela."

"Take my house."

"Your house?"

"As a bolt hole. It's empty and neglected now, anyway. I'll get the family solicitor to give you the keys."

"Oh, okay."

"Use it when you need to, both of you."

"But it's a bit of a long way to cycle..."

"You'll need a car—you shouldn't be using a bike now, anyway. I'll get some money released to you—five thousand should do. I've still got a bit put by for a rainy day, and they don't get much rainier than this. Go and buy a little hatchback with an automatic gearbox."

"Yes, thanks. I'd find a manual difficult."

"What about driving on the left?"

"I manage a bike."

"Of course. Anyhow, a car will help you get here without using the train."

"That would be great."

"Lucy, it's nothing. You're making all the running here. It's the least I can do… for the only," he looked down and swallowed hard, "the only friend I have in the world."

"Friend?"

Dastra looked straight back up into her eyes. "A lot more than that, a lot more…"

Lucy smiled appreciatively.

"This is so unfair, when you think of what we had. For a few days, it seemed too good to be true, and now I'm stuck in…"

"I know, but as my dad always said at the worst times: "Things can only get better."

"I don't see how they can get much worse."

Lucy looked up. "Is there anything I can get on with at the house?"

"Thanks, yeah. Get the solicitors to upgrade the alarm. It needs to be modernized, with panic buttons and infrared stuff. It's all wires and magnetic switches at the moment. I think that Shackerstone's mob will have trashed the place, so it might need tidying up. Use what you need, the electricity and gas are all being paid for on direct debit. But the housekeeper and gardener…I guess they won't have been since I was nicked. Get them visiting again."

"We won't stay there all the time."

"I know. Weekends would be enough, just keep it in use. I want something to go back to if I get out."

"Not 'if'. 'When' you get out… Will it…"

"Will it what?"

"Will it be the same?"

"Between us?"

"Yes."

"Better, I hope. I mean, this is some loyalty test. Most women would have run off long ago."

"Yes, but most aren't pregnant."

"No. Sorry."

A small tear appeared in Lucy's starry left eye. "I'm sorry, it's been difficult. I didn't know whether you would want to end it between us before we get hurt even more. I could get the baby adopted in the USA."

"Lucy, I've got to be open and direct here. It would finish me if you left me now. And as for the baby... well, please, can we see closer to the time?"

"At what point should we..."

"Don't think about that yet. Let's decide after my appeal. My brief is very hopeful about some aspects of the case."

"Brief?"

"Attorney."

"I see. So?"

"Firstly, the press coverage when you came up. He says it makes for an unfair trial. The risk is that it will just turn into a retrial on the same facts."

"In the U.S. that sort of publicity would be normal. I don't know that you will get far with that."

"No, maybe not. I have doubts."

"Do you think Shackerstone planted the hairs?"

"Unless I took her up to the house, which is as near impossible as I can imagine, they must have been taken there, accidentally or otherwise."

"And the semen?"

"That's a hard one."

"Yes. I couldn't get my head round it, but I've had an idea."

"Yes?"

"I reckon they used a syringe on you to extract some from you."

"Okay. It makes sense. I had a big pain in one of my bollocks when I was caught."

"Bollocks?"

"Testicles."

"Yes, but I took this up with DS Khan. He said it isn't that simple and he's right. I spoke to a medical student. It doesn't come ready mixed. The fluid comes from your prostate gland and the sperm come from your... bollocks." She said the word with a poor attempt at a London accent. It came out sounding Australian.

Dastra frowned. "So that doesn't help much."

"Well, you might not think so, but I've given this a lot of

thought. Your forensic team is only looking for DNA, not the quality of your fluid. It is possible that the killer took some sperm from you, and mixed it with a strong sugar solution. The laboratory tests aren't looking for the sugar. All the killer needed to frame you was to hit the right spot."

"That would explain the swelling I had. He would need to know what he was doing though."

"He might know a lot: wasn't Jack the Ripper an expert at anatomy?"

"It's one of the theories. He was never caught."

"No, he wasn't. Do you think Vlad will be?"

"I hope so. I hope he carries on—not for the victims, but for me. He's my only other hope."

"What a horrible reality for you to live with," Lucy replied, glumly.

"Time's up," said the warder.

Dastra looked hard at Lucy. "I'll write to the solicitors, they will get in touch with you. You should have access to the house within a few days."

"Don't lose heart. I'll be back in two weeks."

"I'll look forward to it. I've nothing else."

"I know. I'll be here. I love you."

"I love you."

He swallowed hard as Lucy got up to leave. She turned slowly at the door and smiled. As she turned away the door banged shut behind her.

"Dastra, back to your cell."

"Sure."

He got up and walked out as the warder swung the door open. The warder laughed, walking behind him. "They were right."

"Who?"

"The papers. She's the best-looking visitor we've ever had. Bet you miss getting your cock inside her."

"As you've just been listening, that wouldn't be a lawful bet… insider trading I think they call it."

"It must make it hard for a lifer like you, missing that, imagining other blokes having her, eh? I bet she's already putting herself about with some reporter. She'll only be after a story, you know that."

Dastra sensed a wave of anger pass over him. He clenched his fists and gritted his teeth to force it back down with the bile. A physical reply would be worse than futile.

"Is she a good shag? I bet you've had some fun putting a baby up there, eh? That's one impaling I'd like to do myself!"

Dastra turned and gave the warder a knowing wink. "That will keep the bastard guessing," he said under his breath.

"I wonder," continued the warder, "what she sees in a half-bake like you, eh?"

"So do I."

They turned up some stairs to another door, and walked out along a corridor. Their journey took them through a normal wing where all the prisoners were locked in their cells due to lack of staff. One cell was open while some vomit was being cleaned out. Dastra didn't see the prisoners inside as he walked past, but somebody had seen him: "Vlad!" echoed a voice. "Vlad!" it taunted.

"Kill Vlad!" echoed another voice from behind a cell door.

"Kill Vlad!" went another, duller sounding and more distant.

"Kill Vlad! Kill Vlad! Kill Vlad!" echoed rhythmically. The boredom of the lockdown suddenly found a release for its frustration as hundreds of voices joined in the chanting. Thumping feet and banging plastic mugs joined in as Dastra walked on. In spells of duty as a station jailer, he had endured this sort of taunting and banging regularly, but the difference was that at the end of the shift one went home. It was quieter in the isolation wing, but the chant could still be heard as Dastra was shown back to his cell. The door clanged shut behind him as he sat down on the lower bunk. Lynch was in the top bunk, reading a magazine. He didn't move, but immediately started talking. He had the remains of an Ulster accent, softened by twenty years of living in England.

"Ah, the Impaler returns amid a chorus of his appreciative fans. She came then, your American beauty."

"She did."

"Will she come again, or has she dumped you?"

"She'll be back... I think."

"For a while..."

"What?"

"They all visit for a while, and then they drift away, even your own family. They lose interest. Don't be hurt. My advice is to get ready for it."

"I suppose you're right."

The chanting died away in the background.

"It's part of the punishment: loss of all your relationships. The only lasting one is your cellmate... and God almighty. It's a piss-take the three of us being stuck here."

Twenty

Question (Superintendent Hinx): "So you dealt with the life imprisonment file for the prison service?"

Answer (DCI Shackerstone): "You know the rules. It has to be in within twenty-eight days—I did it while we wound down Operation Klingsor. The policy decision was that we would just keep the HOLMES system ticking over for the forensic results, and then put the three original killings to Dastra later."

Q: "So no doubts?"

A: "None. I think the thing that dispelled any we may have had was the way Dastra helped that I.R.A. bloke in prison with his appeal."

Q: "But wasn't he uh, fitted up? Allegedly."

A: "I understand it was a technical thing and Dastra sorted it out for him while they were sharing a cell together in the isolation wing."

(MPS enquiry into Operation Klingsor.)

The following Saturday, Lucy drove Michaela cautiously up to Prospect of Peshawar in her newly acquired used car, a bright-red Rover Metro. Lucy found roundabouts difficult, but cycling had given her road sense. Armed with keys, alarm instructions and a "dos and don'ts list" from Dastra's solicitor, they opened the iron gates and drove in, locking the gates behind them before traveling on up the gravel driveway. Once safely inside the house, Lucy discovered that a lot of cleaning had already been done. The solicitors had said they had been on to Mrs. Herbert, the housekeeper, and she had clearly put in some of the days she had been paid for since June. The garden had also been noticeably swept and tidied.

Lucy could feel that the house was damp and cold after standing empty for weeks. She found that the power was on and after some trial and error, got the gas-heating going. They both wandered through the house looking at things, opening cupboards and scanning book titles.

"Hey, have a look at this book, Lucy," called Michaela from the library. Lucy made her way from the conservatory. "Look; *"Dracula—the story of Vlad the Impaler"*. I'm sorry, but it makes you wonder…"

"Michaela, he's also got hundreds of other books: look, *"The Yorkshire Ripper"* and *"The Sinking of the Titanic"*. We're not going to blame him for those too, are we?"

"Oh, no. I weren't saying that. It were… just that it were a coincidence."

"In the piano room you'll find beautiful impaled butterflies. He bought them because he liked the colors. I'm sure if you look into anyone's life closely enough, you'll find something that you think confirms your suspicions."

"Maybe it's just being here. The atmosphere… you've got to agree it's a bit creepy."

"And apart from the occasional clunks from the heating, unnaturally quiet."

Michaela looked slightly alarmed. "Like there's some sort of presence here?"

"Not like that. Something is missing that was here before."

"Barney for a start."

"Something else. The clocks have all wound down and stopped ticking. That's the next thing we'll do. We'll wind some life back into all the clocks, then I think we should water some of the surviving plants in the conservatory."

After winding and watering, Lucy eventually found herself drawn to the upstairs, curious to see the four-poster bed again. Michaela felt all the time that they were about to find another body and hurried up after her.

Lucy found the master bedroom and the bed. The room was stuffy and she opened the windows. The bed linen had been freshly laundered and Lucy sat down on it, sinking into the old feather mattress.

"When he gets out I'm going to live up here and play Lady of the Manor."

"That'll be fun."

"I'm going to sleep in this room."

"Tonight too?"

"Why not?"

"I'm sorry, but this place still gives me the creeps. If you are in here, do you think I could share the bed with you?"

"Oh, yes. I don't think I'd want to be alone, at least not until they fit the new alarm with the panic buttons and so on." Lucy lay back on the bed. "Lady of the Manor at last, but no Lord of the Manor."

"Yes. It's so sad, Barney not being here. I wonder what he is doing now?"

"Probably sitting on his bed, unable to leave it."

Lucy and Michaela spent the night huddled together in Dastra's grand bed, listening to creaking noises and hooting owls. They talked until about two o'clock, discussing whether either could find the courage to live here alone.

Lucy awoke early and, leaving Michaela sleeping, donned a dressing gown wandered downstairs. The piano room was warm in the oblique morning sunlight, and Lucy sat at the piano, playing.

"Aren't you cold in only that thin nightdress and gown?" Michaela's voice startled her.

"No, it's quite warm over here with your back to the sun."

"I'll make some tea."

Lucy played some Chopin, before moving on to her beloved Beethoven. Michaela came back with her tea and a coffee for Lucy. "It all seems such a waste, all of this and Barney locked away for his whole life."

Lucy stopped playing. "He'll get out. Mark my words."

"Ah. I've forgotten the sugar."

Michaela trotted back to the kitchen, but returned agitated, without the sugar. "Lucy, it's the prison. There's been a riot; it was on the old radio in the kitchen. They've murdered at least one person on the isolation wing, and there's chaos."

"Barney!"

~ * ~

Lucy and Michaela drove to Wemstone prison, arriving at a police cordon just before ten. The outer perimeter seemed to be well controlled by police and prison staff. Within the walls there was smoke rising and men sitting on the high roofs of the blocks.

Prison and police officers, called in from weekend leave, formed the teams necessary to retake the prison. This was taking time, and every available police officer who could be stripped from patrols was being redeployed to the long perimeter wall. It still wasn't enough, and finding suitably trained public order officers to assist in the reestablishment of order in the prison was proving to be a slow business. Yardley wasn't on call for the weekend, and a superintendent from a neighboring division had been called in from home. She was predicting that it might be midnight before they could assemble sufficient staff and equipment.

On the outside, there was nothing Lucy and Michaela could do except to watch police units arrive. At dusk, they returned fretfully to the house and waited for news on the radio.

Lucy and Michaela had gone to bed and were trying to sleep when the first wave of officers stormed the prison to re-establish control.

Twenty One

"We were working in the prison allotment doing some winter digging when the riot started. We heard shouting and saw some flames above E-wing. Barney and I knew we would be dead if we were caught, so we hid in the steel shed. Barney managed to lock us in, using a piece of wire. A mob tried to force their way in to get tools, but they failed. Later that night we decided the safest thing was to try to get out over the wall and be picked up by the police. We tried two places, forcing the wire up with two spades from the shed. We overheard that some lads had climbed over farther round, so we went round there, blacking our faces with mud so that we looked prepared, and to avoid recognition. I was separated from Barney for maybe three hours, but I found him later coming back in. He had given up when he got badly gashed on some wire. He came back covered in blood and so I helped him wash it off. That's when he got recognized. I was washing him down by the garden tap just as a mob turned up. His face was clean and a white prisoner of about forty, with ginger hair, pointed him out. There was nothing I could do. There were maybe ten or twelve in the group, and they had armed themselves with bits of bed frame sharpened to points. I didn't recognize any of them. They weren't from my block. They just fell on him. I tried to stop them and got two wounds in my chest and another to my right palm. He was spilling blood out like a garden hose. He had injuries to his chest, belly, legs and face. It was lucky that the police raided the prison when they did. The mob scattered and some police got to us. It was the first time in my life I was glad to see Peelers."

(Statement taken from Peter Lynch. Wemstone Prison. October 1998.)

On Monday, Shackerstone's phone rang soon after he arrived in his office off the main CID office. The incident room had been closed since the week after the trial.

"DCI Shackerstone."

"Front counter here, sir. I've got a very lovely lass called Lucy Aybrams to see you. She says she hasn't got an appointment, but she's a very upset young lady."

"Okay. Stick her in an interview room. I'll be down."

~ * ~

Shackerstone walked casually through the door. Lucy was drying her eyes. Seeing her upset and vulnerable like this brought out a fatherly instinct that made him want to put his arm around her. He resisted the temptation and sat down opposite her with a receptive smile.

"Hello, what can I do for you?"

"Hi, I need your help. Barney is in Wemstone hospital. He's been stabbed in the prison riot."

"Oh, I'm sorry to hear that. Well, it will all have to be investigated when order is restored. Don't worry. We'll do our best to find out who did it."

"It's bad," said Lucy, banging the table with the flat of her hand. "He's going to die. A whole heap of them are in the hospital. One is dead already."

"That's sad. What can I say? I'm sorry. But that really isn't something I can help with."

"You could. He could live. So could the other one in the Intensive Therapy Unit. They haven't got enough blood supplies."

"Well, if it's a matter of sending a car to London for some more, I'm sure we..."

"No," Lucy shook her head and fixed her eyes on Shackerstone's. "They need loads of A and AB positive. They're both losing pints all the time from internal bleeding. There isn't enough, there's a countrywide shortage. The doctor said the only way was to get a large group of people down there for a mass transfusion."

"I can't see how I can help."

"Just listen. Barney is the most hated man in the country, so people aren't exactly falling over themselves to keep him alive. But I know he is innocent and I don't want yet another injustice piled on him."

"He's as guilty as hell," replied Shackerstone coldly.

"He can't be. You just don't know him like I do."

"You knew him barely three weeks!" Shackerstone prodded the table hard with his fat index finger. "I've got his DNA inside a murder victim."

"And I've got it growing inside me."

"Listen, love. I can imagine how you must feel, but I'm an honest professional and dedicated copper doing a hard job. He wasn't framed, and if he had been, I would have spotted it. None of us wanted it to be a copper. How do you think we must feel?"

Lucy stood up. "I've got a hunch you've got your doubts. If you knew there was a chance he was innocent, you would get the whole station house down there to save their colleague. You'd get his old precinct, Harlesden or whatever it is, out here too."

"I think you'd best go."

Shackerstone got up and opened the public door to show Lucy out. She stopped at the door and turned to look across her right shoulder at him. A breeze from the main front door blew her red hair wildly about her head for a second. Shackerstone thought her lips were about to break into a seductive smile, but they thinned as she drilled her eyes into his again. He saw the muscles in her face tense and her eyes narrow. "I guess the funeral will be next week. I'll be there on my own, apart from the press doing their Bride of Dracula bit. As the pregnant girlfriend of one of your murder victims, *I'll* be needing some victim support."

Shackerstone's mind raced back into the protective spirit with which he had sat down. He stared blankly at her. He visualized her standing in the autumn rain as the sole mourner at the mercy of dozens of photographers and reporters. He wanted to be there to defend her. He could see himself pushing them away. He could imagine himself on TV blocking the lenses of cameras with his ample, dark hands. A strange pang of guilt struck him as he recalled his own brief career in press photography.

"I'll, uh…"

"Do you think you could send Reshard Khan? I really don't want to see you there, even if you've had second thoughts by then. You won't be welcome, not even if you've managed to charge someone."

Shackerstone swallowed hard, trying not to reply in a way that would cause more harm. He fumbled for words.

"But… where are you going now?"

"Back to the hospital. You were my only hope. I'm going to sit with him now until the end."

Shackerstone took a deep breath and tried to say something supportive. The only word that came out was "Sorry." Lucy walked away from him briskly, flicking her hair round behind her with a shake of her head. Shackerstone watched her walk through the foyer and out by the heavy glass doors at the front. He closed the interview room door slowly and deliberately, as he would do in the presence of a corpse. He sat down in the room and tried to collect his thoughts. It was two minutes past ten and he already needed a stiff Scotch.

The inter-office public address uttered the familiar "bing-bong" tone.

"DCI Shackerstone to the Superintendent's office please."

Shackerstone wasn't yet into the routine of a divisional DCI. He needed to be in Yardley's office at ten along with the duty officer to brief the Superintendent about the crimes over the weekend. He got up and walked swiftly back upstairs to the CID office, collecting the crime data that had already been prepared for him. He was still distracted by Lucy and his unease must have been clear when he entered Yardley's office. The early-turn duty officer, Inspector Bardy, was briefing Yardley about the prison riot.

"Sorry I'm late, sir. Business at the front counter."

"Everything okay?"

"Fine, sir."

"Okay, Brian, I was just getting the latest on the prison from Fred."

"Yes, as I was saying, the three who went over the wall have all been captured by our own dog units. If they had headed for town they would have got away with it, but they struck out into the woodlands to the north. The dogs had a field day. Anyhow, the prison is under control again, but there are four in the hospital with stab wounds. Two are in the Intensive Therapy Unit and unlikely to make it beyond the next few hours."

"I'm going to need to have a word with you afterwards about that, sir," interrupted Shackerstone. "There may be a policing requirement later in the week for one of the funerals."

Yardley nodded. Bardy carried on. "There are press outside the prison, but the prison authorities are dealing with them. I've spoken to the prison governor, and all they will want from us now is assistance in investigating the major crimes. Our prison liaison chap is already down there identifying scenes with DI Graham. Superintendent Smith, who dealt with the prison overnight, has gone off to bed and I had a message that she would give you the full debrief later when she's awake."

"Thanks. Fred. Anything else?"

"Yes, a missing person I was handed over from night duty. Inspector Windsor didn't like the look of it at all. DI Graham was called at home for advice. In fact, it was this job that led to the dog unit being where it was when the prisoners went over the wall. Anyhow, this is what we have: white female, twenty-eight years, Francesca Porterer, apparently healthy and happy with no domestic problems. Two kids. Went on a girl's night out Saturday night, in her car, only two miles, expected back by husband at eleven. We did the usual and let it run on until Sunday when most of the Saturday night missing come home, but no joy. Sunday late turn shift got the ball rolling with some road searches, but there was no trace of her or the car. Night duty couldn't help too much because of every copper in the force being up at the prison, but a dog unit searched the woods between home and the restaurant she used. Her family says it is totally out of character and all the girlfriends from last night have been contacted. I hope she has gone off with some bloke or another, but it looks rather…"

"Depressing?" commented Shackerstone.

"Horribly like the work of Dastra."

"Yes, if I didn't know he was on the critical list, I'd have suggested he had gone over the wall from prison."

"Critical list?" asked Yardley.

"Yes, that was what I wanted to discuss with you. Lucy

Aybrams came in. Dastra's been badly stabbed in the riot, he's one of the two in the Intensive Therapy Unit. As Fred says, he's likely to pop his clogs in the next few hours. There will have to be a bit of protection for her at the funeral when it comes."

"She came in to tell us?"

"No. It was something else. Can we get back to Francesca Porterer?"

"Sorry, yes. Fred?"

"There isn't much to tell. The dogs were called off to the back of the prison. An early turn team will finish the search."

"Nothing found then?"

"There was something that they reckon one of the dogs found her scent on, but it wasn't much use. It was a broken doll, in the road between the restaurant and her home. A car had gone over it. Night duty CID took it over to her husband. He'd never seen it. The dog handler swears by his dog, says he is sure the dog is picking up her scent on it."

Shackerstone was trying to think the doll through, but was getting nowhere.

"What do you think, Brian?"

"I don't know. Maybe it's some sort of wind-up."

"If it's connected with Vlad we have a problem, maybe several problems."

"Dastra did Sarah Carothers. We can prove that," said Shackerstone.

"But what if... no... we're moving on too far. Porterer will come home."

There was a silence broken by Inspector Bardy. "This doesn't help explain why she would get out of her car and touch a doll by the road before disappearing off the face of the earth."

"That's just dog section. They can't show she touched it," said Shackerstone.

"They might be proved right though. SOCO Gray is dusting it now for her fingerprints. Night duty CID has brought in some personal things of hers from home for comparison. She hadn't got any form, so we've no records of her prints."

"But if the prints are hers, it proves..."

"It proves she handled a doll on the way to or from the

restaurant, which at some point has been broken, apparently by being run over."

"I don't know what the relevance is, but if her dabs are on that doll, it all sounds too bloody sinister to me. I must do some thinking."

"Do that, Brian, and let me know of any developments. Anything else Fred?"

"That's your lot, sir."

"Anything from the CID, Brian?"

"Not a lot. One robbery in the shopping center Saturday, caught on CCTV, and two domestic burglaries. The main jobs for the CID will be the prison investigation and the missing person."

"Okay then, we'll call it a draw there."

Shackerstone and Bardy stood to go, but Yardley muttered something under his breath that Shackerstone just caught.

"Stay a moment, Brian."

"Sir?"

Bardy shut the door behind him. Shackerstone sat back down.

"Josh Gordonstown has passed his promotion process," said Yardley, raising his eyebrows.

"Good for him. Where's he moving to?"

"He's not. F-MIT needs restructuring and he's getting the top job. From there he can have a crack at Assistant Chief Constable."

"I hope I'm retired by then."

"And Aybrams, what did she want?"

"Blood, sir."

"Blood?"

"Barney and another prisoner are leaking pints. The blood bank is acutely short today of the types and quantities needed. It would take something like a police division or army base to do the job. Nobody's going to want to volunteer."

"No." Yardley thought for over a minute, staring vacantly at the ceiling as he did so. "We need to think a bit more long-term over this one. We need to look at four months down the line. Dastra has got an appeal together. If the unthinkable happens and this missing person is connected in some way to the Klingsor case, he might just walk free. Indeed, we should consider all possible outcomes, including a possible scenario that he might just be innocent. How will we look if we put him in there to get sliced up by the opposition?"

"He might be dead already: as I say. they've only given him a few hours. She was going back to the hospital to be with him."

"The press will love that if he gets cleared posthumously."

There was a knock on the door. It was SOCO Gray.

"Mr. Shackerstone, the duty officer said you would want to know this. The doll in the road: Porterer's prints are on it, and they've been split by the breakage. I guess she threw it from her car."

"Thank you. Thank you very much."

Gray retreated from the office and Shackerstone and Yardley stared blankly at each other, letting the information sink in. Yardley spoke first.

"How do you feel about Dastra now?"

"Huh. I feel like a probationer constable at my first Crown Court job. You listen to the defence case and the prosecution case and you believe both at the same time. I know he did it. Now I've got reason to think he might not have. It is as stark as that."

"There's old wisdom in there, Brian."

~ * ~

Sitting by Dastra's bed, Lucy watched the hospital staff disconnect equipment from the lifeless prisoner in the next bed. She sensed it would only be a matter of time before the same would be done to Barney. Once the final disconnections were made, the staff unlocked the wheels and rolled the bed away from its position. They wheeled it out of the room, and the prison officer who had been guarding the man followed on down to the mortuary. Lucy felt angry about the need for the prison warder to stay with the body, unaware of the need for evidential continuity for the coroner. It seemed to her that even death didn't free the prisoner from the system.

Only one young blond prison officer sat in the room now, and he could see that his presence was unnecessary in terms of preventing escape. Lucy remained by Dastra's bed watching the monitor as his weakened heart tried to pump the last few pints of blood round his vital organs. His skin was cold and paler than she had ever seen it. His head was propped up by a pillow, and tubes and wires ran to and from his body to the machines that were nervously monitoring or prolonging his life. A blue blanket had been pulled over him to cover the worst of the injuries, but Lucy could see the bloodstains creeping through the bandage on his shoulder. Others were rising up through the blanket and across the white sheets from several points, including the back of his left leg. A large white cotton dressing covered a gash to his right cheek. His right hand rested cold and limp in hers.

"Darling, I hope you can hear me. I want you to know how sorry, how very, very sorry I am it has ended like this. Michaela gave blood, but they wouldn't let me because of the baby and I'm the wrong type. I think by the look of things it has all come back out of you now."

The prison officer got up from his plastic seat and muttered under his breath. "I'll be outside." Lucy looked at him and smiled in appreciation, before continuing talking to Barney. "I know this isn't fair or just, and I know, I *know* we can't turn back the clock. I want you to know how good it was... the short time we had. I was so in love, so very, very much. I couldn't believe it. I still can't." Lucy smiled weakly as she pushed his hair from his forehead.

"I don't think you could believe it either, could you? I will always remember your face, as long as I live—that time when I went back to the station house on Saturday to find you. You were almost like a little boy on Christmas morning opening a fantastic present that he had always wanted." She stroked his hand with her fingertips, willing him to respond. "In a way, you know, you look like a little boy now, peacefully sleeping, far from the world. Maybe it's best that way. There's no suffering where you are now, none at all. I know in my heart that you're not Vlad, and some day I'm going to show the world that you're not. I promise, even if it takes my whole life. If it means I have to, I will flush Vlad out myself. And I know you will be there, by my side, in spirit, helping me along."

Lucy looked at the heart monitor. Dastra's pulse was becoming fast and thready. "I need to tell you that I feel a sort of guilt, right back to the start. Me finding the bodies brought us together. You would have never gotten involved in whatever happened near Goring if you hadn't been in so much of a hurry to get back to me for the concert. I bet you would have taken more care of yourself, like you must have done on the job in London."

Tears started to flow freely from Lucy's eyes. She gripped his hand tighter. "I'm so sorry, my love, this is so unjust. How can they let you go like this? If only they knew. If only they knew you like I do. They can't see the good person. They've been looking at the underbelly of life for so long that they can't see the good in anyone. They judge a man by his defects, and now they've driven events to this!"

Lucy sat back and listened to Dastra's breathing. It was shallow now, but even. Lucy became quieter. "Sorry, I didn't mean to upset you. I'm still here. Don't go yet. I just wish we had gotten married as soon as we fell in love. Marriage on impulse. My dad would have gotten really mad at me, but I would have talked him round. I wonder if we would have married back home or here in England. Who knows? And we shall never have that day now. So I'm glad, I'm so glad we made a baby. That way you have left something, something of us. Someone for me to see you in as it grows up. Someone who can walk tall to the school bus on the day I get your name cleared. I bet it will have your eyes, Barney, and that funny twitch you get down the left of your face." Lucy screwed her face up and tried to imitate it.

"I will bring it up to be proud of its dad. You know the only photos I have got of you are ones I've found at the house of when you were young. I'm going to keep them and I know you'd say yes. They won't mean anything to anyone else; they'll just get slung on a fire in a house clearance."

The heart monitor became erratic. Lucy sighed and moved closer to the bed, laying her head down on the bloody blanket. "I'm sorry, my darling. I'm sorry it was so short, but it was lovely. I wish I could die in you place and save you from this. I wish this was like something from a Wagner opera, and I could die here too, with you, like your mom and dad did, like Isolde. That would be..." Lucy's words tailed off. She felt she had so much to say, but at the same time, couldn't find the words to express herself. An alarm started on Dastra's monitor. His pulse had gone. Lucy looked up and saw that the screen showed a ragged green line.

"Oh, no!" cried Lucy. Two doctors crashed through the doors with a stainless steel trolley of medical equipment and, most importantly, blood bags. "You'll have to move, now. We may be able to save this one."

Lucy hurried out into the corridor and directly into Shackerstone. He steadied her, gripping her by the shoulders, and looked earnestly into her eyes.

"I got the blood!"

"It's too late. He's flatlining."

"If they can restart him, he'll live. I did as you asked. I asked the whole station. We've found enough of his type."

"Why did you change your mind?

"I haven't. I still know it's him." He put his hands in his pockets and looked at the floor. "But that still doesn't make it wrong to help him. Anyhow, my boss leaned on me a bit."

"Why come yourself, then? You know how," Lucy struggled to continue, "you know how I feel."

"A black man's blood's as good as anyone's," he said, trying to change the direction of the conversation. Lucy studied him and replayed her only two previous encounters with him. The Old Bailey had been the more bizarre, and the protective way he had sent Khan off with her had reinforced her first reading of him. She had picked up the signals, and turned them back on him earlier today in order to persuade him to help Dastra. To her surprise it had worked, but she still wasn't sure why. "It's me isn't it?" she said in a loud whisper "You're doing this like you did the ride from the Old Bailey. It's me, isn't it?"

Shackerstone shrugged and looked into Lucy's tearstained eyes. He didn't have to say yes—she read it in his face. He forced a smile, but his eyes betrayed a strange sadness.

Twenty Two

Question(Superintendent Hinx): "You didn't enter any of this on the decision log."

Answer (DCI Shackerstone): "Klingsor was officially closed. All I had was a prison with a riot, and at the same time a missing person case that looked a bit odd. Some prisoners went over the side and the first I knew about Dastra was when Lucy, Lucy Aybrams came to the nick."

Q: "Which nick?"
A: "Wemstone police station. Where my office was."

Q: "But you knew Dastra had a talent for escaping?"
A: "He was good with locks, but I totally dismissed the idea of him getting out then going back in. Mr. Gordonstown didn't agree with me because his examples of his best work submitted for the Chief Superintendent's promotion process were largely based on this case."
(Tape extract from MPS enquiry into Operation Klingsor.)

Shackerstone knocked on Yardley's door.

"Come in."

He opened the superintendent's door and walked in with a tabloid newspaper.

"Hello, Guv."

"What can I do for you, Brian?"

"Have you seen this?"

Shackerstone unfolded the newspaper and showed the headlines to Yardley. Under the title, there were only three clearly readable words across the whole of the front page, standing out in white against a black background: BLOOD FOR DRACULA. A piece of tiny newsprint in the bottom right corner of the page directed readers to turn to page four for the story. Shackerstone sat down and read the article aloud. "'Vlad the Impaler, David Dastra, recently convicted murderer of Reading newlywed Sarah Louise Carothers and widely suspected of more killings, has received literally gallons of human blood in a transfusion at Wemstone General Hospital. One of the prisoners injured following rioting and rooftop protests at Wemstone Prison, Dastra is said to have received over twenty pints of blood to sustain him. Officers from his former police station queued up to supply their murdering ex-colleague with blood after he received cuts at the prison.' Cuts? He must have at least half a dozen stab wounds. They make it sound like he nicked himself shaving. 'Several other prisoners in the notorious beast's wing were injured in the disturbances, and one has since died from complications resulting from his wounds.' Why they can't say he died from his wounds, I don't know.

"It carries on: 'While the efforts of the police appear to be noble and unbiased, it has been revealed that Wemstone police chief Ian Yardley paid his unwilling subordinates an overtime bonus to give blood. What we ask is why taxpayers' money is being spent in this way when our overstretched police force needs to watch every penny it spends? The decent thing would have been to leave Dastra to die peacefully in his hospital bed, and save the country a fortune in prison costs. Supplying blood to this vampire at the taxpayers' expense can only add insult to the families of his victims. The Chief Constable was unavailable for comment as we went to press, and the hospital stated that Dastra still hasn't come out of his coma.'"

"Bastards! They never so much as asked me for a comment."

"They have a point. We were sticking our necks out. Has the Chief Constable been on?"

"I briefed him on the day. He supports my decision. In fact, between you and me, he was quite impressed with it. He felt it was all very ethical, the way the force is going. High moral values in the face of hostility, except the use of the overtime. He wasn't so impressed about that… but there you go."

"Well, I think his approval is about all we will achieve. Even if this other job is a Vlad killing, Dastra is still in the frame for Sarah Carothers. There can't be any release. All we've done is to keep him alive to go back in again, if he ever wakes up."

"He's that bad?"

"Hard to say. They reckon there's little brain activity."

"Which brings me conveniently to another thing, Brian. Josh Gordonstown and I would like you to handle the local end of the prison investigation."

"But boss, I've got half a dozen jobs on the go, as well as this Porterer business. It looks like a Klingsor case and we need to show it isn't."

"I know you must feel some anxiety from this. Porterer is still just a missing person until we find her. I know what it looks like, and I know we made our recent decisions on Dastra based on what may have happened to her."

"So we must push on with the case."

"Detective Chief Superintendent Gordonstown is happy with operation Klingsor. I asked about firing up the case again and he has put some pretty strong arguments to keep it wound down for now. There are no lines of enquiry open. We want you to do the prison riot. The Home Office will be working with you. It will still be related to Klingsor, especially if our man wakes up: he's your chief witness."

"I can't imagine he'd be very cooperative. Lucy Aybrams looks at me as if I've just killed Bambi's mother."

"She could look at *me* any way she chooses. I envy the young fellow who wakes up to that."

"Even from a coma?"

"Especially from a coma."

Yardley watched as Shackerstone shut his eyes and tipped his head slightly back as if imagining something. "Well?"

Shackerstone opened his eyes. "She's very lovely. There's no doubt about that. I know every shred of evidence is stacked up against him, but in a small way, you were right. It does make you think twice about the case. However, when I get her out of my head, all my doubts go away again. I know he did it, one hundred percent."

"And if you found Francesca Porterer on a spike, where would you be then?"

Shackerstone was silent for a moment and bent forward, placing his elbows on his knees and looking at the floor. After a few seconds he looked up at Yardley, his head cocked to the left.

"Buggered."

"And our risk management would have paid off. Well, if he comes round it will have."

"He'll be in hospital a few months if he doesn't peg out. His injuries are pretty horrific."

"At least he's a prison service matter. We can't afford a twenty-four-hour guard on him. All we are doing is one telephone call per shift to check his condition. He's got one prison officer, round the clock. The only fly in the ointment is Lucy Aybrams. The prison service asks for a female constable from here to search her whenever she turns up. It's bloody stupid, with him in a coma and her up the duff."

"I suppose she could leave something down the side of the bed. Mind you, she would have had plenty of opportunity when he was dying."

"I don't suppose she would have thought about it then."

"No." Shackerstone got up. "Shall I leave the paper?"

"No, the missus will already have bought herself a copy for the scrapbook."

Brian Shackerstone hurried back to his own office and after thinking about what he intended to say he phoned Gordonstown. The phone rang for half a minute, and Shackerstone was about to put his receiver down when there was an answer. "Detective Chief Superintendent Gordonstown."

"Sir, it's Brian Shackerstone."

"Hello, Brian."

"Congratulations on your promotion, sir."

"Thanks, Brian. What can I do for you?"

"Operation Klingsor. Do you not think I should get it rolling again?"

There was silence for a few seconds.

"No, Brian. Klingsor is done and dusted. I know what you think about this latest missing person, but a hundred and one cases look like that one. It's a connection too far. You and I know Dastra is our man, just look at the strength of the evidence." He paused. "I know where you're coming from with this—your last *ever* big murder investigation—and you're trying to keep the embers glowing."

"Not without some justification."

"It's much too soon to judge whether Klingsor needs resurrecting. And I tell you what, Brian. Fingers will be pointed at both of us if we do."

Shackerstone thought for a second. "They can point. It's a good job."

"That's right. Let sleeping dogs lie, Brian. You can finish your murder detective career on the prison investigation. If you want to help Dastra, get the blokes who cut him up."

"Yeah, thanks for your time."

Twenty Three

Question (Detective Inspector Graham—Interviewing):
"How was Lucy chosen?"
Answer (Suspect): "She was chosen by Shackerstone."

Q: "At some point, you made a decision."
A: "It wasn't my choice. Shackerstone chose her for me
when I was far away from all the action.""
(Extract from evidential tape transcript.)

Lucy visited Dastra every Saturday, but although he was now pumping eight pints of blood around a healing circulation, he still hadn't woken from his coma.

The doctors at the hospital were professional, but cold and unhelpful when she managed to speak to them on the telephone. On a Saturday, she could never get to speak to anyone about Dastra's condition, although a pair of nurses had sat down with her some weeks previously and explained that he was in a persistent vegetative state.

When Lucy arrived on the seventh such consecutive visit, she was told that no female police officer would be available for over an hour. She enquired at the nursing station as to whether Dastra's doctor was on duty, and for the first time got a positive reply. She asked if it was possible for her to see him while she was waiting, but was given a polite, "Sorry, too busy." Lucy enquired after the doctor's name, and was told "Dr. Walker".

After telling the prison guard she would be back in an hour,

Lucy took the elevator to the ground floor and waited in the hospital canteen where she bought herself a coffee and sat down with a magazine that failed to occupy her mind. Determined to speak to Dastra's doctor, she moved to a different table so she could easily observe the name badges of staff coming into the room. Lucy kept this up for an hour without success at what appeared to be a fairly busy time. As she sat waiting, growing more despondent, she hatched another far more sure-fire plan to speak to Doctor Walker. She found a telephone by the entrance to the canteen. She dialed nine and spoke to the paging service.

"Doctor Walker, please."

"Which one? Gynaecology, urology or neurology?"

"Neurology."

"What's the message?"

"Meet me in the canteen. L."

It worked. Lucy returned to her table, and a handsome, serious and confused looking doctor strode into the canteen trying to work out who had paged him. He was about forty-five, with gray-streaked black hair and a careworn face. Lucy read his name badge and rose from her seat. "Dr. Walker?"

Walker's face searched for the source of the voice, finally finding Lucy's face among the many in the restaurant and approached. "Yes, I'm sorry. Do I know you?"

"Lucy, Lucy Aybrams."

Her name clearly didn't register immediately, but what did register was Lucy's face. Like other men before, he was taken in and pleased to sit down at her table.

"Yes, Lucy. How can I be of help?"

"You're treating my boyfriend."

"I am?"

"Yes, our paths never seem to cross."

"Obviously not. What is the patient's... what is your boyfriend's name?"

"David Dastra"

"Dastra. Are you a reporter?" Walker made as if to get up, but with no real intent. Lucy put her hand on the back of his with some urgency. "No, Doctor. I'm not a reporter. I really am his girlfriend and I'm having his baby."

"I'm sorry, I'm a little surprised, that's all. There has been media interest."

"They have shown a lot of interest in me. Until a week or two ago they were following me everywhere. My face has been in a lot of newspapers over the last few weeks."

"Sorry, I don't get the time to see them. You're a new face to me... is that a corneal graft?"

"Well spotted."

"It's still a very beautiful face, in fact the graft makes it more interesting."

"Thank you." Lucy smiled as if being complimented for the first time in her life. "Barney, David Dastra, can you tell me what the prognosis is?"

"Sure. Can I get you a coffee first? I need a wake-up drink."

"That would be nice."

Walker got up and brought back two coffees. He sat down and smiled as Lucy fumbled trying to open the plastic milk pot. "The case of David Dastra. I don't suppose you'll be too happy if I call him Vlad?"

"No."

"Okay, we'll leave that one. It looks like he's in a persistent vegetative state. I can't say which way he will go. A rare few make a total recovery, most fade away. At some point we will reach a critical decision whether to stop feeding..."

"I know he's in a coma, I just need to know if there's anything that can be done for him. Can he be operated on? Are there any drugs? That sort of thing."

"Nothing at all."

Lucy sat back and folded her arms. "I don't want to be rude here, but I guess what I want to say is that he doesn't have many friends. It would be easy to decide to leave him when something might work."

"I could feel mildly insulted at the suggestion. But you do have a point. I can assure you I'm giving you a thorough professional opinion. And that and the care would be the same for anyone else whoever they were."

"That's very reassuring. Thank you."

Walker smiled as if satisfied at keeping Lucy reasonably

happy. She watched his gaze, dwell on her eyes and sensed his temptation to keep her there a little longer. He spoke after a moment's silence, hesitantly, she thought, tentatively. "There is, of course, something that often works in these cases, but it's probably impractical with all the security."

"Tell me."

"Stimulus. A lot of patients respond to being talked to for hours, or to their favorite music."

Lucy replied enthusiastically. "That would be something I could do. Barney was really keen on music and there are loads of CDs back at his house. I could bring in a portable CD player—would the nurses change the CDs?"

"I could ask them to. It wouldn't need to be twenty-four hours a day, just a few hours at a time would do."

"I could bring in all sorts of stuff. We have similar tastes," said Lucy, her voice rising excitedly.

"That's okay, but don't go for a load of different things, think hard about something you know he really liked, perhaps a tune that he couldn't get out of his head."

"I'll look through his collection. I know there is something that kept him awake."

"Try that. Do you want to go up and see him now?"

"I do, but I've got to wait for a lady cop to come and search me."

"Well, come back up to the ward with me anyway. I'll sort out the nursing staff for playing music."

Lucy and Dr. Walker returned to Dastra's ward by way of the lift. Outside his room a fat female police officer waited, arms folded, talking to the prison guard. The officer smiled as Lucy arrived. She had done the same job for Lucy before.

"Shall we go into the disabled loo again?"

"Yes, okay."

They went into a large lavatory off the ward corridor.

"Okay love, I'll just do the light once-over, routine pat down. If you smuggled in an angle grinder he wouldn't have a use for it."

"Thanks."

The officer patted her down and rummaged through her handbag. Satisfied, she opened the door and escorted Lucy back to

Dastra's room. "See you in five weeks' time then."

"Five weeks?"

The next time I'm on Saturday early turn.

"I understand. Thanks."

"Things may have changed for the better by then."

"I hope so. Thanks for the thought." The officer nodded to the prison guard who opened the door to Dastra's room and entered with Lucy. She settled down on a hard plastic chair by the bed. Dr. Walker came in and made a theatrical display of checking charts and equipment. Dastra looked far better colored than he had done in the Intensive Therapy Unit, and apart from some dribble by his otherwise dry lips and many weeks of hair and beard growth, he looked as if he was in normal sleep.

"There has been a slight improvement in his general condition. His pulse is a lot stronger and the last vestiges of internal bleeding have stopped, and you'll notice we have taken the drain out. He was a fit young man. An older man or an office worker, or even a doctor, might not have made it. The problem is in my department: the brain. The fittest body in the world is no good if it is brain-dead, and we just can't tell."

"But you'll keep him alive?"

"We'll keep him going through the physical recovery, but at some stage..." He pulled up a chair and sat down side-on to Lucy. "At some stage we may have to make a quality of life decision about continuing to feed him if we're sure he is brain-dead. If he recovers, he still has a long life inside prison ahead of him and he may need a lot of care, which Her Majesty's Prison Service isn't really set up to provide."

"I know, but you see, he's been framed. He'll be freed on appeal soon."

"Let's concentrate on getting him better." He patted her leg and got up. "Bring the music, as soon as you can. It's really all we can do for the time being."

The previous weeks had exhausted Lucy's capacity for one-sided conversation with Barney, and after Walker left the room, she sat silently watching him for half-an-hour before relating the suggestion about the music to him. The following day she brought in a CD player with some CDs. Lucy telephoned the hospital each weekday evening that week from her flat in Oxford but was told that Dastra had not reacted to the music.

She visited the hospital the next Saturday. Dastra still hadn't reacted to the music, and the staff and prison officer assured her that they had been playing it to him. Lucy overheard the prison guard whistling the finale to Sibelius's second symphony and took this as a certain indication that they'd told the truth. She continued her evening calls to see if Dastra was awake, but on Tuesday, her telephone went out of order, but she continued on Wednesday night from a callbox in the street outside. Feeling this was getting nowhere, she decided to wait until Saturday.

Twenty Four

Question (Detective Inspector Graham—Interviewing): "Didn't she resist?"

Answer(Suspect): "You bet. That's the fascination. It would be no good drugging any of them. She kicked and screamed right to the bitter end."

(Excerpt from evidential tape transcript.)

"You're where?" said Shackerstone, fumbling with the receiver of the phone in his office. "Hold on, Reshard, I'll just shut the office door." Shackerstone stretched the handset cable and closed his door.

"I'm back at the bypass with Tim. A call came in from one of the surveyors this morning. He said there was a patch of ground he felt we needed to look at."

"And?"

"It's a rectangle about six feet by two. I'm not saying it's very fresh, but everything else has a very fine growth of grass shoots just coming through."

"And this stands out?"

"Yes, quite a bit. There's no grass. I reckon if we had looked two weeks back we would have missed it because the entire site would have been uniform in appearance. We have to get a PolSA search team down to have a dig. The shape is perfect... for a grave.

"Thank the surveyor. Stay put and I'll get some uniformed bods down to guard the area. I'll have to negotiate with the road builders too. Let's pray this will take us somewhere."

Shackerstone put the phone down, took a deep breath, and hoped.

~ * ~

After twenty-four hours of work, the remains of Francesca Porterer were carefully removed from a limed grave at a depth of five feet below ground level. Her skull was separate from the rest of the body and lying between her feet. O'Toole performed the post mortem that Friday afternoon, and Shackerstone's worries dissolved when he discovered that she hadn't been impaled.

After identification of the body by dental records, Shackerstone called on her family at home personally, accompanied by a family liaison officer to break the news. The investigator knew, for her devastated husband, who for weeks had been slowly coming to terms with the fact that he would never see her again, the revelation that she had been beheaded would haunt him for the rest of his life.

~ * ~

On Friday, Lucy and Michaela arrived late in the evening at Prospect of Peshawar to a ringing phone. Michaela answered it as Lucy switched the house alarm off. "It's for you, a nurse at the hospital."

Lucy raised her eyebrows and took the receiver from Michaela.

"Hi. Lucy Aybrams."

"Hello, this is Staff Nurse Adams at Wemstone general hospital—we've been trying to contact you since late last night."

"You have?"

"There is someone who wants to speak to you."

"Okay?" Lucy looked a Michaela quizzically. There were noises on the other end of the phone and a heavy, breathy voice said "lee…us."

"Sorry, I didn't catch that."

There was a long pause. If it hadn't been the hospital, Lucy would have cut the call off as a heavy breather. "See-bay-lee-us," panted the voice "Second sim-fun-ee."

"I think it's Barney!" whispered Lucy excitedly to Michaela.

"Are you there?" said a female voice on the other end of telephone.

"Yes, yes I am."

"He's awake. He woke up Thursday night, still a bit confused... thinks he was injured last weekend."

"Can we come up and see him?"

"It's after visiting, but in the circumstances, okay if we can get a lady police officer out here. At least the car park will be free."

Lucy put the receiver down and hugged Michaela with joy. "I knew he'd come round. I just knew it."

They were forced to look at Dastra through the window of the room until a female officer arrived just after 10:30 p.m. Michaela submitted to a search as well, so that she could go in with Lucy. A fresh prison guard had just arrived for the night shift, and he went with them. Lucy went over to Dastra and immediately grasped his right hand. He was fully propped up, managed to open his eyes and smiled appreciatively.

"Oh, Barney. This is wonderful. We were so worried."

He tried to say something.

"Sorry, I didn't catch that."

Lucy moved closer and listened. His breath smelt dry and stale. He struggled to force his eyes open.

"Hurt," he panted "I... thought... I... was... dead... been... how... long?"

"Eight weeks."

"Prison... riots... Peter?"

"Your friend? Yes, he's okay, still in hospital under guard." Lucy looked at the prison guard for confirmation and he nodded in reply. Dastra took several breaths before starting again.

"House... you... stay... there?"

"Both of us, every weekend."

"Press?"

"Nearly all gone. They used to follow me here, but we're old news now."

"Good."

"Michaela is here."

He tried to move his head, but his neck was stiff from lack of movement. He forced his eyes right over.

"Good... to... see... you."

"You too, Barney."

He closed his eyes and relaxed. "Sibelius," he said. Lucy smiled.

"Yes. I remembered our conversation in your car. We both said it kept us awake. I hoped it would wake you up."

"It did. Now I can't get... back to sleep." He smiled, opening his eyes again.

"You had a very long sleep. You won't need much for a while I think."

"Do. Pain. Hurts to be... awake."

"Where does it hurt?"

"Face... chest... back... leg, all hurt."

"I guess they will. You were stabbed all over. I don't know any more. The prison guard said Peter Lynch was with you. Nobody else has told us much."

"Tell him about the blood," Michaela suggested.

"Oh yes. The hospital ran out of blood, Michaela gave you a pint, but it wasn't enough, so I went and talked your old boss round. He sent a whole precinct load."

"Shacker... stone?"

"Yes, and I think there's something going on there."

"Last week?"

"No, Barney, this all happened nearly two months back. Look how much beard you've grown."

"Two months?"

"You've been out for a long time. Don't you remember anything?"

"Bits... but not much, thank God."

Twenty Five

Following recent public inquiry criticism of police it has been decided by the Association of Chief Police Officers that all recent and current murder investigations will be subject to review by experienced independent senior murder detectives. This in no way implies criticism of any investigation, but is being done to ensure that there has been consistency of approach and that the families of victims have been treated fairly regardless of race, belief, sexual orientation, disability or gender. Operation Klingsor, on which you were the Senior Investigating Officer will be subject to review by the Metropolitan Police.
(Extract from file sent to Detective Chief Superintendent Gordonstown.)

On Monday morning, a forensic result file was waiting on Shackerstone's desk. He read it and let the news sink in before reaching for the telephone to call Gordonstown at headquarters. The phone rang first and Shackerstone answered it.

"DCI Shackerstone."

"Hello, Brian, it's DCS Gordonstown."

"Ah, I was just about to call you, I…"

"I've got some bad news. The Chief Constable has ordered a review of Operation Klingsor by the Metropolitan Police."

"Why?"

"Every job is being reviewed, but of all the bloody police forces in the country, I get our magnificent friends from the smoke."

"The Met… yes… but I doubt that there will be a mutual

dislike. Anyhow, we did a good job. We got a result, and the evidence will be tested again at Dastra's appeal."

"Appeal?"

"In only three weeks' time."

"Is there any risk of it being successful?"

"Not on anything we did. It's just the subsequent developments that bother me."

"Like your beheaded lady?"

"Yes, I've a forensic file in front of me."

"What does it say?"

"Firstly that they have recovered some oil-based cosmetic from her face. Her husband says all she ever used was lipstick. The boys have checked her house—she owned nothing like this stuff."

"Can we trace it?"

"We'll try, but the main issue is the soil under her toenails. It is identical to the Vlad samples. No error"

"Oh."

"My intuition said she was a Klingsor job—but if she is, it does make the Dastra conviction look a bit wobbly."

"We can't afford it to be wobbly."

"Coincidence?"

"Do you know how small an area the soil comes from?"

"No."

"It's virtually unique and not very local. Comes from hills round Goring."

"But very near to where we caught Dastra."

"Yes, but a good drive from here. Porterer must have been transported from Wemstone, killed near Goring, and then returned to the bypass site for burial. And she, or someone, made her face up and not with anything she had at home."

Gordonstown mused, "Perhaps she had a friend somewhere. And then there's the timing of her disappearance."

"During the prison riot."

"I wonder if Dastra actually made it out over the wall."

"It doesn't seem very likely and it's a different M.O. And it doesn't really explain him going back in and getting half killed. Incidentally, he has come round."

"Mmm. Still we had best keep an open mind on the case."

"There is something, though."

"What?"

"The day I first met him he was doing a trick where he broke out of a cell at the nick."

"Interesting... I need to think about that one. Is there anyone who might have assisted him?"

"He was with his cellmate, an I.R.A. bloke, when he was found stabbed."

"So he could have got out with him."

"And persuaded him to take part in a murder, then go back inside?"

"No... you're right. That's completely illogical. It would need to be someone he really trusted to supply him with transportation, but who he can spin a convincing story to in order to cover the time he spends killing. We know he acts alone."

"His arrest told us that much."

"What about the girlfriend?"

"Well, she drove up to the prison."

Gordonstown spoke with deliberation, "So in theory he could have escaped, flagged down Porterer, did the killing and the burial, then gave Aybrams a cock and bull story to get her to drive him back to the prison."

"To go back in?"

"The perfect alibi...he wasn't counting on being attacked."

"It's a bit thin."

"*Thin* might be all we have to keep our original result safe from scrutiny. I wonder if she uses makeup."

"Lucy's got good skin. I doubt it"

"We need to search her flat and Dastra's house again."

"It's still very shaky. We'll need at minimum an exact match on the makeup first."

"Brian. There's already enough reasonable suspicion to pull Lucy Aybrams in. Our colleagues in the Metropolitan Police are being publicly crucified over their failure to arrest the suspects for the Stephen Lawrence murder early enough to preserve forensic evidence. It won't happen here, not with the Met about to review my biggest job. We must act quickly!"

"Not in my book."

Twenty Six

Question (Superintendent Hinx): "So you arrested Lucy Aybrams?"

Answer (DCS Gordonstown): "Yes. We knew she would visit Dastra at the hospital at the weekend, so effectively she came to us."
(Tape extract from MPS enquiry into Operation Klingsor.)

The sergeant behind the custody office desk at Wemstone was relaxing, and wasn't familiar with either of the two detectives or the female prisoner they were bringing through the caged entranceway.

"Detective Chief Superintendent Gordonstown and this is DI Simons from HQ." The sergeant sat up, hardly glancing at the warrant cards.

"What can I do for you, sir?"

"Stand there," said Gordonstown to Lucy, pointing to a spot just in front of the sergeant's desk. Lucy did she was told, standing with one arm straight and the other arm across the top of her bump. DI Simons spoke next. "Sarge, during a prison riot at Wemstone Jail recently, one Francesca Porterer was abducted and subsequently murdered. Forensic evidence has come to light suggesting that this murder is connected with others for which David Dastra is the suspect, and for one of which he has already been convicted. There is soil evidence to suggest Dastra escaped from prison and murdered Porterer. Officers on duty at the prison riot state they saw this female, Dastra's girlfriend, in the vicinity of the prison, with a car. I have reasonable grounds for believing she may have assisted him."

Lucy glanced alternately towards each of the three men, uncomprehending. The sergeant leaned back and looked as Simons. He made no attempt to enter any of the details into the computer in front of him. "Is that it?"

"Yes, Sergeant." The word "sergeant" was spoken with emphasis as if to assert his authority.

"Can I have a word in the side office? Sir!"

"I'll take this," said Gordonstown. He followed the sergeant into a small room and shut the door behind him. Lucy heard voices being raised in the room, but couldn't make out what was being said. After about five minutes, both officers emerged red faced. "Right," puffed the sergeant sitting down. He spoke directly and clearly to Lucy.

"I'm authorizing your detention here for the purpose of obtaining evidence by questioning you."

"We want to search both of her residences, too, under section 18," added Gordonstown.

"And also for the purpose of preserving evidence in this case," continued the sergeant, with a sarcastic emphasis on the word "case".

"Your surname please?"

"Aybrams."

"Can you spell that for me please?"

"A-Y-B-R-A-M-S."

He began typing into the computer.

"Thank you. Your first names?"

"Lucy Catherine, Catherine with a C."

"Address?"

Lucy gave her Oxford address.

"Date of birth?"

"January 31st, 1978."

"Place of birth?"

"San Francisco. USA"

"Can you stand over there? I'll check your height."

Lucy stood by measure on the wall.

"Five-foot-eight," said the sergeant.

"Right. While you are in custody you have certain rights: You have the right to have someone informed of your arrest, the right to consult a solicitor free of charge and the right to consult the Codes of Practice governing the treatment of persons in police detention. You may do any of these things now, but if you do not, you may still do so later." He handed Lucy a printed explanation. "Do you wish to exercise any of these rights?"

"Yes, I want a friend told I'm here and I would like an attorney... a solicitor."

"I'll call you the duty solicitor."

"Could you please call me John Aaronovitch?"

"Certainly," smiled the sergeant. "As you are U.S. National, I'm obliged to inform the U.S. consulate of your arrest under a consular convention. As you are pregnant I will also call a police surgeon to establish that you are fit to be detained."

Lucy said nothing. The sergeant produced the form from a computer printer and asked her to sign for her rights. He took Michaela's details and made a short phone call to get a female officer to the custody suite to search Lucy. The phone rang back to the sergeant about a minute later. "Right... right. She won't be back for an hour? Okay, well, if she's willing to, great."

He put the phone down.

"I've got a female detective coming down to do the search." He smiled with obvious satisfaction. Gordonstown shot a glance at Simons, but waited by Lucy until the door connecting to the rest of the station opened. DI Nicola Graham walked into the room in a business-like way and then gave a look of surprise at seeing Lucy. Her eyes flicked from Gordonstown to Simons, and Gordonstown spoke.

"DI Graham. What a... pleasant surprise. Can you search this young lady for me?"

Graham looked a little flustered then motioned to Lucy to follow her into a female cell. She made sure that she pulled the door fully closed and pushed on it to check. She spoke softly.

"Hello, Lucy."

"Hi. Searching again?"

"I'm sorry about the pregnancy test business. It wasn't my idea to use it."

"No?"

"It was Mr. Gordonstown. What has he got you in for?"

"Assisting Barney to escape from the prison and murder somebody."

"What?"

"I don't really understand. I'm just scared."

Graham was silent for a second. "Okay. I've got to do this search. I'll just pat you down and take all your loose property. The sergeant must list it and you'll get most of it back straight away. When I get back upstairs I'm going to make a few calls. Please try to relax. I gather you have a solicitor on the way?"

"I've requested John Aaronovitch."

"I'll check that, then I'll make a call to him myself." Back in the main custody suite, the sergeant listed the personal items in Lucy's presence along with the contents her handbag. He bagged a few sharp items and some headache tablets from her bag and asked her to sign the custody record, then escorted her to a cell.

"I'll call your friend and Mr. Aaronovitch. Just sit tight."

Lucy sat down on a blue plastic-covered mattress in a cell that smelled of sweaty feet and stale food. The sergeant slammed the heavy steel door shut and Lucy was left alone with a lidless steel toilet and a wall full of graffiti for company.

~ * ~

Bulging in shrunken, olive-green fishing overalls, Detective Chief Inspector Brian Shackerstone stepped heavily into the custody suite at Wemstone police station just as Detective Chief Superintendent Joshua Gordonstown was putting his arrest notes through the date stamping machine to authenticate the time of completing them. Simons was relaxing, arms folded, sitting on the waiting bench.

"Detective Chief Superintendent Gordonstown." Shackerstone spoke in mock surprise. Gordonstown spun round and immediately reddened.

"Brian... rather fishy, aren't we?"

"Well, something *else* may also be, and we need to speak."

"Not now, Brian. I'm about to go out for two premises searches."

"On my job?"

"On *our* job, Brian. I have full supervisory rights on this one. This is my decision."

"Without consulting me?"

"I did consult you, but you disagreed and I respect that. However, in the end I have the final say."

"But there isn't enough evidence, is there? Did you know she was with another girl at the prison? I have them both on prison car park CCTV. Have you brought the other girl in?"

Gordonstown paused and reddened again. "She can tell me all that in interview."

"No she won't," said a London accent from the main door. It was Yardley.

"My office please, Josh."

Gordonstown looked heavenwards and followed Yardley out of the custody suite.

"I'd like to be a fly on the wall in that office," mumbled Shackerstone.

"It doesn't sound like your man is on side," suggested Simons, from the bench.

"He isn't. Neither am I. That's why I called him in," said the custody officer, smugly.

"But Gordonstown will just pull rank on Yardley."

"He can't," said Shackerstone sitting down on the wood bench. "The law says the local superintendent has the final say, regardless of rank. If Yardley says she goes free, off she goes."

The telephone rang. The sergeant took it. He smiled broadly.

"It's her brief. Aaronovitch."

"That will put the cat amongst the pigeons."

Shackerstone was called to Yardley's office, where a heated debate had clearly just taken place. Both men were now seated and Gordonstown was red-faced and sweating.

"Explain for DCS Gordonstown's benefit what the state of play is on Aybrams. I've already looked on HOLMES."

Shackerstone sat down on a hard chair. "I've traced three pieces of CCTV footage of her with her friend driving firstly through the town center, parking up in the prison car park, and then returning by the town center. Nobody else was visible in the car, and while there was the possibility of someone hiding in the boot, there was no discernible difference in the rear suspension height between the different shots. If Dastra had been aboard, both girls would need to be in on the plan, and he would have to have been let out before the car had passed back through town."

"You didn't tell me this," interjected Gordonstown.

"I got it yesterday…"

"You set me up! Shackerstone's payback?"

"Bollocks. I didn't expect you to arrest Aybrams without consulting me."

"You'd already blown me out."

"You brought this on yourself, Detective *Chief* Superintendent." Shackerstone's tone bordered on insubordination.

"Gents!" Yardley snapped. "Mistake over. Let's learn and move on like grownups."

Shackerstone wasn't finished, but his voice was quieter. "The make-up has been analyzed and it's not of a type commercially available in the U.K."

"How about America?"

"It contains a suspected carcinogen that's banned in most countries, including the USA. It's a huge job to find out where it comes from, but we're still on it."

"And you don't think Aybrams might have a pot of it?"

Yardley waved it off. "Give it up, Josh. There isn't a shred of reasonable suspicion to arrest her. The only thing linking her to the makeup is that she's female."

Gordonstown silently seethed as Yardley telephoned the custody suite and ordered Lucy's immediate release.

After Aaronovitch had spoken to Lucy in an interview room, Khan was directed by Shackerstone to offer her a lift back up to the hospital. She accepted, and after signing for her returned property, she found herself being driven back to the hospital in his battered Nissan.

"Sorry about all that. Shackerstone had expressly told Gordonstown you weren't to be arrested."

"So why was I?"

"I don't know. There's some sort of turf war going on between them. This latest murder is making them both fret over Barney's conviction."

"And so they should. He was framed."

"I know what you think."

"What's this about soil, then?"

"I can't tell you."

"Yes, you can. It was one of the reasons Detective Simons gave for my arrest."

"Okay. The soil from the dead lady is the same as the stuff from the others."

"That's brilliant. It must put him in the clear."

"Not directly. It's only soil, and Gordonstown, and to some extent Shackerstone, both think Barney got out of prison to kill her."

"And went back in? That's dumb."

"It might be possible. It's a first class alibi."

After a pause for thought, Lucy continued. "Can I ask how she was murdered... was she impaled?"

"No. She was beheaded."

"Hell! What sort of man does that?"

"Very much the same sort that might do impalings."

"So, let me get this straight. Because you all think Barney did the impalings, you think he did this one too?"

"I only discount the impossible."

He drove into a police bay at the front of the hospital, and put a printed card in the window that identified the car as being on police business.

"I had best come up with you, or you will need searching again."

"Thanks."

"There is something," he said as they got out of the car.

"Yes?"

"Don't say where you got this from."

"I promise I won't."

"None of his semen from the Carothers case was found inside his pants. It was only on the outside of his trousers."

"Pants?"

"Underpants."

"That might help my theory about the attacker getting semen from him. Can I ask you a question about the latest case?"

"Go on." Khan selected the floor as the lift doors closed.

"Was the latest victim abducted from her car?"

"Yes, probably. Why?"

"How many doors did it have?"

"I'm not sure. Four, I think."

"Like all the others, yes?"

"True, but four door cars are common enough... and yes, I know Barney's wasn't."

"Yes, but Barney wasn't a victim... at least not in the sense that the others were."

"If you accept that."

"Anyhow, a succession of four door cars is very unlikely if you look at the probability."

The door opened on Dastra's floor.

"So you think there is a four door connection?"

"Well, what proportion of cars over here have four doors?"

"About two-thirds, I guess, if you include all the ones with a fifth door at the back."

"We've got the three victims I found, then Sarah and this latest one. Five in all. The probability of all five being four door cars randomly selected is two thirds raised to the power of five."

"Which is?"

"Let me think... Eight times four... thirty two over eighty one times three, that's two hundred and forty three—thirty-two over two hundred forty three. In other words, it's less than one in seven!"

"I'm impressed."

"But you see my point. Four doors aren't random. They are likely a factor in the abductions."

"I'll pass it on."

Twenty Seven

*Question (Superintendent Hinx): "Can we move on to
Dastra's appeal? You were quite confident of the outcome?"*

*Answer (DCS Gordonstown): "Totally. So was Brian
Shackerstone. We had Dastra nailed down by every piece of evidence
we had. It appeared to us that he was just hoping against all reason.
The only weakness I could see in our case was that there had been
no semen deposits inside his underpants. A pretty minor point."*

Q: "Which didn't get past the appeal judges."
A: "And quite right too."

*Q: "But he must have been well prepared to get an appeal
together so quickly. It was what? Just over three months. Just before
Christmas."*

*A: "Counsel stuck in for a certificate from the judge straight
away on the basis of the adverse press coverage, and he granted it.
After that we still expected at least six months wait. You only usually
get a quick turnaround for short sentences, but somehow a gap came
up for Dastra. Anyhow, we had little to prepare. It was the same for
his legal team and Aaronovitch moved very quickly. I know it wasn't
the quickest ever appeal, but it was still very fast. The Crown
Prosecution Service and us... well, everybody wanted it out of the
way quickly. It suited Dastra too, because he was kept in hospital
while they tried to reattach his left hamstring and sort out some of
his scarring."*

Q: "His hamstring?"

A: "Sliced through in the prison riot. I think the surgeon joined the ends back together and when I saw him, he had a cast with his foot pointing down like a ballet dancer. Anyway, it meant he went straight from Wemstone General to the Appeal Court."

(Metropolitan Police Service enquiry into Operation Klingsor.)

When Michaela called her to the telephone, Lucy waddled to the sofa and sat down carefully, easing herself back to be comfortable with her bump. "It's Peter Lynch," Michaela murmured, holding out the phone.

Lucy flicked her long red hair back behind her right ear before taking the receiver from Michaela. She put it up to her ear and spoke cautiously. "Hi. Lucy Aybrams speaking."

"Hello, I'm Peter Lynch, Barney's old cellmate. You might have seen me on the telly last month."

"Oh, yes." Lucy relaxed. "Punching the air outside the Appeal Court. How are you?"

"Adjusting to being out. It's really weird. I've lots of people who want to know me, but no real friends left from old times. Barney's one of the few mates I can count on with my back to the wall."

"I know he owes a lot to you."

"And me to him. He's a genius with locks."

"So I've heard."

"Anyhow. I was doing a bit of thinking about his appeal result tomorrow. Will you be going?"

"Yes. I couldn't really be anywhere else."

"No, I guess not. Well. It's just a practical thing. I'm going, of course, to support my mate. I wondered if I could join you up there."

~ * ~

The Law Courts in London's Strand would have been to Lucy's architectural taste if her mind hadn't been on the appeal. The ornate mock-Gothic arches and vaults hide a labyrinth of corridors and courts up spiral staircases and through dark wooden doorways.

Lucy and Michaela had travelled up by train. Dastra, clean-shaven and with his hair trimmed, was brought up from hospital by prison van with his wheelchair folded up in his compartment with him.

Gordonstown, Shackerstone, Graham, Khan, Shanter and Hunt sat in the body of the court during the proceedings, which had gone on for three days and had now been adjourned for lunch on the final day. Prison officers had trouble moving Dastra around the cells in his wheelchair, so gave him his lunch in a room off the court.

The appeal case hadn't sounded particularly good in the cold light of reality, so Lynch, Lucy and Michaela found themselves without much of an appetite for their lunch. When they returned, Lucy caught Gordonstown smiling smugly at her. She scowled back.

It was just after four when the judges returned to the courtroom. One of them read the judgment out, peering at the documents through reading glasses.

"The appellant has submitted four grounds on which he feels his convictions for rape and murder should be quashed.

"The first is on the facts of the case. The appellant's semen was found in the victim and on his own clothing, but not on the inner surface of his underwear. The victim's vaginal fluids were not found on the appellant or on any of his clothing. His claim is that given these pieces of negative evidence, he could not have had sexual intercourse with the victim, and therefore his conviction for rape is unsafe.

"The second is also as to fact and arises out of the first. If intercourse did take place, and the appellant asserts that he has no memory of these events, then the absence of any semen on the inside of the appellant's underwear means that he continued with the murder, disposal and carrying of the body with his penis still on the outside of his clothing, giving obvious risk of injury, which medical evidence shows did not take place.

"The third appeal is as to fact. New evidence discovered since the original trial on a recently murdered young woman places the location of the murder at or near the same place as that of Sarah Carothers. The claim being that since the appellant was in prison at the time he could not have committed this murder himself, and since police throughout have been working on a psychological profile of a single suspect, the appellant claims reasonable doubt on his own conviction.

"The fourth appeal is as to fact. On the second Tuesday of the case, two national newspapers published stories referring to the appellant's relationship with an American student at Oxford University. This was the penultimate day of the trial and the summing up took place on the next day. Although the trial judge made reference to the jury that they should not be influenced by the article, the appellant's view is that the judge should have stopped the trial on the basis that adverse publicity made a fair trial at that time impossible.

"The appeal judges dismissed the first appeal, as there was no other reasonable explanation for the semen inside the victim other than the occurrence of sexual intercourse. Cleansing may have been possible at the scene, especially if this was in a house, as was suggested by the existence of further forensic evidence at the appellant's home. Expert opinion on vaginal fluid gives a clear possibility that intercourse is possible under conditions of force without significant amounts of the fluid being present.

"The judges dismissed the second appeal on the basis that there were circumstances where cleansing of the penis could have taken place after intercourse. The judges were concerned that on this and the first point, the prosecution withheld the material fact that no semen had been found inside the defendant's underwear. The effect of this knowledge on the case was felt to be marginal and was unlikely to result in a different verdict by a jury. It is nevertheless a poor reflection on the diligence of the prosecution."

The judge peered over his reading glasses at the police officers before continuing.

"The judges were not impressed by the third appeal, and found the logic tenuous. They felt that they were being asked to believe that the presence of albeit somewhat unusual soil under a murder victim's toenails that matched soil from the appellant's own case would be sufficient to cast doubt on his conviction. The obvious and single conclusion must be that the crime took place in the same vicinity, and no more. The third point is therefore dismissed.

"On the fourth point, the judges have had considerable discussion. We, as appeal judges, have had to put aside all emotion. This has meant disregarding the considerable suffering that the victim's family have endured, and we do not do this lightly. We have a primary duty to act with legal correctness.

"Given the adverse publicity already in the press together with the quite proper and lawful speculation about the cases with which the appellant was not charged, the jury should have received stronger direction earlier in the trial. The behavior of two newspaper editors in publishing articles about the relationship between the appellant and his paramour in which the appellant is described as, 'The Beast' or 'Dracula' is most reprehensible and proceedings against those papers should inevitably follow. Given that reasonable and balanced prosecution and defense cases were presented to the jury, with prosecution evidence of hairs from Mrs. Carothers actually supporting the defense of consensual intercourse at the defendant's house, the possibility exists of considerable undue external influence being placed on the jurors. Miss Aybrams's testimony was also key to Mr. Dastra's alibi, and therefore central to the defense case. The newspaper articles undermined her credibility in a manner that portrayed her in a conjectural light inconsistent with the evidence presented to the court. Any juror reading those articles could have been seriously influenced. This part of the appeal is therefore upheld."

Peter Lynch leapt from his seat and punched the air. Lucy's eyes brightened as she focused on Dastra who, open-mouthed, gradually let his face break into a cold smile. There was a hubbub of conversation in the court, but no cheering. Lynch sat down, with an abashed but amused shake of his head.

"Silence in court, please. We conclude that the appellant did not receive a fair trial and his conviction is therefore unsafe. We have given long and serious consideration to the issue of a further trial. Although we have grave doubts about the case, and a retrial would be in the broad public interest and the *apparent* pursuit of justice, it is not possible, given the adverse publicity suffered by the appellant, both at the time of the trial and subsequently, to ensure a fair and proper retrial. It is therefore with some reservations, that we must allow the release of the appellant."

"No!" came a shout. It was Sarah's husband. Lucy ignored him as the sound of dozens of conversations filled the court and reporters made a commotion exiting the room. Gordonstown was looking dejectedly at the floor, but Shackerstone followed Lucy with his eyes as she pushed her way past people to get to Dastra. Peter Lynch and Michaela followed her, but John Aaronovitch, who had been sitting closer, got there first.

Dastra got up from the wheelchair and balancing awkwardly on one leg, hopped to the rail with his plastered leg resting on its toes. Aaronovitch grasped his right hand with both of his and shook it vigorously. "A proper result."

"Thanks, John. Thank you so much."

"That's my job."

Dastra watched Lucy pushing her way through the crowded court towards him. The prison guard by him stuck a pen in his hand to sign a form returning his personal effects to him, and he scribbled a signature on the form while paying little attention to it. Lucy came up to the guardrail, eased her bump onto it, and embraced him, sending pen and paper spilling across the floor. He silently hugged Lucy with eyes closed.

"This is an interesting result," commented Aaronovitch, shaking his head. "I'll be dining out on it for months."

Dastra let go of Lucy and he hopped back to his wheelchair.

"Thank you, John," said Lucy "You've done so much work."

"Team effort, Lucy, and you played a very important part."

"I hope so, and kind of you to say that."

Peter Lynch and Michaela had deliberately made slower progress through the throng of barristers, press, families and police in order to give Lucy her moment with Dastra.

"That's the second best news I've had all year, Barney-boy." Lynch leaned over the guardrail to grasp his hand. "Can he go?" he asked the prison guard. The guard motioned with his open hand.

"That's it Barney. We're out of here."

Lynch stepped forward and patted Dastra on the shoulder. "Now for our greatest escape yet!" Lynch pulled the chair away from the divider behind it and spun it round to grab the handles. He wheeled it straight for the main door of the courtroom and out into the corridor. Lucy and Michaela hurried along behind as Lynch drove the wheelchair hard at knots of press people in the way. "Gangway!" They scattered like chickens in front of an onrushing car.

Near the front entrance, Lynch pushed Dastra into a corner and blocked access to him from behind. "We've got to move fast. We'll have press and possibly angry victims' families outside. Michaela, maybe they won't recognize you. Could you slip out quietly and hail a cab?"

"Sure."

"Then, when we see you've got one, we'll run the gauntlet."

Dastra pointed backward at Lynch. "I suppose it would be stupid to say something like, 'You've obviously done this before.'"

"Bloody right!"

Michaela glanced at the front doors and turned to Lucy. "It's pouring out there. Can I use your brolly?"

"What's a brolly?"

"Umbrella."

"Of course, yes." Lucy took a folding umbrella out of her shoulder bag.

"I'll come back and cover you when I've got a taxi." Michaela pulled the umbrella hard down to cover her as she strolled down the shallow steps of the court through the crowd of press and public and out to The Strand. Hailing a taxi took only a few seconds. "Paddington station, please, and could you wait? I'll be right back with your fares."

"Okay, love" he replied, starting the meter. Michaela dashed back, but Lynch was already at the entrance arch with Dastra. He bumped him down the broad steps as the press tried to close in, but once again momentum ruled the day. Microphones were thrust at Dastra, but Michaela pulled the umbrella down over him and fended them off.

"Comment on the result, Mr. Dastra?"

"Mr. Dastra. Were you framed by the police?"

"Mr. Dastra. Some will still see you as Vlad. Any comment?"

Dastra said nothing and was glad to reach the wide and welcoming door of the taxi. He got up and hopped in as Lynch folded the wheelchair.

Lucy was far behind, having spotted Shackerstone on the steps of the court.

"You've got a lucky result, Lucy."

"Have I? Have I... *indeed?* You would call that a *lucky result?"* she shouted back at him, the rain running down her face. "He nearly died! I wanted him back whole."

Shackerstone shrugged, but didn't walk away.

Lucy hurried down to the taxi as Michaela was getting in, folding the umbrella awkwardly in the doorway as a crowd gathered round. She passed it to Lucy then slammed her door. Lucy assisted Lynch in collapsing the chair, then repulsed a pair of burly reporters with thrusts of the half-opened umbrella as she slid in next to Barney. Lynch piled in, pulling the other door smartly closed, crushing the fingers of one reporter, who howled in pain.

"Mr. Lynch. Any similarities with your case?"

"Paddington Station, please!" said Lynch a loud voice, then motioned the driver to pull out. The headlamps of two motorcycles, shimmering through the raindrops, drifted into the stream of cars behind them.

"Driver, at Paddington, take us into the station concourse, as far in as you can get, then at ten past five do a U-turn and take us to Marylebone Station." Lynch produced a twenty-pound note and slid it up and down through a crack in the plastic barrier between them and the driver's compartment.

"Marylebone?" said Lucy. "My ticket is from Paddington."

"Don't worry, we'll get another. There's a train at 5:20 To Wemstone. We'll jump on that. These two on bikes behind us will have called all their mates to Paddington."

Dastra sighed and smiled with satisfaction. "So that's why you gave our destination away. I am impressed. This is like a military operation."

Lynch winked.

Michaela asked, "What do we do at Wemstone?"

"We'll never get there. We'll *buy* tickets to Wemstone, then get off early at High Wycombe, where I parked my car this morning before catching the train up to meet you."

"Then home for tea," added Dastra.

Twenty Eight

Question (Superintendent Hinx): "For the benefit of the tape, tell me how you came to investigate the shooting at Dastra's house in December 1998."

Answer (DS Trimble): "Dastra's place was on my patch and I was late turn CID. Local uniformed units took the initial call, and I went up there as soon as possible."

Q: "What did you find?"

A: "Dastra said he had been there alone when a shot was fired at him. Lucy Aybrams had returned to Oxford. The bullet appeared to have entered through a window at the side of the house, by the piano, and then embedded itself in the tall wall at the side of the room. He said it missed his head by millimetres. I got the folk from the lab up there and they worked out a trajectory. The shot had been fired from inside the garden, from the lawn at the side of the house."

Q: "Did you suspect Dastra had done it himself to get some police protection?"

A: "One keeps an open mind. I had swabs taken from his hands. There was nothing to be found on the grass. They dug a .22 bullet out of the wall, but the impact had destroyed any chance of getting rifle marks off it."

Q: "Did you consider a search of the house to see if Dastra had a rifle?"

A: "Of course, but his house had been turned over when he was first arrested, and with the tabloids on his tail, he wouldn't have had much chance to acquire an illegal weapon."

Q: "Did you offer any advice?"
A: "To Dastra?"

Q: "Yes."
A: "I took a good look round his garden wall. There were places someone could slip over. I went back with a Crime Prevention Officer and a Tactical Advisor from the force firearms unit the following afternoon. We did a written risk assessment of the whole plot. If he could get his wall repaired, and made secure with barbed wire and some sort of alarm, then nobody could get into his garden other than by the gates. The gates were already set up with an intercom, but the CPO suggested a CCTV camera too. The only way to get a shot at the house from outside the wall would be from the woods at the back, and then the only clear view would be into the piano room again. All he had to do was keep the curtains shut along the back. The CPO added a few touches like security lights."

Q: "Was Dastra happy with this?"
A: "No. He wanted an armed team there twenty-four hours a day, which to be honest might have been a better idea. We could have kept tabs on him and protected him at the same time."

Q: "Why wasn't that the recommendation?"
A: "DCS Gordonstown phoned me in the morning and told me there would be covert armed surveillance, because they wanted to catch him trying another murder."

Q: "So Dastra was left flinching behind his curtains."
A: "You could say that."
(Metropolitan Police enquiry into Operation Klingsor.)

Yardley ran the briefing in his office. "As I'm sure you are all aware, Dastra reported a shot fired at him last night. There are also a number of other issues we need to resolve." There were nods from Shackerstone and Gordonstown, sitting on the soft chairs. Nicola Graham had brought in a hard plastic chair from another office.

"For a start, the court judgment is far from clear and it looks like we have been told to treat him as only technically not guilty. Sarah Carothers's husband is going for a civil action so he can get compensation from Dastra."

"Rightly so. This shooting is either a ruse to gain sympathy or a nutter having a pop at him," said Gordonstown. "We need to get back on Klingsor and keep tabs on him until we can put him away again. I just hope we're close enough to stop the next killing. Given our criminal psychologist's view on Vlad, I'd put Aybrams on the potential victim list. We know what Vlad did to his would-be princess."

"All too well, but we don't have a hope of protecting her," protested Shackerstone. "She's bound to go to him at weekends."

Gordonstown shrugged. "I think not, after this shooting, at least not until he's improved his security. A local team is going up to survey the place this afternoon."

Yardley had already made his mind up. "So I think all we can do to cover ourselves is to put a surveillance team on him. That'll give him a bit of protection into the bargain."

"So they'll be tooled up?" asked Gordonstown.

"They'll have to be. The risk assessment more or less dictates it."

"Good. That was easier to agree that I thought it would be. Thanks, Ian."

"Ah, yes. The next thing is a call received from him this morning. Apart from a good moan about the shooting, he has got something of a press siege going on up at his house during daylight, with half a dozen paparazzi outside his gates."

"Serves him bloody right," said Gordonstown.

"So I'm going to ask the local superintendent down there to sort out some PCs to go up to the gates when he wants to come in and out. Or anybody else for that matter. That way our surveillance team gets advance warning of his leaving."

"But he can't get far, surely, without help?" said Gordonstown.

"He can, he's getting his car back from storage," replied Shackerstone.

"But he's got his leg in plaster."

"His Porsche is an automatic and his right foot is fine. He can get anywhere by road. All he has to overcome is the thought of there having been a body in the boot."

"That would only be a problem if he were innocent. If he put Sarah there, there's no reason why the car should give him the creeps."

"I think I'd get rid of the car either way."

"God knows what he will do, but with what we've got at present we need teams in fast cars."

"A Lotus Carlton, a Jag and some bikes," interjected Yardley. "It's the best we can do. The other thing is his status as a police officer."

"What?" they both said in unison.

"Oh yes. Under police regulations Dastra gets reinstated and he gets all of his pay back to the day when he was found guilty."

"The victim's family won't like that." Gordonstown shook his head.

"If you're not guilty, you're not guilty. The regulations were designed to protect coppers from false allegations by criminals."

"But he's hardly fit for work, surely," Graham stated flatly.

"Nor is he likely to be for a long while. Nevertheless, he is reinstated as of Tuesday and I'm writing to him to tell him so. He will be shown on sick leave as long as he keeps the doctor's certificates coming in."

Gordonstown frowned. "Can't we shove him on half pay?"

"Not for six months, and if it turns out that he is totally innocent, the chief constable will probably treat his injuries as received in the execution of duty. He can stay off sick and he won't go on half pay for a long time."

Shackerstone sat back "Well blow me down. I think I might just join him."

~ * ~

Dastra cautiously opened the trunk of his Porsche as the diesel engine of the storage company's low loader echoed into the distance down the lane beyond his gates as it receded into the evening countryside. Professionally cleaned and serviced, the Porsche gleamed under the harsh security lights at the front of the house. His detective's eye scanned every detail of the largely empty space inside the trunk. All the trim and carpets had been replaced as he had requested, the CD player had been swapped for a newer one, and he lifted a corner of a piece of carpet to establish that the deeper recesses of the car had been thoroughly steam cleaned. The car was freezing cold, colder than a mortuary. Of one thing there was no doubt; Sarah's body had been in this very space, yet he had no recollection how it had got there.

He closed the boot and limped briefly back to the house to set the main alarm. Within a minute, he was easing himself into the driver's seat, resting his bad leg at the side of the transmission tunnel and throwing a crutch onto the passenger seat. He turned the key part way in the ignition. The fuel gauge rose to show *full*. He clicked the key one step further and the V8 engine fired and spun into life. He watched the oil pressure gauge rise. A gray-white cloud of vapor condensed around the exhaust in the cold air. Dastra took out a single CD from his inside jacket pocket and slotted it into the main CD player slot in the dashboard. The cabin filled with the opening bars of Sibelius's 2nd Symphony. He selected *drive* and rolled the car down the driveway towards the gates, opening them with his remote control. As they closed behind the Porsche, he wound up the lane to the main road, and turned towards Wallingford.

He didn't speed to start with, but waited five minutes until the engine was fully warmed up. It was during this five minutes that he first saw distant headlamps in his rear-view mirror. Once the engine was at operating temperature, he began to push his speed up as the road meandered along the Chiltern hillsides. He watched the speedometer rise to sixty, seventy, then eighty miles per hour. The lights kept pace. He pushed harder, the Porsche only beginning to reach its designed cruising speeds of above one hundred miles per hour. The lights kept pace with him, two hundred yards back, but then turned off abruptly.

"Who next?" mumbled Dastra under his breath.

A single light now replaced the twin headlamps. He had been handed over to a motorcyclist. There was little chance of him outpacing a bike on these roads, so he eased his speed down until he reached the broader and more gentle curves of the Wallingford by-pass. Here he accelerated away from the bike, pushing his speed up to one hundred twenty, and only slowing for roundabouts and to overtake other cars. The bike could keep up with the Porsche on the main sections, and when overtaking, but the handling of the car on the slippery and potentially icy roundabouts gradually gave Dastra a four hundred yard lead. The last roundabout on the by-pass came up quickly in Dastra's windscreen, and he forced the car all the way round it at speed in order to backtrack his original route, but slowly behind two other cars. The motorcyclist was slowing down for the roundabout, trying to ascertain where Dastra had gone. Dastra surmised that never having seen the strange lights of the Porsche from the front, the motorcyclist would have to guess which exit Dastra had taken, and would guess wrongly.

Five minutes later and there was still no bike in his rear-view mirror. Dastra cruised on across the Oxfordshire countryside, Sibelius filling the cabin of the car. He felt free at last, if only temporarily.

~ * ~

Swinging himself back out of the car under his security lights, he pulled the crutch from the car, and limped to his front door to pick up a second one he had left propped there. He was fumbling for a door key when a bright flash fired. He looked left, and was then caught in a sustained burst of five powerful discharges from a flash gun.

Even though Dastra was powerless to pursue, the photographer behind the flashgun receded quickly into the bushes as Dastra's eyes tried to recover from the dazzle. Dastra found his mobile phone and called the police, before letting himself into his house.

PC Peter Ainsworth, a local officer, arrived only ten minutes later in a police car and went off into the grounds alone in the dark to investigate. After fifteen minutes, he returned to the house and Dastra, still on crutches, ushered him through to the kitchen to make him a mug of tea.

"Well, Mr. Dastra."

"Call me Barney. I am actually still a paid copper in Central Southern Police."

"Sorry, Barney, I've followed a path right down to the bottom of your estate and over the wall at the bottom. That's where he came in. You've got to get your security improved."

"It's in hand. I've got a security company sorted out. They're putting triple barbed wires along top of the whole length of the wall, with an alarm."

"That'll keep them out. Anyhow, I tracked our photographer across a field on the other side."

"You did?"

"Then down to the Reading Road. He was sitting in a car in a lay-by with a mate. You should have seen their faces when I came over the fence right next to them."

"I would have enjoyed seeing that."

"I gave them the gypsy's warning, and stuck them in the book for a bald offside front tire. We can't allow that at this time of year."

"Good. Thanks. I owe you one. You've got more bottle than I would have, tracking someone at night round here."

Ainsworth looked quizzically at Dastra. Dastra thought perhaps he was considering to himself what his host had been convicted of doing in the darkness somewhere. Dastra, propped up against a cupboard, handed him a cup of tea.

"Thanks, uh, Barney. This'll put some feeling back into my fingers. Can I ask you something?"

"Fire away."

"Did you do it?"

"That's pretty direct."

"I'm a direct bloke. Your photographer just now will back me up on that one."

"All right, you can have a direct answer. No I didn't. I know what the evidence looks like, but I didn't, and furthermore, I couldn't have."

"You don't sound sure."

"They whacked me on the head. All I remember is going into the woods. Then I woke up in my car with Sarah in the boot."

"But wasn't your Harry Monk inside her."

"Harry Monk? This is a bit far west for cockney rhyming slang."

"Born and bred in Clapton, mate. But wasn't your spunk in her?"

"Allegedly, but I had a bollock like a balloon the next day. Lucy reckons chummy took some with a hypodermic."

"Sounds a bit farfetched."

"I know. But there is another factor, which nobody looks at. Look at me. Am I a good-looking bloke?"

"This isn't a gay chat-up line is it?"

"Ha! No. Please, tell me. I won't be embarrassed."

"I guess you're pretty average. We both are, like you're an average looking bloke."

"Precisely. So I had pulled the best looking bit of totty in Southern England."

"Oh, yes. I was sort of hoping to get a butcher's hook at her."

"She's gone back to Oxford. You'll have to get a look another time."

"That's a pity."

"Anyhow, would you have stood her up?"

"Not a chance. She looks like every man's dream."

"So you see my point."

"I do."

Dastra asked Ainsworth to carry both their teas into the piano room while he made his way along behind. They then sat down with their mugs and continued the conversation.

"Are you on duty Friday or Saturday?"

"Friday late turn."

"She's moving in for Christmas. I've managed to convince her that it's pretty safe up here again, and she's got loads of college work to catch up on. If you feel you need a 'butcher's hook' that badly, you could arrange to be the unit that sees her in. She's coming up at six, and I'd rather she felt that you were someone I knew, and we weren't up here without a friend for miles."

"No problem, I'll be here at six tomorrow, subject to..."

"The exigencies of duty."

"Indeed."

~ * ~

Ainsworth was as good as his word, and after seeing Lucy in through the gates past a single reporter shivering in the dark, he drove his black-and-white police Metro up the drive behind Lucy's similar but less distinctive red Metro.

Lucy got out of her car quickly, initially concerned by the presence of the police car. Ainsworth swung his legs out of it, but remained seated.

"Are you here to arrest one of us?" said Lucy approaching the driver's door.

"Blimey. No! I called round to see Barney the other night. I thought I'd make another social call." Ainsworth got to his feet.

"Oh, a friend, that's good. It's just that your colleagues seem to like arresting both of us. Can you help me get a suitcase out of the trunk?"

"Sure."

Pete Ainsworth slammed the door shut then went to the back of Lucy's car and lifted out a large suitcase then helped her with another that lay across the backseat. Dastra arrived at the front door on his crutches. Ainsworth carried the suitcases into the hall.

"Thanks Pete, I appreciate that."

"Me too."

"And now you're going to offer your local bobby a mug of rosy."

"Rosy?" asked Lucy as she shut the front door.

"Rosy Lee… tea."

"Sure," said Lucy, making her way to the kitchen. Dastra took Ainsworth to the piano room and sat down heavily on the sofa.

"Bloody hell, mate," whispered Ainsworth. "Crumpet or what? She's even better than in the papers."

Dastra maintained a serious expression on his face. "You can see what I mean though. You wouldn't stand it up, would you?"

"Listen, chum," said Ainsworth, sitting down on the edge of the sofa. "Standing it up ain't the half of it. I wouldn't let it out of my sight. If you ever get tired of loving it, give me a call."

"So do you believe me that I'm not Vlad?"

"Definitely. Quite the reverse, in fact. Some women are worth dying for. She'd make me a serial victim, not a serial killer."

Twenty Nine

Question (Superintendent Hinx): "So the armed surveillance of Dastra continued right through Christmas and the New Year."

Answer (DCI Shackerstone): "Of course. We were just waiting for the next killing. It was driving me mad that it was going to be Lucy."

Q: "But he was in plaster. He was virtually an invalid."

A: "The plaster came off just after Christmas. He was still on crutches over the New Year, but I considered that this might have been for effect. Luckily Lucy went back to live in Oxford before the term started, so we only had to fret about her when she stayed with him at weekends."

(MPS enquiry into Operation Klingsor.)

The surveillance team driver stroked the bristles on his chin before continuing with his debriefing. "About one in the morning and I am heading west on the M40 motorway taking over from Jon on his solo motorbike. He goes on past the Marlow turnoff and the target goes up the slip road. I'm pushing it hard to catch up with him."

"Obviously very hard," commented Shackerstone, with a bitter edge to his voice, looking at the other surveillance team officers in the room for some sort of confirmation. The Klingsor team listened intently as the driver of the Lotus Carlton continued with his account. "Well, yes, boss. Jon said he was touching one-forty up the hill on the M40 out of Wycombe, so we were up to one-fifty just to close on him. I pick up the taillights of a Porsche 928 on the up slip, apparently doing a right around the roundabout at the top. The lights are about to change to red so I push on at about a hundred on the slip road, when I see the target in the left hand lane, turning towards Marlow. I'm on the wrong Porsche, Guv. It was just bad luck. I mean, 928s aren't exactly thick on the ground at any time, and in the dark, this was virtually identical. I hit the brakes and I'm ready to do a left, and if I hadn't hit that patch of ice, I would have made it. The bend is tighter than ninety degrees, and the next thing I know the car is stepping off to the right. The front offside wheel clips the curb and that's about the last I see. The garage sergeant from traffic police says we were still doing seventy. There's a load of impacts on the Carlton and we roll over a few times, I guess, landing upright across the slow lane and the hard shoulder."

"I passed out, Guv, don't remember anything until I was out of the car," said the passenger in confirmation.

"Anyhow," continued the driver. "I could see the target reversing up at speed, and flames shooting out from under us—big engine fire. I couldn't get out—neither of us could. The impacts had crushed the seatbelt stalks between the seats and the transmission tunnel. The target comes flying past us in reverse, blocks the road behind us, and gets out. All I see is him silhouetted against his car lights with no crutch or stick, rock music pumping out of his car. From what had been said by Mr. Gordonstown, I'm expecting to get my throat cut. Either that or I'm about to be burnt alive. Worse still, I actually see the knife come out, one of those Swiss army jobs, and I nearly shit myself. I'm trying to get my pistol out when he says 'Okay, chum, I'm a police officer, are you injured?' I breathe a sigh of relief and say I'm not too bad and to get me out pronto. He cuts the strap and then pulls me clear. He then does the same for Terry, and that's when the fire starts to really go. Terry comes to his senses and runs clear, but our man, still limping, has his sleeve go up and burns the skin on the back of his hand. He comes to the hospital with us for his burns. We've both got whiplash and some cuts and bruises."

"Nothing too bad though, except the whiplash," added the passenger.

"Our man, I had a chat with him up the hospital and I don't

think he's in a good way generally. He's lost a bit of weight, and I heard him tell the triage nurse that he was on antidepressants. He seemed pretty shaky even considering the accident. I mean... he was a lot shakier than either of us. Anyhow, I took pity on him and got a police driver to bring his car back here to the nick, to save him a garage fleecing him for recovery."

"Thanks, I got SOCO White to dust it down as an insurance against future events," said Shackerstone.

"Guv, I don't think there *is* a future in this. We've been up his tail pipes since the week after he came out. He's had press follow him and the girl about and camp on his doorstep. We even ran into one in his garden before his razor wire got put up. He's only had a few visits, some from Lynch, and a few from the local beat officer. When he's away from the house we haven't lost him for more than a few hours in total and then in short intervals. I'm sure his speeding has sweet F. A. to do with escaping us—it's just that night rides are his big escape. The faster he goes the less likely he is to get shot at and if you get close enough you can hear music thumping out of his car. When he's in his drum he sits where we can see him in that big room on the left with the piano—the one where he's supposed to have killed Sarah Carothers. When Aybrams stays, she dotes on him. We've seen them spend Christmas together with Lynch staying for a few nights. Anyhow, I think she's the biggest thing in his life... she would be if she were mine." There was some laughter from the other members of the team. "Anyhow, she must be, with a kid on the way."

"Perhaps we should clip his wings and do him for the speeding."

"We have already had two of our motorcyclists come off."

"And we've fleeced the Police Authority of a written-off Lotus Carlton," Shackerstone added.

"But, Guv, the garage skipper says the ice was the main factor—well, that and the speed. I'm sorry, but to be honest it was a bit of bad luck. I don't even think he rumbled we were Old Bill."

"He might have been cleverer than we thought."

"Well, for my money he's still one of us. Nobody would have criticized him for driving off. It's a bloody miracle he even saw us." There were nods from some of the surveillance team.

Shackerstone continued, "Right, thanks for bringing us up to date. Now there's a bit you need to know before all this goes public. I'm on the telly again Wednesday night on Crimewise. Early last week we finally got a result from our searches for Porterer's car, after trying lakes and rivers near Goring to no avail. Detective Chief Superintendent Gordonstown suggested that, as we have established that Dastra had no help from Aybrams, he might have used Porterer's own car to take her body for burial, before slipping back into the prison. Therefore, the car might not be far away from her burial site. Well, PolSA found it six miles back along the unopened bypass, where the road has already been finished off. It was down a steep embankment in some bushes at the edge of a copse. We reckon our man buried the body and drove the victim's car along the site until he found the paved section then drove it as far back towards the new junction with the M40 as he could. He dumped it and probably hitched a lift on the main motorway.

"There was little of forensic value in the car. All the windows were smashed so it had been well washed by rain, and a lot of leaves and earth had been blown through it. The shit hit the fan a bit with a second car about a hundred yards farther back, in the same sort of condition. The difference was that this one had traces of burnt skin in the boot, and we discovered it was registered to a missing student from Warwick University: one Alexandra Robinson. She was reported just after Dastra got let out. Sorry guys."

"No, Guv. He hasn't been out of our sight for long enough."

"So you say," snapped Shackerstone. "You'd best be sure— your logs will be his alibi. Anyhow, PolSA took another look at the bypass and got ground radar on the short section that hasn't been finished. No luck there, so they looked in the woods where the car was found. Yesterday they got a result...a body is being dug out of a clearing as we speak. Post mortem this afternoon." Shackerstone let the information sink in for the benefit of the surveillance team. "Well, I want you lot to rack your brains for any...and I mean any...possible times he could have dumped her and her car there. We think if the car came in from anywhere, it came in through the small works unit up by the new junction on the M40. It's less than a mile."

"I suppose if he didn't use his car, in theory he could have got out over his wall at night on foot," suggested a DS from the surveillance team. "Once his razor wire was up we had more trouble getting in and out to the house, then the alarm trigger wire effectively locked us out. Still, in a way he's made it into a bit of a prison. I guess he could have slipped over the wall with the alarm switched off, but it would be very difficult. Back when your victim went missing Dastra was in plaster and on two crutches."

"He was. Nevertheless, such is the level of paranoia over Dastra being a free man, that there have been reported sightings of him from helpful busybodies far and wide. We've even got good CCTV of a bloke just like him shopping in Hungary!"

~ * ~

Shackerstone had been sleeping badly and wasn't in the best frame of mind by the afternoon. He didn't find the post mortem particularly easy, and after taking a cursory look at the blackened face on the slab, its scorched lips parted by a bright pink swollen tongue, he took a whiff of the odor and retreated to an anteroom to wait for O'Toole's opinions. It was a lengthy examination and O'Toole came out after three and a half hours.

"I can understand you staying out for this one Brian. It's enough to put you off roast pork."

"We've got a possible ID on her... a student from Warwick. She was reporting missing before Christmas. Alexandra Robinson... Sandy to her friends."

"Okay then, this one's female as you know. Approximately twenty years old, white... originally, five foot four inches, light build, skin heavily burnt, and she was still alive when the burning commenced."

"Shit."

"That's only the start of it. By marks on the body and lack of burning along patches down the spine, I'd say she was burnt alive while chained to a wooden stake."

"To a stake?"

"There is quite a bit more...and it's not pleasant."

"Is it ever?"

"The fire had been put out, obviously, or we'd only have ashes and a few of the larger bones. Her body had been quenched with water soon after death."

"Okay... and?"

"There are unusual injuries to her fingernails, fingers and toes, and rope burns on her wrists and ankles which suggest that she might have been subjected to torture."

"Right."

"I followed up the torture line. There is a lot of damage to the shoulder joints. I think she may have been hoisted up by her arms tied behind her back. The Inquisition called it the *strappado*."

Shackerstone looked hard at O'Toole. "Bit of an expert on the medieval, aren't you?"

"The macabre is my business, luckily for you. Your lads have photographed all the injuries and your SOCO has done his bit. There's still histology and entomology to come... let me know about entomology, I need to cross-reference with time of death for professional verification. Your lads say they could be done in a couple of days."

"I'll have the results phoned through. Once they are in I'm going to have Dastra in for interview. Can you give me an approximate date of death, so I can check his whereabouts?"

"Hard to say... burning doesn't help... three to five weeks, and tortured in the forty-eight hours before death. The wounds haven't had time to heal."

"I'm back on the television tonight for another appeal. Can't you give me anything else?"

O'Toole pushed his glasses hard onto the ridge of his nose, looked blankly at Shackerstone and shook his head.

~ * ~

Shackerstone made a confident and unflustered appearance on Crimewise, asking for public help on the movements of Francesca Porterer and Sandy Robinson. As requested before the program, the announcer didn't question him on the innocence or guilt of Dastra, or if he had any suspects. Millions watched, and undoubtedly, millions drew their own conclusions.

Thirty

In the cross-hairs I can try
To shoot the baby in the eye
Baby squeals and then it's dead
My airgun pellet in its head.

Wait for mum to find the prize
Her offspring dead before her eyes
She screams and sobs and screams again
It echoes on inside your brain."

(Extract from small red notebook, exhibit BS14, found in glove box of vehicle exhibit BS2.)

Detective Sergeant Martin Buckler had been on the Metropolitan Police Obscene Publications squad at New Scotland Yard for six months. Today, an amusing perk for him was to introduce an hour-long tape of the most obscene and shocking clips of pornographic film that the squad could find for the benefit of a group of recruits fresh from finishing police training school. As most of the practices portrayed on the tape would beggar the belief of even the worldliest viewer, he knew the officers would return to their new postings with a fresh outlook on the depths of human depravity that would harden them for the rigors ahead.

After introducing the group to the tape and explaining everyone's right to walk out if they felt uncomfortable with the content, he went and worked in an adjacent office (having watched the tape several times before), listening to the nervous laughter and giggles as minds were opened to bizarre sexual fetishes. After fifty minutes, he returned to the room to watch the faces of the probationers. The video soundtrack issued a series of screams. Buckler watched the faces of the recruits become variously expressionless, reddened or pale. The screaming on the videotape continued.

"Bloody hell," said an older male recruit, looking away.

"Please feel free to leave," said Buckler. "Don't feel there's any peer pressure to stay. It gets a lot worse than this."

"Is she really being tortured?" asked a woman officer.

"We think so," answered Buckler.

"God, that's disturbing."

The tape continued. There was some foreign dialogue, followed by some crowd noises.

"Have they dubbed the crowd noise over, Sarge? There don't seem to be more than three actors, the girl and the two hooded monks."

"It's dubbed for sure and the dialogue has been put into Serbo-Croat. We don't know what the original was."

"Oh, no, I can't watch this," said a male officer. He got up and left the room without looking back. A female officer got up and walked out after him. The others watched for three grueling minutes and then Buckler stopped the tape.

"You're probably among only a handful of human beings alive today who have ever watched someone being burnt at the stake. I'm sorry to show you that, but until a week ago snuff movies were an urban myth. All the others have been clever fakes or hurried clips of Balkan war atrocities. This doesn't quite fit the supposed legend of the snuff movie: the actress should be a willing young would-be star who plays along until she realizes she is going to be killed. It looks like they take an unwilling victim from the outset and get the acted part from another source. This one was edited into a longer and genuine 1978 film about Joan of Arc. The victim was obviously picked for her likeness to the original actress."

"Sarge?"

"Yes?"

"Did you see Crimewise last night?"

"No," replied Buckler with a smug smile. "When you've been in The Job a while, you'll find crime programs are a big turnoff."

"Well, I think she's a murder victim from Central Southern Police."

"That's right," said another, "I knew I had seen her before."

Buckler tried to protest. "Sorry guys. But this isn't an English film."

"Sarge, her body was found burnt. It was one of two. The other was beheaded."

"Beheaded? That's... very interesting. We've got another film..."

After DS Buckler had left the recruits to look at some hard-core pornographic magazines, he took an elevator to another floor to obtain some photographs of the two murder victims from Central Southern police's Internet pages. The lift on the way down was crowded with a group of independent advisors on their way out of the building from a meeting. In the mirror at the back of the blue-carpet-lined elevator car Buckler noticed the hearing aids in the ears of one of them.

"Excuse me, sir?"

"Yes."

"Can you lip-read?"

"Very well, but why?"

"Can I borrow just half an hour of your time? It's very important. It could solve two murders."

"Certainly, I'll just have to speak to my driver... I'm afraid she'll have to feed the meter."

~ * ~

A phone rang in the Wemstone incident room. The phones were staffed for the hoped-for calls arising from Crimewise, but few calls had come in. Tony Shanter took the call.

"Incident room."

"Is that the incident room at Wemstone?"

"Yes, it is. DS Shanter. How can I help?"

"Hi. This is DS Buckler from the Met's Obscene Publications Unit. I've got a video your squad needs to see."

"Oh yes?" said Shanter, evincing disinterest.

"Yes. It's of your two latest victims being murdered."

Shanter sat up. "Are you certain?"

"I watch these things for a living. I'm as certain as I can be. I've got their circulation photos from your force Internet site for comparison."

"But videos? Snuff movies?"

"More or less. Most unusual ones. It appears that the producers like to hide the killings in historical costume dramas. Your victim Porterer looks like she was marched to the guillotine as Marie Antoinette. Your second lady, Sandy Robinson, starred briefly as Joan of Arc. There's quite a bit of torture and then later in the film they burnt her alive at the stake. And I mean actually alive."

"But videos? Shit."

"There's a lot more you need to know. The films are dubbed into Serbo-Croat, and the snuff sequences edited into older films with the rest of the story. It's a perfect cover for moving them about, and how many of us search a genuine two hour film for three or four minutes of snuff?"

"How long have you had the films?"

"A week. They were seized by police in Croatia and copies sent out via Interpol as a fishing exercise to see if any of us know where they came from. We never even considered an English connection. Well, there was nothing in the film to suggest they were from here, at least not until now. In fact, I was so unsure that I pulled in a deaf bloke off an advisory group to lip-read the victims. I've got him doing a transcript."

"Thanks. That could be very useful. I'm still having trouble taking all this in. I don't suppose there are any films of impalings as well?"

"No, sorry, I guess you're thinking about the Vlad jobs."

"Yes, it might have given us a clearer picture on our prime suspect."

"I'll push that one back to Interpol. Something might turn up."

"Can you get the videos up here? It's pointless all of us coming to you."

"I'm getting copies done now. I'll get a car to run me up."

"How long?"

"An hour."

"I'll start calling the troops in. The top brass need to see this."

~ * ~

Brian Calver observed the reactions of the team as they watched the videotape on a large TV monitor. He cast his mind far back to when he had been Shackerstone's parent constable, showing him the job back in 1970. To harden him up, Calver had taken him to a grisly post mortem and Shackerstone had vomited on the mortuary floor. He knew Shackerstone would be first to get up, and he wasn't wrong. Shackerstone nearly ran back into his office, before pouring himself a Scotch. With his large dark hands trembling, he splashed some of it onto his desk.

Gordonstown followed him into the room. "I'll have one too, Brian." Shackerstone got out another glass, and seeing Yardley also leaving the officers crowded around the television, he set out another glass and sat down behind his desk.

"DI Graham!" he shouted. "You need to be here. DS Buckler. Tony."

As Graham entered, ashen-faced, he pulled out a fourth glass and after ensuring all had a full measure, he passed them to his guests. Buckler wandered in with Shanter.

"Scotch, Sarge?"

"Thanks, but no."

"Tony?"

"Guv."

"Shut the door, then. Take a pew everyone."

They found seats and settled down silently, sipping their whiskies. Nobody said anything for over thirty seconds, and it was Nicola Graham who spoke first.

"How are we going to tell the victims' families? Not to mention the press."

Yardley spoke with deliberation. "You're right. We'll need a bloody good press strategy on this one. We can't release our copies, but every hack in Europe will be on the hunt for them and any others once the story breaks."

Buckler offered, "We've no idea on the numbers out there and it's impossible to know."

Gordonstown lifted his glass and rotated it in his hand, watching the golden liquid clinging to the sides. "I think we need to keep it under our hats for now, Ian. With luck, we'll get the bastards soon and we can keep the whole lot *sub judice* until after the trial. I can't see how releasing any details about the films can advance the investigation much. They tell us the girls were murdered. The only face you get to see apart from the victims is a side-on shot of the bloke who rapes Porterer in her cell. We can always release his face as a still as if it has come off a CCTV."

"But, Guv," said Graham, "we need to establish a location... there must be a temporary studio somewhere. These people need equipment, lights, costumes and all that sort of gear. This isn't some amateur job and a lot of the snuff footage was well filmed. You've not seen any like this before, have you, Sarge?"

"No, these two are the first we—"

Gordonstown cut him off. "But there are no clues in the film. The backgrounds could be painted, except the cell they were both in—that looks pretty real or they would have changed it around. I guess the technical bods could get rid of the people and make up composite pictures of the scenes. We could release those as stills but it might give away too much to the press."

Behind his desk, Shackerstone put his hands together as if praying, and pressed them hard against his lips in thought. Eventually he picked up his glass, hand shaking. "Our criminal psychologist said chummy would have no pride. He was barking up the wrong tree there. They've got pride by the spade load."

Yardley grimaced, "You know, I'd never realized how much blood shoots out when someone is beheaded."

They all looked at the floor, deep in thought. Shackerstone downed his drink.

Gordonstown came in with false enthusiasm. "Come on everyone. We need to get on with an investigation strategy. We need some technical analysis of the film to give us some clues as to the crime scenes. We'll get some stills of the costumes and the suspect. We'll need some more stills of the equipment... the guillotine and the rack for a start. Some theatrical supplier somewhere must be able to give us a link back to our suspects. The other route is back through the chain of supply of the film."

Buckler agreed. "We can help there."

"Good. Anything else?"

"Geology, Guv," said Shanter. "We've still got the soil off both bodies. We do know the scene is in a building with that clay on the floor."

"Good. Yes. Very good, and it all fits. Porterer was on her knees a lot... it accounts for the clay under her toenails. And we found out just this morning that Robinson had the clay baked into the gaps between her toes. It all adds up."

"Except we have visited every building on that clay. There were only twenty-seven. We'll have to take a second look now that we have seen the film, but I wouldn't hold your breath. We must look at the doll business again too."

"Yes, we'll go over that again with much greater resources. Someone out there knows where it came from."

"And the impalings, Guv?"

"Oh, yes. We've got to take another look at those."

Shackerstone agreed, "Yes, the clay soil is the same."

"Which means we go looking for more films," continued Gordonstown.

"We'll do our best, sir," Buckler added, "but it will take time."

Yardley continued with a bitter edge to his voice. "Where does this leave Dastra?"

"A possible member of the film crew? More to follow? Who knows?"

Yardley tapped on the table. "Face the facts. I can understand why you both need to keep Dastra in the frame...you both have a good bit riding on the original result, even if he is free now. However, this film changes everything. We know now he probably couldn't have done Porterer, and God knows, Josh, you've made a fool of us trying to prove that he did."

Gordonstown frowned. Buckler made a polite exit with Tony Shanter as Yardley continued, "And he stood up that girl of his, the best looking bit of crumpet ever to be dragged into our custody office."

"It wasn't quite dragging."

"Anyhow, from where I sit, Dastra is looking more innocent

by the day. The Robinson job must clinch it."

"He shook our blokes off his tail a few times—he might have joined his chums at this cell somewhere."

"Get real! He's been under constant surveillance... unless he slipped out at night to a second car. This was when he was still in plaster and on two crutches."

Gordonstown's frown deepened as the weight of Yardley's arguments wore him down. Yardley continued, "Okay. I know he isn't out of the woods yet, but he's heading that way. And I'm not prepared to carry on spending a fortune in overtime having a surveillance team following him about twenty-four seven. They've wrecked a bloody Lotus Carlton and crashed two motorbikes. All we have to show is a lot of unusable evidence of speeding offences!"

"Ian. Please. Keep the team on him."

"Give me one reason why I should, Josh."

"Because two out of the three scenarios still have him as a suspect and he might kill again."

"Then *you* pay for further surveillance."

"I would, but my surveillance budget is shot. Can you leave it on until the picture is a bit clearer?"

"It stops on Sunday. That's my best offer... the officers have already been warned to be available. Sir."

"Thanks for nothing."

Yardley got up and left with an air of contempt, saying nothing more. Gordonstown turned his attention to Graham and Shackerstone, waiting for Yardley to move out of earshot.

"Yardley is full of shite. At the moment, Dastra is still a possibility, either as an accomplice or as a copycat. If he is an accomplice we could get back through him to the others."

Graham replied tersely, "Or we could be wasting our time, sir. Covering earlier mistakes..." She got up and walked out, shutting the door behind her.

"We've got to look after ourselves on this one, Brian. Nobody else will..."

"We? You dig your own grave! In the beginning I... I was convinced he was our man. I still believe he did Carothers. But the rest, it doesn't fit anything."

"Don't let it get to you, Brian."

"Get to me?" Shackerstone stood up and leaned over his desk, arms locked straight and hands resting in the whisky splashes. "Get to me? Get to *me*! It's been getting to me since we dug up the first bodies. I can't sleep at night from worrying about whether Dastra is our man. It was you who kept the fucking pressure on me to keep him in the frame when I started to have doubts. I still think he could kill Lucy. Until today I didn't know what to think. I'm not eating. I'm losing weight. I'm hitting the fucking bottle. My mouth is permanently dry and I sleep at best two hours a night. All I can see is the faces of the victim's families and the face of Lucy Aybrams accusing me of setting Barney up. Now, get this straight. I'm going to see heads coming off! I've managed to get half a dozen inmates at the prison charged with his attempted murder, and I'm still on a guilt trip like a bloody round the world cruise. Somewhere along the line, one of us cocked-up. I don't know where, but I'm not spending another fucking minute watching my back or yours. I've done my best. I've given all I can to this bloody case. I can't think straight anymore."

"Sir?" Khan's voice came from the door. "I know this isn't a good moment, but entomology has come back on Robinson. They reckon she was in the ground two weeks before Dastra was released."

Shackerstone turned to Gordonstown with a look of angry satisfaction. "That's it! I'm going off sick. Right this minute. With stress. You can have Operation Klingsor. And Vlad has shown you exactly where to stick it."

Thirty One

Question (DI Nicola Graham): "Did you make...?"
Answer (Suspect one): "Please let me finish..."

Q: "Go on."
A: "Then comes the trap and the excitement of the hunter cornering his prey. Then the elaborate, yes... ritualistic preparations for the kill... you get to know them... the victims... you know, there is a fascination for seeing the life still in them... knowing you will take it... and then seeing it gone. But first, the humiliation. The rape."

Q: "Go on."
A: "The rapes are special. Sex is about the giving of life; this is about taking it."

Q: "Did you rape them all?"
A: "No, not always. You can't do three in a row, for instance. And then there was that Sarah bird. I took her from behind in the back of the Porsche."

Q: "A bit tight for space."
A: "Her or the car?"

Q: "(Pause) The car."
A: "Then there is the execution itself... the last moments of terror on the part of the condemned... that's a big factor... a selling point... just like the Romans watching the Christians waiting to be

eaten by lions. The process of death... the slower deaths are best...
all oddly fascinating... but the death itself is a release. But that
moment has to be captured. Then it's art."
(Extract from evidential tape transcript.)

~ * ~

"David Dastra and John Aaronovitch for an appointment
with DCI Shackerstone," said Dastra to a squat female reception
officer at Wemstone police station.

"He's off sick. You're expected though. I'll give DI Graham
a ring."

She made a short call before returning to the counter.

"She's sending someone down."

Dastra sat down on a blue metal bench to rest his leg, while
Aaronovitch read the latest posters of CCTV stills of suspects for
local crimes. Superintendent Yardley appeared from a doorway
rubbing his hands. "Barney! Welcome back." He shook Dastra's
hand, half helping him to his feet. "And Mr. Aaronovitch. Perhaps
you'd both come up to my office."

"We'd like to, Superintendent, but my client has an
appointment to be interviewed as a possible suspect."

Yardley gave them both a knowing smile. "My office, gents.
There's something to your advantage... you can speak to acting DCI
Nicola Graham later."

Aaronovitch exchanged glances with Dastra. Yardley
showed them through the station and took them up to his office. The
elevator had been refurbished and now had an electronic voice that
announced each floor. Yardley's office was still much the same and
he seated his guests in comfortable chairs by a low table before
ordering teas and coffees.

He went to his desk and opened the top drawer. He took out
a small black leather wallet and two pieces of paper. "I've been
dying to do this. I just wish Mr. Gordonstown could share this
moment with me."

"Sir?"

"Your warrant card, Barney." He handed the items to him.
"You haven't asked for it back, and as the law stands you have been
entitled to it since the day you won your appeal."

"Really?"

"Not guilty is not guilty, all rights restored. And there is a new car pass and a list of the door codes to the nick. You'll be needing them."

"I will?"

Yardley came back round from behind the desk and sat down on the remaining armchair.

"Did you watch Crimewise on Wednesday?"

"I did."

"Well, a bunch of Met probationers on a day trip to the naughty books squad at Scotland Yard yesterday had also been watching... doing their homework, I guess. Anyhow, they were shown a clip from the nastiest snuff movie The Job can find. They spot that our lady Sandy Robinson is in it... as the victim. I can tell you it was disturbing... the stuff nightmares are made of. She was tortured and burnt alive in a sort of pseudo historical add-in to a genuine film about Joan of Arc. They dug about and found another film with the other victim, Francesca Porterer in it as an unwilling Marie Antoinette with the inevitable outcome."

Dastra breathed in deeply and let out a long sigh. "I don't suppose there are any films about Vlad the Impaler?"

"No, not yet. But I'm sure there will be. It's just a case of waiting for them to turn up. It's not a very western subject. Interpol is putting feelers out and requests have been made directly to the police around the Balkans. The point of all this is that you are in the clear. None of the three suspects in the films is of your height and build. We've had a surveyor come in and do some projections based on the known height of the victims. DI Graham has already eliminated you from being a film star."

Dastra sat open mouthed.

"That's not all," continued Yardley. "We've found out how they trap their victims. You knew about the doll found on the road with Porterer's prints on it?"

"Yes, I was told by Lucy... I understand a WPC had told her."

"This place still leaks like a sieve. Anyhow, our researchers have been trawling crimes all over the country, and we found an attempted abduction in Surrey, a SEPol job, although the train of events began locally. Girl driving home on New Year's Eve, alone, spies what she thinks is a baby in the road. Gets out to look but it's just a doll. Kicks it away, gets back into her car. Before she knows it a biker has smashed her car window, and she drives like the blazes round to her dad's place, just over the border into Surrey. She runs into his house, expecting to be accosted by the guy on the bike. He's trying to stop her to tell her that a dark figure had slipped into her nearside back door while she was stopped. Chummy decamps from the back of her car and off into the night."

"I don't suppose they got a look at him?"

"No."

Teas and coffees arrived and Yardley questioned Dastra about his health and his likely recovery time. He talked to him about the car crash and the burn on his hand.

"Which makes you a victim and a potential witness, and I guess the victim support scheme will want to get in touch with you now we know you're not a serial killer. Anyhow, let's go up to the third floor and speak to Nicola Graham; she'll have a great deal to tell you."

Thirty Two

Question (Detective Inspector Graham): "Okay, that's pretty clear. Tell me about the impaling."

Answer (Suspect): "Hazel shafts are straight and stiff. You need one about as thick as a child's arm."

Q: "Where did you get them from?"
A: "Up in some woodlands above Goring. You cut them yourself, with one of those Swiss Army knives with a saw blade—that way nobody sees you going into woods with a saw. Once you've cut your rod, you slice the wood off one end until you have a point... not too sharp mind... about forty five degrees is enough, and plenty of splinters. (pause) Any sharper and they slide down too fast."

Q: "God! (long pause) For the benefit of the tape, can you say who or what you mean would slide down it too fast?"
A: "Yes. Young women. (pause—sigh)"

Q: (Long pause) "Can you describe how you set about...? Can you describe how you went about obtaining your victims?"
A: "Sure, but it should be obvious even to you lot that you can't tour the countryside with ten feet of hazel rod sticking out of your sunroof. No, you have to get them to come to you."

Q: "How?"
A: "It's almost an urban myth... a lone driver at night sees what appears to be a baby in the middle of a quiet country road. The

trap was improved a bit with some broken glass, skid marks and a bit of fishing line to make the doll's arm move. Your driver stops to check, and she only finds a doll. While she is out of the car her kidnapper slips into the backseat of her car. It takes a lot of care and you mustn't push your luck."

Q: *"How?"*
A: *"For a start, the driver will only fall for it if they haven't heard the story. And you need a windy night to cover the noise of slipping in to the backseat of the car."*

Q: *"Is this why all the cars were four-door?"*
A: *"Exactly. It's too difficult to get into the back seats of a two door."*

Q: *"Why didn't you get into the victims' cars when they were parked and empty?"*
A: *"Because they might return with passengers. The places would be wrong too. Too busy, perhaps. The whole point of getting in on a lonely road was that you could minimize the time between getting in and taking control. You can't risk them turning into home at the next entrance."*

Q: *"So how did you choose them? It couldn't be the first female who happened along."*
A: *"You watch at the turn into your chosen road and then if a possible comes along and turns off, you block the road off and phone ahead. The man at the chosen spot pushes the doll out. Some don't stop. Others don't get out. Some have got the back doors locked. Some aren't pretty enough."*

Q: *"But you nearly got caught."*
A: *"Some arse appeared from a dark farm track after I had slipped into a girl's car. He ran up and tried to stop her driving off, even smashing the back window. I was showered with bloody glass. The next thing I know he is on our tail on his motorbike, and she's driving like blazes to get away from him. She thinks he's the bloody killer! You couldn't believe my luck... the only thing was the driving.*

Twenty minutes pressed to the floor in the back of a car being chased by a bike is the greatest recipe for motion sickness. When she stopped, I wanted to be out like a hare, but I was staggering like a drunk. I can't believe I made it."
(Excerpt from evidential tape transcript.)

Joanna Carter kicked the doll out of the bright patch of road lit by her headlamps and into the featureless woodland darkness of the ditch beyond the verge. Pulling her blue waxed-cotton coat back around her against the wind she ran back to the open door of her Range Rover and got back into the driver's seat, fastening her seatbelt and slamming the door. She flicked her long curly brown hair behind her and pulled away, paying little attention to a smaller car's headlights that had now appeared in her rear-view mirror.

She had driven perhaps half a mile before sensing an intuitive uneasiness. For a moment she thought she had felt a presence in the car but was in the mental process of dismissing the idea when the cold silencer of a large revolver was pressed to the left side of her neck.

"Keep driving," said a flat male voice in her left ear.

Joanna's heart raced. "What?"

"Drive!"

She didn't dare to turn her head. Her mouth began to go dry. She tried to catch sight of her passenger in the rear-view mirror: a black silhouette against the headlights of the car behind.

"Oh God, no! What do you want?"

"Keep driving. Go left here."

The car behind followed. Joanna's adrenaline rush made her think fast. She touched a button on the door and the driver's window lowered, letting in the road noise and the wind. She let her arm drift up ready to try to make some sort of signal to the driver in the other car.

"He's with me," said the gunman.

"What do you want? Please. I've got plenty of money. You can have it all. Please don't…"

"Keep driving."

"Look, I've got over five hundred pounds in my bag."

"Keep driving. Turn into the gap in the field on the left."

"Please. No! What are you going to do to me? Please."

"Turn. Now. Bitch!"

Joanna reluctantly slowed the Range Rover and began to turn into the field. She stamped hard on the accelerator. The car straightened up and struck the end of a dry stone wall by the right gatepost. There was a double bang as the revolver discharged through the windshield, accompanied by the split-second punch of the driver's airbag. Joanna's unwelcome passenger hit the front seats with a cry of pain that she missed in the temporary deafness caused by the airbag explosion. Stunned for a moment, she tried to free her seatbelt. In the confusion there was a hand reaching in from the window and a rag being pressed hard over her face. She turned and stared in wide-eyed terror at a ski-masked figure by the door. The hard purity of a chlorinated hydrocarbon seared at her mouth and nostrils.

She instinctively tried to claw the rag off her face, but her assailant seized the fingers of her right hand and twisted them away over the side of the door. Her left hand had more success, and for a moment she pulled the pad away enough to let out a determined cry. The passenger twisted her left hand away into an arm-lock. The pad was back over her face and her body began to twitch as she struggled to break free. Her back arched involuntarily, forcing the front pockets of her jeans against the bottom of the steering wheel. Gradually Joanna's body stopped twitching and relaxed as she surrendered her consciousness. Her last sensation was losing control of her bladder.

~ * ~

Joanna was awake and her head hurt. She eased her eyes open, but it made absolutely no difference to her vision. It took her a moment or two to realize that she wasn't waking at home in her own bed. Her own bedroom was dark, but the darkness was in no way as total as the darkness that now surrounded her. The next thing she realized was that she was lying on a thin mattress, quite naked, and covered by a thick but coarse blanket. Her surroundings felt damp and cold, and there was a mixed smell of stale sweat and urine. She got up cautiously and wrapped the blanket around her, pushing the bulk of it over one shoulder. For a moment she tottered uneasily on a cold steel floor while blood rushed from her head. With one arm rigidly outstretched and fingers widely splayed, she felt her way forward into the utter blackness. Within a few careful steps, she touched a metal wall. She turned right and moved slowly around the room, finding the four corners at intervals of about twenty feet. Her heart sank as she reached the last corner. She had never passed a door. She started to scream. And scream. And scream. And no other living thing heard her.

Thirty Three

"Take the bitch and make her see
How the end for her will be
When she sees she's going to die
Let her scream and let her cry
Be there for her final breath
Be her company in death."
(Extract from small red notebook, exhibit BS14, seized from suspect.)

After a night getting the Carter investigation rolling, Nicola Graham made a call. "DC Dastra?"

"Yes?"

"Hi, Barney, it's DI Graham. I need some help."

"From me?"

"It's important and it might help you."

"I'm listening."

"I've been reviewing all the original evidence and I've found something. I want you to deal with it."

"But I'm still off sick. Gordonstown said if I return I can't be on the enquiry."

"That still applies. But you're the one person likely to be able to action this within a day."

"A day?"

"We're one hundred per cent sure they've taken another woman. She piled her car up, and there's a gunshot from inside the windshield. SOCO White has found traces of Trichloromethane and two strange sets of fibers and hairs in the car. As far as I'm concerned, they are filming her now. I need you to deal with this action, on the hurry-up."

"I can't... I can't even think about The Job. Anyhow, why me?"

"It's the geology. There's something odd about the soil samples. According to the report attached to the data, the samples all had a lot of lime in them."

"We always knew that from the burials."

"That's what everyone thought, but the sample from your car had similar levels, and as far as we know Sarah hadn't been near a limed grave, unless... Anyhow, everyone missed it."

"I can't see it helping me either way."

"Hell! Forget yourself for one minute."

"Sorry."

"I've got a thirty-year-old mum out there about to be topped in a way we are only likely to find by seeing a video after a few weeks. Her name is Joanna Carter. Her husband is being comforted by the FLO team now. Her kid is off with the in-laws. We need a lucky break... a big one... but I believe in creating my own luck. The soil is supposed to be unique and we have searched every building on it. We now realize that the original soil from the scene of the crime had traces of lime in it before the burials took place. Right now, you are my only hope and I'm sticking my neck out. I need a result. Get your arse up here and collect this action."

~ * ~

Joanna listened carefully for any noise in the absolute darkness. She had no sensation of the passage of time, but she guessed she had been listening for several hours when she heard footsteps and voices. The sound seemed to be getting closer, but some way below her. There was a loud metallic clang somewhere in the middle of the room, followed by a bright light being shone in her eyes. After such total darkness, a match struck in the room would have hurt, but the flashlight caused her to shut her eyes tight against the pain.

A few seconds later, a hand seized her hair and dragged her towards the middle of the room. She screamed and kicked out, but felt a second person taking her around the waist. She was then dropped through a hatch and landed awkwardly on a mattress in a brighter space. Before she could open her eyes, a blanket was thrown over her head and her hands tied behind her with some thin nylon rope.

"What's happening? Where am I?"

There was no reply.

"Please. Please. Can I have my clothes back? I'm cold."

"We have clothes for you," whispered a man's voice through the blanket. "Lovely clothes."

Large hands took her by the shoulders and guided her forward. She sensed a cold and muddy floor under her feet, and that they might be guiding her along a passage. She heard the echo of a voice in the distance and sensed from the slap of feet on the floor that there were two people walking with her.

"I'm very frightened. Please, I want to go home."

There was no reply, but her guide pushed her on for another minute or so. He stopped abruptly and turned her to the right. She was pushed forward about six feet, and then the rope round her wrists was loosened. She felt the heavy hands leave her shoulders. There was the sound of a metal door slamming behind her.

Joanna struggled with the rope and let the blanket fall from her. She was in a windowless room about twenty feet square and ten feet high, lit by a bright row of fluorescent lamps running across the top of the wall above the metal door. These, however, were the last trace of modernity in the room. The other three walls were made of bare gray stone, and the surface was punctuated by iron fastenings and two rusty lengths of chain. From the wall ahead of her there projected two iron manacles, close together and about six feet up.

Joanna pulled her hands from the rope and picked up the blanket, pulling it over her shoulders and wrapping it around her body.

"There is food," said a voice.

Joanna spun round to speak, but the room was quite empty.

"In the corner. Bread. Biscuits. Eat!"

Joanna isolated the sound to a small speaker up high above the door. Next to it, a small closed circuit TV camera appeared to be following her movements.

"What do you want?" she shouted.

"Eat!"

"No. I don't want to. I want to go home. Can I have my clothes?"

"Clothes are on their way, but you need to eat."

"Clothes first."

"As you wish."

Joanna sat on the floor by the food. A sealed bottle of mineral water caught her eye, so she opened it and after tasting it cautiously, she drank it.

"Your clothes are here," said the voice on the loudspeaker.

"Where?"

The door opened and a short, dark haired man of about twenty-five walked in. He carried what appeared to be a long ball gown on a coat hanger, covered by the thin polythene used at dry cleaners. He hung the dress up on one of the iron staples, smiled weakly at Joanna, and left the room, slamming the door behind him.

Joanna got up and walked over to the dress.

"It's your size," said the voice.

Joanna put her arm out from underneath her blanket, lifted the plastic cover, and looked at the dress, puzzled. It was gray and trimmed with fur. A bright crimson underskirt gave it volume and made the bottom of it spring out away from the wall.

"I don't understand," she shouted. "What is this?"

"A nice pretty dress."

"Why?"

"Beautiful women must have beautiful things."

She stroked the fur, admiring the dress but then got a grip on the reality of her situation.

"You didn't abduct me for a fashion show. For heaven's sake. What is this all about? Why am I here? Who are you?"

"That is unimportant. Please put the dress on. We can do this the easy way, or the hard way. Either way, you end up doing what I want."

"Look, I think you have made a mistake and grabbed the wrong lady. Just let me go. I don't know where this place is, and I haven't seen any…"

She realized that they had let her see the man carrying the costume. A deep intuitive fear told her they weren't planning to let her live.

Thirty Four

"...and he will insert himself into the investigation. This is because he needs to feel some control over the forces he fears most; those who have been set to hunt him down."

(Extract from report of Dr. Rob Holt made in June 1998 for Operation Klingsor.)

Gordonstown was at DI Graham's door.

"Nicola."

"Good morning, boss. Come in."

Gordonstown sat down on the chair by the door.

"How are things?"

"There's not much more than I told you yesterday at the press briefing."

"I need everything. I'm already using this latest development to fight off a review on the rest of Klingsor by HQ. I need to be up to speed."

"Okay."

"And you had Dastra in earlier."

"Yes. He can come and go. You approved his return to the main CID office when he eventually returns from sick."

"Yes, but between you and me, I still have him somewhere in the frame."

"Last night we gave him an alibi. He would have been pushing it hard to do this one: he was phoned at home by DS Shanter at 9:30."

"But what about with that car of his?"

"He did have a window, the last half hour or so of the possible interval... but he's still twenty percent disabled."

"Not too disabled to save two officers from a car crash."

The telephone on the desk rang. Graham picked it up. "DI Graham."

"Ma'am. DC Dastra."

"Oh, uh, good. Any news?"

"I've had a hunch. I took the findings back to our expert. He agrees."

"With what?"

"The lime has probably come from mortar, between bricks."

"Not quicklime?"

"You add quicklime to water to get lime. The result is chemically identical, what differs are the other particles present. It looks like our scene is below a brick wall and over the years water has washed the lime out into the ground. It must be very localized."

"But no idea where?"

"No, but it would need to be a big structure to account for the concentration."

"What about a building site?"

"That's what I said. But our man said he would have expected a whole host of other things: sharp sand, cement, plasticizers, that sort of thing."

"No other ideas?"

"I'm sorry, not really. But I have some thoughts and need to dig around."

"Keep on. Operation Klingsor will pick up the tab. Let me know just as soon as you get anything."

"Will do."

Graham put the handset on the cradle.

"Das... Expert opinion on the soil. I found out some more about the lime."

"Oh?"

She explained the anomalous result from the Sarah Carothers murder as Gordonstown sat impassively.

"Good. Very good. We all missed that. Easily done, though, given the weight of other evidence, and I'm pleased with the way you handled the press conference. I don't think the press will connect this Carter disappearance with Vlad. Not yet, anyway."

"I'm still not happy with the press strategy. If it was down to me I would tell everything."

"If we go public with the truth behind the videos we will almost certainly kill Carter."

"But with respect, if we had gone public about the dolls, she might never have been taken."

"They would have tried something else... they watch TV too!"

~ * ~

The next day the fluorescent lights in the incident room were still glowing brightly at midday, holding back the leaden gloom of the heavy rain clouds outside. Tony Shanter answered a ringing telephone. "Incident room. DS Shanter. "

A voice on the other end was shaky. "Sarge. Barney. DC Dastra."

"Oh. Hello. How are you keeping?"

"Okay. I'm on my mobile. Is anyone from an outside team there?"

"No, Barney. They're all out on actions. We're just entering stuff and doing some housekeeping. On a day like this it's better being indoors."

"Yes. It's bloody pissing down here. Listen, this is mega important. I think I might have found the suspect's studio. In fact, I'm about seventy-five percent sure. I'm standing in a wooded area near Goring by the entrance to some old Ministry of Defence bunker. It's at least a mile from where we were looking."

"I don't want to dampen your enthusiasm, but what makes you think that?"

"Sarge, trust me. Send armed backup, now!"

"But, why?"

"Someone is down here, in the bunker! Please... get me some armed backup down here. I'm feeling totally exposed, with them being tooled up, and I'm getting bloody wet. I think this is just short of an urgent assistance shout. At the very least I need some armed assistance on the hurry-up."

"Okay. I'll get things jacked up here, but on an officer safety front, I'll get Older Brian to call you every five minutes. Give me a grid reference…"

~ * ~

Reshard Khan and three other detectives picked their way down the hillside, splashing through puddles and slipping on damp leaves on the trail behind twelve officers from the armed response unit. They had gone several hundred yards into the woods before the man at the front motioned for everyone to stop. He raised his arm above his head then pointed to Dastra, shivering and wet under the dripping trees. Some of the armed officers fanned out into the wood as the rest gathered round Dastra.

"Am I glad to see you lot!"

"What have you got?" asked the Inspector from the armed unit. Dastra waited for the detectives to walk up before raising his voice against the rain.

"If you look just behind me in the bank you should just be able to see an entrance into a derelict Ministry of Defence bunker. The hasp on the doors is unfastened, but there's a rusty but well-oiled padlock in the loop. I've tried the doors but they seem to be fastened from the inside. Did you bring the door buster team?"

"Up by the road, we wanted to secure the area first. I'll give them a shout." The Inspector moved away to talk into his radio. Khan stepped over to Dastra, holding a blue clipboard over his head as a substitute umbrella.

"What makes you think this is it?"

"I'm not one hundred percent, Sarge. But this is a good bet."

The rain stiffened and Khan's clipboard deflected some towards Dastra, so he tilted it back.

"Why?" he shouted.

"We knew the clay was from near a brick structure, yet we had searched every building on the clay. The trouble with geological strata is that they can dip under the ground. I reckon the top of the clay is fifty feet down hereabouts, so this wouldn't be in the area we were searching. There is an entirely different layer on the surface. Anyhow, I got onto the land registry to see if there were any tunnels hereabouts, then I tried the Ministry of Defence. They have a half a dozen old sites round here. I've tried two others but you can see why I like the look of this one."

The Inspector returned. "Do we have any idea of a layout?"

"Yes, Guv. I haven't got a map but this was described over the phone."

"Go on, but speak up."

Dastra raised his voice to a shout. "The complex is laid out around two passages in a cross shape, with a circular chamber at the center. This entrance is on the left arm of the cross and it is about two hundred feet to the chamber. There are various rooms off the corridors…"

"What about other entrances?"

"There's one higher up near the top of the hill, but it is connected by an old elevator, which even if it still worked, wouldn't move without power."

"Have you checked it?"

"No point. No power."

The two men from the door-opening team arrived with their case of hydraulics and tools.

"Okay," said the Inspector. "Let *us* secure the complex and then we'll call you in."

The door opening team moved up to the doors, which were under a brick arch about seven feet high and set into the hillside. Across the door, they clamped a wide bar from which trailed two hydraulic hoses into a rectangular blue case. One of them activated a valve on the case and they stood back in expectation of the door being burst inwards. The clamps broke some bricks free, but the door merely bowed slightly, the metal groaning under the strain. Neither man said anything, but they moved the bar and tried again nearer the ground. The team eyed the doors nervously, but again the bar made no serious progress.

"The steel door bends too much. I need to pin it with some wedges from the van. It'll be slow and noisy," shouted one of the two. "Is that okay?"

"No choice. Go on!" the Inspector shouted back. One man from the door team went back up to the road and returned minutes later with a sledgehammer and small toolbox. After a short discussion, the other man started hammering small metal wedges between the door and the wall. Finally, the bar was reset and the hydraulics restarted. The door bowed in again, but this time something broke and the door flew inwards with a hard clang that rung out above the drumming of the rain. The door opening team stood aside. Eight of the armed team, machine pistols up with integral lights shining, ran into the dark tunnel shouting "Armed police!"

The detectives and the door team stepped into the tunnel entrance to get out of the rain and watched as lights flickered ahead down the passage. Echoes of "clear!" and "armed police!" rang out as the team took control of each room, advancing into the darkness.

"Listen," said Khan, as the detectives moved away from the sound of the rain.

"What is it?"

"A low hum, like an engine."

"A generator!" blurted out Dastra "Shit! This must be it. They may be able to use the lift."

"Where is it?" shouted Khan.

"Inside, turn right at the chamber and keep going."

"Where is it on the surface?"

"Up to the road, right and then first left, down a track."

Khan said nothing more but ran back out to the three armed officers left guarding the entrance. Dastra and the others continued in, flashlights lit.

"There's only one way to find out if it is a generator."

"How?"

"Find a light switch."

They fumbled around the walls feeling for switches, during which time Khan returned.

"Two armed bods are racing up the hill. They'll seal off the elevator."

"If our birds haven't all flown."

Fluorescent light suddenly flickered down the passage.

"Got it."

"Who did that?" echoed the voice of the armed Inspector from far down the passage.

Khan shouted, "There's power, Guv, which means they may have got out by the old lift."

"Right. Send two of my..."

"Done, Guv."

"We'll still treat the place as occupied until we have cleared it."

"Okay."

There were a few minutes as they watched lights going on down the passage, the armed officers methodically checking each room and the spaces echoing with shouts of "clear".

The Inspector shouted them forward. "All right, come down the passage as far as the chamber and take a look. We've got your crime scene!"

Khan turned to one of the other detectives. "Best start a scene log, right here. Put the cordon tape just outside in the woods, then get local units to create a bigger cordon. Run the log here in the dry. I'm going in with Barney. Simon, go back to the car and get us the incident crate... we'll need suits at the bare minimum. Any joy from the top of the lift shaft?"

Fifteen minutes later, three officers in blue paper suits, gloves and overshoes arrived in the circular chamber at the center of the complex. They stopped, wide eyed, to look at a wooden scaffold and silver backdrop. One of two studio lights lay toppled and broken on the ground. Khan scanned the dome above, and was strangely heartened to see a long gray nylon rope dangling from a pulley. The detectives skirted the film set and moved to the next entrance on their right, where the armed officers were walking back towards them along the passage.

"It's all yours, gents," said the Inspector. "There's nobody here. I think they got out in the lift. My lads have found some fresh tire marks, but that's all. Oh, and someone has found some Tudor-looking costumes hanging up on a rail. One of them is shredded..."

"Where's the generator?" asked Dastra.

"Yes. Back near the elevator. It vents up a pipe in the shaft."

Khan looked at the ground and shook his head. "They must have done it."

"Yep," said Dastra.

"Poor bitch," added Simon.

"But there's always hope."

Khan changed the tone of the conversation. "Damn. I've made a balls-up. Barney, you need to get out of here because of forensic contamination."

"Okay, Sarge."

"And call DI Graham. I doubt if she knows yet."

"Knows what?"

"That she's just got the most important crime scene of her career."

Thirty Five

Question (DCI Shackerstone): "So just get to the point. Why do you want me here? DI Graham said you wanted to say something that you could only say with me present."

Answer (suspect): "You've been unwell... over me, haven't you?"

Q: "That's private."
A: "I know I hurt a lot of people, but that doesn't affect me. But it affects you, because you couldn't stop me."

Q: "Can we get to the point?"
A: "You can save some more hurt."

Q: "I've saved a load by nicking you."
A: "This isn't over yet. You'll have to get your poor frightened survivors into the witness box. I'll do a deal; in exchange for some small pieces of knowledge from you, we can keep them out. I'll plead guilty."

Q: "Oh! Right... You will? Okay, I'm up for it."
A: "You were a photographer once weren't you?"

Q: "Yes, you know that already."
A: "Your photos were good. You generally find that schwar—blacks tend to be arty in the musical way."

Q: "If you say so."
A: "Your photos appeal to artists. Do the movies appeal to your artistic side?"

Q: (long pause) "I had to follow your trail. It wasn't art, it was carnage."
A: "Bloody good canvas, though."
(Excerpt from evidential tape transcript.)

In the large central chamber of the bunker complex, Detective Inspector Nicola Graham dressed in mandatory blue paper suit, gloves and overshoes, called together Khan, a crime scene coordinator and SOCO White for the a briefing. Down the radiating arms of the complex, more blue-suited officers worked in near silence. Initial forensic work had swept a clear path through the studio, avoiding the exhibits which had by then been cordoned off with "police do not cross" tape.

"Okay, I've begun a PolSA search of the entire complex in order to identify areas of forensic value. From here on, this is the order of play. We'll need to video the lot before we go further, and do most of our forensic work in situ. I need to establish that there will be sufficient fuel for the generator, and establish a dry suiting-up room back near the entrance, once one has been swept for evidence. I'm not happy that Dastra came in, Sarge."

"No, ma'am," said Khan. "But he had the layout and it *was* his work and his find."

"I know, but we could have eliminated him. I know none of you will have put your hoods up, so his hairs will be everywhere. Still, we might get some dabs or other stuff which help one way or the other."

"Is Detective Chief Superintendent Gordonstown on his way, ma'am?"

"He's at HQ. He'll be down when…"

There was a scream from down the left hand passage, and a female search officer started swearing loudly.

"I'm covered in shit!"

There were a few more noises, followed by a man's voice saying, "It's okay. It's okay. We're police officers…" A search officer jogged back towards the chamber, but Nicola Graham was already running towards him with the others following close behind. A female search officer stood with soft feces and urine trickling down the side of her face and the hood of her paper suit. Two male colleagues had climbed an iron ladder up a short vertical shaft above the passage, and were cowering beneath a solid metal cover as something was banging repeatedly on the other side.

"I think we've found our victim," said the dirtied girl from the search team. "She's got a metal potty, and it's going to take a while to convince her we're Old Bill."

"I'm a negotiator. I'll have a go," said Graham. "Get back to the surface and call an ambulance for her."

Graham let the officers climb down before taking a police mag-light and ascending to the iron cover. She eased the cover open and shone the torch into the chamber. There was no sign of Joanna, but Graham couldn't risk opening the cover further and scanning the room because of the risk of attack.

"Joanna. Joanna Carter?" There was no reply. "Hello. Don't be frightened. I'm a Detective Inspector from Central Southern Police. My name is Nicola Graham. I know what you must be thinking. You are thinking that I am somehow connected with the people who brought you here. I'm not. Just let me assure you of that. I am here because of you. I know you probably think that it would be a million to one shot that the police turn up, but some clever detective work has brought us here. The bad guys have gone and only police are here now… lots of us. My colleagues are part of a Specialist Search team and they were here to help me find you. They are all police officers, and trained to search structures thoroughly. That's how they found this void. There are dozens of other officers examining this site, and the reason we are all in blue coveralls isn't that we are the bad guys in a James Bond movie. It's so we don't contaminate any evidence.

"We are here to make *you* safe. To rescue *you*, Joanna. We found your Range Rover. We think we know how they trapped you. We have been on their trail, but we didn't find this hiding place until today."

There was silence.

"Joanna. I can call you that, can't I? Your husband,

Richard… he can be here soon. I can get him brought from Amersham. I'm sorry but I've forgotten your child's name. She's four years old, though and safe with your in-laws. They're worried sick. I've called for an ambulance so we can have you checked over. Is that okay? I thought it seemed like a good idea. We have worked out that this is some sort of film set. Have they tried to film you at all?"

"Yes," came a hoarse whisper.

"Were they all men?"

"No. There were two ladies-in-waiting."

"Ladies-in-waiting?"

"You want to help them get me back to the scaffold. You only want my head. I won't put it up. Don't you see? There isn't going to be any Anne Boleyn!"

"Anne Boleyn?" Graham paused to think.

"But they'd be costumed. As I explained I've got a police forensic suit on."

"I can only see your head."

"Can I come up a bit higher without you having a pop at me?"

"A little."

Graham slowly moved up a rung. "I'm going to shine a light at the badge on my suit. Can you see it clearly, Joanna?"

"Yes."

"I'm going to take the flashlight away me and put it down so that it shines at the ceiling to give a gentle light for us both. I don't want to shine it in your face. Is that okay?"

"That's good."

Graham put the light down and waited for her eyes to adjust. She could just make out a shape crouched in one corner.

"I'm going to trust you with something I never give up, Joanna. I'm going to take my police warrant card and throw it over to you. You can check who I am. Then you can bring it back over in your own time, or you can throw it back. It is up to you. I'm throwing it now."

Graham tossed her warrant card over. Joanna moved to pick it up. Graham watched as the shape in the corner rose and walked towards her, shrouded in a blanket. Nicola Graham would never forget the cold fear she saw in the face that slowly penetrated the circle of light. Nicola forced a smile, and the white spectre smiled back. Joanna Carter was safe.

~ * ~

Long after Joanna had left the tunnels for the security of a hospital in Reading, Detective Chief Superintendent Gordonstown arrived in a paper suit. Nicola Graham was dictating to an officer who was writing in a decision log.

"DI Graham. Well done. How did you find it?"

"The problem with the soil results from the first investigation. I gave it to DC Dastra, that's why he came in."

"Dastra? You stupid tar—I gave strict instructions that he..."

Graham waved Gordonstown into a side chamber before replying in a hushed but assertive voice.

"Listen. I'm not the one who missed the soil problem. Dastra was my only fast-track solution. I took a risk. His intervention has saved Carter's life."

"And he led you here himself?"

"He did. I know he could have had knowledge, but either way, Carter is safe. And partly down to her."

"Yes?"

"They tried filming Anne Boleyn's execution. She wouldn't put her head up for the headsman's sword. They lost their tempers with her and slung her in a side room. She's a tough lady. They tried to dope her up, but before she was too groggy, she tore her costume to shreds. From the little we've got out of her she's seen some faces, two males and two female 'extras', but nobody like Dastra. I rather hoped to eliminate him on forensics as well."

"Hoped?"

"He came in with the first officers. If nothing else his hairs will be here. We couldn't have prevented him or the others from bringing them in on their suits anyway."

"That's a pity; it means we can't get him either."

"We probably couldn't anyway. If he was a victim, too, his traces might be in here."

"You need to investigate how he went about solving this. Who he called. We need a full account from him."

"Okay, but we must treat him as a potential victim, whatever other views we choose to take. The specialist search team found something at the bottom of the lift shaft. A large scale Ordnance Survey map covering his house."

"Yes, but that could…"

"Guv, there's a penciled line round his garden wall. The map has been there some while, and it's pretty greasy from the lift workings. It could have been there from when Dastra was nicked or from when he was shot at."

"If you believe he was."

"The point is it shows us at some point they felt the need to mark it. And we don't know why."

"No dabs on the map?"

"It has been in the shaft a long time. We might get lucky."

"So we can't prove it *isn't* his."

"In my risk assessment they know where he lives, they probably went there to leave the hairs from Sarah and they've deliberately attacked him and left him in the frame. Someone has taken a shot at him, he has just unearthed their hide and we know they are armed. However differently you and I may feel about him as a suspect, we need to give him some protection to cover our backs in the decision log."

"They could have topped him any one of a number of times since he was released, in spite of the security at his house."

"Not if they spotted us watching him."

Gordonstown scratched his head and walked a few paces away, before turning and coming back to speak. "Mmm. His house is like a fortress as it is. All right, we'll stick another armed unit on him, round the clock. Run it for a month. This time we'll keep him happy by telling him about it."

"It'll cost a fortune. Operation Klingsor can't afford…"

"We won't have to. Witness protection will cop it. They're over halfway through the year and only a quarter of the way through their budget. It's one of those windows of opportunity we get at HQ every so often. We can watch him and get our people to give his security a good going over."

Thirty Six

Question (Superintendent Hinx): "So what did you think then?"

Answer (DCI Shackerstone): "Once I had decided he was innocent, I didn't have to lose sleep about him being on the loose and about to murder Lucy. I guess my main problem was coping with having put him inside."

Q: "So you returned to work?"
A: "Yes, I was still dosed up on antidepressants, but my doctor said it would be good for my recovery if I wasn't sitting about thinking too much at home. I've got some pastimes, like fly fishing. But The Job was the best therapy for me."

Q: "Fly-fishing? That's interesting..."
A: "Why? Because I'm black?"

Q: "No, not like that. It's like The Job... fishing for clues."
A: "Right."

Q: "Sorry. We digress. Were you surprised to be let back on the squad?"
Q: "I was. I didn't think DCS Gordonstown would let me near it."

Q: "Do you know why he let you back on?"
A: "He had given himself a lot of the credit for Barney's

conviction in his promotion submission. With me back he could delegate some of the blame if the wheel came off Klingsor...not that he ever considered Dastra remotely innocent... even if we had made some mistakes. That's why he wouldn't let me resurrect Klingsor when Porterer went missing. Lucky for us both that I kept it going on a small scale. I had covered his back."

Q: *"He told us that in his interview."*
A: *"That was very gracious of him. We don't... we don't see eye to eye at all now."*
Q: *"When did things start to go wrong?"*
A: *"When we found Francesca Porterer's body. Josh wanted so badly to show that it was Dastra, that he didn't play the part of an active SIO. He tried to run it like one of these lone maverick TV detectives, so he charged off and nicked Lucy without checking the most up to date evidence we had that put her in the clear. In his eyes I had shown up a senior officer and trust went downhill from then on. Even when Dastra looked guilty after all, I wouldn't believe it. With the atmosphere as it was nobody was more shocked than I was when Josh took me straight back onto the squad. Ironically, it was well timed."*
(Taped excerpt from MPS enquiry into Operation Klingsor.)

"Oh, and Brian, we've had to tell Jeff Carothers to drop his civil action."

"I bet he wasn't happy." Shackerstone peered out through the Venetian blinds of Gordonstown's office into more slate gray morning weather. Twinges of his own misery fluttered somewhere behind his breastbone.

"Carothers still thinks Dastra did it. Anyhow, now I've brought you up to speed, there's a fair bit you can do for me."

"Go on, boss. I need to be busy."

"Good, this will be up your street; The Chief Constable is rather pleased with Dastra. He wants to give him a commendation."

"And?"

"Well, Brian. The press loved the Carter rescue story, but most didn't give Dastra much more than a mention. I know that it means very little at our level, but the Chief is worried that Dastra is going to refuse the compensation offer from the police authority and go for a lot more for the harm to his reputation. He wants something of a fairly public coverage of him being exonerated... full regrets... that sort of thing."

"What's been done already?"

"Public Affairs tried a press release, but they fell afoul of the old rule: on a slow news day the press go for a good fireman story or a bad cop story. The good fireman got it."

"So where do I fit in this?"

"I want you to do the story. You're at the coal face. They might listen to a senior detective from the squad."

"Gladly. You know where I stand. I know why you wouldn't want to do it yourself."

"Precisely, and I understand you have some connections in the press world."

"Oh, right. Yes. In fact, one of my old chums has gone to a new magazine, *Celeb Dot Mag*. They do the pictures and a short article in the magazine, with in-depth follow-ups and discussions on their website. That will be easy to arrange. He's been badgering me since Dastra came out of prison. He'll want all the usual pictures of the loving couple in their lovely house and all that stuff."

"Good. That'll keep the Chief Constable happy."

Shackerstone got up to leave and then stopped, frozen for a few seconds as if deep in thought. He turned back and sat down again. "Idea."

"A good one?"

"Could be. Up until now, we have been chasing our suspects, letting them strike, and then hoping for forensics."

"Traditional reactive police work."

"Now you've got a constant armed guard on him. It can't go on forever and we've got bugger all forensics from the bunker apart from a few fibers from the costumes."

"So what's your point?"

"My point is that the magazine article could be used to announce that the armed guard is now over and we are satisfied there is no risk to him. Then we put an armed surveillance team in the woods and shove some stooges in the house to create the illusion of movement. Stick Barney and Lucy in a safe house, perhaps a room in an Oxford college."

"This will cost a lot more. I don't know if… no, they're well under budget. I know where you are going with this: you hope the suspects will surface at Dastra's house."

"Yes."

"One of your fish rising to the fly?"

"This is harder than that. When they aren't feeding, you use a fly called a Monty… a special sinker that tempts them to feed. The magazine article will be the Monty. There are risks and weaknesses. I'll develop the plan. The last thing we want is him or her being picked off at the safe house or kidnapped. I will speak to the surveillance people. We need to draw our suspects out at Dastra's house and nowhere else. And I need to check timings with my mate so that we drop the overt guard when the magazine comes out."

"Aren't we forgetting something?"

"Sorry. What?"

"The consent of Dastra."

"Yes. Could be a problem, but Lucy will probably be up for it."

"So who will get the consent? I don't think that I…"

"I was planning to call in at his house tonight anyway. It's Lucy's twenty-first birthday."

"And how would you have remembered that?"

"I looked it up on her custody record."

Gordonstown gave Shackerstone a look that said he didn't want that brought up again. "Still chasing crumpet then… even ones young enough to be your daughter?" Shackerstone smiled, and Gordonstown let a wry smile slip back. "Get fishing, Brian."

~ * ~

Lucy's mother brought tea and coffee into the piano room just after the end of the six o'clock television news. Dastra tried to relax in front of the television but found himself nervously checking the curtains for gaps. Lucy's mother took a cup of tea to the armed officer in the library. He was reading one of the books to alleviate the boredom. She returned to the piano room as the gate intercom sounded. Dastra flicked the remote control on the TV to show a view from the gates.

"Who is it?" asked Lucy.

"You won't believe this. It's DCI Shackerstone. Alone."

"What does he want?"

"I'll ask." Dastra pressed the intercom. "Hello, uh, Guv, what can I do for you?"

"Personal call, Barney, just a bit of welfare."

"No search warrant then?"

"No. I promise. I have... a present for Lucy." Shackerstone held his hands up as if to show symbolic empty-handedness, although he was holding a small box in his left hand.

Dastra looked at Lucy before activating the gate.

"Let him in then," she said, raising her eyebrows.

"But, I can't, he's..."

"Please. He isn't all bad."

"*Timeo Danaos et dona ferentes.*"

"Sorry?" said Lucy's mother.

"I fear the Greeks, even when bearing gifts." Dastra leaned over and pressed the intercom. "Drive on up, Guv. I'll open the gate."

Shackerstone's white Citroen ground up the drive and round the flowerbed before he called at the front door. The armed officer answered it, but Dastra made his way to the door, still limping slightly, to meet him.

"Guv."

"Barney." There was an awkward silence. "Can I come in for a moment?"

"Sure. Sorry. Yes, come on in."

"Is Lucy here?"

"Yes, she is, but we've, uh, we've got her mum here."

"Oh. Sorry. I suppose I could leave this and call again, but I think this is reasonably urgent. It will only take five minutes or so... but I need to see you both."

"You'd best come through then."

Shackerstone nodded to the armed officer and followed Dastra to the left through towards the piano room.

"Back at work then, Guv?"

"Yes, first day back today."

"You're fully recovered?"

"I'm getting there. Your saving Joanna Carter was a big help.

That's partly why I've come over." They entered the piano room. For a moment, Shackerstone thought that the slim blonde rising from an armchair was Lucy, but there was no bump, and the hair was much lighter and shorter.

"Guv, this is Lucy's mother, Vanessa."

Shackerstone offered his hand and she shook it. "Brian, Brian Shackerstone. Pleased to meet you Mrs.—" He stared blankly at Vanessa Aybrams in the manner he had done on the first occasion he had met Lucy. He was trapped in another daydream. Vanessa broke the silence.

"Hello, Brian. I've heard a lot about you."

Shackerstone snapped back to the present. "Sorry. Yes. Nothing good, though."

"Well, that's not entirely the case. Lucy told me about you arranging blood donors for Barney and getting her released when she was arrested."

"I have my moments, but I'm not generally flavor of the month." As Vanessa sat back down Shackerstone turned to Lucy and smiled. "Hello, Lucy. Happy birthday."

"Thank you." Lucy didn't attempt to get up and Shackerstone was uncertain whether to shake her hand or not, so stood awkwardly for a moment. He suddenly remembered the present and handed it to her. "Oh, this is for you."

Lucy opened the small box and found a pair of diamond earrings. "Oh, thank you, they're lovely. Sit yourself down." Lucy pushed her long hair back and held them up to her ears, seeking the approval of Dastra and her mother. Shackerstone sat down opposite Lucy. "You know… you and your mum…so alike."

"Like a big sister."

Shackerstone turned to Vanessa. "You must have been a young mum."

"Last year at college, just like Lucy."

Dastra eyed Shackerstone with suspicion, hoping for the small talk to end and for him to get to the point. He coughed to get Shackerstone's attention then raised his eyebrows expectantly.

"Oh, yes, I've got something I need to tell you both and it's taken a bit of courage to come up here."

"Shall I leave you three alone?" asked Vanessa.

"No. You can hear this, too, and I could do with a witness." Shackerstone moved forward slightly on his seat and motioned to Dastra to sit down next to Lucy. Shackerstone put his palms together and put his index fingers to his top lip as if thinking. He paused, stroked his chin, and then let his hands drop to his lap. "Look, I made some mistakes in this investigation... big mistakes. I want both of you to know that I am totally convinced now of your innocence in this business, Barney. And I am really pleased that you are going to get the CC's commendation."

"I am?"

"Didn't you know? Gordonstown was supposed to tell you. You can read into that what you want. All I want to say to you both is that I am truly sorry for being an accessory to screwing up your young lives." Shackerstone looked at the floor as if fighting back a tear. There was an embarrassing silence, broken after Dastra leaned forward and put a hand on Shackerstone's shoulder.

"Thanks, Guv. I know a lot of people would feel bitter, but convincing you in particular is a big milestone. I'm, well... very glad you came up. Honestly. Although, you can understand that I'm a bit taken aback."

Shackerstone looked up, clearly happy that Dastra had made it easier for him than it might have been.

Lucy spoke next. "We've got some news, haven't we, Barney?"

"Oh, yes. Gosh. Lucy and I are getting married on Saturday."

"Right. Brilliant. Congratulations. Of course, that's why Mum is here. No Dad though?"

"We're divorced," said Vanessa. "He's not too happy about all this. He wanted to give Lucy away with the full white church wedding treatment."

"So who'll give you away?"

Dastra replied, "It's a registry office job. Lucy's a bit far gone for church. We'll get it blessed in church after the baby is born."

"That way I will still get the dress," added Lucy.

"Good," said Shackerstone. "Your dad will be proud."

Vanessa rose. "Would you like coffee?"

"Tea, please, coffee makes me a bit shaky."

"Me too," said Dastra, with a forced smile.

Shackerstone watched as Vanessa walked gracefully to the kitchen. He turned back to Lucy and Barney. "There's something else I would like to do for you both. I want to go on record saying you are in the clear, Barney. I've got a mate who works for one of those celebrity magazines and it would make a good story. He will have to do some photos... in fact it would be super if he could cover the wedding."

Shackerstone was mildly surprised when Dastra readily agreed: "That would be okay. Security is the main thing. I don't want to be a male Lorna Doone."

"Quite. Security. Yes. DCS Gordonstown and I have discussed this armed guard business."

"I knew we'd get round to real business eventually."

"Sorry. That isn't the reason I came. He gave me this as an errand when he knew I was coming up."

"Okay."

"You realize the armed protection can't last indefinitely."

"That has been worrying us both."

"And we're still no closer to catching our suspects. So, with your permission we would like to try something that might flush them out."

"Yes?" said Dastra, slowly.

"It has been suggested that we announce in the magazine article that we believe the killers are well away on the run and that we have taken off the armed guard. In fact we will replace them with constant covert armed surveillance."

"But the risk? What about Lucy and the baby?"

"It's you they're after. They could have had Lucy at any time since she found the first bodies."

"I don't want her widowed and my kid orphaned. That's aside from having a natural aversion to being killed."

"But you're at risk now anyway. We know they've got access to firearms."

"Yes."

"The plan I have in mind would make things considerably safer for you. We want to move you both out for a few weeks."

"But this is our home," protested Lucy.

"I know, but I want you to consider this. I've already made some enquiries, and there are some rooms going to be freed next week at Corpus Christi. The college people are willing, and it'll be better for Lucy's studies. You can both move in while the surveillance team simulate your comings and goings. We'll get hold of some skinny stooges to double for you both."

"Skinny?"

"They need to look your size with body armor on. I know we won't get much in the way of facial likeness... you are both pretty distinctive...but we're not expecting them to get close. The static target will be a dummy. We can't risk the officers. Oh, and we'll need to borrow your car, Barney."

"Yes, and obviously I'm not keen about all this."

"I've spoken to some of our technical bods and they reckon at this time of year, with no leaves on the trees, they could fill the woods with electronic stuff and have a good chance of picking up intruders at a reasonable range. The wall is alarmed, but in some respects we will be best served letting them get inside it, then springing the trap. If they don't fall for it within a month or so, I don't think they'll ever come back."

"They've always moved pretty swiftly."

"So that's the plan. What do you think?"

"We need to give it some thought. I have serious concerns."

Lucy took Dastra's hand and turned to Brian. "I told Reshard on the way back from the Old Bailey that I would gladly do anything to catch Vlad. Well, within limits, I'm ready."

Dastra stuttered, "But... but... right. Okay. If you are happy. Okay, we'll go for it. When will it start?"

"Next Wednesday when the magazine comes out. Can my mate cover the wedding and get some shots of you both here?"

Dastra hesitated, got a quick nod from Lucy. "Okay."

"I want him to take some views that make the place look wide open to intruders. They'll probably send a journalist along to get a few quotes from you. I'll confirm Saturday with an e-mail and call you when it is confirmed."

Vanessa returned from the kitchen with a tea for Shackerstone.

"Brian wants us to move out for safety," said Lucy.

"But this is like the Tower of London."

"I'll explain later."

Lucy cast a concerned look at Brian. "You said you would get something off to the magazine tonight. Won't you come with the people from the magazine on Saturday?"

Shackerstone sipped his tea before replying. "No. I'm busy. Fishing. It's therapeutic, keeps my mind off murder, and like Barney's art, I've discovered that it's an antidote to The Job."

"But Brian," Vanessa continued, "you must come to the wedding. Barney will have no family there. A colleague would at least be something."

"Not this colleague, eh, Barney?"

Dastra looked uncomfortable for a moment, then said, "I'm not like that. I would truly appreciate it if you came, Guv."

"And I would have a partner for the photos," added Vanessa.

Shackerstone smiled. "Okay. I'll be there. As you all insist."

Thirty Seven

Question (DCI Shackerstone): "Is this relevant?"
Answer (Suspect one): "You need the deal. I don't. A few weeks at court is nothing out of a life sentence."

Q: "Okay. (pause) My art was still photography. Yes. I thought I was talented."
A: "On the evidence, yes. So, to the question."

Q: "You'll stick to your word."
A: "Yes."

Q: "But why should I believe you? You can change your mind in court."
A: "This is on tape. If my word is broken, you can play it to the jury and they will hear that a complete shit is in the dock. You see, some blokes have to know the way everything is. Everything. Even watching death. Now, some more things about you. Why did you give up being a photographer?"

Q: "I couldn't make enough money."
A: "Because of your color?"

Q: "It was a white man's game then, with a lot of barriers for a black man. I only made a lot of money from one photo, and not when I took it. She was..."
A: "Killed. Then everybody wanted your photo. There is an

insatiable appetite for the tragedy of beautiful women on their way to death. Like the Princess of Wales before her car crash. So... did my movies appeal to you?"

Q: "Did your work appeal to me? I found none of it artistic, especially the executions proper. They were flat, like news coverage. I believe that you got excited with those."

A: "Clever chap. Yes, it was exciting. Art went by the board. It became reportage...a medieval newsreel. It was their terror. People who were going to be dead in a few minutes. It's not the same in a film with actors. It's only fascinating if you know you are watching the real thing... like when you see something on the news. The Romans knew what it was like in the Coliseum and they couldn't get enough of it."

Q: "How about you. Is it a sexual thing?"
A: "(long pause) Yes. How about you?"
(Extract from evidential tape transcript.)

On Saturday evening the hired tables from the wedding reception in the piano room were being packed away and around thirty guests from Oxford University and the police were relaxing around the house. The photographer had started to put his equipment away in readiness to leave when Shackerstone found him in the hallway.

"Colin?"

"Brian. I wondered where you had got to. Not quite the sort of society wedding I'm used to, but I always relish a challenge."

"Have you got plenty of shots here at the house?"

"Loads. There wasn't a lot of opportunity at the registry office, but I've got dozens here, and I've used the house and grounds as you suggested. That Irish bloke Lynch made a good best man."

"Yes. Very odd, that, a convicted terrorist at a police wedding."

"We like odd. It sells magazines. No doubt the bride and groom can tell my colleague all about it tomorrow when he comes up for the interview. The proofs of the photos should be ready by then."

"I was thinking..."

"You always did too much of that." He leaned down and put a large format camera into an aluminum box.

"Could you do a couple more shots?"

"Why? I've got loads."

"But you haven't got any in the piano room."

"Because it's full of tables and chairs. I have far more of them both than I need anyway. You were right, she's very lovely. I hope I've done her justice. I'll let you have some of the proofs."

"Thanks. Listen. The tables are gone now. They're putting some of the furniture back. I just want a couple more shots."

"All right, as a favor to an old friend. In the piano room?"

"Yes. I know it's dark now, but please give them your best shot. I'll give you a hand."

"You're welcome to take them yourself."

"Really?"

"Of course." He handed Shackerstone a roll-film camera body. "I'll show you what to do for exposure. Things haven't really changed much in thirty years. And I still use roll-film for large format work; the color saturation is better than digital, so you'll feel right at home."

"Have you got some black and white film?"

"Black and white? Yes, if you want." He rummaged around and handed Shackerstone a loaded film holder. Shackerstone clicked it onto the camera.

"How about a red filter?"

"Very good for skin tones, but her lips will look pale. Try orange."

"Light red. I'll get her to use purple lip color."

Colin found a large square filter and Shackerstone slid it into an attachment at the front of the camera lens.

"I really appreciate this."

~ * ~

Lucy Dastra was getting tired of the interview, and her bottom was going numb as she sat with her new husband in the piano room on Sunday talking to the journalist from *Celeb Dot Mag*. Brian Shackerstone hovered protectively in the background, but Lucy felt a wary sense of him intruding too much into their lives. He had taken her mother back to Heathrow Airport in the morning, but Lucy would have preferred for Barney to have done this simple job for his new mother-in-law. As the journalist closed his notebook and clicked off his tape recorder, Lucy rose from her seat and shook some life back into her legs.

"I must say we're honestly very pleased to get this story," said the journalist, laying each print out on the top of the grand piano. "We're going to use this one of you the registry office, we think."

Lucy, Barney and Shackerstone gathered around the piano.

"And we're delighted with these shots back at the house. Pity about the time of year. More natural light would have helped. This is a lovely one of you, Lucy. But too much bump, I think."

Lucy picked up the photograph. "I see. Am I really that big?"

"The camera does its best not to lie."

"Does its best? I thought the camera never lied."

"In skilled hands even a camera can be economical with the truth. For instance, this is my favorite."

He produced a black and white print of Lucy's smiling face resting on her folded arms on the top of the piano, with a dull reflection of her in the dark polished surface. Her long hair was lightened, almost to white. Her blue eyes appeared dark gray and her skin appeared luminous and ghostly. The room beyond was bright and thrown slightly out of focus, although the main features, like the great beam across the ceiling and the French windows were clearly visible. "I understand this was your work, Brian."

"Yes."

"It's slightly spooky, I think, but we'll publish it because my editor loves arty shots. And I love this one of Lucy with the baby clothes. You took all four of these black and whites of Lucy, didn't you?"

"Yes."

"Fantastic pictures, like I say, almost surreal."

"Red filter."

"Such wasted talent."

"I left photography behind a long time ago."

"Pity."

"The police forces of this country are littered with wasted talents. We've got psychologists, lawyers, engineers, pharmacists…"

"And geologists," added Dastra with a smile.

"Yes, geologists, historians, artists, poets, musicians, you name it. It's a bit like the French Foreign Legion."

"I'll have to do an article on it sometime. Anyhow, your black and white pictures will almost certainly be in the main article in the next issue, and they will be attributed to you." He scooped up the proofs and put them back in a large envelope. "Well, that's it. The magazine will be out midweek as usual."

Once the journalist had gone, the bride and groom collected their bags and waited for darkness before Shackerstone drove them to Oxford and their safe house at Corpus Christi College. As Lucy watched the bare winter trees drift by the car windows, she prayed that Shackerstone's plan would work quickly, and that she would be safely back in Prospect of Peshawar before the baby was born.

Thirty Eight

A press cutting from Celeb Dot Mag *read:*

"*Relaxing in their large country home in Oxfordshire, the Dastras discussed with me the events of the last year. Barney, referring to the overturning of his life sentence, said, 'I owe virtually everything to Lucy. If Lucy hadn't been at my trial, the tabloids hadn't done their"Bride of Dracula" story, it all might have played out differently. Although it may have swung the jury, there's still a good chance I would have been convicted on the evidence available at the time. Then when I was stabbed in the prison riot, Lucy persuaded the police to give blood for me and the other prisoners. Then to cap it all she got the staff at the hospital to play Sibelius CDs to me to bring me out of a coma.'*

"*Lucy led me through their home, which Barney recently inherited following the death of his parents. It is a large mock Elizabethan house, but needs refurbishment. Lucy has plans to restore parts of the house to their original condition. I asked her what she plans to do after her baby is born. She said 'I need to do my final exams and get my degree. I want to teach little children, so I guess I will have to go back to college part-time and get a Post Graduate Certificate of Education. Between us, we should be able to afford to restore this place. And after all that has happened we need to spend some money on security—all that keeps the world out at the moment is a bit of wall and some barbed wire. This is a lovely spot, and I wouldn't want to live anywhere else, but it is pretty remote for southern England. In the USA it is normal for houses to be miles from anywhere, but being half a mile from the nearest village and surrounded by forest is enough here to make this place very secluded.'"*

PC Martin Kennedy checked the lawn of Prospect of Peshawar through a night scope. "Is this night four or five?" PC David Hampton, a few feet away but looking out from the opposite side of the hide, was in no mood for another night of Kennedy's complaints. "Shut up. We've only been here since eight. That's no more than an hour."

"It's like watching bloody paint dry."

"See if you can leave ten minutes between each comment, and keep it to a whisper."

Kennedy whispered again after twenty minutes. "This is all bollocks. Talk about planned on the back of a cigarette pack."

"You're getting paid. All you've got to do is stay awake."

"I won't be doing that soon."

"You volunteered to get trained for this... nobody asked you."

"But where's the action?"

"Hopefully as far away as possible."

"I'll get some shut-eye then."

"If someone gets in without us spotting them, your life won't be worth living. Now give it a rest."

Kennedy needed more distractions, so spoke softly into his radio headset. "Alpha from Charlie. You awake?"

"What do you think?"

"Just checking. Anything doing?"

"All quiet over here. Joe and Tracy are making a good show of activity in the piano room."

"Anything for a peeping tom?"

"I heard that!" came the voice of PC Joe Michaels. PS Tracy Sparks could be heard laughing in the background.

"When are we off to bed then?"

"A couple of hours. We've got some videos to watch."

"Dirty videos?"

"Charlie from Bravo. Cut the crap."

"Sarge."

The banter died down for the next hour, but Kennedy's boredom surfaced again at around ten o'clock.

"Alpha from Charlie. Seen any interesting badgers?"

"Shut up. We've had an activation."

"Probably my badger."

"Shut the fuck up. I've got a suspect male, in the woods to the east. Could be a poacher. Four hundred yards from the wall."

Kennedy and the others remained silent. After ten minutes Hampton called Michaels.

"Delta from Charlie... you monitoring this?"

"Yes. We'll keep the shadows moving on the curtains."

"Echo. Are you standing by?"

"Standing by."

An uneasy silence descended on the whole surveillance team, eventually broken again by one of the officers from Alpha.

"He's moving back and forth. There are too many trees but I think he's moving away. I think it's a poacher. Shit."

"What?"

There was a long silence.

"Alpha from Charlie. Are you okay? Alpha from Charlie, come in please."

There was a long silence. "All units from Alpha. Somebody has stepped right over me. He's heading towards the section of wall at the back of the house. I think he's got a rifle and we're still getting glimpses of his back through the trees."

"All units from Bravo. Let suspect two get close to the wall and then move in. It's quiet out there so keep it that way until the challenge."

"Bravo from Alpha. Sarge, we've got to close up. We'll lose them both."

"Okay. Keep your heads down."

The airwaves remained eerily silent for another ten minutes with each of the officers listening only to the night time woodland noises and the thumping of their own hearts. Eventually Alpha broke the tension in a measured whisper.

"All units from Alpha. Number two is close to the wall. We're fifty meters off."

A shot cracked through the night air of the woods, smashing

a window in the piano room.

"What was that?"

"All units from Alpha. Not, repeat not our suspect. We've got... wait... come here chum. We're police... put the gun down. Yes, all units from Alpha. Suspect two is out rabbiting with an airgun. The shot came from suspect one."

"Alpha from echo. We're rolling."

"All units from Delta. Dastra dummy has been shot in the head. No injuries."

"Stop! Armed police!" echoed a voice from the direction of the shot. The team waited for an update. "All units from Bravo. One arrested with one firearm secured. All units to remain vigilant for other suspects. Try to secure his firing point for SOCO. We'll take our man down to the road. Well done everyone."

~ * ~

In the morning Brian Shackerstone visited the custody suite to inquire about the prisoner shown on the whiteboard as "male anon firearms Klingsor".

"Not forthcoming then?" asked Shackerstone of the custody officer.

"Stroppy bastard according to night duty. He's in a sleep period now. Didn't get his head down until two."

"Good. That'll give me time to prepare. Has he asked for a solicitor?"

"Yes."

"Can you get them here for ten? That'll give them time to consult before the interview."

"Okay, Guv."

"I'll go and read the officer's notes. I think we've got this one banged to rights, down to the .22 rifle."

~ * ~

One hundred miles away, PC Bob Dray sat bored at the wheel of a traffic car on a police observation point by the westbound carriageway of the M20 in Kent. In the passenger seat sat spotty and skinny PC Simon Moles, a probationary constable who had been sent to traffic division for a two-day training attachment. Dray usually patrolled alone, but the company on a bright winter morning was more than welcome. After over twenty-eight years in the force, he felt he could teach Moles a thing or two. A sudden increase in traffic signaled the offloading of a channel tunnel train or cross-channel ferry.

"Here we go."

"Sorry, Bob?"

Dray shifted the Vauxhall Carlton into *Drive*. "I fancy that Ford Granada and caravan." he said, pointing to a car and trailer up ahead.

"Why?"

"Intuition... anyhow, we don't need reasonable suspicion to check his license. We'll check his documents and fish for the rest." Dray let the traffic car speed up on the hard shoulder before joining the main carriageway. He accelerated hard, but it took nearly a mile to catch up with the car and its trailer. Moles checked on the license plate and was told over the radio said that it was registered to a catering company in Maidenhead.

"Okay," said Dray. "Hit them now."

Moles activated the blue lights and two tones. They watched as their quarry drifted onto the hard shoulder, braking gently. Moles got out and went to the driver's door. He leaned down and looked in. There were two other men in the car, but he only asked the driver to get out. They walked round to the grass verge where they were joined by Dray.

"Just a document check, sir."

The driver smiled. "No problem. I've got them all here in my pocket." His accent was cultured and precise. He unfolded his license, vehicle test certificate and insurance. Dray busied himself examining the details, but with a second eye for imperfections. Moles walked back along the car, looking at the tax disc, tires and the general condition. The front passenger looked ahead, but the man in the back seat wound the window down.

"Problem?"

Moles didn't answer directly. "Just come through the tunnel?"

"The ferry. The trailer has got butane gas."

Moles saw an up-to-date copy of *Celeb Dot Mag* and concluded that the man was being truthful. There were no opportunities to buy magazines on channel tunnel trains. Moles wandered to the back of the trailer and peered in through a window. There were lights and tripods bundled on the floor. He wandered back as Dray was about to let the driver go.

"What's all the kit for?"

"We are a freelance film unit. We've just done a filming in Eastern Europe."

"Interesting work?"

"It can be. I would bet it's like for you police... it has its ups and its downs."

Dray looked at Moles, wondering what his line of thought was going to be. Moles motioned the driver back towards the car. "Thanks. We're done. Drive safely." Moles and Dray watched the driver get back in and they got back into the traffic car as the Granada pulled away towing the trailer.

"Bob?"

"Yes."

"I've got bad vibes about that caravan they're towing."

"You'll need more than that to look inside it. Sadly, real copper's instinct was banned by the Police and Criminal Evidence Act." Dray accelerated down the hard shoulder and joined the main carriageway.

"Bob, do you know anything about that business up in Central Southern Police with that DC who got nicked for a load of murders."

"Yes. But he only copped one, and then he got out on appeal."

"And everyone thought he was still the killer, then it all changed a couple of weeks back."

"Did it?"

"It's in a confidential bulletin from the intelligence unit."

"Yes?"

"There's something about identifying the backgrounds to some snuff movies. Then there was this business in all the papers with a kidnapped woman being held in some disused underground fortress."

"And the DC led everyone to her."

"That's it. Well, we've got a film crew. On the backseat of the car is a magazine doing a story on him."

"That's not enough."

"If you were on a ferry, coming back to England after a spell abroad, would you buy *Celeb Dot Mag* as your first purchase?"

"Probably not, but these are film types. It still isn't enough, young man."

Moles looked out of the window. *Intuition. Intuition.* Dray gave some encouragement. "Take it apart. Maybe there's something you picked up without realizing it."

"I don't know. You stopped them on intuition. Why can't…"

"And we've gone as far as we can. We need more now."

"Well, the guy in the back said they had come from Eastern Europe."

"So?"

"Wouldn't you say the exact country…unless you had something to hide, and none of them sounded English—the accents were precise but the turn of phrase was wrong."

"Like what?"

"One called the caravan a 'trailer'."

"Good, but not enough…"

"I've got it. The car is registered to a catering company. They were a film unit."

"Much better. For what it's worth, the documents were a little too perfect. Too new."

"So you'll pull them over?"

"It's not a lot, but we'll run with it. What power are we going to search the caravan under?"

"I don't think there's anything we can use in the circumstances."

"I'm not sure myself, but that drain pipe is dripping a lot…"

"Sorry?" Moles looked at the back of the trailer. "So what?"

"They could be transporting unlicensed industrial waste. That or wildlife offences like possessing bits of badgers always give us more powers than dealing with serious crime. Let motorway control know we want to stop them again and ask for some backup. We'll hang back for a few miles."

As his inexperienced apprentice spoke awkwardly into the radio, Dray let the police car drop back through the traffic, but maintained visual contact with their prey. They followed on past the exits to Maidstone while a second unit raced to their assistance.

"We're going to have to pull them in the next mile or so," said Dray.

"Why?"

"If they're headed for Maidenhead, they'll take the M25 clockwise. The spur from here is eighteen miles long with one exit near the start. If we have to bring them in, it's a long way back from the next junction."

"Let's go for it. I'll check our backup." Moles spoke timidly and slowly into the radio handset. "Motorway control from Motorway Two Zero Bravo."

"Twenty Bravo... go ahead," came the fast and confident response. Moles tried to speed up to show more expertise. "Approaching slip to M25. Can we go car to car with Motorway Two Zero Delta?"

"Go ahead and call them."

"Motorway Two Zero Delta from Motorway Two Zero Bravo. Your location? Over."

"Bravo from Delta. About six miles and we'll be up your tail pipe."

"Mo, uh Delta from Bravo. We need to stop before he gets far onto the M25 spur. We'll keep him talking."

"Bravo. Received. We're doing one hundred and twenty."

"You're getting the hang of that, young man. We'll make a traffic officer of you yet."

~ * ~

Back in Wemstone, the incident room team was gradually picking up more and more information about the previous night's events around Prospect of Peshawar. Rumors were flying round the office and the receiver, DS Tony Shanter, was irritated at not being kept informed of the situation with the prisoner. He passed the time reading some completed actions before marking them for the indexers. A phone rang and the officer answering it transferred it across the room to one of the indexers. Shanter listened, hoping that a half-heard conversation might shed some light on the arrest downstairs.

The officer doing the indexing picked up the phone to answer a call. "Wemstone nick, how can I help you? South East

Police? A vehicle stop on the M20? You say they came off the ferry? Is there a reason for the stop? Young and keen, eh? Give me the index... hold on while I key it in... That's interesting. It's in the system. Let's have a look. Oh, just a roadblock the inquiry team did last year up here... one of hundreds. No result I can see on my screen here. Good try though... Yes... no... we think we've already got someone for that. No? Oh. Really... *Eastern Europe*... and the caravan they're pulling is full of film gear?"

Tony Shanter was up from his swivel chair and closing on the indexer. "Keep them on! I've just processed a note about some tracks left near the underground studio that included some sort of trailer or caravan."

"Sarge. Did you hear that this one's full of filming gear?"

"Yes. I got that. But our blokes wouldn't be heading from..."

"Sarge," came a voice from an analyst. "I've just searched HOLMES for trailers. There's another entry in the system. Dastra's original interview. He lost his personal radio near a campsite."

Shanter thought again. *Assume nothing.* He picked up a phone and called the custody suite. "Hello... DS Shanter here. Any news on the shooter at Dastra's house, at interview? DI Graham has something for me? Yes, please put her on." He paused to listen to Nicola Graham. "Shit. Sarah Carothers's husband was the gunman?" He slammed down his telephone and snatched the handset from the indexer. "Sorry. DS Shanter here. This is important. Your crew need armed backup."

~ * ~

Dray pushed the Carlton up to ninety miles per hour in order to close in on the back of the trailer. Moles flicked the blue lights and two tone siren on again. The trailer's brake lights lit up as it drifted onto the hard shoulder and came to a halt. Dray stopped behind it, and both he and Moles put their hats on and got out.

"Motorway Twenty Bravo from control. Urgent message." There was a pause. "Bravo from control. Urgent message from Central Southern Police. If vehicle is a possible then subjects may have access to firearms. Are you receiving me?"

Moles and Dray were out of earshot. Dray spoke to the driver again. "Sorry to stop you again, Guv. Your caravan is leaking a lot of fluid."

"Sorry, officer. I expect it is the waste from…"

"Waste? Quite. My colleague and I have reasonable grounds to suspect that you are carrying industrial waste. I must search your trailer."

"Industrial waste? But that's ridiculous."

"Open the van please, sir. There's a good fellow."

The driver got out and walked round to the near side of the trailer with Dray following. Moles waited near the trailer door. The driver fumbled with some keys and opened it. "You're sure you don't need a warrant?"

"We don't," smiled Dray, with the *just try me* certainty of an official who knows he is in the right.

"Fine. No problem. We've been searched at three different borders. Go ahead."

"Three borders? We'll have to be very thorough indeed to match them. PC Moles? In you go."

Moles stepped in and saw that the floor of the trailer was piled high with collapsed tripods and lighting stands. He clambered over the pile and started lifting the seats of the trailer to reveal the storage boxes beneath. Lights, leads, recording equipment, two cameras and dozens of videotapes filled the eight different boxes around the trailer.

"I need the toilet," said the driver, still by the door. "Will this take long? I could use the toilet in the trailer."

"Okay," replied Dray "It's not you we're searching."

The driver stepped inside the trailer behind Moles and began close the door behind him. Dray instinctively put his foot in the door. "No need to close it."

The driver turned politely. "Sorry, the toilet compartment folds out over the door. I won't be a moment." Moles appeared at the door. He was uneasy with the request, but realized he had no power to search the driver. "I'll just check the toilet compartment before you go in."

Dray nodded and let the door close. Inside Constantin Raglisevitch locked the door and pulled the folding cubicle out for Moles. He backed into a narrow space by the tripods and waited for Moles to lean forward over the portable toilet. He eased a slim five-inch gravity knife from his back pocket, let the blade drop out of the handle and locked it into place. His heart beat slightly faster, but he had killed many Bosnian Muslims at Srebrenica in this way and it was virtually second nature. He would wait for the officer to stand up and then seize him in a neck lock, before bringing the knife up under the back ribs, slicing from side to side once through the skin in order to sever a major blood vessel. Death would be quick and the neck lock would ensure silence. The second officer would come in to help his colleague and would suffer a direct and fatal stab to the throat.

Moles straightened. Raglisevitch moved in behind him and slid his left arm around his neck, choking off any sound. Moles's hat dropped forward onto the toilet as the knife was pressed up hard through his nylon jacket and through his shirt. Moles didn't crumple.

"English police don't die so quick," whispered Raglisevitch. Then he felt the sharp pain of the knife across his own fingers. In the hard and unhesitating strike into Moles's back, Raglisevitch had allowed his hand to ride over the narrow hilt as the tip of the knife stuck fast in the multiple layers of Moles's covert stab-resistant vest. The pain now seared into the sensitive bundles of nerves in his hand. There was a loud click above the noise of the traffic as Moles dropped down and drove the end of his telescopic baton into Raglisevitch's right thigh. Raglisevitch released both neck and knife, screaming with pain. Dray, hearing the scream, flicked out his baton and smashed the curtained window in the door, showering the two occupants with glass.

He fumbled with the door catch, and within seconds Raglisevitch was dragged across to the grass verge by his hair. Moles spun out and moved towards the Granada, swapping his baton to his left hand and arming his right with a small gray tear gas canister. The man in the back of the car was opening the nearside door to go to the aid of the driver. Moles blocked the door, but used the gap to discharge some tear gas. A siren burst in above the noise of the traffic as Motorway Twenty Delta pulled in hard just ahead of the Granada. With tires trying to grip on the loose surface of the hard shoulder, it ground to a halt then reversed hard to block off the only means of escape. The two officers hurried out, but the fight was over. Dray was sitting on Raglisevitch's back while applying rigid handcuffs. The two passengers from the Granada were out on the verge coughing and rubbing their eyes, with Moles standing well back from them shouting above the din of the traffic, baton still raised.

"You have just been sprayed with CS crystals. Do not rub your eyes. The effects are temporary."

Thirty Nine

Question (Superintendent Hinx): "So who took the prisoners on?"

Answer (DCI Shackerstone): "We did, but SEPol, sorry, South East Police had got things moving and found the tapes in the caravan, and some handguns inside camera equipment boxes."

Q: "How did they come to light?"
A: "The lad who stopped them, he used a bit of gut feeling. He got the caravan towed in to a traffic police garage while the prisoners went off to Ashford. No cross contamination. A SEPol forensic team did the rest. It was a goldmine of evidence: there were costumes, cameras, videos, lights, tripods, books, knives, chains, hypodermics, rohipnol, chloroform, you name it. The makeup we found on Porterer, even dolls and fishing line."

Q: "What costumes?"
A: "Some Tudor gear, male and female. Then some Victorian, again male and female. Different sizes."

Q: "What did you conclude from these?
A: "Costumes for the films. The Tudor stuff we knew about and we linked the fibers to the underground studio, but the Victorian stuff we could only guess at. Gordonstown had his Jack the Ripper re-enactment theory. We could never prove what they intended, as they weren't very cooperative."

Q: "You said books?"

A: "History. Mostly foreign stuff, but it covered the movies and a lot more. There were some books in English, but they covered hundreds of different historical deaths and murders."

Q: "Including Jack the Ripper?"
A: "Well, yes."

Q: "Tell me about the forensic evidence."

A: "Good and bad. The fibers were great—a positive link to the bunker. That clay was there in the carpet, on shoes, on the feet of tripods and lighting stands. Dastra's hair was there, and his blood, in a big stain under a rug. He must have been lying there after they bashed his head. The grease on the car's tow ball matched the line we found on the back of his jacket. He must have been lifted into the trunk at some time. Blood from two of the girls, too, right down in some of the recesses of the caravan and the trunk of the car. There were dozens of sets of prints—our three suspects and half the border guards between here and the Ukraine. It looks like different frontier checks had been done and some reasonable searches of the inside on some occasions. The guns were inside false bottoms of camera equipment boxes. Previous searches hadn't found them. They ignored the videos and costumes because they were exactly what you would expect to find in a film unit. SEPol were the first to search the caravan with an idea of what to look for."

Q: "No other prints?"

A: "None of any use, although, importantly, no prints of Dastra's. His hairs and blood, but no prints. It appeared that Dastra had been there, but knocked out. Lucy's hypodermic theory with his semen looked good at the time too. Everything seemed to come together."

Q: "What about the address the car was registered to?"

A: "A small lockup on an industrial estate. Cars came and went, according to the neighbors. No forensics... clean as a whistle."

Q: "So any ideas where they did the editing and production of copies for sale?"

A: *"Not at that time, but everything pointed to Europe. The Slovakian police did some good work and found the lot just after we got the team weighed off at the Old Bailey."*

Q: *"Yes. Can you cover the video finds?"*
A: *"Of course. We found the masters of the Marie Antoinette and Joan of Arc films. There was the incomplete footage of Joanna Carter being set up for the execution of Anne Boleyn. The real finds were two different versions of the Vlad the Impaler film—they were very disturbing, and I mean, extremely nasty."*

Q: *"I know. I've viewed the second one."*
A: *"We don't need to cover any detail then."*

Q: *"No."*
A: *"The man they impaled, Terry Amsterbild... we identified him. Missing tourist. Body never found, although we knew approximately where to look."*

Q: *"Unexpected, though."*
A: *"Women were the interest; he was there to add realism. The extra woman they impaled in the second version we identified through Interpol in Hungary. She was the young wife of one of the film distributors. He decided to make a few pirate copies of the first version with our victims on it. The Vlad team found out and popped over to Hungary. They added her to subsequent copies of the film as a warning to anyone who might double-cross them."*

Q: *"So the films filled in a lot of the whole picture."*
A: *"They were a major result. The lab proved that the first version was a master and also which of their cameras it was recorded on. It was stone cold proof. All that was missing was a film with the Sarah Carothers murder on it, and the two actresses Carter saw in the bunker. We found traces of Dastra's and Sarah's blood and hair. We found that Raglisevitch's hair matched one of the many in Dastra's car. One of the other suspects had left his hair in Robinson's car and some clothing fibers in Porterer's. We were*

there. We charged them with the lot. It had all come together."

Q: "Even the magazine."
A: "Particularly the magazine. Moles saw it on the backseat of the car. It was the trigger."

Q: "What was your conclusion about the magazine?"
A: "I'll have to check the policy file. Yes. Here it is. Suspects may have intended to target the Dastra residence, as per earlier decisions, risk assessments and armed surveillance."

Q: "What about identity parades? Just cover the results for the tape."
A: Joanna Carter picked out two of the three in the underground studio—and we got the third banged to rights on a load of his hairs. Nothing on the actresses."

A: "You were satisfied they weren't coerced."
Q: "Entirely. Carter's account had them actively involved in the scene where she was supposed to be beheaded."

Q: "Would you cover the issue of the semen please."
A: "We tried to get a match on Raglisevitch's DNA. The stuff inside Francesca Porterer had deteriorated a lot, so it wasn't an evidential match, but we broke him in interview. He was an out and out racist, so using DS Khan tuned him up a treat. He lost his temper and ended up trying to punch Khan, but before he did, he let out a great tirade of evidence."

Q: "No doubts then?
A: "Not from me. There was something though."

Q: "What was that?"
A: "Gordonstown still wasn't happy with Dastra. He had a nagging suspicion. His mind was on the Victorian stuff and Jack the Ripper."

Q: "Did you discuss it?"

A: "We did. He always had Dastra as a suspect and he thought the next variation to the M. O. would have been a Ripper killing."

Q: "He wasn't far out."
A: "Ironic really. He was spot-on. For a while, anyway..."
(Extract from Metropolitan Police enquiry into Operation Klingsor.)

Bronze twilight punctuated by the orange glow of sodium lamps filtered into Shackerstone's office through the Venetian blinds. He walked in and flicked the fluorescent light on. Gordonstown followed him and sat down.

Shackerstone peered out through the blinds. "The sweet, dark moment of a good result."

"Pity about your trap, though," said Gordonstown.

"I got Carothers trying his avenging angel bit. He has confessed to both shootings up at Dastra's place and a string of firearms offences, so I've charged him with the lot. Mind you, a jury would probably let him go."

"Actually, we've had a bit of a cock-up on that front."

"What?" Shackerstone's good humor evaporated.

"His remand in custody went a bit pear-shaped. His counsel made an application to a judge in chambers at the Courts of Justice."

"I know, but we've got loads of grounds to keep him."

"Our man got directed to the wrong room. He sat outside for three hours waiting to be called. Luckily, they postponed the hearing for him, but when he went back today, the judge wasn't very pro. Carothers is back out."

"So where does that leave Dastra?"

"I can't put armed surveillance on him again. I've put a special scheme with the local control room. They are set to have an armed unit to Dastra within a fifteen minutes response time. Carothers has got a bail condition not to go within six miles of the house, and his gun is in the evidence store."

"That should do. Have we told him about the arrests?"

"Yes."

"He'll stay away."

Forty

Question(Superintendent Hinx): "Did DS Tony Shanter inform you of the information from the photographic shop in Aylesbury?"

Answer (DCI Shackerstone): "He did."

Q: "What do you recall him telling you?"

A: "He said that a shop assistant recognized Dastra's face from the TV. He was in the shop buying an accessory."

Q: "What accessory?"

A: "A red filter for a camera lens."

Q: "And that didn't ring any alarm bells?"

A: "With hindsight, it does, but at the time I dismissed it. There had been so many false sightings of Dastra."

Q: "Was it entered on HOLMES?"

A: "No. Tony came to me to tell me that he wanted it on, but with restricted viewing. As far as I was concerned we had got our suspects and Dastra didn't feature."

Q: "So it wasn't followed up."

A: "No. I planned to ask Barney about the filter, but I never got round to it. I thought that if it really was him, then he might have got the idea of using it from me."

Q: "Did you know he was interested in photography?"
A: "He could have taken it up. He was arty, and he had a new kid on the way."

Q: "Do you not think that it would have saved a lot of grief if you had put it in the system and acted on it according to basic principles?"
A: "Yes. It was... it was a fatal error."
(Extract from Metropolitan Police enquiry into Operation Klingsor.)

Lucy sat on a stool in front of the old mahogany dressing table in bright morning light looking carefully at her face in each of the three mirrors.

"Barney, have I got freckles?"

He rolled over and rose slowly out of the four-poster. The normality of his naked form contrasted sharply with Lucy's bloated belly and heavy breasts. He walked over and crouched slightly, placing his hands round the tops of her arms. Putting his head over her right shoulder, he looked at her reflection. He raised his eyebrows.

"Gosh, yes. More than freckles, they look brown and sort of joined up."

"What do you think caused them?"

"I don't know. It has been sunny these last few days, but I suspect it's something like the brown line running down the middle of your tummy. It must be a pregnancy thing."

He stood up and Lucy swung round to face him.

"Look at the line now."

Dastra saw that the tea-colored mark that had developed down Lucy's swollen belly was now much darker. He knelt down and put his hand over her navel.

"It's not moving much."

"It can't once the head is engaged. I'm sure it is going to be any day now."

"But it isn't due for another ten days."

"I hope it comes sooner. My skin is so tight. I think that if you put in a pin I would explode."

He sensed that she was trying to make a point about the

pregnancy, and the fact that he was going out that evening to speak at a formal dinner. "What time have I got to pick up Michaela tonight?"

"About four, she said, at Reading."

"You know that'll be cutting it fine."

"Yes, but you know I don't want you to go to London."

"But we've had all this out umpteen times. I've got to. I won't be asked next year because I will be old news."

He stood up and went to get his clothes ready for work.

"But darling, I'm worried."

"I'm on the end of a mobile phone. If you have a show I'll be home within an hour, I'll be with you for the birth, I promise. Nothing is more important than that."

"So don't go then."

"You won't be having it tonight or tomorrow. It's not due yet. You just…"

"You're going to say that I don't want you to go."

"Yes. You think that they are the wrong sort of company."

"I like Peter."

"But the rest? You were the great protestor once. What happened?"

"I married a cop."

"Fair point." He went off to wash and shave. When he returned Lucy was lying on the bed with the phone pressed to her ear.

"As soon as you can. That would be wonderful. Will you book now? I know, but at least they won't be busy at a time like this. Let me know. Bye, Mom."

Lucy reached out and dropped the phone onto its cradle.

"Mom? Isn't it the middle of the night out there?"

"Yes, but I wanted to tell her about the freckles. She says they're a sure sign that the baby is on its way. She had them with all three of us."

"And she's coming over?"

"As soon as she can. She's booking a flight now. She's so excited I can feel it from here."

"Good, I'm pleased. We'll need her here."

"First grandchild." Lucy got up and walked over to him. She

took hold of his arm and looked into his face. "I'm sorry. Look, I know your Mum and Dad would have been pleased too."

"They would. That's why I'm happy your mum is on her way. She's the only one I've got now."

Lucy put her arms around his neck and kissed him, turning her bump to one side so as not to push him away. "And you won't go tonight?"

"I've got to. You'll have Michaela, a mobile phone and a landline. I can be back in a jiffy if it all starts."

Lucy let go and sat down on the bed. "It isn't me I'm worried about."

"Don't worry about me. I'll be fine."

"But you aren't. You've been… very moody these last few days."

"I know. It's nothing. Perhaps I might be getting stage fright over doing my speech tonight."

"Then don't go."

"I must. Tonight is something that I *must* do. I must see it through." He kissed Lucy on the forehead. "I've got to go. My mobile is on and Mrs. Herbert said she would be in at midday. She's a better cook than I am."

"Come home as soon as you can."

"I'll try to slide off around three or four, but the office is covering Hemel Hempstead's calls today so that they can have an end of job party for one of their cases. I think I'll have to have a party when The Job eventually gives me my compensation."

"I'm sure the delay is just a budget thing."

"Or the case review. Perhaps the check is in the mail."

"I'll come in handy. You'll phone me if you get bored at work?"

"I'll phone you anyway, if only to keep you from going up the stepladder again to finish painting the nursery."

"Telling off accepted."

~ * ~

Brian Shackerstone was on the bank of a broad, still lake, fishing for rainbow trout on a sinking fly. His mobile phone vibrated and he flipped it open.

"Shackerstone."

"Brian. It's Joshua Gordonstown. Where are you?"

"I'm enjoying a nice and rather expensive day of fly fishing. I guess you're going to cancel it."

"The exigencies of duty, Brian, sorry. I've got a nasty triple murder at an address north of Hemel Hempstead. They're all off for the day and your office is supposed to be covering."

"A murder? What about F-MIT or my on-call DI?"

"Your on-call DI has busted his ankle playing squash and I reckon I owe you one more murder scene after Klingsor. I'll start the ball rolling, but I'll need to know how long you will be."

"I'll need to clean up. I won't be in a suit."

"Get here as you are. Not too fishy, though."

"Okay. I'll be an hour if the traffic is good. Where is it?"

"It's a bit off the beaten track. I'll give you directions."

~ * ~

Brian Shackerstone's Citroen bumped up the unmade road through the trees and past several impressive gateways before coming to rest opposite a uniformed officer standing by some blue and white cordon tape. Some cars were parked along the verge, and the last of these was Dastra's black Porsche. Shackerstone drew his car up behind it and got out into the dappled spring sunlight, still dressed in jeans and a sweatshirt. Dastra limped ashen-faced out from a driveway between tall hedges.

"Hello, Guv, nasty job this."

"So I understand. You'd best give me a quick briefing before I go in."

Dastra went to the back of his car and took some exhibit bags from the boot. Shackerstone cringed at the thought of the cross-contamination issues there would have been if Dastra hadn't had his car steam cleaned.

"Middle aged couple, Mr. and Mrs. Hughes. There's also a dead old lady upstairs in a bed. Shot at close range. Mother to one of them we think. Anyhow, he's a scrap metal dealer from West London. It's some sort of gangland hit. Mr. Gordonstown has been on to the National Criminal Intelligence Service, and our man wasn't called Hughes. He was a nasty piece of work called Wilmershott who turned Queen's evidence in the eighties. He got a load of major league armed robbers and drug dealers banged away. It looks like his fellow villains have blown his new identity and paid him back."

"A real *supergrass*, or at least, a demised supergrass."

"Very much so. Some guys from the Met are being called up to attend and get the ball rolling with possible suspects, but they will be an hour or two as they were off duty."

"I know the feeling. What's the M.O.?"

"Police radio alarm bypassed. He and she have both been hooded. He's been stabbed several times and so has she. He got one in the neck, right under his chin. There's blood everywhere. It's up the walls, all over the floor and the furniture; I've never seen anything like it. Whoever did it wanted to send a pretty strong message."

"Right."

"They've really turned the place over, too. Papers all over the place, drawers out, paintings taken down off the walls, as if they were looking hard for something. Perhaps they thought it was in a safe."

"Anything else. Any… horrible surprises?"

"Gosh, yes. There are a couple of things. His belly has been skinned—from his ribs down to his penis. Chief Superintendent Gordonstown is trying to find out if he had a tattoo or something and our suspects have taken it as a trophy. DS Khan has made a few calls, but nothing doing yet."

"You said a couple of things."

"Oh yes. The wall above the body has had blood spread all over it and the word "GRASS" written in two-foot tall letters spelt out by wiping a rag right across it. Like I say, a pretty strong message."

"Interesting… You're using the plural for our suspects. Any reason?"

"Sorry. I missed a bit. Dr. O'Toole is inside. He says the killings are by more than one person because the stab wounds are bunched. If one person is stabbing they strike anywhere, but with more than one they get in one another's way, so they are restricted to…"

"I know about bunching, thanks. I'd best go and do my bit." Shackerstone looked away towards the house as if deep in thought. He pressed his bottom lip up hard against his top lip and began to frown. He looked at Dastra. "Have you got an extra-large blue suit for me?" Dastra took one from the open trunk. Shackerstone leaned against the car's rear bumper while he put the suit on over his jeans and T-shirt.

"How's Lucy?"

"Pretty close to her time, we think. She's developed these funny freckles, almost overnight."

"Yes?"

"Her mum says they're because the baby is due any day. She's flying over from the USA tomorrow, I'm picking her up from Heathrow."

"Oh, good." Shackerstone's tone brightened. "You should have her here at a time like this. If you get stuck, I'll gladly pick her up. Is Lucy alone at the moment?"

"No. Mrs. Herbert should be there tidying up and doing some cooking. Why do you ask?"

"If it could be any time, you need to be with her."

"I've got this Injustice dinner up in London."

"Oh, that. So Lucy will be alone tonight?"

"No. A good friend of ours is coming up, and she's staying for the rest of the weekend. Lucy will be okay without me. There's a mobile phone as well as the landline. I'll go straight back home in good time if anything starts—and all the indications are that it is a pretty healthy pregnancy."

"But you're still going to give your piece at the dinner?"

They both sensed the atmosphere between them change.

"Guv, I know what you must be thinking. I'm not going to point any fingers at anybody, I'm just going to attack the system."

Shackerstone screwed up his eyes and looked hard at Dastra. "Thanks, I appreciate that, but if I could order you not to go, I would."

Shackerstone stood straight to zip the suit up. Dastra moved in closer to him to speak in a quieter but more assertive tone.

"Guv, tonight I will be with people who will listen and believe me. I have to do this."

Shackerstone nodded, giving a forced smile. "I'll see if we can release you as soon as poss."

Shackerstone turned away and they both walked across to the

gateway and along a taped route down the side of a curving gravel drive towards the crime scene. The brick-built, two-story house was wide and imposing, with a frontage of at least seventy feet, and ornate white pillars either side of the door. By its style, it was less than ten years old. The up and over door to the double garage was up, and the police route into the house was through here, as the main door awaited examination. DS Khan logged exhibits on a plastic sheet covering an old table.

"Reshard."

"Boss."

Shackerstone stopped to slip overshoes on, and to pull up the hood on his suit. Dastra handed him a pair of gloves.

"I won't come in, boss. I've seen enough. Mr. Gordonstown was in the main lounge just to the back of the house. That's where Mr. Hughes is. Malcolm will be with Dr. O'Toole examining Mrs. Hughes in a room off to the right. The old lady is in a bedroom above us. And SOCO Gray has got a team doing the whole house, room by room."

"Thanks."

Shackerstone disappeared into the house for about forty-five minutes, while Dastra waited in the garage, assisting Khan with exhibit bagging. Dastra had wandered up the driveway and out onto the road when Shackerstone emerged with Gordonstown, the two arguing with one another in loud whispers. They walked briskly towards Dastra, ducking under a cordon tape. Gordonstown smiled at Dastra. "Okay, Barney... off you go. The real Met will be here soon and Mr. Shackerstone has asked me to let you slide. I suppose you'll be giving me a mention tonight."

"Not at all sir, that won't be my tack. I won't be blaming you—or Mr. Shackerstone. It was the system that screwed us all... the way we do things. Even if I did blame you, sir, I wouldn't condemn without good evidence." Dastra raised one eyebrow to make his point.

"Good. Neither would I," he replied, winking.

"See you tomorrow, sirs."

Gordonstown folded his arms and watched Dastra get into the Porsche and reverse it into a side turning before accelerating away. Shackerstone turned to him.

"Okay, boss. What are you looking so smug about? And why did you call him all the way from Wemstone? You could have got a local PC to drop off the exhibits stuff."

"I needed to ensure he got away for his speech tonight."

They walked back in to the front garden. "And there's obviously a bit more."

"Okay, Brian. I shouldn't tell you this but... You have just said goodbye to DC Dastra... for good."

"For good?"

"We've got him for another murder."

"What?"

"A murder up in Yorkshire, a week back, a prostitute. She had his hairs in her hand."

"But... it must be another job by this other lot."

"So you think that one is still on the loose?"

"Must be."

"You're right, and he's just driven off."

Shackerstone stared coldly at Gordonstown, shaking his head firmly.

"But, we know they stitched him up."

"No. They planned it that way with him, to cover each other's tracks. Granted, he wasn't there for every job, but his traces were found far more frequently in the caravan and the underground studio than would have been reasonable for the short times he was supposed to be there. And it was all a bit too convenient him giving us that, wasn't it?"

"Oh, come on, Guv. If he was guilty, it took him months to tell us about the bunker."

"Or just a few hours, and not until after they had escaped. All they lost was a few bits of kit and our man looks like the hero riding to the rescue of the fair maiden."

"But Barney, he's married, kid on the way... he's got so much to lose."

"He's a cold-blooded pathological killer, Brian. He could yet do Lucy in. That's why he needs to be lifted now, before she gives birth."

Shackerstone shook his head. "Sorry, it just seems wrong."

"Just calm down and listen, Brian. We know that despite the

films, our man still likes playing Vlad. He even added an extra killing to the film…"

"But that was abroad. Barney was…"

"In England? He was still on shift work in the Met and on a four-day leave break when she went missing. He could easily have gone out to look after his little empire."

"But surely there would be some records of him crossing?"

"I've got SEPol and the airports checking. We'll find the day… don't you worry. Anyhow, Dr. Holt gave us two stories about Vlad that could put young Lucy as a victim. Indeed he probably planned this from the moment he met her."

"What? Holt wasn't even close…"

"Either he disembowels his princess who tricks him into believing she is pregnant…"

"Which can't apply now."

"No. But the ingredients are there."

"But they're potty about each other."

"They were. It sounds a bit cool now."

"It's just a phase. Once she's had the baby…"

"He would have killed her. Possibly by impaling her and sewing the baby to one of her nipples."

"And then surely get caught?"

"The net was closing, Brian. He knew that we would have got him eventually. I reckon he would have done her and the baby at home then skipped the country."

"The net?"

"Oh, yes. This Yorkshire job has got full corroboration. He was caught on a speed camera on the M1 in Leicestershire and his registration number was taken curb-crawling about an hour before the body was found." Gordonstown stopped for a moment, watching Shackerstone's reactions, but then continued at a quicker pace, his tone angrier. "Listen, Brian, he's stuffed. All our bloody farting about has cost another girl's life!"

"This is hard," muttered Shackerstone, shaking his head and looking at the ground. He looked up again and took Gordonstown's eyes. "When is he going to be nicked? Today?"

"At this posh dinner of his in London. I couldn't do this locally. Too many risks: Our bods deliberately cocking up the procedures for him, the sort of thing I got from you when I had Aybrams brought in. I've rustled up a surveillance team... a few people I can rely on from HQ. That's why I kept him here. They'll follow him from the bottom of the lane and keep as close a watch as they can on him and Lucy at his house."

Shackerstone looked down the empty road. Dastra's Porsche was out of sight. Gordonstown's glib satisfaction was still droning in his ears. "They can keep tabs on him until he's ready to be nicked by Yorkshire at this dinner. I hope he enjoys it... may be his last meal on the outside."

"But, Guv, Lucy is about to drop. Her mother is flying over tomorrow."

"That's the welfare angle sorted then. She can stand in for him at the birth."

"I'm sure Lucy will be delighted."

"And don't get any funny ideas about tipping Dastra off. The only people in the force who know about this are me and ACC Complaints. Even finance don't know why we've delayed paying out his compensation, and all the surveillance team know is to watch closely and wait for Yorkshire police. I've told you more than I should have."

"Yes. And for what? Personal bloody satisfaction, or do you still resent me being on F-MIT?"

"It's not a black thing, Brian. Honest. You're the best black DCI..."

"I'm the only fucking black DCI!"

"True, yes, but it's just satisfaction at proving you wrong, white or black. There's no need to play the bloody race card."

Shackerstone shook his head. "Then you should have kept your gob shut just now."

"No." Gordonstown started to make each point with a stab at Shackerstone with his right index finger. "It was worth it to see the look on your face. I've waited months for this moment, and the next few hours will be my reward, Brian. I'll be on your shoulder until he is well on his way up to London. Yorkshire police are coming down by train, and all the Met have been told is that they are backing up a high profile arrest. Yorkshire will brief them on the spot. A quick arrest, across to St Pancras, straight on a train up to Leeds. Not a chance then that any of his ex-Met chums can throw him a lifeline. And I'm ensuring you won't either, because if he isn't nicked tonight I'm going to have you investigated for tipping him off and for the all the other bloody mistakes you made on the Klingsor job."

Shackerstone walked away shaking his head, trying desperately to find a hole in Gordonstown's reasoning. He spun on his heel, looking abruptly back at Gordonstown.

"Sir, can I call his wife. I'll only speak to *her*. I won't warn him... you can listen in. I just need to touch base with her."

"I'll consider it. In the meantime I need to borrow your mobile phone. Mine is on the blink. I'll give it back to you later."

Shackerstone reluctantly handed over his mobile phone. Gordonstown checked the battery indicator, then pocketed it before continuing. "Can we get on with this job now? Operation Klingsor is history now, and I'll get you back off this case by midweek. Believe me. This job is going to be this year's big case. It will run and run while I dig around London's gangland, stepping all over the Met's toes. This is just the kind of opportunity I need."

Forty One

Question (DCI Shackerstone): "How about you. Is it a sexual thing?"
Answer(Suspect): "(Long pause) Yes. How about you?"

Q: "No. It's a protection thing. I wish I could have saved…"
A: "But does it turn you on?"

Q: "I'm asking the questions."
A: "The deal. There is a need to know… you haven't told everything."

Q: "(pause). Okay. I find them sickening somewhere in here… they keep me awake."
A: "But you need to look again, don't you?"

Q: "I suppose so. Yes."
A: "Because of the art, or because you get turned on?"

Q: "Neither. I think it's a kind of fear thing. I need to confront them. A lot of cops are like that… it's almost a hobby with some. (pause) Is that enough?"
A: "Enough what?"

Q: "Is that all you wanted to ask?"
A: "There is another question. A philosophical one…"
(Extract from evidential tape transcript.)

Dastra was home soon after three, but Mrs. Herbert insisted on staying to prepare a meal for Lucy and Michaela. Lucy wanted to try some more emotional pressure to make him stay at home for the evening, but he remained darkly silent. Eventually he put on old clothes and boots and went out into the garden. Taking some seed potatoes down to a small area he had prepared just off the lawn towards the gateway, he spent a slow hour planting them and clearing his head.

At about four o'clock Lucy waddled awkwardly down from the house and across the lawn towards him. The day was still sunny, but a light breeze was tugging her dress, accentuating her bump.

"Darling, you'll need to get ready if you're going to get Michaela at four."

He stabbed the spade in the ground as if he was about to lose his temper, but Lucy's smile calmed him.

"That's four rows of Wilja, second earlies."

Lucy nodded. "Good exercise."

He stepped out of the mud and wiped soil from his hand. When he was satisfied his right hand was reasonably clean, he took Lucy by the hand and helped her back up to the house. He showered and dressed up in a dinner suit. He made several attempts to tie his black bow tie, and only succeeded on the seventh with some help from Lucy. She had given up trying to dissuade him from going to the dinner, and after finishing his tie and checking his appearance, she sent him off to fetch Michaela from Reading station.

~ * ~

When Michaela stepped off train, Dastra was already on the platform waiting for her. They kissed like old friends and he offered to take her bag. Seeing him still limping, Michaela declined, so he walked her out to the car park. He opened the trunk of his car.

"What's all this?" asked Michaela.

"Exhibit bags and stuff; I've been on a job today. A triple murder up near Hemel Hempstead... not very nice at all."

"I thought you looked a bit stressed."

"I suppose you've seen me stressed out often enough to know."

"I reckon I know you as well as anyone, except Lucy. Is she

okay?"

"She's blooming, but she gets very tired from carrying the baby. I hope it comes soon."

He shut the lid and they both got into the car and were soon on the road back up from Reading towards Prospect of Peshawar, moving slowly behind a large blue farm tractor. Michaela watched his growing anger with the lack of progress.

"You must be getting quite excited about the birth."

"Yes. I suppose so. It seems we've come a long way in ten months. Mind you, Lucy is getting fed up. She just wants to get the birth out of the way. Her Mum is on the way over."

"I know, Lucy phoned me."

"I guess she spoke about tonight. She's not too happy about me going out."

"You can understand that, though."

"Of course. It's just something I have to do."

"Lucy can see that too. Deep down I think she wants you to do it. I think she's just a bit nervous with the baby so close."

Dastra saw a chance and pulled out, accelerating past the tractor. He continued to add speed to the car as it raced up the hill. Without warning, a yellow Renault pulled out of a narrow road on his left. He braked sharply, the Porsche lurching sideways as the wheels locked up.

"Madman," he shouted, as if the driver could hear him.

The Renault continued to pull out slowly then drive equally slowly up the hill. Dastra drove up close behind the rear of the car, weaving from left to right.

"Barney, don't," protested Michaela. "It's probably some country yokel who never goes out."

He shook his head and eased back. The car in front pulled to the left without signaling and slowed almost to a stop. Unfortunately, as Dastra went to overtake, the car started a slow U-turn. Dastra braked again as he watched the car cross just in front of his front bumper and use the full width of the road and the lay-by to turn about. The driver didn't even glance across at him, but stopped the car in the same lay-by as where Dastra's press intruders had been caught, and started to examine a map.

"Lost?" commented Dastra, moving off.

"It happens to me all the time."

He accelerated hard into a wooded section of the road and up to the small roundabout at the top of the hill. A minute later his progress was checked again as he coasted down the lane towards his gates. Now a large left-hand drive American car was moving slowly in front of him.

"You know, this must be day of the lost driver. This guy can find nothing down here except our house, a nice view and some fields. In fact, with a car that wide I doubt if he'll fit."

"Tourists, I expect. Seeing the sights," suggested Michaela.

"Are we on the Oxfordshire tourist trail?"

The American car maintained its speed and drifted on past the gateway. The days of constant surveillance on him crossed Dastra's mind, but the type of car was wrong. He activated the remote control and sped up the gravel drive. Mrs. Herbert's car was gone and he parked close to the front door. Lucy waddled out to greet Michaela and kissed her as she got out of the car.

"Hi. Good to see you. Did you have a good journey?"

"The train part was good," answered Michaela, looking at Dastra. "We seemed to be behind a lot of weekend drivers on the way up from the station. Anyhow, that's enough about me. Gosh, Lucy, you've got so…"

"Big?"

"Well, yes. Any day now then."

Lucy clasped her hands. "I can't wait."

Dastra took Michaela's case from the car and put it on the front step.

"I'm sorry, ladies. I must go. My mobile's on. I can be back in no time and you've got the details of the Café Royal."

Lucy nodded as if in resignation at the inevitability of him going. She put her right wrist on his left shoulder and held him by the back of his head.

"I'm worried for you. That's all. We will be fine here in British Fort Knox. If I do have to call an ambulance, the main problem will be them getting through all the security."

"I'm sure it won't come to that. I must go."

"Oh," said Lucy, changing her tone and dropping her arm. "DCI Shackerstone phoned."

"Yes?"

"Yes. He was a bit odd again, like he sometimes is with me. He was checking that I was okay, and he wanted to check when my mom is arriving."

"I guess that's why he called. I told him about her earlier at the crime scene. I think he carries a bit of a torch for her."

"He was still odd, though. A bit formal, as if someone was listening."

"He will still be at work. Gordonstown is with him. Darling, I must get cracking."

He kissed Lucy and got back into his car before rounding the flowerbed and driving back down to the gates. Lucy and Michaela watched the gates open and the Porsche 928 accelerate out into the lane.

Forty Two

Question (DI Graham): "Did you have absolutely no regard for her?"

Answer (suspect): "There was some, but she was just a tool in the end, like the rest."

Q: "But she was nine months pregnant for heaven's sake!"
A: "That was why... why great speed was needed."

Q: "But... but, the baby... didn't you have any feelings?"
A: "It was a trip. Life to death. This was very personal... the child was... family. But Lucy. (long pause) My fascination with her made the transition from life to death more... alluring."
(Extract from evidential tape transcript.)

Blustery clouds gathered in the early evening as Michaela and Lucy finished their dinner in the piano room. Mrs. Herbert had cooked it and left, assuring them that she would be back tomorrow to check on the progress of the birth.

The phone rang as Lucy and Michaela drank coffee. Michaela answered it, but turned immediately to Lucy.

"It's that Chief Superintendent Gordonstown," she whispered, passing the phone to Lucy.

"Hello, this is Lucy Dastra."

"Hello, Detective Chief Superintendent Joshua Gordonstown. We have met before."

"When you arrested me."

"Yes, sorry about that. No harm done, I hope. Is DC Dastra there?"

"No, he's gone to London. He's doing a talk. He left around five."

"My mistake. He told me earlier. I'm sorry to disturb you. I'll, uh, speak to him tomorrow... it can wait. Oh, by the way, good luck with the baby."

"Thanks."

"Goodnight."

Lucy replaced the receiver. "Second odd call of the night...I think he was checking whether Barney had actually gone."

"Why would he do that?"

"Barney has put a lot into his speech tonight. I think Gordonstown is worried that he might feature in it. I suppose he was hoping something—like me—might have stopped Barney going."

They finished their coffees and Michaela washed the dishes before Lucy showed her to the upstairs room they had prepared for the baby.

"We don't know what gender it is yet. I want it to be a surprise. That's why we chose yellow."

"It's sunny. Like the baby's mother."

"Thank you. I hope it's a sunny child." Lucy sat heavily on the bed and showed Michaela some baby clothes and toys she had bought, before turning the conversation round to Dastra. "You said yellow was sunny like me."

"Yes?"

"What color would you put in for the father?"

"I didn't mean it like that. I wasn't missing him out. It was just a comment."

"Be hypothetical then."

"Don't know. Black would fit him right now. Twice I thought we were going to have a road rage on the way up from the station."

"I can believe that. He went out for one of his long drives the other night. Something's bugging him, I know, and I don't think it's the baby. It's something to do with the murders, something that keeps picking at his mind, but he won't share it with me." Lucy and Michaela walked down the stairs and back to the piano room.

"He's had a strange year. There must be a lot going on in that head of his."

"I know. I just wish he'd share some of the burden. That's what marriages are for, aren't they?"

"That and babies."

"Ouch!"

"What?"

"A contraction... you have these occasional practice ones. They're quite normal. It doesn't mean the baby is due. But..."

"What?"

Lucy stood still and smiled. "I think I've just had a show."

"Oh, God. How long will it be now?"

"Don't jump the gun, I need to check myself."

Lucy waddled off to the bathroom to examine herself. She came back with a nervous smile on her face.

"We'd best call Barney. It will be hours yet, but he'll want to come back." She sat down carefully on the sofa.

"What about calling the maternity unit?"

"They can take me at an hour's notice. Just call Barney, please."

Michaela tried Dastra's mobile but only connected to the answering service. She tried the Café Royal. "Hello. Yes. I need to contact a friend urgently to tell him his wife's about to go into labor. David Dastra, he's giving a speech tonight at the Injustice dinner." Michaela paused while the person on the other end checked a list. "What. Are you sure? David Dastra. Not listed."

"Tell them to try Barney Dastra," suggested Lucy.

"How about Barney Dastra, yes... bugger. The line has gone dead." Michaela pressed the phone cradle several times, but the line was quite silent. The silence was broken by the bleeping of the intercom from the front gate. Michaela answered it, looking into the unit.

"Hello?"

"Open up." crackled an agitated male voice.

"Move back from the camera so I can see you."

"Can you open the gate?"

"It's that man, Lucy. Jeff Carothers."

Lucy, wincing from another contraction, looked up in alarm

at Michaela. "Call 999, he's supposed to stay away as part of his bail conditions."

"But the phone's dead."

"Try the mobile, it's in the hall."

Michaela ran out of the piano room, through the library and into the hall. Lucy moved over to the screen by the intercom. She could see Carothers's face distorted by the wide-angle lens. He was clearly talking excitedly, but Michaela had flicked the sound off. For a moment, Lucy thought she could see a figure standing behind him. Lucy's attention suddenly switched to the windows at the front of the piano room. "I think there's someone on the drive."

Michaela came back in, mobile phone in one hand. She went up to the window and looked out into the fading daylight. "It's okay. Thank goodness."

~ * ~

Lynch found Dastra in the gentlemen's toilets at the Café Royal in London's Regent Street, sweating and breathing hard.

"Barney-boy? What's the matter?"

"Oh, Pete, am I glad to see you? It took me ages to find a parking spot, and it's about a mile away."

"You've cut it very fine. We're going in to the banqueting room in a minute. Did you have to run?"

"If you can call it that... Paralympics "fast track limping" might be closer."

"Take a minute to get your breath, Barney-boy. You're a star player tonight, everyone can wait."

"I'm dead nervous and my heart is going nineteen to the dozen."

"Chill out. Have a Scotch or two."

"No, I can't get tanked up. Drunk driving is a sacking offence for coppers—even though it isn't yet for Members of Parliament."

"That's the way the establishment looks after itself. You see better when they've jumped all over you."

"I can, and I want to put some of that idea into my speech. But my mouth is going dry already."

"Just try to relax. You'll be fine once you are on your feet, and we've got a meal before that."

"I haven't got much of an appetite. I've just come from a really nasty triple murder."

"You and I have been through a lot worse times than tonight, Barney-boy. Just cool down."

~ * ~

Dastra followed another after-dinner speaker called Robin Kaminski, from the USA, who told the story of how he had secured the release of a prisoner on death row. The story mirrored Dastra's, and forced him to adjust his speech.

There was polite, but limited applause as Dastra got to his feet. He took a casual roving glance around all the faces looking at him, as if challenging someone to speak out. There was silence. He scanned the hands slowly turning wineglasses, and the deadpan expressions of some of the more notable celebrity "miscarriages". This was it.

"As you know I have been asked to speak tonight as much because I am the latest freed victim, as because I am probably the only serving police officer here."

There was hissing from a few of the audience, followed by general nervous laughter.

"I know we're not in the top spot for popularity, especially here in London. I suspect that many of you will have taken interest in the Stephen Lawrence inquiry. I'd like to be able to claim that my own police force would never have made such a dreadful mess. Unfortunately, I know too well that they can. Yes, as I am still on the payroll of Central Southern Police, you could say I have a foot in both camps, and I am sure many of you feel that I am amongst both the stitchers-up and, sadly, the stitched-up." Dastra paused and took a sip of brandy. "But I put it to you all, that there are plenty of other stitchers-up here tonight, whether they be the judges, the barristers, solicitors or even the TV news presenters."

His speech had been well practiced, but although he was happy with his delivery, his audience seemed distant, as if still suspicious of this latest celebrity. There was even some slight heckling, but he got his point home none the less. He talked for about twenty minutes, and tried to end with his main points.

"...therefore, I must finish with a message to you all, and to all honest coppers... No Shortcuts!" There was polite applause.

"If you want a first class justice system, the resources need to be at the sharp end too. Underfunded and overworked coppers make a breeding ground for expedient corner cutting. The bottom line is that we who have suffered have all paid instead of the taxpayer. Thank you."

There wasn't thunderous applause, but there were a few cheers, including at least one familiar Irish voice. As the applause died down, Dastra let himself relax back in his seat. He was the last speaker and he watched in strange detachment as people drifted off home or out to the bar. Eventually he decided to join the latter group. As he was waiting to be served, he was approached by a previous speaker, the tall, balding, avuncular Robin Kaminski.

"Say, Barney, pleased to meet you." Kaminski gave Dastra a firm handshake.

"Pleased to meet you, Robin."

"Great speech. You spoke from the heart."

"Thanks."

"Your first go at public speaking?"

"Except in court, yes."

"You did well. We all get butterflies when we start, then suddenly you're there."

"You forget your nerves."

"That's about it. Say, I've been taking a great interest in your case. I'm delighted you've been cleared. And I am very interested in getting more information on the guys you've got in custody."

"There's not much I can give you…it's all *sub judice* at the moment."

"I've heard a bit, like the snuff movies. But you've got the right guys?"

"Oh, yes, one hundred and one percent. There's enough to be sure of several murder convictions for each."

"A stroke of luck, wasn't it?"

"Good police work."

"So your trap didn't work."

"Trap?"

"Don't be coy with me, Barney. You tried to tempt them up to your home."

"Well spotted. It worked, too, but on the wrong man. The

husband of one of the victims."

"So I heard. Still, your wife must be besotted with you to put herself up as the next victim."

Dastra paused. "Lucy?"

Kaminski stroked his chin and stared for a second at Dastra. "Yes. Lucy."

"Lucy? No. We had stooges in the house."

"But the killers were supposed to think Lucy was there... weren't they?"

"Not particularly. It was me they took a shot at."

"Yes, but that was the husband of one of the victims. He was aiming for you, but you were using a proxy for Lucy to tempt your movie makers into surfacing to make a film of her."

Dastra grimaced, "Gosh, no. I was the bait. Lucy was incidental. They could have got her at any time."

"Not until after the idea had been planted in their heads."

"Idea?"

"The idea of killing her on film."

Dastra shook his head. Kaminski nodded knowingly.

"Sit down, Barney. I'll get you your drink."

Dastra sat down by a table, confused and worried. Kaminski returned with two drinks, and the notebook computer he had been using for his presentation.

"You were using Lucy to bait them with a possible rerun of the Manson murders, were you not?"

"The Manson murders?"

"You've never heard of Charles Manson?"

"Yes. Vaguely, it was before I was born."

"Right. Back in 1969, The Summer of Love. Charles Manson brought it to an abrupt end."

"He did?"

"He led a strange kind of hippie group near Los Angeles. He called them his "family". He partied with the rich and famous, and was hoping to break into the music scene through a man called Terry Melcher, the son of Doris Day."

"But what has Lucy...?"

"Please hear me out. This guy Manson seemed to have a mesmeric hold over the people in the family, and he himself believed that the lyrics of a Beatles record called Helter Skelter were telling him to start a race war. He wanted to start a fierce backlash against the black community by sending his followers to murder some rich white people."

Kaminski's computer screen lit up and he selected a file with some photographs as thumbnail images. "He seemed to have decided that Melcher wasn't helping him to become famous, so he instructed a follower named Charles Watson and three of his female groupies to go round to Melcher's Beverley Hills house in Cielo Drive and kill everyone inside. Unfortunately, it had changed hands some months earlier. Inside was actress Sharon Tate, heavily pregnant. With her was a former boyfriend Jay Sebring... he was the guy who did the funny haircuts for the gladiators in the movie Spartacus, and two other friends, Abigail Folger and Voytek Frytowski. Her husband, director Roman Polanski was waiting to fly home from Europe. Take a look at this picture of Sharon." Kaminski clicked on a thumbnail and the screen was filled with a photograph of a stunning, honey-blonde actress. "She was shorter but otherwise generally similar to Lucy apart from hair and eye coloring, but the hair wouldn't be difficult to change for a movie, especially if you used black and white. They're both in the same league of good looks. Then take a look at these other shots of her. Do some of the settings look familiar?"

"The photos they used in the magazine. It's as if..."

"The magazine copied the settings deliberately, right down to lightening her hair in the black and white shots. Surely that was the true bait?"

"Not that I knew." Dastra let the images sink in, along with the feeling that he had somehow been betrayed by Shackerstone. "This is unbelievable."

"Your photographer must have been in on the scheme. I can't believe you didn't have..."

"It wasn't the main photographer who took those particular shots... it was... my Detective Chief Inspector."

"The same cop who put you away?"

"Shackerstone. Yes. I just don't..."

"Shackerstone?"

"Yes?"

"One of these photographs…" He clicked the cursor on a thumbnail and it filled the screen with a smiling and beautiful blonde with the background deliberately out of focus. "…is attributed to B. Shackerstone." He clicked on a button and a "properties" window appeared. "*B. Shackerstone, London, 1969.*"

"I knew of his name from the investigation, but I never made the connection until now. It looks like he had a former career."

"I knew he was a photographer."

"Barney, this is what you were up against if you hadn't caught your culprits." Kaminski's manner seemed to brighten with intellectual excitement. "This is a police picture of the Manson murder scene… it's pretty disturbing…"

"Yes. Gosh."

"Concentrate on the ceiling beam. It's a lot thinner than yours is, but it was essential to the crime. They used it to hang Sharon up by the neck. You can see it still round her neck where she's lying in the photo by the sofa." Dastra looked at the bloody and lifeless pregnant corpse lying in front of a sofa draped with the Stars and Stripes.

"So what did they do, exactly?"

"The four of them went up to the house one night with specially sharpened bayonets…they had put a cutting edge down both sides. Watson had a long Buntline Special revolver. He climbed a telephone pole and cut the phone line. Then they went over the fence and ran into a young lad leaving in his dad's car. His name was Steve Parent, very much the forgotten victim in the whole saga. Watson shot him four times, then they broke into the house through a window and searched it for victims. They found the four young people around the house, Sharon was relaxing on her bed. They herded them into the lounge and after looping the rope over the beam, they tied the ends of the hanging rope around Sharon's neck and Jay's. Watson sent one of his companions out when she got cold feet about the enterprise and she later gave state's evidence."

"I don't think we'll be getting any of that from the Vlad team."

"No? Anyhow, Jay objected to the brutality shown to Sharon so Watson shot him dead. Voytek and Abigail put up a fight, and both were killed. They made it outside, but not far enough. This is

Folger on the lawn. The nightdress was originally white. It went totally red from the dozens of deep stab wounds she received."

Dastra sucked at his teeth. "Nasty…"

"Which brings us back to poor Sharon, who by now had surely lost her mind. Her guests were all dead and now it was her turn. She never had a clue as to why it was all happening. She pleaded with them to take her with them and allow her to have her baby and then kill her. Every instinct was to protect her unborn child. She was losing so much, Barney… a bright career in front of her, fame, fortune, family, everything… but still she put the baby first. D'ya know what one of the girls said?"

"Go on."

"'We don't care about you or your baby, bitch. You're gonna die, so you'd better be ready!' Her own baby was back at Manson's commune. Sharon pleaded with them to cut the baby out after killing her, but they couldn't care less. Anyhow, they started stabbing with bayonets, catching her on the cheek first, then puncturing her chest and back, to a depth of five or six inches. She bled to death, and one of the killers left the scene licking the blood off her hands. Strangely, though, they never stabbed the baby. It was delivered stillborn but otherwise untouched at the autopsy." He produced a post mortem photograph of the actress on a mortuary slab.

"Very gruesome. I don't think I need to see that sort of thing with Lucy about to drop."

"I'm sorry, Barney. I felt sure you must have been part of the plan."

"But how did Manson get them to do what he said… to murder without a motive of their own?"

"Hard to say. At the trial he seemed to have some odd hold over his followers, to the extent that when he carved a swastika in his forehead, they all followed suit. They were all sentenced to death, but the death penalty was suspended for a few years in the 70s and so they're all still serving life. I think his grip has relaxed after thirty years."

"So you're telling me that in the USA at the moment you can get executed for a one-off shooting, but a bunch of multiple killers are serving life?"

"Hard to swallow, I know. That's the USA. The best justice

money can buy."

"I used to believe in the death penalty, and I guess I still do for the likes of our Vlad team, but now I've been on the receiving end of a miscarriage…"

"You're not so sure."

"No, I'm not." Dastra pondered for a moment. "Still, we digress. Has Manson shed any more light on the killings?"

"No. He just sticks to a claim that as he wasn't present at the killings, he can't be guilty. Anyhow, some think it was a struggle for group supremacy between Manson and Watson, others that the family treated him as a sort of messiah and would do anything he asked of them. What we do know is that he referred to his victims as pigs. He dehumanized them in advance of the crime, just like Hitler and the Jews. They even wrote PIG in Sharon's blood on the front door of the house as they were leaving."

Dastra leaned back and folded his arms. "It's all pretty disturbing stuff, Robin, and I'm genuinely grateful to you for pointing this out. I'm wondering now what to do about my DCI. I'm in a difficult position. I guess I'll have to make a formal complaint against him… one of my own senior officers."

"Sorry to be the messenger."

"That's okay. If I had known a few weeks ago, I would have been a very worried man. Still, there you go, all safe now." Dastra emptied his drink and plonked the glass down hard on the table. "Anyhow, how did the Manson lot get caught in the end?"

"Luck again. One of the girls was arrested for something else and bragged to another girl in the cell with her that the police had screwed up the investigation: evidence lost, and they failed to connect it to the other Manson killings."

"There were more?"

"Oh, yes. Manson wasn't too keen on what his disciples had done. He didn't feel it was brutal enough. He decided to supervise the next night's killings personally. Only a few miles away, but in a different police jurisdiction, a couple called Leno and Rosemary LaBianca were hooded and trussed up in their own home by Manson himself, who then went out for a bite to eat while his disciples did the serious part of the evening's killing. When they had finished they wrote, 'Death to Pigs' on the wall, and 'Rise', and 'Helter Skelter', misspelling it, all in the blood of their victims. Look at this photograph." Kaminski brought up a crime scene photo on his computer. "The words allegedly came into Manson's mind from the Beatles' lyrics. He had never heard of a Helter Skelter in the English context, and used the American meaning. Interestingly, the killers also carved 'War' on Leno LaBianca's abdomen."

Dastra's thinking drifted back to the Hughes crime scene of that afternoon. He was listening less intently to Kaminski's words.

"Like I said, one of the factors was that the police in L.A. publicly disconnected the two cases, despite the obvious links. The second killings at Cielo drive were initially blamed on a drug deal going wrong."

"Robin, you said the LaBiancas were hooded?"

"Yes."

"And the suspects wrote in blood on the walls?"

"Yes, as I say…"

"And Leo?"

"Leno."

"Leno's belly had 'War' scratched on it?"

"Yes."

Dastra felt a sweat break out across his forehead and the back of his neck.

"Listen, today I was at a crime scene just like that. The words were different—but they could have been written over to throw us off, and the guy's belly had been skinned—I guess so they could conceal what they had done. But everything else was there."

Kaminski looked up from the computer. "That's very interesting, Barney."

"There's one more thing."

"Go ahead."

"There's a thumbnail of a car in your collection. Was that Steve Parent's?"

"Yes. An AMC Rambler."

Dastra's last clear thought at the bar table was the large American car bumping past his gate earlier that afternoon. Intuition did the rest. He didn't even recall running from the bar and down the wide staircase When he arrived in the lobby area, he didn't know what to do. His mouth was going dry, the back of his neck was sweating and his hands were hot.

Calm down. Phone her.

He pulled out his mobile phone and pressed the four buttons to AutoDial. "I'm sorry, this line is out of order," said a pre-recorded voice. He tried button 5 to dial Lucy's mobile. It rang four times then went dead. Dastra felt his stomach begin to churn. He made the next call to his local police station from a badly needed toilet cubicle. The telephone rang for five minutes before he got an answer. The officer on the other end was disinterested and uncooperative, even more so when Dastra gave his details.

"Listen, mate, the whole area has been knocked out. Some piece of switching gear has blown. There are thousands of houses without phones tonight. We have loads of central station alarm calls triggered by the line failures."

"Has mine been triggered?"

"Let me have a look. Umm, yes, as you would expect. Still, unless there is a corroborating second call, you know the policy: We treat them as false alarms."

"I'm on a special scheme. My alarm should be treated as an instant armed response."

There was a brief silence on the other end.

"It was. It was boshed today by a senior officer."

"Boshed?"

"Yes, he said it was no longer needed."

"Listen, that must have been a mistake. There is a risk to my wife... a real one. I can't go into detail, but I've just received some info here in London that she is going to be murdered tonight."

"Really?"

"Yes, really. It's too complicated to explain, but just get someone up there."

"I can't do that just on your say-so. I'll have to speak to the duty officer and get back to you. He's out on a call."

"Just get an armed unit up there."

"I'll do my best. Someone will take a look, mate. Don't worry, I'll sort it out."

From the noncommittal tone of the officer, Dastra didn't trust that much would be done. He finished using the toilet, washed his hands and splashed water on his face to cool himself down. He went out into the hotel reception and standing near the main entrance doors he tried to call Shackerstone. His home line was out of order too. He tried his mobile number. He didn't want to sound too panicky and when he only obtained voicemail, he left a short message.

"Guv, this is Barney. I think today's killing is another snuff movie. Someone is doing a copy-cat of the Charles Manson murders. I am going home A.S.A.P. I just think he may be after Lucy. Call me back on my mobile. Urgent."

He tried some others on the squad, but knew most were out drinking. Dastra's final attempt was to raise Khan, whose mobile was also switched off. He sat down in an armchair and tried to find Khan's home number in his pocket diary. He became aware of two men uncomfortably close to him.

"David Dastra?" said a Yorkshire accent.

"Sorry, yes. I'll be with you in a sec…"

"I'm Detective Chief Inspector Fotheringhay and this is my colleague Detective Sergeant Halgill. We're from Yorkshire Police." Dastra looked up from his diary.

"Please, just let me make this call."

Fotheringhay leaned across and snatched Dastra's mobile. "David Dastra, I'm arresting you for the murder of Sonia Popelcinski in Leeds on the fourth of March."

Dastra leapt to his feet, his mind still on Lucy and barely registering what was being said.

"Sorry, Leeds? I don't understand."

Fotheringhay continued "You do not have to say anything, but it may harm your defense if you do not mention, when questioned, something which you later rely on in court. Anything you do say may be given in evidence."

Dastra stood open-mouthed for a second, but his mind clicked back to Lucy.

"Listen, this is some sort of cock-up. I think my wife is about to be murdered by someone and I need to get to her fast. I can't come with you. It's impossible."

DS Halgill slipped a rigid handcuff onto Dastra's right wrist. Dastra tried to spin away but found himself face down and pinned to the armchair while his other wrist was secured behind his back. Peter

Lynch emerged from the dining room. The few other people in the reception area were either backing away or looking on. Lynch ran up and pulled Halgill back by the collar.

"Barney-boy. What the fuck is going on?"

Halgill brought his elbow up and butted Lynch hard in the face, sending him sprawling to the carpet. Fotheringhay pulled Dastra up to his feet and started to march him towards the main door. Halgill backed away from Lynch and began to follow them. A Metropolitan police van with two officers waited by the curb outside. Dastra was bundled into the cage in the back. He breathed in deeply and tried to collect his thoughts. He knew that in the next few minutes he would have an opportunity to explain his predicament to a Metropolitan police custody officer, so spared his breath and started to think hard about what he would say.

Five minutes later the back doors opened, but not in the back yard of a Metropolitan police station. They were in a side street by St. Pancras mainline railway station.

"Thanks, gents," said Fotheringhay to the crew of the van.

"What's happening?" Dastra demanded as Halgill guided his head under the low doorway from the cage. Halgill got Dastra standing upright before answering. "We'll book you in with British Transport Police, and then back to Leeds for you by train."

"You can't. You don't get it do you. I have got to get back home. My wife is in danger."

Fotheringhay stepped around the back door of the van. "Don't you ever give it a rest?"

"Not when I'm about to be arrested again for something I know nothing about and my wife is about to be murdered!"

The van driver appeared at the rear of the van and shut the doors. Recognition sank in as he was about to turn away. "You're thingy...Vlad isn't it?"

"I was, yes. But I was cleared. This lot are about to..."

"There you go. I always had my doubts. Goodnight, gents."

The van driver got back in and drove away. Dastra turned to Fotheringhay again.

"Look. Listen."

"Come on lad, let's get walking."

"I'm a bit slow. I've got a leg injury from prison."

They started to lead Dastra down a passage at the side of the station.

"Listen. Have you ever heard of the Charles Manson murders, in the USA?" There was no answer. The detectives pushed Dastra on. "I've dealt with a murder today... a middle aged couple. There was blood all over the walls, and something had been written in blood and rubbed off. They were hooded and he was stabbed in the throat. It was a copycat murder."

"If you say so, lad," said Fotheringhay.

"Well, tonight I've left my heavily pregnant wife at home with her best friend. I reckon she's going to get a call from the same people, and they want to film the rest of the Manson murders."

"So you think from just one job you've been on today, that your wife is the next port of call?"

"It isn't one job. For fuck's sake. It's part of the Vlad killings and some of the crew are still loose!"

"We know that, lad. That's why we are here. We've got you banged to rights for one in Leeds."

"But I couldn't have. Tell me how it..."

"I'm not falling for that one. That'll start the twenty-four-hour detention clock ticking. Just wait until we get back to Leeds."

"What about booking me in?"

"British Transport Police will book you in at their office here. We've got forty-five minutes before our train."

Dastra sighed, but hoped that the custody officer at the BTP station would listen to him. Fotheringhay and Halgill led him down the passageway and into the back of the police station. They were let in to a brightly lit corridor with a bench down one side. There were several other officers ahead of them, apparently waiting to have prisoners booked in. Halgill held him by the arm while Fotheringhay went ahead to speak to the custody officer.

"DCI Fotheringhay, Yorkshire police. I've got one I need to house for forty minutes or so."

"You'll have to wait your turn. Take a seat on the bench."

"But we've got a train to catch."

"I'm sorry. If you don't get booked in, it will have to be a pocket-book entry. Just make sure you get the times."

Fotheringhay came back and spoke to Halgill. "Take a seat.

If it gets to be longer than half an hour, we'll skip this and take him on to the train. I'm going to find a tea, do you want one brought back?"

Halgill nodded. Fotheringhay slipped past the queue of officers. He spoke quietly to the custody officer to get the code for the door into the rest of the station and then saw himself out of the custody area. Halgill pushed Dastra down so that he was sitting on the prisoners' bench, still handcuffed behind his back.

"Can I get out of these for a while?"

"Just wait your turn."

"But I need a leak."

Halgill pulled Dastra to his feet. Holding him by the shoulder, he led him through the other officers until he could get the attention of the custody officer. Dastra deliberately turned away so that his face wouldn't be seen.

"Can my bloke use the toilet?"

"Use the second cell on the left, mate."

Halgill led Dastra down a side passage and into an open cell. He bent down to undo the handcuffs, and Dastra saw his chance. Through either unfamiliarity or misplaced trust, Halgill didn't remove the cuffs in the arms-length fashion he had been trained to. He fumbled with the lock and as Dastra felt his left arm go free he raised it gently but as far as possible from the chromed ring of the cuffs before bringing his elbow back hard into Halgill's face. Halgill grunted and let go of the other cuff to put his hands to his nose. Dastra spun round and punched him left-handed across the right jaw. Halgill dropped unconscious to the cell floor. Dastra sat down on Halgill, took the handcuff key from the open cuff and put it in the keyhole of the right hand cuff.

"Sorry, mate. This isn't personal." Dastra undid the handcuff on his right hand, then rolled Halgill over and took off his raincoat, recovering his mobile phone in the process. Putting the coat on, he buttoned it up to cover his bow tie. He found his own police warrant card and, shutting the cell door behind him, looked cautiously out into the main corridor. Other officers seemed to be busy with writing up the notes of their arrests. Dastra took a deep breath and marched confidently back out past them and past the custody officer's desk. He turned back to the busy custody officer in a casual way and showing his warrant card, said, "Sarge, has DCI Fotheringhay come through in the last hour or so?"

There was a brief moment of uncertainty from the sergeant, but the warrant card photograph reassured him. "You've just missed him. He's in the building. But his colleague is in with a prisoner."

"It's the DCI I need. Can you give me the door code?"

The sergeant whispered the code to Dastra. He tapped it in, opened the door and walked through, hiding his limp and praying that he wouldn't meet Fotheringhay coming back the other way. He asked an officer for the way out, and within a minute he walked free out into the street.

His car was now over a mile away. He looked left and right to see if he could find a taxi. One rolled past but it was occupied. A few vehicles behind it a large Metropolitan Police Territorial Support Group van full of officers was cruising slowly along the street. It changed direction and headed towards him. He froze as it braked sharply and two officers piled quickly out of the sliding side door.

"Dave Dastra?"

Dastra's heart was in his throat.

"I thought it was you," said one. "We were at Harlesden together."

Dastra's mind was recovering from the prospect of being arrested again. He didn't try to recognize the officer.

"It's me, Ralph O'Brien."

"Oh, Ralph, nice to see you. I need an urgent favor."

"Fire away."

"I need a lift, just a mile or so."

"We'd best ask the skipper."

They walked round to the front passenger as the second officer got back in via the sliding door. Dastra started speaking to the sergeant.

Dastra flashed his warrant card. "Look, you know I'm in The Job, Central Southern, and ex-Met. Ralph here will vouch for me."

"That's right, Sarge."

"All I need is a lift to my car. It's in Portland Place. I just need to get home and bloody quickly."

"Jump in mate, clear a space, lads."

Dastra let out a great sigh as he was bundled into the van.

"Vlad on our carrier, eh?" said someone in the back.

"Stick you pedal to the metal, Jerry," said the sergeant to the driver.

"Uniform 191 from MP," came a voice on the vehicle radio.

"Go ahead, MP," replied the Sergeant into a handset.

"Can you attend St. Pancras BTP to assist with a lost prisoner?"

"Received."

"We must have just missed that. That'll cost someone two days' pay," said a voice in the back. The carrier cruised under the Euston underpass and then turned left towards Portland Place.

"Where's your car?

"Down here on the left, the old Black Porsche."

"The five litre, is it mate?" said the officer next to him.

"Uh, yes."

"That'll get you home bloody quick."

"I hope so."

The door opened.

"Good luck, mate!"

"Yeah, good luck."

He got into his car and started up the engine. Lucy's first gift of Beethoven's mass in C started pouring from the six speakers in the car. He reached to switch it off, but changed his mind. "That'll calm me down a bit."

He waited for the carrier to drift out of view then shunted the car back and forward using drive and reverse, pushing the other cars away. The movement triggered an alarm on one of them. By the time the third horn burst had begun, Dastra was in a wide U-turn .

He accelerated sharply up the street and at the top took a left into a wide crescent, then left again onto the Marylebone road. As he dashed along it he concentrated on anticipating the traffic lights correctly. The enforcement cameras could flash for all he cared.

The traffic lights across Baker Street were green, and he watched with delight as the remaining lights all the way ahead as far as he could see turned green in unison. He accelerated hard, the long nose of the car lifting slightly as one by one, he put the lights behind him. The last set of lights before the Westway flyover turned orange as he approached. He used the kick down and the gearbox dropped into first gear at about fifty miles per hour. The sudden lurch forward shot him across the junction as the lights went red. He kept his right foot down. The car went up into second at seventy as it lifted on its suspension over the crest of the flyover. Eighty, ninety, one hundred, the car shifted up into third as he shot up the long slope on the main Westway.

Dastra settled in his seat and began flashing his headlights at drivers blocking the offside lane. If they didn't move, he swept past them on the inside. He was down in Acton and off the flyover in a forty miles per hour three lane section before he knew it and still doing over one hundred miles per hour. The double flash of a speed camera pulsed at the Porsche as Dastra leveled out. Voices on the Beethoven CD started singing *"Gloria in excelsis Deo"*. The lights at Acton were going red as he jumped them, and he eased off as traffic merged back to two lanes. Two more lights and he would be on a clear run to the M40 motorway. As he reached the railway bridge at the crest of the hill the traffic lights were green, and he knew that the next set would be phased green on the same cycle. He pushed the accelerator to the floor and both lights were past him. Three lanes. Another speed camera flashed.

The music was entering a complex fugue of voices as the Porsche climbed to one hundred forty miles per hour, rounding the long curve under the bridges by London's Polish War Memorial.

Forty Three

(Statement by PC Mark Jamalia. Alperton traffic garage.)

"*Just after starting my night shift I parked my marked police Vauxhall Vectra on the Polish War Memorial roundabout on the eastern bridge section, facing south. I was out of the car and directly over the A40 westbound offside lane and facing traffic coming down the hill from Central London direction. I was using a correctly functioning radar speed gun and taking readings from vehicles coming towards me. At 10:17 p.m., I saw a dark vehicle, flashing its headlamps and approaching the bridge at speed. I took a reading from this vehicle of one-forty-seven point five miles per hour. I saw that the vehicle was a Porsche 928, black in colour, and noted the registration mark (see original note). I returned to my vehicle and drove down onto the A40 in pursuit, circulating the description of the vehicle over the main set radio. When I reached the main A40, the vehicle was already in the far distance, and I followed its tail lights for about two miles, but never caught up, losing sight of the vehicle near the junction with the M25. A PNC check revealed that the car was registered to David Dastra, of an address near Henley. I passed this information on to Central Southern Police by radio, in order for them to be alerted to the vehicle.*"

A solitary police traffic car sped down the slip road from the Polish War Memorial after Dastra, the blue lights punching out into the dark bronze sky. Outmatched, the car soon drifted away in Dastra's mirrors. The straight run past Northolt aerodrome allowed him to open up the car to one hundred and fifty-five miles per hour, at which point he found his judgment and concentration were strained to their very limits. At least it kept his mind off Lucy.

As voices on the CD began to sing *"Credo"*, the Porsche blasted onto the M40 motorway.

At this speed Wycombe in six minutes, the turnoff to Henley one minute later.

All was going well. There was light traffic on the motorway, and if a police traffic car were to chase him, he would gladly have it chase him all the way home.

A yellow light flashed on the instrument panel. Dastra tried to scan the gauges, taking his eyes off the road for only a split second at a time. Temperature and oil pressure were normal. Fuel was low. High-speed travel had pushed up fuel consumption.

The CD played on. *"...et unum sanctum, catholicam et apostilicam ecclesium."* For the sharp turn where the Lotus Carlton had crashed, Dastra dropped his speed to less than fifty. As he drew closer to home his thinking came from a more rational frame of mind. There was, after all, a good chance that police would be with Lucy by now. They would have discovered that she was safe. He would be the embarrassed panicky husband with a trail of speeding tickets leading back to Central London, followed by an almost certain driving ban.

All the same, he kept his foot down. This narrower, two lane dual carriageway was empty as he plowed past Marlow and swept up to the roundabout on the Henley turn off. On the winding single carriageway road to Henley his only hope of speed was constant overtaking into the teeth of oncoming traffic. His car managed this with ease, and five minutes of driving brought Dastra down into Henley as the Beethoven CD reached the *Benedictus*. Across the bridge over the Thames, the town center traffic lights stopped him briefly, but then he tore on through the narrow streets of Henley and out onto the Wallingford Road. He found himself stuck behind two slow Land Rovers at the top of the hill, the rear of which had two Labradors in the back, illuminated under the canvas cover by Dastra's headlights. There was a line of traffic coming the other way so he tried the police on his mobile phone. The battery was nearly flat. He turned off the music as he spoke to the control room.

"DC Dastra, inquiring about the call to my house."

"Yes, mate. We sent a unit up, double crewed. There were no problems, they've given an 'alarm fault, lawful occupier on premises' result for the call."

"Are they still there?"

"No, mate, they've already given a result for the next call they had been assigned to." Dastra tried to ask more, but his mobile phone went silent as the battery finally gave up. He clicked the music back on. A last speed camera flashed as he took the turn into a country lane, then a sharp right into towards his house as voices on the CD solemnly sang, "*Agnus Dei.*' The house was lit up high on his left and he approached the drive in a more cheerful frame of mind.

The beat of the music caught the pulse between light and dark as the lights of his house flickered through the passing trees.

He took a deep breath and began to smile. Everything seemed normal again. All his earlier thoughts and the panic now seemed totally irrational. He turned his mind to his arrest by the Yorkshire officers. What had happened in Leeds? And how would he justify his escape and assault on Halgill? Surely they would follow him here and arrest him again with even more force.

Something unexpectedly struck the roof of the car with a light but sharp whipping noise. He stopped, turned off the engine and extinguished the headlamps, waiting for them to rotate back into the car. The car was silent now apart from the whipping noise and the whistle of the wind. He eased the door open. The noise of wind rushing through the trees filled the cabin. Dastra fumbled around in the gap and felt a cut telephone wire flapping against the side of the car.

He returned to a state of panic, his heart pounding. He clicked the door shut and rolled the car forward down a slight incline until it gathered speed and he was able to go through a gateway leading into the field opposite the gates to his house.

He got out and limped back across the road, pulling off Halgill's raincoat. He couldn't climb his garden wall easily because of the height and the razor wire. Making his way left along the line of his own wall, away from the road, he reached a point where the ground rose and shortened the height he needed to climb.

Decision time. Dastra flopped Halgill's raincoat over the

razor wire. The trigger wire stretched, but no alarm sounded. In the dark scramble to get over, he caught his ankle on some of the wire but the wound was sharp and clean so he barely noticed it. Landing in the wooded part of his garden he limped slowly through soft earth among the trees and up towards the house.

Quite suddenly, in the dark, he walked straight into something that shouldn't have been there—a hard, metal shape several feet long covered in branches and leaves. He pushed the foliage aside, and in the splintered shafts of light from the house saw that he had found a police patrol car. Now his worst fears were realized. With palms hot and sweaty, and mouth completely dry, he peered into the empty car. The window was open and he felt around inside. There were two hats in the foot wells, in amongst the smashed remains of the fixed main police radio.

His stomach churning more now—Robin Kaminski had told him what was coming.

The police car was in a dip in the woods below the edge of the front lawn, through which the main drive passed on the right. He could see another shape about half way up the drive, and on the right a large, wide car, American by the size of it, and probably the one he had seen earlier. From Kaminski's account, he knew to expect a body in it so crept forwards to seek confirmation. As he got to the edge of the lawn he suddenly recalled the spade he had stuck in the ground earlier. After skirting the lawn towards the drive, he fumbled about in the dark and found the spade still upright in the potato patch. Picking it up mid shaft like a weapon, he crept slowly towards the car again.

The lawn was on a convex slope, and as he moved across it to the drive, he saw two men silhouetted about twenty yards from the house next to a shape on the ground. One of them appeared to have a modern silenced machine pistol slung from his shoulder on a strap. Dastra stayed down in the shadows and skirted the figures. He looked hard, his eyes adjusting to the scene, and made out a bloody body on the lawn. It couldn't be Lucy. It wasn't pregnant. In fact, it looked like a man in a light shirt and dark trousers.

Oh my God, It's a cop! Dastra turned to his right and caught the vague shape of a body lying across the large front seats of the car.

Then, above the wind, there was a terrifying, and terrified, hollow scream from the house. It was Lucy.

"Please no! I don't want to die yet. Please don't kill me. Please let us have our baby. Please no, I..." Her cry was cut off abruptly.

Dastra ran, pounding footsteps covered by the echoes of the scream. He was a virgin at killing, but running at one of the two men from behind with the shovel raised like a sword he almost beheaded the first with the sharp edge. The other man turned to cry out but Dastra knocked him sideways and landed on him, trapping the man's arms under him in the sling of his gun. Dastra's hands scrambled ineptly for the man's throat as Lucy screamed again in a mindless frenzy from the house. Dastra's arms, strengthened by months of supporting himself on crutches, forced their way to their goal. He crushed the stranger's windpipe using every last ounce of his grip, and stayed there for an agonizing minute, filled with Lucy's screams, until he felt no heartbeat at the throat.

There was another deeper scream from the house, Lucy again, but now of bleak and empty despair. Dastra rolled the stranger's body over and took the machine pistol. He kept his head down and raced on, stumbling, catching himself, continuing toward the source of Lucy's screams. The piano room. He went up to the left end of the house, aiming for the side of building, avoiding the crunch of his feet on gravel. Closer now, he crept toward the veranda, triggering his own security lights. He froze. There was no reaction from within. His heart raced hard as he stepped over a small raised flowerbed and under the veranda, tiptoeing onto the paved area by the French doors. Curtains blocked any view inside, but a set of doors towards the rear was damaged, as if it had been burst open in a struggle to get out. The doors had been closed again as far as the damage would allow, but shafts of light from within indicated that the curtains were open. Dastra crept along to the damaged door and peered through a broken pane into the room beyond.

His jaw dropped.

Lucy, in a short and unfamiliar nightdress, was hanging by her neck from a white rope passed over the great central beam. Her toes were twitching, trying to find the floor, and her face was reddening with trapped blood. A thin, smiling, wild-haired, good-looking man of about twenty-five was hauling on the rope and apparently shouting something at Lucy. A short, brown haired woman of about twenty held a long knife or bayonet against Lucy's breasts, and a second woman with a similar weapon stood back, gesticulating. The male stood, apparently uncaring, in a widening pool of blood coming from a body by his feet. Dastra's view of this body was partly obscured by the back of his own sofa, now draped with a Stars and Stripes flag. He stretched his neck to glimpse the face on the body. Pete Ainsworth, his white shirt heavily stained with blood, his dull, dry, lifeless eyes gazing across the floor. A grotesque and vast spattering of blood, like a bizarre piece of modern art, marked the great wall that divided the piano room from the main house.

Dastra eased himself round to see further to his right. Near to him, a dark haired man sat with his back to the side windows among a number of studio lights, apparently directing the action from one of Dastra's kitchen chairs. Another man to his right was working a video camera and beyond him on an armchair, cowered Michaela, eyes shut and quite still, gagged and bound, hand and foot. Dastra moved away from the door trying to figure a way to get control without compromising Lucy and Michaela.

The youth let go of the rope and Lucy fell down so that she was kneeling at his feet. Lucy coughed hard to clear her breathing and started sobbing heavily.

"Please don't kill me, please."

The thin youth pulled her long hair back and lashed out at her face with a carving knife, catching her on the left cheek.

"Stop!" yelped Dastra from his dry throat as he pulled the doors wide and stepped into the room. "Everybody keep absolutely still."

Dastra held the machine pistol up shakily as his hot palms sweated hard against the metal. "Back off. *Now!*"

The youth backed away from Lucy, who clasped her hand to her face, bright red blood pouring out between her fingers.

"Lucy, take their knives," ordered Dastra. Lucy was out of her mind with terror and was beyond doing anything. The man in the chair turned slowly to face Dastra—the face was Dastra's own face, the slightly longer hair, his own color. The eyes, the nose, the mouth and the general shape—undoubtedly his. It was as if he were looking into a slightly distorted mirror that made him look fatter.

"My God... You!"

There was a click at the back of his head. "Don't move!" said a foreign and distinctly eastern European voice. "Put the gun on the floor."

Dastra dropped the machine pistol.

"Kick it away."

He kicked it to his right, towards the camera tripod as a heavy blow to his shoulder and neck sent him sprawling.

A voice gritted, "he has killed Ion and Nicolai... Martina found them." A kick struck him in the belly and someone sat down hard on him as strong hands bound his wrists.

"Perhaps that makes today even," said the director with an odd Cockney accent. He rose from his chair and aimed a kick at Dastra's face, catching his right cheek as he tried to avoid the blow. The man on Dastra's back moved off him and pulled him up by the hair. The director kicked him hard in the groin. Dastra cursed at the pain and the other man threw him back to the floor.

"Stop it, please!" screamed Lucy. The director ignored her.

Dastra's doppelganger spoke cheerily, "Hello, brother. Surprised?"

Dastra looked up from the polished wooden floor and nodded. Blood and mucous bubbled from one of his nostrils. "Just let her go, take me. Just let her live. It must be me you want."

"It is."

"So kill me, not her."

The director looked across at Lucy, still roped around the neck and kneeling at the feet of the youth. "But she's my star! This will guarantee her fame forever... y'know, they'll write books about her. The price? Just her life, and yours, of course! A small price for eternal fame." The director swung a kick at Dastra's legs.

Dastra gasped as his hamstring took the force of the impact.

"I need this memento, so film it!" said the director, motioning to the cameraman, who swung the camera around to comply. The director's voice betrayed a sense of urgency. "Look, we've killed two coppers, saving me from using my actors in that essential role. Fake deaths are never as good. And we've knocked out the telephones for miles and cut the lines to your house. You're fucking stuffed."

The brother, fatter than Dastra, walked away to the piano, the camera following him. He lit a cigarette and puffed briefly, then continued his quick fire commentary.

"Before topping him, we got your copper chum here to radio that all is well, and also that he has finished his next assignment. We're listening, too, you see." He paused and eyed the room. He turned to the man who had come in behind Dastra. "Get back out there with Martina and listen, I'll deal with this." The man nodded and left the room the way he had come in, closing the broken doors behind him. The three actors waiting for directions to proceed with Lucy's murder perched uneasily around her, Lucy restrained by the rope around her neck.

The director looked across at Lucy. "Nice touch... dying in front of your old man!"

Lucy, watching him through tear clouded eyes, tried to rationalize what was being said, but blind terror at losing everything left her with only with the a final appeal. "Please, please leave us." A labor contraction made her wince and bend over.

"In a little while... after you are meat."

"But, I... please. We've done nothing."

The director, whose voice had betrayed little anger until now, turned on her. "Shut the fuck up! You won't say what I want, then you gob off as it suits you. You Yank women always talk too much. Shut up and play your fucking part."

Lucy tried to say something, but the youth tightened the rope, choking her off. It wasn't asphyxiating her, but to Barney it looked like she'd lapsed into unconsciousness. The director turned back to him.

"Skarrow is our surname, you *and* me... y'know... and I'm Chas, your very slightly elder identical twin. We are good London East End stock, probably Jewish immigrants a few generations back, but who gives a toss? Mum died giving birth to us, down in Kent. Dad had done an armed blagging, and had booked a ferry across to France so that the team could meet up in Spain with the proceeds. Mum was eight months gone, and the stupid git decided to risk taking her, because he had another couple in the car who he thought could help. The stress started her off, I reckon. It looks like she popped me out in the back of the car, then he panicked and dropped her at a hospital in Ashford. He took me over to Spain with the other couple, and when he contacted the hospital by phone, he found out that Mum had died. Y'know I never thought I might have a brother until I got sent back to England for a private education. We played your school at rugby. I was in the crowd while you played scrum half. I knew from then on. I tried to trace what had happened, but the only record was of a thirty-eight year old bitch dying in a maternity unit at Ashford on my birthday. I tried to find a record of my birth, but instead I found yours, with no mention of me. Some of the rest I got out of Dad when I last visited him inside. Even he didn't know about there being a second brat, never mind an identical twin."

"Sad," added Dastra sarcastically from the floor.

"Sadder for him... he died last year from cancer. A man shouldn't die in prison. That's why I killed that fucking grass Wilmershott and his family."

"Who?"

"Hughes to you. Grassed up, you know, turned Queen's evidence on all the team in Spain about ten years back. Dad was extradited but I got left in Spain. Spanish passport, of course." He blew a smoke ring and leaned on the piano. "So why am I going to kill you both? I've always liked a slow death, as long as I can remember, although my first killing was instantaneous. When I was thirteen, I had a .22 air rifle with a telescopic sight. I shot a new-born baby dead in a pram in someone's garden across the road in Spain. Straight through the eye and into the brain. Then I waited, and waited. The mother came out to check on it later. I was still looking through the crosshairs. She screamed on and on like it was the end of the world or something. I can still hear her in my head."

"And that wasn't enough?"

"No, too quick. She ran indoors. I wanted to be there with her, watching her suffer. And y'know Spain is a good place for sadists. Bullfighting... I love the ritual. Do you know much about the Inquisition?"

"Enough."

"Ritual. Torture and the burnings. I wanted to see films about it, but they aren't thick on the ground. Then I saw a home video from the Bosnian war where some Serbs got some Bosnian girls and raped them stupid and then they cut them open. Great film, but done on the cheap. I hit on a business idea… they act, I direct. So I recruited some financially strapped talent from all over Europe. The more war-torn the area, the easier the pickings. You were my only contingency. You were hard to trace, but I went through your old school. Then when I discovered you were a cop with family out here, you were the perfect cover. If anything ever happened, I could always "stitch you up" as your mates would say, with our family DNA. But I never understood how you ended up actually working on my case. How?"

Dastra said nothing, trying to play for time.

"I asked a question."

Dastra raised one bloody eyebrow. "Work it out."

"I can't." He moved towards Dastra, puffing hard on the cigarette. The end glowed bright and he took it from his mouth, and held it sizzling against his forehead. The burn loosened Dastra's tongue. "I transferred out here to be nearer to home. I'm guessing you chose Oxfordshire in order to be nearer to me." Skarrow put the cigarette back in his mouth.

"In part, but I still had to draw you out of London 'cause we can't operate there. Y'know it's hard enough in England as it is."

"So, how did…" Dastra's voice tailed off. The smoke from the cigarette suddenly reminded him of carbon monoxide poisoning.

"I killed your new parents and made it look like an accident." Dastra was silent, remembering that the deaths had taken place in this same room. "Easy. And it seemed fair. I'd lost both parents. It seemed right that you should share the pain. The only gamble was whether you would actually move out here. Even if you didn't, I could be sure that your comings and goings would put you in Oxfordshire at the right times. How did you end up on my case?"

"I'm a detective. They were short of detectives."

"So just a coincidence, but not so unlikely. I had wondered if you had been drawn to the case out of fascination, whether we have similar traits." He smiled thinly.

"No. I was picked out of the blue."

"Pity. Y'know, the three bodies Lucy found were our first kills here. We impaled a Dutch bloke as well for the story. He's still under the bypass. Y'know, if no bodies had been found, you'd have been safe for longer. Once they had been found, it was wrap-up time. Then you got too close to us. Your mate came and knocked on the caravan doors, but we kept still. Then we slipped out a few minutes later and we saw you digging. Then, like a gift, you leave your copper's walkie-talkie behind.

"We knew you'd come back so we trapped a victim first, that night. You didn't return till the following day, when we gave you a nice hard crack to the back of the head. Y'know, we weren't intending to impale our next victim because that film was done. The papers had already nicknamed me Vlad, so I decided on one more impaling, but not before I had left our Skarrow DNA inside her. We dumped her body in the boot of your car and I lifted you into the driver's seat, too concussed to remember anything. I guess some of my spunk rubbed off my trousers onto yours... nice piece of luck, that.

"Blame Lucy for the mess you got yourself into. If she hadn't found the stiffs, she wouldn't have kicked things off. And of course, it was her star turn at the trial that triggered off your release. She is so lovely. Y'know, faces like that should not be allowed to get old. Now her face will be preserved forever." The director leaned his head to one side to examine Lucy on the sofa.

"Fainted, I think... The other killings you know about. You find the studio and our next victim. Then my second trailer with all my props gets picked up on the M20. We'd been to Romania for Christmas and to restock with period clothing and other things lost from the bunker. Y'know, it's dirt cheap to have costumes made in Romania. I had to drive on past when they got stopped in the van. We were going to do a Jack the Ripper reconstruction. Mary Kelly. Shame.

"Of course, I still needed to work, so without props and a studio we had to go modern. I went up to Yorkshire and re-enacted a Yorkshire Ripper killing. Y'know I've left our hair in her hand too. I even hired a black Porsche 928 and stuck false plates on it... and a trail of speed cameras and a visit to a garage with security cameras. I was banking on you being out of the way by tonight."

"I very nearly was."

"Really?"

"I was arrested."

"Police screw-up again? No surprise there, eh! Anyhow, I bought this magazine with some photographs of you and your wife in this room. After we lost all our kit, I racked my brains." He threw his head back and sucked his bottom lip as if savoring his knowledge. "Y'know, Charlie Manson fitted the circumstances perfectly, right down to the beam. Two of the shots were even set up and photographed like originals of Sharon Tate. Maybe the photographer was thinking along the same lines."

"He was. That's why he used a red filter to lighten her hair. This is a trap."

"The dead cops prove there's no trap here, but I accept that the red filter is true...we're doing the same trick. It also makes the blood look very bright on black and white jobs like this one. This was far too good an opportunity, and I'll be able to make mega bucks in the USA...it's nearly the thirtieth anniversary. I'll stuff these scenes into a copy of a recent documentary about Manson and there'll be thousands of fascinated voyeurs jerking off to a replay of the murders just like the Romans watching at the Coliseum, and all excusing themselves to anyone who might catch them that it's intellectual curiosity.

"I had to be quick, mind, in case the baby came. I trawled the Balkans for skilled extras to help out. We did the LaBianca killings first, out of sequence. It would have been difficult to do them once the alarm was raised after tonight."

"But how did you find Hughes... or whatever his name was?"

"Wilmershott? I found him last year after a five-year hunt. I was just waiting for the right thing to work him into. Pity he lived in the same police patch, but I had hoped the 'grass' business would cover my trail.

"I knew from the press you would be out tonight. I expected Lucy to be here alone so I brought along actors to play the other deaths, we even have the springy stage knives somewhere here." He glanced about as if to locate them. "The death of the caretaker's friend, we filmed soon after arrival. It was piss-easy as there was some mad idiot shouting into your entry phone when Ion was up a pole cutting your phone wire. We dragged him in and shot him."

"He was Sarah Carothers's husband."

"So I've done a husband and wife? Practice for doing you two. Y'know, it was a gift finding another girl here, and another having two police officers arrive. This chap here was brilliant, performed like a method actor.

"Still, there were no brave knights for the Manson victims, and Lucy, being a California girl, knows what is coming, more or less. I've shown her some stills to get her in the mood. Y'know; she should die last, but I need her to play her part well, and applying pain to her friend here seems to help her focus on her final performance. Once Lucy is dead, we'll chase her friend out of here and stab her to death on your lawn. I will sort out the scene order in the editing stage."

"Listen... listen," Dastra pleaded, coming up onto his knees. "What about the baby?"

"What about it."

"If you kill us it will die."

"And your point is?"

"It's yours!"

"Uh?"

"Your DNA." Dastra looked around at the others in the room, as if they might provide some peer pressure. His eyes came to rest on Lucy. "You've already shown that our semen is identical. The baby is as much yours as it is mine."

"So it is mine to murder, too. You know I do babies."

Dastra's eyes snapped back to his twin. "Your nephew or niece... and genetically your son or daughter."

"I already killed your adopted parents. A nephew or niece is fuck-all."

"But you had a motive for them. The baby is just a prop. Stab Lucy with a stage knife and kill me if you must, then go."

"Spare Lucy and kill you?"

"And spare Michaela too. It's one film. You've got LaBianca. Lucy and Michaela can act their parts. Who's going to be able to tell..."

"I have a better idea," said the director, flatly. "I let you live."

"Me?"

"According to the Manson case pathologist, the unborn baby

lived off oxygen in the placental blood for maybe ten to twenty minutes after the death of its mother. Your baby could be all you can salvage from this. After Lucy and her friend are both dead, we will depart. I have a light aircraft waiting a few miles away and I know you will not follow us because you will be busy cutting into Lucy's womb to save your baby. What will your police colleagues make of you up to your arms in your wife's blood?"

The director rolled his head back and Dastra noticed him twitch down the left side of his face. Dastra's stomach clamped down hard on the remains of the food had eaten in London. The stark reality of the limited choice before him pushed him to the edge of vomiting. He tried hard to relax but that only made it worse. All that stopped him bringing up the contents of his stomach was a change in tone from the director and the sudden crystallizing urgency of the fatal situation before him.

"Y'know, time is short. As you can see, the first injury has been done with a cut to your wife's cheek. Time to finish."

Dastra tried a last plea. "This is so bloody unfair. You are robbing her of everything…"

The director gave him a severe look and a nod to his actors. One girl seized Lucy's head by her hair and shook her hard.

Lucy had fainted into a safe and protected corner of her mind. She was walking barefoot through green fields in bright sunlight, aware that something was amiss, like a storm gathering in the distance, but far away. The pain in her scalp brought her sharply back to consciousness. Her reawakening into the nightmare of the present caused her heart to race and her mind to refocus in bitter sharpness on the bleak wild terror of what lay ahead in the remaining moments of her life.

The youth helped pull her off the sofa into a kneeling position.

Dastra started pleading again. "Look, I have loads of money. More than I need, I can pay you. Just leave us and go away, I can't call the police if I wanted to."

The director got up and took a large mauve polka-dot silk handkerchief from his pocket. "I will have to shut you up before we continue, or you will spoil the scene. You can't do a take two on a live killing." He bent down to tie the gag but Dastra spun away.

Pocketing the handkerchief again, he grabbed Dastra's hair and
smashed his face down hard on the wooden floor. He then tried to tie
his feet with a piece of cord that he produced from another pocket.
His conversation was now directed at Lucy "So that we do the job
properly, Mrs. Dastra, and so that you play your part well, I have
made a deal with your husband."

"Have you hell," Barney shouted, trying to kick out at
Skarrow. The cameraman stepped over and knelt hard on his back
while Skarrow tried to get the cord around his ankles.

"Your husband," continued Skarrow, his breathing becoming
a little labored from struggling with Dastra. "Your husband will be
given a chance to cut your baby out." He paused to puff. "After the
filming is over and we have finished with your services. You'll be
quite dead, of course."

Lucy saw Barney struggle to speak, but all that escaped from
his mouth was a grunt.

"You'll be dead, and I know you'll be interested in your
offspring. Barney will live, and if he does the job well, so will your
brat."

She watched as Skarrow stepped round to the other end of
Dastra and took the polka-dot handkerchief out of his pocket again.

"The only cooperation I need from you, Mrs. Dastra, is one
word as you die. It would help greatly if you could say 'mother'."

Dastra twisted his head round and took a last glance at Lucy,
her head lolling forward in total resignation to her fate. A tear mixed
with the blood flowing from her cheek, and Dastra watched as a
great drip of tear and blood fell to the floor. Its motion seemed to
slow. Activation of the security light outside picked it out as it fell.
He knew he was in one of those awful moments when fate was in the
balance and the entire world seemed to move like a car with all the
brakes on, sliding on a strange surface, the driver praying for the
tires to bite and the motion to stop.

The great red drip splashed in the lake of Pete Ainsworth's
blood.

"Lucy, Lucy, I'm so sorry. I love you."

Lucy nodded, and gave Dastra a final look of wide-eyed
terror. "Save the baby," she mouthed. Skarrow tied the gag tightly
across Dastra's mouth, the knot pressing behind his right ear and

tangling in a length of hair that tugged painfully at his scalp. Lucy looked up and gave him a last look, and nodded slightly through her tears. The cameraman got off Dastra's back, lifted his camera tripod and put it back where he had been earlier, making slight adjustments.

Skarrow started giving cold instructions in a low voice. "Okay, roll the camera. Slobba, you stab her first, then the others go straight in. You know where to slice, just don't block the camera too much. Mrs. Dastra. If you want the rest of your family here to live, I need a 'mother' from you as you go down for the last time."

The youth raised his knife high and plunged it down into Lucy's right shoulder. It ground between two ribs and opened a hole into her upper right chest. Dastra saw a wide arc of blood drops fly from the knife as it flew back for the next strike. Lucy gave a deep moan. There was a dull popping sound heralding a fatal injury somewhere—probably her lung sac. Unable to bear any more he turned his head round hard to the left toward the open French doors, tears streaming from his eyes, knowing he would have to endure working alone in the middle of the night's carnage trying to save his unborn child.

Forty Four

Question (DCI Shackerstone): "Is that all you wanted to ask me?"

Answer: "There is another question. A kind of philosophical one."

Q (BS): "All right."

A: "Who do you think is nastier? The Roman circus master who plans kills for profit and the pleasure of thousands, or the so-called professional who decides to tempt him to play a private role out of public view in one of his own fantasies?"

Q (BS): (noise of table being struck) "You think you are so fu— smart. You think you have committed the perfect crime and got caught out by a bit of bad luck. Well, let me tell you something, the perfect criminal selects his own circumstances. The big flaw in your plan was that you were led by the need to relive historical events, so that was exactly where I led you with Manson. The perfect crime, no. But to me, the perfect bloody criminal." (loud noise followed by long pause) "It's experience, Skarrow, and you haven't got it."

A: "Obviously not."

Q (BS): (sigh) "We use our past to steer through the present. You ran into someone with the wrong past."

A: "Yes, very philosophical."(long pause, sigh). "One last question." (pause) "Do you always take the day off?"

Q (BS): "No, not any more. I had taken this week off to go down to Cornwall for the eclipse."
Q (DI Graham)): "Listen. Mr. Shackerstone has answered all he needs to. Now you can explain for the tape."

A: "The ninth of August. It was thirty years ago today, Mr. Shackerstone, wasn't it?"
Q (BS): "It was..."
(Extract from evidential tape transcript.)

The bookshelves filling one wall of the modest flat in Marlow had many hundreds of books on them, and on wide subject matter: history, photography, biography, cooking, fishing, rugby union and non-fiction crime. There were, even to the most casual observer, too many books on crime. This was, however, the home of a detective. Yet, there was another, more disturbing aspect to this collection: Over twenty-five books were on the same case in 1969 and its aftermath. By the fireplace, and directly connected to these books was a candid black and white photograph of a beautiful smiling actress. Brian Shackerstone had taken it as a young press photographer in spring 1969, outside her English home in Eaton Place Mews, London. It was a head and shoulders shot, with the background thrown deliberately out of focus. Four months into a pregnancy and the actress appeared to be blooming. It was an excellent photograph, and established him on his career as a photographer in a white male dominated profession. On August ninth, 1969, events in Los Angeles made the value of the photograph leap as Brian Shackerstone dwelt darkly on the murders at Cielo Drive. He had weeks of nightmares and in a spirit of great animosity, he threw his press career away and joined another white male dominated profession with the intent of becoming a murder detective.

Now the whistling of the wind at the windows of the flat was broken by the chug of a car's diesel engine and the whine of the power steering as he swung it into a parking bay. A slight thump signalled a misjudged bollard and a new dent in the front offside wing. The engine stopped and Shackerstone, still dressed in jeans and a sweatshirt, ran from the car, through the entrance door and up the stairs to his flat. He had tried to call Dastra from three different public phones on his way home from the Hughes house, but all had been out of order. Fumbling, he opened his flat's door, and then went directly to his house phone. It was dead.

"Shit."

Shackerstone took the now lifeless mobile phone that he had lent to Gordonstown from his pocket as he strode into the kitchen searching for the charger. He found it in a drawer and connected it back in the lounge before sitting down and switching the phone on. He waited for a signal. A sudden bleep told him there was a message on his voicemail. He thought about phoning Dastra, but decided to take the voicemail first.

"Guv, this is Barney. I think today's killing is another snuff movie. Someone is doing the Manson murders. I am going home A.S.A.P. I just think he may be after Lucy. Call me back on my mobile. Urgent." Shackerstone felt a tightness grip his chest as he let his eyes wander over to the photograph on the wall. He gave the pile of photographs of Lucy on the table a guilty glance and sucked his lower lip in thought. He considered today's scene, then began to wonder how he had missed something he knew so well. Maybe it was over-familiarity. Probably it was his preoccupation with Dastra's impending arrest. Whatever the reason, he could now see LaBianca ingredients neatly hidden in the Hughes scene.

"What have I done?" He ran a hand up his forehead and wiped the sweat over his head. He tried to call Dastra's mobile. No reply, just a message service. He tried Dastra's home number. Out of order. He tried Lucy's mobile. It diverted to a message service.

Because he rarely had to call directly, he didn't have the number of the control room covering Dastra's address. He rang 999, and after explaining the problem, was put through.

"DCI Shackerstone here, from Wemstone, operation Klingsor. I need to know if you have had any calls to Prospect of Peshawar, near Henley, please."

"Oh yes, sir," said a male voice. "The whole area has lost its phones. All the alarms have been activated. Of course, your man's house was on this armed response scheme until today, but it was cancelled."

"Cancelled?"

"A Detective Chief Superintendent Gordonstown phoned in and cancelled the whole thing earlier."

"Bugger. So nobody has gone up there?"

"Well, I wasn't going to send anyone, but DC Dastra phoned in. He was well upset."

"Why?"

"He tried to explain something about another killing, and then we got a second call from a guy called Kaminski."

"Robin Kaminski?"

"Yes."

"He's an expert on Charles Manson."

"So he said. He gave a better explanation than DC Dastra, so I sent a patrol car up anyway."

"Unarmed?"

"It's all right, they've been and gone."

"Thank fuck for that. Everything okay then?"

"Yes, they have given a result for the next call too."

"Good. What did they say about Peshawar?"

"Usual stuff, set off by the phone fault: Lawful occupier on premises. DC Dastra called back for the result. It's all squared up, no grief this end."

"Good. Bloody good." Shackerstone breathed a big sigh of relief. "And DC Dastra, he called in. Do you know where he was?"

"Close to home, I think. His mobile packed up while he was on."

Shackerstone allowed himself a smile of self-satisfaction and quickly decided to drive up to Prospect of Peshawar to warn Dastra privately of the Yorkshire case.

"Just one more thing. Something's bothering me. Did they say whether or not Mrs. Dastra was okay for a telephone? She's due any time and I can't get an answer on her mobile. If it's out of order and she doesn't know it, she will be stuck for an ambulance."

"They didn't mention anything. I'll give them a shout, sir. I'll have to put you on hold."

Shackerstone waited. Two long minutes passed. The voice on the line was now a bit panicky. "Sir. We couldn't raise either of them. I know there are radio dead spots, and I was going to give that as an excuse. But, well…"

"Well what?"

"The burglary they gave a result for—the occupiers have just called in to complain that police have still not arrived."

Shackerstone found goose bumps spreading all over him and hairs rising on the back of his neck. His mouth went dry, as it did in the witness box at court. The extra adrenaline helped him think fast and hard. The options skimmed through his mind. The risks and problems kicked away the wrong ones and a plan began to crystallize.

"Right. Don't send another car. Don't put anything out over the local channel. If anything has happened to your officers, then chummy has got their radios, and that means the force radio in the car as well. I need a tactical firearms unit and as many officers as we can muster on the hurry-up to rendezvous on the road west of Henley by the junction that goes to Stonor Park. Get your duty officer up there."

"I can't. He's covering a fatal car crash at Abingdon."

"Okay. A sergeant can't take this. I'll have to run it. Put the requests in now, get him to give me as many troops as he can, he can phone me if there are any problems. I'll be at the rendezvous point in about ten minutes."

"Yes, sir. What about authorities from senior officers?"

"I will get those as I drive down. Put a message through to Wemstone to call out all the Klingsor team. I hope we are wrong... by God I hope we are, and that your blokes are pissing about."

"So do I, sir."

Shackerstone waited at the turning to Stonor Park with only four unarmed uniformed officers and their two cars for the best part of twenty minutes, before a single van with an acting sergeant and seven officers arrived, followed by a single armed response car with two males and a female sergeant.

They alighted stiffly from their vehicles, bracing against the wind.

"Can't we get a tactical team out?" he inquired of the sergeant.

"They are being called out. It will be an hour at least. PS Dove, sir."

Shackerstone shook her hand. "We have to move on this. It

can't wait, officers lives are at risk."

"Tell us the problem."

Shackerstone gathered all the officers around him.

"Listen in. The information is that two officers going to investigate an alarm at DC Dastra's residence have gone missing. A probably bogus result has been given for that call and the next one. Operation Klingsor has good information from a reliable source." Shackerstone smiled to himself because he was the source. "The Vlad team will surface here to attack Mrs. Dastra."

"Does that mean DC Dastra was Vlad after all, and he's going to kill her?"

"No it doesn't. Barney is somewhere in transit between London and here, we hope. Anyhow, that isn't the issue. We know that our three Vlad suspects on remand were armed, and that any other members of the team are likely to be. We also suspect that the team is intending to make a snuff movie by repeating some of the Charles Manson killings at DC Dastra's house, with Lucy Dastra as the principal victim. There is no more intelligence than that. All the phones are out and a tactical approach to the house needs to be made before we weigh up the situation."

He pulled out a 1:25,000 map and spread it across the hood of his Citroen. The wind tugged at it as the officers crowded round, and tiny raindrops began to darken it in patches. He switched on a small black flashlight to provide better illumination. "Right, I know the location well. My intention is that we park up here," he pointed to a small road junction, "downwind so they can't hear us, and approach the last five hundred yards to the wall on foot under cover of darkness. We should be able to secure the suspects' vehicles, and anybody in them. The three armed officers go over the front wall into the property from the lane, followed by everyone else. If we trip the alarm off, get ready for chaos."

Shackerstone then laid out a set of photographs. "This is Dastra, his wife, Lucy, her friend Michaela, and this is the layout of the Piano Room—note the beam. The action will be in that room because of the beam, to match Manson." He then opened a rough sketch of the house and grounds: "This is the front gate, its circular drive, lawn here and patio leading to the Piano Room through French doors."

The sergeant interrupted. "Sir, with respect, there is a total lack of planning here. If this lot are armed, we need tactical support. This whole thing needs to be properly risk assessed. We can't go in under these conditions."

Shackerstone snapped back sharply. "Listen, Sergeant. If you knew your colleagues were being shot dead at the far end of the street you were in, would you stay put and wait for a risk assessment, or would you do what you joined to do?"

"But that's a spur of the moment thing. We've got sufficient information to plan ahead here."

"This is time critical and we have the facts including officers missing or at severe risk. We are in the golden hour, trying to get a spanner on jelly. The filming could be happening now. The longer we wait the more chance they have of getting away with it."

"And if we steam in there without the support we need we could all end up casualties."

"So which is more important? Our lives or the lives of those we are sworn to protect?"

"In my book, ours."

"So you risk your own life driving at a hundred miles an hour to get here, then suddenly want to play the bloody health and safety ticket?"

Dove paused to think, her arguments slipping away. She played her final card. "But, Guv, this is totally against all procedures."

Shackerstone was up from his car hood and advanced until he was toe to toe with Dove. "You joined the force to fight crime and show bravery, not cower three miles away while your colleagues get butchered! The force has spent a small fortune on teaching you all that 'SAS style knees bent running about looking like a female Rambo' stuff. I'm quite prepared to go up there on my own with anybody else who has got the balls to go to the aid the aid of their colleagues and the public we are supposed to be fucking serving!"

Shackerstone reddened. The sergeant took a step back, and fiddled nervously with her holster. She swallowed hard, and for a moment, Shackerstone thought he saw tears welling in her eyes.

"Sorry, Guv. I'm with you. I'm just not happy. Okay, let me sort out the tactics. They won't be brilliant, but, yeah, well, time is pressing. Has everyone got body armor and access to the tactical radio channel?"

"Not me." grunted Shackerstone.

"There's a spare set of armor in the back, Guv." said a PC. "You'll need one of these baseball caps, or we might shoot you."

"Yes," said Dove under her breath. "We might."

~ * ~

Under light rain, armed police sergeant Angela Dove dropped the MP5 from her shoulder and trotted slowly along the shiny wet tarmac of the lane. Behind her in the moon shadows of the rustling trees lining the sides of the road, Brian Shackerstone panted heavily in body armor, followed by a line of fitter, younger officers. Dove rounded the last bend towards the house. There were no cars in the lane. She looked back towards Shackerstone and shook her head. He caught her movement in silhouette against the dappled lighting from the house. He knew her meaning, but pushed his hopes on in the belief that the suspects' vehicles would still be on the driveway.

Dove motioned to a field to the right, and her two armed colleagues and six unarmed officers trotted into it. Her intent was that nobody should cross the gateway to Prospect of Peshawar. The officers she had just detached were to move through the field and then cross the road farther down beyond the entrance. Dove would take herself, Shackerstone and the others to the left of the entrance and cross the wall in the woods. She stopped and gave a signal with her hand for the others following to do the same.

"We've found a car. Dastra's, in the field across from his house." said a voice in her earpiece.

"Anything else?" she said, above the wind noise.

"No, it's unlocked but empty."

Shackerstone had no radio.

"What was that?"

"They've found Dastra's car."

They moved on to the left and as the road turned slightly right to pass the entrance to the property, slipped into the woods about thirty yards along the wall. Dove was hoisted onto the shoulders of two officers and used a small pair of night vision binoculars to peer over the wall at the house and garden. "No sign of a police car," she said loudly to Shackerstone. "But there is a big

American car on the drive—so it looks like they're here."

He screwed his face up as he let this information sink in.

"Shit. Can you see a body in it?"

"Yes, but I think…"

"The car is a prop to match the Manson scene. They would have to leave it. Are you sure you can see no other cars?"

"Nothing. Just the American car."

There was a call on the radio from the team on the right. An officer by Shackerstone plucked his earpiece out and held it to the DCI's ear.

"We can see the front of the house from here. No movement. It all looks dead. There are two, maybe three shapes on the lawn about fifty feet out from the house, probable bodies, no movement except wind blowing the clothes and someone has written PIG on the front door. I guess that's for our benefit. I think that our blokes have had it. This has happened, Sarge. This is a crime scene."

Shackerstone let the earpiece drop. Dove dropped down from the wall.

"Did you hear that?" she asked.

"Yes," replied Shackerstone, picturing the carnage inside the house. "We're too late." He put his hands in his pockets and leaning against the wall with one leg bent and his sole back against the brickwork he stared dejectedly at the ground. Drips of rain ran down from the peak of his baseball cap and dropped down on the dark earth where his eyes were staring into nothing. He wanted to die. He would have preferred dying heroically while saving Lucy, but in any case, his police world seemed to be grinding him into oblivion.

"Guv," whispered Dove. "We have to take the scene. Let us do this properly and professionally, by the book. We can still do that much for the victims."

"Can't you see?" replied Shackerstone, "It's all over. We can walk right in."

"Listen, we have agreed a tactical approach. There will be unsecured weapons in there, guns and knives. There are a thousand things in there that could put us all at risk. Please, do it my way? Sir?"

Shackerstone half heard her. His mind was already several steps ahead in the planning process of scene preservation. He needed a forensic team, a photographer and a doctor to pronounce life extinct, better still O'Toole, who could get right down to the job of examining the corpses. He would need lights, covers, hundreds of evidence bags and most of all, a team of experienced and well-trained detectives. Those same detectives would need the emotional resilience to be able to cope with the death of a colleague they had once sealed a false conviction against for murder, and the grisly death of his pregnant wife.

Shackerstone felt a long way from being a dispenser of justice; indeed, he sensed a deeper, but still unclear sense of guilt. He had ensured that Barney and Lucy had been splashed across magazines in order to draw a possible suspect out, and sensed that his scheme was coming together long after he had discarded it. Gordonstown had caught him off balance today with the plan to arrest Dastra—so he hadn't seen the Hughes killings in the wider picture. Ultimately, it was Shackerstone who had led Dastra to be away tonight, leaving Lucy isolated in the house with her friend. Could he have avoided it? What else had he failed to do? Shackerstone was tired from the day's efforts, and was now predicting a long stay. He could foresee himself still there in the midmorning, numb with tiredness, briefing Gordonstown on the case and the inevitable post mortems. He tried to imagine what he would tell him, but suddenly snapped back into the present.

"Carry on. Let's get the pain over."

Dove transmitted on her radio. "Mickey, are you by the wall yet?"

"Yes, ready to go."

"Stick to the tactical plan. I know it looks as if it is all over, but keep it quiet and secure the scene. Rendezvous on the front lawn."

They cut the wires and one by one the team went over, Dove leading, gun in hand, and a line of unarmed officers following. Shackerstone stayed behind. He called the local control room on a mobile phone borrowed from Dove.

"Hello, DCI Shackerstone here. Yes… Prospect… I'm just outside the wall now. It looks like our blokes have had it. I'll give a SITREP soon, but it looks like the suspects are long gone. I need some roadblocks put in. I don't know what we are looking for, but stop everything on the three main routes out of here. The suspects must have video equipment, lights and that sort of stuff. They might even be in a police car. Yes, and there will be a lot of blood on them. Use the armed units that are coming, these blokes will be tooled up... stinger... good idea—puncturing their tires will slow them down. Keep radio silence, they have probably got access still... phone your PCs on their mobiles, or go back-to-back. Don't let them hear us setting up... A helicopter! Well done. From the Met? Bloody good work. Ours is broken? Twenty-five minutes. Get them to use their thermal imager on the woods, you never know. Right, I need to get some more resources rolling. All the Klingsor team need to rendezvous at about fifty yards back from the gate. Get our Home Office pathologist out... O'Toole. I'll need photography and forensics. Lights. Tape. See if you can try again to get a late turn Police Support Unit up from a town center, perhaps with some searchers on board. Do your best. Thanks. Try to second-guess me, Sarge. I'm going to need all the help I can get in there. Cheers."

He wandered back along the wall to the gateway, deciding to wait until Dove's team opened it. He rattled the gate pointlessly, appearing in silence on the unwatched monitor in the piano room, only a foot from Lucy, motionless on the sofa. He peered up the drive towards the car. He caught sight of a figure signalling to him from the edge of the woods to his left. It looked like Dove.

Trotting back along the shadow of the wall, he let his eyes adjust to the dark again, and searched for the place where the others had climbed over. Finding the break in the wire, he eased himself up by his arms onto a moss-covered capstone and dropped onto a soft bed of earth and pine needles, catching the arm of his sweatshirt on the wire as he fell. Panting hard from the exertion, and still encumbered by body armor, he moved quickly into the trees and towards Dove and the rest of the team.

Crouching in the shadows, Dove was still committed to a tactical approach, cold scene or not. She couldn't hear anything of the other team going over to the right, which reassured her that the silent approach was being played out correctly. Shackerstone rattling the gates had irritated her, but the wind in the trees had covered the noise. Her signals to him had the desired effect, and she could see him joining the rear of her group. They got up and skirted the lawn, staying down from the lighting around the house. Keeping off the gravel drive, Dove shone a light across into the American car.

She looked back at Shackerstone and nodded her head firmly as if to confirm the body. She stopped and crouched down, signaling the others to do likewise. Shackerstone carried on past the others and crouched down beside her.

"A white male body in the big car, I think there are more over there," she whispered, pointing out shapes on the lawn to their left. "We will wait here for the other group to move closer to the right end of the house."

Shackerstone felt something wet on the ground under his hand, he drew his hand up to his nose and sniffed it. Blood. He reckoned that this was part of a trail left by the fleeing killers that would lead all the way back to the gate, just as it had at Cielo Drive. This thought alone was sufficient to make him become totally disinterested in tactics, and his overwhelming desire to confirm what he already knew in his heart to be true drove him to rise up from the grass and walk slowly to the bodies. "Sod this," he muttered.

"Guv, Guv, no!" whispered Dove, but Shackerstone was either not listening, or hadn't heard her above the wind. He walked slowly across the lawn, his small black flashlight in hand. He stopped to shine it at the bodies and was disconcerted by what the dull yellow beam picked out: The dead police officer he had expected to find. The others were in some way wrong. The next body, also male, bluntly hacked at the back of its neck didn't belong in Shackerstone's picture of the scene. The other corpse, male again, lying twisted and spattered with blood had perhaps played some part inside then had been dragged out. Shackerstone scanned the lawn for the body of a woman, and although he saw none near him, he knew one would be somewhere out in the shadows on the grass. As he stepped over the partly beheaded man and the bloody spade, he spied the glint of a shiny object in the grass picking up light from the house. He shone the light down, the beam encompassing a large black revolver with a long silencer.

The detective in him told him to leave it, but shadowy movement of figures along the line of the drive reminded him of the tactical need to secure it. He took a plastic glove from his trouser pocket, put it on his left hand and replacing the gun with an old pencil to mark its position, he picked the gun up by pinching the trigger guard on either side. He looked back across to his right and saw rapid movement by the other team through the confused shapes and shadows of the trees and outbuildings. Shackerstone found a property bag in his back pocket and dropped the revolver into it. He sealed the bag carefully, shielding it from the rain with his body, then dangled it from his gloved hand.

He paced steadily and silently up to the house, fully prepared for the sights and smells of the lifeless flesh and fluids within. Stepping over the flowerbed at the left of the piano room, he followed a trail of blood under the veranda. Lights shone brightly beyond the closed curtains, and a security light above him suddenly flicked on. It made him start, but it was a small impact on a mind already filled with the expectation of further horror. He breathed out deliberately and regularly, preparing himself for a shock. The calming exercises he had learnt during psychotherapy were needed now, but were beyond his mental reach. A peptic lurch in his stomach told him to go no further. He could rest here until the detectives arrived, and then play the part of the detached professional as he supervised the scene examination. A nervous tremor in his sweating right hand signaled that the battle between fight, flight or freeze was being fought out in the reptilian depths of his mind. There was however a small source of calm.

The presence of a bright environment is a greater reassurance to police officers than to many others. Bright lighting is associated in the police psyche with crime prevention and the arrival of officers and resources at an incident. Light seems to heal the interruption to society and to put a stop to the progress of a night-time incident. Its presence at a crime scene clears the shadows and washes away the imagined mysteries the mind creates in pools of darkness, replacing them with cold facts. The activation of this security light, despite making Shackerstone's heart jump, was a small familiar crutch. In his internal battle, one side drew strength from it, and he briefly gazed into its dazzle for comfort.

Forty Five

Question (Hinx): "What were you thinking?"

Answer (DCI Shackerstone): "What was I thinking? I was thinking ahead to Lucy's post mortem. Have you ever been at a PM on a pregnant woman?"

Q: "I've seen one."
A: "Have you seen one that was about to drop?"

Q: "No."
A: "I have. Killed on the way to hospital in a crash. They deliver the dead baby."

Q: "I know."
A: "That isn't what does my head in, sir. It's the unwanted milk leaking out of them. All that wasted good intent by Mother Nature."

Q: "So you hadn't worked out where DC Dastra would fit in?"
A: "No, I had assumed he would be dead. What I saw was an incredible shock, hence my reaction."
(Extract from Metropolitan Police enquiry into Operation Klingsor.)

The hard rays of the security light under the veranda at Prospect of Peshawar clawed into Shackerstone's eyes and forced him to snap back to reality. Breathing deeply, he pulled the peak of the black baseball cap down slightly to shield the glare.

A broken set of French doors to his right hung slightly open and the curtains were drawn apart. As always, he moved quietly for the dead. He noticed the sets of bloody footprints on the paving leading away from the doors and stepped over the trail so as not to disturb any evidence.

Through the imprinted dazzle of the security light that still lingered on his retinas he found himself observing everything in almost obsessive detail. Even the peeling paint in the frame of the French doors caught his eye. He looked at the rough surface of the paving at his feet, and the way the blood had dropped into the tiny valleys like a miniature flood, leaving the high points in a mottled yellow pattern. His subconscious was at work again, trying to distract him from the terror within. His eyes followed the trail towards the doorway.

Then, above the wind and the rustling of the trees, he picked up a man's voice and an eerie, almost disembodied sobbing. The sounds bit into his attention and turned him to look in through a broken pane. He noticed the grand piano first, pushed back to his left. The sound told him someone was still alive. He eased the left hand door open with his nails so as not to obscure any fingerprints and scanned the room.

There was a lot to take in, and with a studied preconception fixed in his mind, he couldn't be sure for a moment what was real and where his brain might be adding to fill in the gaps. The dazzle spots in his eyes were fading, but still cast doubt on his momentary interpretation of what he saw.

Most of the expected scene was there before him. Lucy's bloody face struck him first, the blood washed away by her tears in clear paths down her cheeks. He saw the rope around her neck and a vast blood-spattered area away beyond her. A Stars and Stripes flag was there somewhere, draped across the sofa. Somewhere in his scan of the room, he caught Dastra's eyes looking at him terrified and surprised. In a fine spray of blood droplets, a long, bloody knife was being raised above Lucy and Shackerstone knew he had to stop it.

Intuition had forced his subconscious to move the revolver from his gloved left hand to his right. Shaking and fumbling to find the trigger through the plastic forensic bag, he brought the gun up and aimed at the figure's chest, steadying the weapon with his left hand. He squeezed the trigger and hoped for the best. The gun gave a heavy jerk upwards, bursting the bag with a dull popping sound.

A heavy flowerpot shaped bullet slammed into the murderer's jaw as he brought the long bloody knife back to stab Lucy a second time. He fell back, eyes glazed, arms flailing, and stumbled over a dead body behind him. The only sound he made was a breathy hiss as his lower jaw disintegrated and large fragments of jawbone drove hard back into his voice box. A jet of blood burst away from his throat, arcing up and out.

As would have been the case with most police officers in England, Detective Chief Inspector Brian Shackerstone had never fired a pistol before, let alone anything with such a kick. The recoil jarred his wrist, but the pain registered only slightly as he stumbled into the room and brought the revolver up again, steadying it with his gloved hand. The tattered shreds of the plastic bag sat up in Shackerstone's line of aim, but his second shot hit the knife-wielder squarely in the chest as he fell back to the left and away from the two women. The third bullet went high as Shackerstone's wrist weakened, drilling into the shorter woman's neck and bursting away the opposite side of it in a shower of shredded red flesh. Her body crumpled, and the bayonet she had been wielding a second earlier clattered noisily across the wooden floor. Shackerstone moved on leftwards, his wet soles slipping momentarily on the shiny surface.

He dropped his aim for his next shot and it thudded into the center of the second woman's chest. Her arms flew back as the force of the shot carried her away from Lucy, dropping her and her knife on top of the body of the officer Shackerstone vaguely recognized as Peter Ainsworth. Outside, there was a shout of "stop!" followed by a double shot above the wind. There was a short scream from a female, then silence.

Two men to his right were moving as he advanced into the room. He spun to the right, gun still braced before him. "Stop! Armed police!" he blurted. The cameraman, slipping a small videotape cassette into his jacket with his left hand, reached for the surrendered machine pistol with his right. Shackerstone's next bullet hit home, smashing the video cassette near the hub of one of the spools, pushing a tight spiral of iron oxide tape into the cameraman's chest and out through a messy exit wound in his back. The force lifted him and threw him against the French windows. "Shit," said a voice outside as the bullet spun on lazily in a mist of blood accompanied by a long ribbon of videotape out past the closing police officers. The cameraman's body slid down in its own blood on the polished floor, and in doing so kicked away a leg of the camera tripod, toppling it over its other two legs. The extra weight of the tripod hammered the lens of the camera hard into the floor, shattering the fragile red filter into shards.

The director half-rose from the kitchen chair, photographs falling from his lap, his hands opened wide and rising in a sign of surrender.

"Barney?" mouthed Shackerstone. No. The details were wrong, the hair more wild, the face and body were fatter. Dastra himself, gagged and bloody, grunted at Shackerstone's feet. There were shouts outside. They heard Dove shout, "Don't move, armed police." There were the cracks of two rounds from her gun, and the grunt of someone falling.

Shackerstone was trying to make sense of it all. Dastra's double blurted out "I'm not armed, don't shoot."

Shackerstone scanned the room for the living. The girl he had shot in the neck was gurgling blood into another growing pool on the wooden floor. Michaela was gagged and bound on a chair by the camera, Dastra, the real Barney, was handcuffed and kneeling on the floor at his feet, Lucy was hunched over the bloody Stars and Stripes flag on the sofa, and finally in front of him was Dastra's double. Shackerstone couldn't stop returning his eyes to him. "Just stay there," he ordered, motioning with his gun. He kept the gun on the director and crouched down behind Dastra to try to free the cuffs.

"Get me some help in here!" Shackerstone fumbled with his bunch of house keys and found a handcuff key. He released one of the cuffs and dropped the keys for Dastra to finish freeing himself.

Dastra took the gag off, but said nothing. He took the other cuff off and after untying his feet went over to untie the rope from Lucy's neck. Her cheek bled less now, but the wound to her chest bubbled bright fresh blood. Dastra stemmed it with the flag, but she winced with pain. Dastra backed off.

"Where is it?"

"The baby," Lucy gasped between desperate pants. "And my chest. I'm going..."

"I want some help!" screamed Shackerstone again, holding his gun up.

"Wait, Guv," came a male shouting back. "We're just securing the..."

"Be quick! I've got one prisoner, possibly two, and some serious casualties in here."

"Two minutes and I can get you a medic."

The bodies brought Shackerstone's mental focus to the director, who was now standing slightly forward from the kitchen chair, his arms still half raised.

Surely, here before Shackerstone was the central figure of all the terror of the last two years: the impalings, the beheading, the torture, the burning, the butchered couple, the girl in Yorkshire and now two dead police officers. To the list of brutalized and now lifeless victims, Shackerstone added the web of anguished and mentally scarred families and friends for whom there would never be any parole. He added the miscarriage of justice, Dastra's needless suffering in prison and his own sense of guilt at his part in putting him inside. He added the long sleepless nights of his own breakdown, the terrified look of Michaela in the corner of the room, and last but not least in his mind he added the terror of Lucy amplified by his personal obsession.

"Are you Vlad?" he demanded of the director through clenched teeth. "Are you... bloody *Vlad*?"

"Yes, I am." He returned an empty stare.

Shackerstone turned his head slowly to take a look at Lucy: The color had drained from her face as her blood ran unchecked into her lungs, and Shackerstone watched her body go limp as she slipped into unconsciousness.

Dastra was panicking, unable to save her. "Lucy! Lucy!" He shook her and then drew his hands away as they trembled with his uncertainty as to what to do next. Dastra shouted, "She's dying. What do I do?"

Shackerstone needed to help. He instinctively checked the French doors to see that nobody was coming in. Steadying his aim at the center of the director's throat, he gradually squeezed the trigger.

"*You* can fucking die, chum." Skarrow's right hand flew up and at the same moment the firing pin clicked on the soft hollow in the back of a spent cartridge.

Shackerstone had counted five shots, and he was right. He had no knowledge of the first round of that load being spent on Peter Ainsworth. Skarrow was already stumbling over the chair and within a second crashed out through the set of doors his cameraman had just expired against. Shackerstone, trying to follow, stumbled across the tripod of the video camera, clicking his empty gun pointlessly after Skarrow. He ran out after him, leaving Dastra, Lucy, Michaela and the still-gurgling actress in the room.

"He's mine," screamed Shackerstone against the wind. Dastra could hear shouts of "Stop. Armed police!" as officers went to assist. At the same moment, there was a noise as the front door burst open and officers began a rapid search of the house. "In here!" shouted Dastra. Two officers appeared in the doorway from the library, scanning the room with weapons raised.

"Here!" shouted Dastra. "She's dying in front of me!"

They lowered their guns and hurried in. One of them unzipped a green first aid bag as the other assessed Lucy. "Is the upper chest the only major injury?" asked the other of Dastra.

"I think so, and I think the baby has started, too."

"Sucking wound. We've got to seal it to re-inflate her lung. Let's get her up on the sofa." The three of them lifted her body up carefully and rested it along the length of the sofa, her head and chest raised on cushions. The officer with the medical bag stuffed another cushion under her knees to raise them. The other officer summoned help on his radio.

"What about the girl behind us?" said the officer with the bag.

Dastra replied, "Suspect shot by police."

The officer ripped away the blood-soaked material covering Lucy's wound and pressed his hand over the hole.

Dastra's voice was shaking, "She's dying isn't she?"

"Not if we can help it! Now make yourself useful and go and help the lady in the corner."

Dastra backed away and tottered over towards Michaela. He picked his way over the dead bodies, and noticed as he rose that the upper air in the room was becoming ripe with the odor of abdominal contents. He untied Michaela and took her gag out.

"It's over, babe."

Michaela, her face bruised, stumbled to her feet, seized him and silently hugged him hard. After a few seconds, she held him away slightly and looked up through her tears into his bloody face. "Oh, God! What was... what was..."

"Later."

"But Lucy."

An officer shouted across the room, "We've got an air ambulance coming from Oxford, ETA ten minutes... wait... there's something else." The officer listened to his radio while his colleague stuck a very large sticking plaster over Lucy's knife wound. "There's a suspect adrift."

"Another?" replied Dastra.

"The bloke the black detective was chasing. They've both gone into the woods, down the hill towards the main road."

"*The yellow Renault!*" Dastra knew exactly where Skarrow would be heading. "I know where his car is. Can we get someone down there?"

"The other drivers are in the woods chasing him."

"I've got wheels."

"Then get after him!" The medic was checking Lucy's pulse. "Please stay with us, love!"

"I must stay with my wife, just in case."

"In case she dies?"

"In case she comes round. I want to tell her..."

"She won't come round, mate, not this side of hospital and better if you leave us with your lady. There's nothing useful you can do here, so piss off and catch the bastard. Now, go!"

Dastra ran to Michaela and put his hand on her shoulder. "I'll be less than ten minutes. But go with her if I don't come back. If... the worst happens... she wanted to save the baby."

"I know."

He leant down and pressed the switch to open his gates. With his face aching, Dastra slipped out the door and half sprinted across the lawn, through the opening driveway gates, out into the lane, and across to the field where he had stashed the Porsche. He dropped into the seat and started up the engine. Beethoven burst back into the *Agnus Dei*. He flicked the headlights and wipers on.

The choir sang softly, *"Qui tolis peccata mundi."*

"Who endures the sins of the world," murmured Dastra, slamming the car into drive and spinning it round on the grass. He was out into the lane in a second, turned left, turned again at the top by the police cars, winding through the woods down towards the lay-by. Beethoven was dying down to "Dona nobis pacem" when Dastra drew up about eighty yards behind the parked yellow Renault. A blue Ford Transit van sat squarely in front of it and facing the same way. The lights of the Porsche rolled back as Dastra extinguished them. He turned the music down. The car engine would be inaudible above the wind and he could safely leave it ticking over.

"Dona nobis pacem," whispered from the speakers. There was no sign of Skarrow, but Dastra guessed correctly where he would be heading. He imagined him running down the open hillside with Shackerstone leaping after him in the moonlight, the wet spring grass cushioning each step.

"Dona nobis pacem," reached its final bars as a dark figure came stumbling down the hillside and vaulted the short wire fence. Dastra knew it was his brother. Hairs stood up in a great wave beginning at the tip of his scalp and rippling down to the extremities of his body. "Yes, give us peace," he murmured. The figure stumbled across a ditch at the edge of the road, gained its balance, leapt up and flicked open the trunk of the Renault. The interior lights silhouetted him lifting a small pistol and pointing it back towards the field.

The Porsche surged forward as Dastra forced the accelerator pedal hard into the carpet.

Skarrow expanded in his windscreen as he flew faster and faster towards him. For a brief moment, Dastra saw yellow flashes emerging from his brother's gun. Skarrow was concentrating on trying to shoot his pursuers and was late to notice the fast approaching shadow of the large black sports car.

The thick bumper collected him at about forty miles per hour just under his knees and immediately the impact whipped him hard over the rear bumper of the Renault. The impact shunted the Renault forward into the van, and its bright yellow trunk lid flew into the air as the crumple zone collapsed. Dastra recoiled from the impact back against his headrest. Skarrow's screams filled the empty road as particles of glass fell like heavy sparkling drops mixed in with the evening's drizzle.

The meager light from the Renault flickered as Skarrow thrashed back and forth, pinned between the two vehicles. Stunned, Dastra let the bloody windscreen come into focus. On the outside, Skarrow's blood mixed freely with the rain, while a spray of identical blood from Dastra's nose had burst out over the dials. He staggered out of the car, winded and breathing hard. He noted that Skarrow held his empty hands out to him in a pleading gesture.

"Kill me, kill me," hissed Skarrow. "Please kill me."

It is something of a mystery to those charged with the job of investigating assaults by police officers on suspects, that so many occur at the end of a chase. There is nothing abnormal in this at all. The abnormal response for a human would be to run their quarry to ground and then fail to strike. This is the difficult emotion faced by police officers, and unable to switch off this natural hunter mode at a moment's notice, many feel the need to grapple in some way with the hunted.

Dastra limped around to the broken but living remains of Skarrow and seized the top of his dark hair, pulling his head back hard and leaning over the crushed trunk of the Renault to peer with his own wild eyes into Charles Skarrow's.

"Nicked!" Dastra bounced his brother's head hard on the back window of the Renault and let go of his hair. There was a cough from the field, followed by a low moan.

"Fuck me. That hurt!" It was Shackerstone's voice.

"Guv?"

"The cunt's shot me," croaked the voice from the darkness of the open field. Dastra limped round the car and tried to spot Shackerstone. Flashlights from two pursuing officers flickered down the hillside towards them.

"Over here, Barney. Help me up."

"Don't move. I'll find you."

"Here. Over here. I'm okay…"

Dastra made out Shackerstone's shape lying on the shiny wet grass.

"Guv?"

"It bloody hurts, but the vest has taken the brunt. I think I've broken some ribs."

"Grab my arm."

"Thanks. I feel like I've been hit by a train."

The light picked them out as Dastra helped Shackerstone get to his feet.

"Stop! Armed police!"

"DCI Shackerstone and DC Dastra!" They stayed still, Shackerstone leaning on Dastra, until the armed officers had closed on them. Angela Dove shone her light on their faces.

"They're ours," she shouted back across the field. "Suspect still adrift."

"He's not. One detained, down by the car. He needs an ambulance."

Dove jogged down to the car and climbed awkwardly over the wire fence. Dastra helped Shackerstone down towards the cars.

"Suspect secure," she shouted up across the field. Dastra and Shackerstone arrived at the wire fence at the same moment as two armed officers. They helped Shackerstone get over the wire and the ditch and into the road. Skarrow was lying across the hood of the Porsche, eyes wide open, watching the officers.

"That's one hell of a PolAcc," said Dove, shaking her head.

Shackerstone, panting hard, crouched down at the side of the car and tilted his head to the right to look into Skarrow's face.

"Hurts, doesn't it?"

"Yesss."

"Serves you fucking right." Shackerstone stood up and turned to Dastra. "Well done, mate," he said quietly, putting a hand on Dastra's shoulder. Dastra looked sideways at Shackerstone, the magazine photographs coming to mind. Silence hung over them for about twenty seconds, broken only by gurgling noises in Skarrow's throat and strangely similar noises from under the crumpled front of the Porsche. The hard beat of helicopter blades suddenly pulsed the air overhead. A bright light flooded the scene from above as an air ambulance hovered above the field and began to settle, blowing a fine silvery spray of raindrops with its downdraft.

Dove turned to face the helicopter. "He won't find anywhere to land there, it's too steep."

Shackerstone shouted, "They've seen Vlad! They think they've been called to help *him*!"

Dove moved quickly up to the fence and stood on the bottom rail, motioning the helicopter for it to go on up the hill to the house. It rose sharply into the air and disappeared over the woods. Dove stepped down. "You must get back up there, that'll be transport for your wife to hospital. My guys can guard the scene here."

"I'll stay too," said Shackerstone. "Better call some more units down here and an ambulance for our suspect."

"There aren't any mobile units free. That's why I came," said Dastra.

"And now you've wrecked your car." Shackerstone leaned against it, breathing hard, and slowly let himself slide down until he sat on the wet road. "Can you find your way back up there through the woods?"

"I can find the wall, but it's too high to climb from this side." Dastra glanced up towards the dark silhouette of the woods while dabbing his bloody nose with a tissue.

"There's a set of step ladders somewhere up there that your visitors used. I saw them when I jumped over."

"We've just used them," Dove added, "but we'll never find them in time. Do you think we could get the Transit van going?"

The exhaust note of a car echoed farther down the hill. Dove and Dastra exchanged glances as headlights lit up the lay-by. Dove moved into the road, gun held high in one hand, the other waving the car to a halt.

"Hello, sir," she said with a smile as the driver's window lowered to reveal a perplexed and worried man. "I'm going to make you an offer you can't refuse..."

~ * ~

"Thanks mate," said Dastra, as the car jerked to a halt behind one of several emergency vehicles blocking his driveway. He got out of the car, and biting back the pain in his leg, he ran up the driveway, trying to make out the jerky shapes in front of his house lit by the pulses of rotating blue and red emergency lights. He heard the whine of helicopter engines rising somewhere out to the left on his lawn. A knot of police officers and paramedics dispersed from the source of the noise as rotor blades hacked at the damp air. Dastra waved both arms wildly, but the aircraft lifted a few feet from the lawn and slowly turned away from him. He tried to skirt it to one side, but there was no getting near it as the downdraft threw him down on the grass. He rolled over and watched it lift swiftly into the night sky, the navigation lights blending into a blur beyond the rain as it banked over the trees and slowly vanished.

Forty Six

Question (Superintendent Hinx): "Had you ever discharged a firearm prior to this date?"

Answer (DCI Shackerstone): "Never. I've never had the interest. Guns are for sad inadequate types who want to feel big. Or a tool for a job of work, work I wasn't involved in."

Q: "So you've never served in any of the services or on an armed unit?"
A: "No. Never."

Q: "The complaint against you is that you attempted to murder Charles Skarrow."
A: "I've had the regulation nine notice served on me."

Q: "To which you replied, "I utterly refute this allegation. Has this man got no moral values at all?"
A: "That's right."

Q: "Let me describe to you what ballistics found, then we will give you an opportunity to explain."
A: "Okay."

Q: "When a revolver is fired, it leaves a firing pin mark on the back of the cartridge. If you go round all six and try to fire again on a spent cartridge, the firing pin strikes in the same place, generally leaving no mark. That is, unless, the cartridge has moved slightly, or it has recently been fired, and is now hotter and has expanded slightly. This means that the second firing pin mark, which is rarely perfectly central, might be slightly out of register to the first, giving a microscopic second edge to the indentation. A second mark, on top of the first, but slightly off. Do you follow?"

A: *"Perfectly."*

Q: *"We can never prove, therefore, on a cartridge with a single mark, that a firing pin hasn't hit it twice, but we can clearly prove that it has in cases with the double mark. Now, on the revolver you used, forensics found three cartridges with a visible second mark on them."*

A: *"I see."*

Q: *"Would you take us through, step by step, what happened next. You had just arrived in the doorway here on the plan of Dastra's house. Just take us through your actions and what you were thinking. Account for the double strikes, please."*

A: *"I could see three of them attacking Lucy. I moved in and fired the gun, even though it was still in the bag. All my shots hit, much to my relief. A man on my right, the cameraman, started to bring a machine pistol up. I shot him too. Once. I hit the tape, but the bullet went on through him. Then the director...he just froze. I kept the gun on him and freed Barney from his handcuffs. I shouted for help."*

Q: *"He says in his complaint that you leveled the gun at his head and pulled the trigger. Is that true?"*

A: *"Absolutely."*

Q: *"Oh, right."* (Pause) *"I'm somewhat surprised. Why did you do that?"*

A: *"Well, you have to consider my* Mens Rea *at the time. The facts were far from clear, I was still trying to get the spanner on the jelly. Skarrow was, I believed, armed and capable of killing us both, and as you know he shot me later."*

Q: *"With a weapon he took from his car."*

A "That can't be established for certain. He shot at me after going to the back of the car, which could have been for a reload... we found an empty magazine in the wreck. What I saw before in the piano room was that he had something with him, in his hand, he brought it up and I pulled the trigger. I would suggest his weapon had the same problem as mine." (pause) "Furthermore, in my mind was that he had killed, or supervised the killings of Carothers, the two officers, and now Lucy and her... unborn baby.""
(Extract from Metropolitan Police enquiry into Operation Klingsor.)

Vanessa Aybrams waited by the baggage reclaim at Heathrow Terminal Four, willing her cases to appear on the conveyor belt. The flight had tired her, but excitement at the prospect of her first grandchild held her spirits up. She appreciated that being airborne had kept her in the dark as to developments, but she was prepared for only two possibilities: either the baby had arrived, or it hadn't. The worst outcome would be that she had arrived in the middle of Lucy's labor, and that nobody would be here at the terminal to collect her.

Her luggage appeared in the first batch, and a kindly man helped her load it onto her trolley, which she pushed on through customs. As she emerged into the arrivals hall, she scanned the crowd for Dastra. There were no familiar faces. In looking for him, she missed the handwritten signs held up by cabbies and other people meeting strangers.

"Vanessa Aybrams?" said a voice, almost directly in front of her. She looked, and looked again. A red-haired man in his thirties stood about ten feet away across a partition, holding a cardboard sign with her name on it.

"Yes. That's me."

The man waved her round the end of the partition. Vanessa hurried round to meet him. "Hi. Who are you? What's happened?"

"Hello Mrs. Aybrams, I'm DS Tony Shanter, DCI Shack—"

"But where's Barney? Is everything okay?"

"I'm here on his behalf and there's a car outside waiting for us with DCI Shackerstone in it."

"But..."

"Please. Let him speak to you. I'll push your trolley out."

Vanessa Aybrams knew that there was no good news coming at the end of this. If everything had been all right the detective would be reassuring her.

Outside the main entrance of the terminal, in bright spring sunlight, Shackerstone was waiting in the back of a marked Central Southern Police BMW 5 series area car with a uniformed driver at the wheel. Shanter put Vanessa's cases in the trunk of the car as she opened a back door and got in with Shackerstone. She saw the bandage around his chest, but her first concern was still Lucy. Shanter got in as Shackerstone started to explain. Vanessa's hand went to her mouth.

~ * ~

Two weeks later, alone in the main bedroom at Prospect of Peshawar, Dastra, now bearded, packed Lucy's personal effects into a large plastic crate. At the dark wooden dressing table, he sat for a few minutes, examining Lucy's jewelry before wrapping it in a handkerchief and sliding it into a front trouser pocket. There wasn't much. They hadn't been married long enough.

He opened a stiff drawer at the top right and found a thick CD case wrapped in silver paper. The tag had been written over two weeks before: *To Barney. Happy Birthday. All my love, Lucy.*

"My birthday? When was that?" It had been a week earlier. With nobody else in the world to send him a present, it had slipped by unnoticed among bigger events. He toyed with the idea of opening the present, and while he was doing so, he spotted a large card in the drawer. He put the present down and slid the card out. It was pink and green, with a teddy bear on the front under the words: *"Husband. On Your Birthday"*. Lucy had never got round to writing anything inside. Dastra felt a lump in his throat. He got up and swept the present and card off the dressing table and dropped them into the crate.

He wandered out of the bedroom, distracted by the package and card, and sat on the floor of the unused nursery, leaning on the yellow wall and staring blankly at where Lucy had stenciled boats and bears onto it. He leaned his head back until it rested against the surface, and watched a mobile rotate lazily in the slight draft. The baby should have been here, watching the mobile, focusing for the first time on its new home. Its mother should have been here too. The effort expended by Lucy on the room seemed wasted, and Dastra considered for a moment what might have been, had Skarrow not fallen into Shackerstone's untended trap.

The perfect world Dastra had dreamed of at Prospect of Peshawar, with his beautiful wife and new baby dwelling in the old family home, had been irrevocably broken by his twin brother, now recovering in hospital under a heavy police guard.

He tried for a moment to fight back tears, but a few came anyway, and allowed a small release of the tension created by being in the house again.

"Everything?" said Michaela from the doorway. Dastra took a moment to realize what she was asking. He appreciated her courage in returning to the house, and didn't want to appear abrupt.

"Yes, please, Michaela. All of her gear."

"Are there any suitcases?"

"Use another crate. Can you give Pete a shout? I need him to help me dismantle the baby-bed."

"Okay."

Michaela disappeared and after an exchange of shouts, Peter Lynch arrived at the doorway of the baby's room with pliers and a screwdriver.

"I'm sorry. I was having a peek into the piano room. There are some blokes still working in it."

"Scenes of crime officers. They say they should finish on Tuesday, then we can shut the place up."

Peter sat down on the floor next to Barney, knees up, resting his arms on them with the pliers and screwdriver swinging in his fingertips. "Shut her up, eh? Will you come back? To live, I mean."

"I don't know. It's a real house of horrors now. Could you stay here alone?"

"No, I don't suppose I could, not right now."

"Imagine Lucy up here with Hannah while I'm at work. She's got a lot to put behind her as it is."

"So have you."

"But they didn't try to murder me after killing two cops in front of me and spelling out what they wanted to do."

"No, but you have other... you've got more than enough in your head to go quite, quite mad."

"Yeah. But not like Lucy."

"No."

"Let's get on with it. Lucy wants the crib?"

"Yes."

They both got slowly to their knees and started to take it apart.

~ * ~

In a white and summery dress, Lucy sat out on a garden chair in bright sunlight on the lawn, several feet away from where sandy splotches in the grass marked the extent of recent bloodstains. Lucy held Hanna's head gently to her right breast, stroking her thin hair as she suckled. Her attention on her baby, she blotted out the stitches still holding her deep cut together, spiked and dark like rusty barbed wire across her skin, just a few inches above the baby's head. The cut on her face still had a scab, but the wound hadn't been deep and had begun to disappear.

Lucy, concentrating on Hannah, suddenly felt a shadow fall on her and she started. Hannah sensed the jolt and began to cry.

"Sorry," said SOCO White. "I was trying not to disturb her."

"It was me. Don't worry."

"Sorry again."

Lucy calmed Hannah and managed to get her feeding again, while White stood still. He moved round so that Lucy wasn't in his shadow. "I just wanted to know if there was anything you would like to take. I can get anything you want out of the... room."

Lucy had tried to avoid even thinking herself into the piano room. This was as close as she wanted to get, but there was still some comfort to be had there. "Thanks. I'd like to take all the CDs."

"That's a lot of...."

"Please."

"Of course. I'll find some boxes."

White, clad in a blue oversuit, walked back up to the house and entered through the side of the piano room. A minute or two later, Lucy watched Barney and Peter carry bits of the crib out and load them into the back of a hired Luton van. Michaela emerged as the others went back through the front doorway, the blood now cleaned from the heavy white door. She dumped a yellow crate on the lift at the back of the van and, apparently unaware that Lucy was watching, she walked purposefully around to the piano room, and entered through the French doors. Lucy heard voices and nervous laughter.

That was farther than Lucy was yet prepared to go. She knew the events were spinning round deep in her subconscious, but she couldn't go there. It wasn't fear or memory block. Her mind just wouldn't let her in. It was a reflex, and she knew it was doing her harm. If she went up and looked, she knew it wouldn't connect properly. She wasn't ready, but admired Michaela's ability to cope in her own way.

She didn't know how long she had been immersed in these thoughts, but Michaela was suddenly nearby and talking to her. Hannah was still feeding.

"Lucy. I've been to have a look."

"I saw."

"Do you want to. It's not..."

"Not yet. When I said I'm still numb, like Barney was after he got out of prison, I meant it. No closer today... this will be as far as I go. I don't want to think about it yet."

"We all need to talk about it. Together. You, me and Barney, with Brian Shackerstone, perhaps. He's not got it together either."

"I can't."

"But..."

"I just can't." Lucy's shout woke the baby. Hannah cried, and Lucy turned away from Michaela, trying to get Hannah back on her nipple. Barney, coming out of the front door with a box, peered down towards them to see what was going on. Michaela turned away from Lucy and hurried up towards Barney.

"What's up?"

Michaela had tears in her eyes. "I've upset her. We shouldn't have brought her here at all."

"Perhaps not. We needed to try, so don't be hard on yourself."

"I wanted to look again. I had to. I *needed* to." Her voice trembled and began to choke slightly. "The last time I looked around the room I was waiting to die. I was examining everything as if it was going to be my last view of the world. I looked at everything: The detail on the nightdress, the crumbs on the floor, the paintwork, the cameraman's pocket..."

Barney put the box down and hugged Michaela. "I know. I know, babe. I've been there... twice."

"I'm sorry."

"We'll go soon. We had to come, you and I. But this is enough for today."

"You're going to bring her back?"

"When she's ready. Then we can all talk our way through a proper debrief."

~ * ~

When it came later, it came as a flood. The gates weren't opened by a psychologist or a counselor, but by Barney, fellow victim, husband and lover. She didn't open her heart up on a couch in an anonymous clinic, but on a temporary dais back in the contaminated piano room at Prospect of Peshawar. It wasn't that the location represented safety, but that it was familiar, and the memories of it were now somehow balanced between the extremes of pleasure and pain.

She cried and cried. He painted, biting back his tears and pressing them into the smooth blobs of paint on his canvas.

She relived every moment of that night, over and over, and this self-therapy seemed to be the key. The baby interrupted for feeding, and Barney fed Lucy's sadness into his art in a way his brother could only capture fleetingly and brutally on iron oxide tape.

When their work was done, they left the house as they had arrived a few hours earlier, in Lucy's car, now fitted with a baby seat. They didn't look back.

The builders waiting in the drive with their machines were then free to move in and raze the piano room wing of the house to the level of the surrounding garden.

Forty Seven

Question (DCS Butcher): "So that's why the trials were separated?"

Answer (DCS Gordonstone): "That's right. The female suspect who survived Brian shooting her, was, and still is, paralyzed from the neck down."

Q: "Yes, I know. We had to investigate her allegations against DCI Shackerstone."

A: "Fit enough to allege police brutality but unfit to be interviewed as a murder suspect for up to a year. Makes you sick, doesn't it?"

Q: "It's a strange but necessary double standard. What about Charles Skarrow?"

A: "At that point Skarrow was still laid up in hospital with crushed legs. Their legal team wasn't up for him being added to the first lot of indictments, understandably from some perspectives. So it went ahead without him, but with reporting restrictions so as not to prejudice a future trial. Joanna Carter was the key witness, but her courage was exhausted. When we finally got Skarrow under interview in the summer, I tried to get her to pick him out on an identity parade, but she wouldn't even come into the station. So there was no chance of her giving any evidence at his trial."

Q: "So what did you do?"

A: "I didn't. Skarrow made the running... not literally... he was in a wheelchair. He wanted to speak to DCI Shackerstone, something about art. It was going round in his head. He cut a deal. If Lucy made a statement and came to the trial, he would roll over and plead to the lot. I can't fathom out why that was bothering him or why this was concerning him to that degree. A life in prison waiting to be attacked by any have-a-go inmate would have bothered me more. Still, that's the way with nut...odd psychological types."

Q: "And Mrs. Dastra?"
A: "Dastra, uh Barney, he did well to bring her round. So I charged Skarrow with the lot. Lucy came to the Old Bailey again, and Skarrow was as good as his word. As you know, he kicked off a bit as they were taking him down. He kept screaming across the courtroom to her. 'Was it art? Was it art?' She was as cool as a cucumber. She just shook her hair back and smiled."
(Extract from Metropolitan Police enquiry into Operation Klingsor.)

Brian Shackerstone stared out of his bedroom window into the autumn night, wondering how Charles Skarrow and his compatriots were coping with life in prison. In the darkness his mind drew images of the dead and broken lives left by the Vlad team, and the videos of the killings still circulating somewhere out there in the world.
I did it. I really made a difference.
He relived, as he had done in every idle moment, the second by second trauma of entering the piano room and bringing an end to a crime, in a manner known only to a handful of armed specialists. He still couldn't believe it, and neither could many of his colleagues. Nervous, boozy perfectionist, Brian Shackerstone, riding to the rescue, blasting away with a six-shooter like he meant it and had done it all his life.
"The Police Complaints Authority have ordered an investigation," reported the media.
"They have to," Shackerstone said to himself. "It's routine. I know I broke the regulations, but with thirty years in, they can sack me and I'll still get my pension."
"Come back to bed, Brian," whispered Vanessa Aybrams from the darkness behind him. He slipped into the double bed and

smiled to himself. He couldn't believe how far he had come. Vanessa wrapped herself around him. He blew her long hair away from his mouth.

"A happy man," he said to nobody in particular, "'subject to the exigencies of duty'".

About Harry

Harry Hindes is a serving police Detective Chief Inspector in the UK with 29 years of hands-on experience across many fields of police work. His current assignment is as a hostage and crisis negotiator, but he has played a role in some of England's major investigations, including the July 2005 London tube bombings and the murder of Alexander Litvinenko.

Visit our website for our growing catalogue of quality books.

www.champagnebooks.com

13793890R00206

Printed in Great Britain
by Amazon.co.uk, Ltd.,
Marston Gate.